EVERYBODY'S D(

Everybody's Doing It

Abigail Collins

Psychology News Press

Published in 2019
by Psychology News Press
92a Hoxton Street
London N1 6LP
dcpsychologynews@gmail.com

Typeset by Keyboard Services, Luton, Beds.
Printed by Spauda in Lithuania.

ISBN 978-0-907-63319-8

Chapter One

For Whom The Bell Tolls

I am standing in front of the mirror staring at my reflection. I am in total awe of myself. The kind of awe preceded by shock. The sort of shock and awe that journalists talked about at great lengths when describing both Gulf wars. I am beginning to think that my sleek, sheath-style dress was a terrible mistake. I have literally had to squeeze myself into it and I look more like a sweaty bratwurst than a blushing bride.

The last six weeks have been so stressful that I have lived off of junk food and booze and as a result I have gained nearly a dress size. The fabric of the wedding gown is now rucking across my hips and stomach and I don't have so much of a cleavage as a boob spill on the scale of a major environmental disaster. I heard the stitches cracking as I pulled the zipper up and I know that if I sit down it's all over. My quaking, spreading flesh will create an irreparable San Andreas Fault.

The gown is so tight that I can't even walk properly so I shuffle over to Rob's laptop and Google, *How To Drop A Dress Size Overnight*. I find a cut-price plastic surgery clinic in Turkey where they will wire my jaw and staple my stomach at the same time. It's an absolute bargain and I half consider checking budget flights, but sadly Rob will just have to accept me as I am, for better or worse. I figure I am at least holding to one part of the bargain already.

Rob and I are getting married tomorrow. He is out with work colleagues tonight, celebrating his "last night of freedom". I wish he'd stop using that stupid cliché. It makes me feel like I've emotionally blackmailed him into a life of marital bondage rather than being the woman he really wants to spend the rest of his life with. It's not like I was the one who proposed.

1

Rob already went on a stag week to Budapest last month. Considering that my hen party was half a spa day with my best friend and only bridesmaid Jojo, Rob's repeated rutting seems a little excessive. I'm sure it's just another round of laddish drinking and ogling strippers, with no actual sowing of wild oats – or at least I hope so – but still, it's annoying.

Originally I was going to have three bridesmaids; my cousin Wendy and my brother's fiancée Annabelle (neither of whom I particularly like but Mum insisted), and Jojo. Rob said that he didn't think I needed any bridesmaids as I was the prettiest girl in the world and all eyes would be on me anyway. Eventually we compromised on a solitary Maid of Honour after I burst into tears and then got trapped in the bathroom. The lock, which had been sticking for months, finally got jammed and Rob had to kick the door down to get me out. The cost of replacing the door and fixing the frame would have more than paid for three bridesmaids dresses, but I decided to keep my mouth shut and just be thankful that at least I'll have Jojo by my side.

I'm aware that this kind of imbalance is not the best way to start married life but I am so racked with nerves right now that I can't think of anything else except squeezing into my dress, not tripping over and landing flat on my face while walking up the aisle and avoiding getting horribly drunk at the reception. Anyway, it's too late now; the money's been spent, the invitations sent and the church is booked.

Mum has taken on most of the arrangements, all executed with fevered Churchillian precision. I half expect a battalion of amphibious vessels outside the church. Any time I question her choices she gives me an imperious stare. Consequently between Rob and my mother I feel like a spectator at my own wedding. "The Big Day" now has as much resonance for me as *Match Of The Day*.

Most of my preparation has involved drinking wine with Jojo and moaning about the cake/dress/menu/speeches. "At least you're marrying the man of your dreams," she says with a wistful sigh. "Of course," I say like an automaton, not even convincing myself. Inside I am fearful and full of questions. I know I love Rob, more than I've ever loved any man. I just don't know if I'm still in love. The juggernaut of a year of wedding preparations has flattened anything that might be genuine feeling.

My brother has agreed to be Rob's best man. Everyone except me finds this a really touching gesture.

"Such a family affair," Mum trilled with delight. Patrick wasn't overjoyed.

"How can his own future brother-in-law be the best man?" Patrick whined. "It's not like we're mates. I don't even know which football team he supports."

"Chelsea," I replied glumly.

No doubt Patrick has written a speech that shows me in the worst possible light. He has already let me know that I owe him a massive favour for being, "Wing Man to Robbie-No-Mates."

I know that secretly Patrick feels sorry for Rob. Despite the fact that Rob is good-looking, successful and has lots of acquaintances, he doesn't have any real friends. He is a misfit, which is probably one of the things that attracted me to him in the first place. Rob did ask his closest pal from University to be his best man but Duncan couldn't make it because of the cost of the airfare and hotel. "Anyone would think the guy lived in Abu Dhabi not Aberdeen," moaned Rob. I suggested we pay the expenses, but Rob turned into Groomzilla, ranting that it was a huge honour to be asked and that Duncan was ruining his special day.

I look at a photo of Rob and I on the mantelpiece. He is so handsome. He could have been a model if he wasn't five foot nine. His dark curly hair is flopping over his piercing blue eyes and his jaw is surly and sexy. He hates to smile in photographs. He thinks it's crass. I am draped around his neck, a huge pair of Jackie-O sunglasses perched on my nose, not so much an attempt to look cool but more to hide as much of my face as possible.

Rob says how funny it is that as an actress I am so camera shy. He doesn't understand that the only reason I like playing other people is because it gives me a break from being me.

Rob proposed to me two years into our relationship by scrawling "MARRY ME WHEELER" across a beer mat in a bar in Amsterdam. It wasn't so much a question, more like a Final Demand. I had been so blind drunk at the time that I could barely focus on his face so he asked out loud instead, dropping to his knees as I clung to the bar for support. I said 'yes' immediately, hugged him and then vomited down the back of his shirt. The crowd went wild for us. It may not have been the most romantic proposal but it was memorable.

I suddenly feel very lonely. I text Rob, *Can't believe you're going to be my husband tomorrow. I love you xxxxxxx* I wait for him to text back some reciprocal guff. Nothing. I reason that he's probably in a noisy club and he can't hear his phone. Or maybe he's so pissed that he's dropped it down the loo again (like Budapest). Then I panic and my mind creates a series of catastrophes, ranging from Rob being knocked over by a speeding taxi to him being impaled on a stripper's pole after having a go at dirty dancing himself.

I go to the fridge to pour myself more wine but there's only a thimble full left. I know I should just take a bath and relax, have an early night. Apart from the two kilos I desperately need to lose in the next twelve hours there isn't anything else that needs to be done. Mum and Rob have organised everything on a minute-by-minute basis. Rob has booked me a decent saloon car with an upmarket mini-cab firm for 11.25 precisely (he says that limousines are a waste of money). If he turns out to be a mass murderer I doubt that anyone will be surprised. Mourners will stand over the coffin that contains the hacked pieces of my remains (the bits the Police could find) and say things like, "the signs were all there," and, "how did she not see it coming?"

I am convinced that I won't be able to sleep unless I anaesthetise myself from the stress with a little more alcohol so I nip out for a cheap bottle of plonk. I throw a bathrobe over my dress and take the two-minute walk – or rather waddle – to our nearest convenience store. I grab a bottle of white wine not even bothering to read the label and take it to the counter. Mr Singh, the owner of the shop who never seems to take a day or night off, is by now accustomed to my odd hours and weird habits but my bizarre apparition confuses even him.

"Going to a fancy dress party?" he asks jovially.

"No," I say, without any trace of humour. "It's my wedding dress. I'm getting married in the morning."

Mr Singh looks unsure and is perhaps wondering if I'm playing some kind of practical joke or researching a role or if I've finally had a nervous breakdown. After a few moments his face breaks into a smile.

"Congratulations," he booms. "I had no idea. When's the big day?"

"Tomorrow," I reiterate dismally.

"So is this some kind of English bridal tradition I've never heard of? Aren't you supposed to wear deely boppers and an 'L' plate on your Hen Night?"

Mr Singh wears a turban but has a broad London accent and I'm pretty sure that he knows as well as I do that running around like Miss Havisham the night before one's wedding is completely abnormal. I realise he is making a joke so I laugh but the sound comes out flat and forced. He can see that I'm as skittish as a doped-up race horse about the prospect of my impending nuptials. He looks at me with wise, gentle eyes and I half-consider asking him if he could organise a last-minute arranged marriage for me with one of his relatives. Anything would be better than having no one but myself to blame if Rob isn't The One.

"Who's the lucky fellow?" Mr Singh asks.

"Rob," I say, trying to smile.

Mr Singh draws a blank. "Who?"

Rob and I have been coming into this shop together since I

moved into his flat six months after we met. "The man you often see me with," I qualify.

Mr Singh's eyes grow wide with surprise. "Oh. It all makes sense now. I thought he was your brother."

I wonder what kind of image Rob and I must project for Mr Singh to assume that we are siblings. Love's young dream we are clearly not.

"Wait a minute," Mr Singh says as I go to leave, "I have something for you."

He disappears into the back and returns moments later with a tiny blue porcelain elephant. His kindness catches me off guard and I get a lump in my throat.

"Is this some kind of Sikh bridal tradition?" I ask, hoping that it is a good omen.

"No," he laughs, "just some stock we couldn't get rid of from years ago. I told Hardeep that homewares would never sell." Hardeep is Mr Singh's son. He drives what looks like a rally car with the windows down and the Bhangra cranked up.

I thank Mr Singh and put the tiny elephant in the pocket of my bathrobe. "Elephants are very loyal, Kat," adds Mr Singh. I grasp the cool, smooth china tightly in my hot, sweaty fist and I hope and pray that Rob is my elephant.

Chapter Two

Big Birthday Girls Don't Cry

On the eve of my thirty-ninth birthday I took a long hard look at myself in the bathroom mirror. Three years since Rob's departure and I remained terminally single. Mr Singh's elephant stared down at me judgementally from the top of the medicine cabinet; despite serving as constant reminder that I had been dumped somehow I still thought of it as a lucky charm. The fact that the tiny, fragile creature had survived unscathed when everything else in my life had shattered seemed nothing short of a miracle. Last year during a pub quiz I discovered that not only are elephants polyamorous but they also practice autoeroticism. If only Mr Singh had given me me a swan instead. Or a gibbon. Or a black vulture.

After Rob and I broke up Mum kept pushing self-help books on me with the all the ecstasy of a television gospel preacher. "Katie!" she said waving *The Secret* in my face like it was a Dead Sea Scroll, "since reading this I've lost three inches off my waist *and* won five pounds on the EuroMillions. Twice!" The books had their use: when I couldn't afford to replace my bed I used a pile of them to support the bowing pine slats. *Feel The Fear And Do It Anyway* had been propping up my increasingly substantial arse for the last two years.

It suited me perfectly to rubbish the self-help stuff. As far as I was concerned I wasn't the one who needed to change. Rob had run out on me, he was entirely to blame and I was just an innocent bystander. Rob probably thought of me as collateral damage – if he thought of me at all these days. I doubted it. Far too busy with Luscious Ludmilla, the woman he left me for, to give me a second thought. But somewhere deep inside the despair, in a tiny recess long forgotten since Rob's departure, a quark of hope still glimmered. And that subatomic particle of faith, the one that wasn't damaged by the fallout of rejection nor poisoned by bitterness, wanted to believe that I could get out of my rut just by believing that I could get out of my rut.

I looked at my foggy reflection in the mirror, wiping the steam away and immediately regretting it as my face as it really was zoomed back into focus. I took a deep breath. What if there was something in Mum's books after all? Maybe all I needed to do was believe, like Dorothy in *The Wizard of Oz* – just click my stilettos together and repeat the mantra, *By my fortieth birthday I will be pregnant and married. By my fortieth birthday I will be pregnant and married. By my fortieth birthday I will be pregnant and married.* At least it couldn't hurt to try, I reasoned.

"What could possibly go wrong?" I asked later that night to the small but vital group of friends who had gathered in my local pub to help me usher in the last year of my thirties. Bilal and Benjamin, who had been a couple since the dawn of time, looked at me sympathetically.

"Well done you," said Bil, "Really..." he paused while he searched for an appropriate word, "Pro-active."

"How, exactly, do you plan to pull it off?" asked Ben a little doubtfully.

"I'll just Google what I want, order it and have it delivered. Otherwise known as internet dating."

Jojo looked delighted and clapped her hands, "Finally! Welcome to the party."

I looked at her incredulously, "*You're* internet dating?"

She shrugged. "Of course. Everybody's doing it. How else do you meet anyone these days?"

Could it really be true that Jojo, face and body of a supermodel, heart of a Nobel Peace prize winner, was trawling online for men? Every day I sat next to people on the bus swiping left and right like their lives depended on it. But they were mere mortals. If Jojo had to resort to online dating to find love and was still single what hope was there for me?

"I've been doing it forever," she confessed happily.

I downed my Prosecco. Sensing my despair Bil immediately refilled my glass.

"Any luck?" I asked hopefully.

She tried to smile, "It's been ... interesting."

Ghastly images of unsuitable suitors came to mind; a Kagoul-wearing pigeon fancier, a taxidermist in tweed and a taxi driver with dandruff and a penchant for novelty pens that undressed busty blondes depending on which angle they were held.

"I have an Internet dating profile too," chipped in perennial bachelor Gropey Dave. He liked to think of himself as as Pontypridd's finest stand-up comedy export. We liked to think of him as an ageing, womanising alcoholic.

"Tinder?" Ben asked. It was more of a slight than a question. Dave looked a little affronted.

"Not just Tinder. E-Harmony and Match too. Why are you all so surprised?" he asked innocently.

Ben snorted and I saw Bil kick him under the table. Jojo forced a smile but even she was struggling with the concept of Gropey Dave staying sober long enough to write a heartfelt dating profile.

"There go my conjugal dreams up in smoke," I sighed. "Proof perfect that the Internet is full of sex-obsessed weirdos."

"That's a bit unfair," Dave replied, sounding genuinely but unjustifiably hurt.

"Okay. Why did you join a dating site?" I asked.

He shifted uncomfortably. "To look for girls."

"And what did you do, or intend to do, with these 'girls'?" I asked.

Dave looked sheepish. "Date them and um..."

He paused, wearing that look a dog has when it gets caught stealing food.

"And shag?" I suggested.

"Obviously I wouldn't say no if the opportunity arose."

"I rest my case," I said turning triumphantly to the others as if I was a prosecutor in the High Court and Dave the accused.

"Why are you being so bloody judgemental?" Dave's voice was increasingly loud and a hush fell among our fellow drinkers. "Shagging's not a crime is it? Why can't I be interested in shagging *and* love?"

I saw several women who were obviously on dates now looking with suspicious intensity at their partners.

Ben folded his arms. "It's like I've always said. Women flock to the Internet looking for relationships and men treat it like a giant knocking shop. Two entirely different agendas."

Dave raised his eyebrows. "What would you know about it?"

Ben's nostrils flared, "So because I like cock you don't think I understand anything about straight men and women?"

I tried to lighten the mood. "You don't need to fight over my vagina, boys. There's more than enough to go round."

Ben winced as if something unsavoury had been shoved under his nose.

Dave said, "That explains where the draft is coming from."

Jojo joined in, "And on that note..."

Bil picked up the thread, "A bum one?"

Ben slapped my thigh, "Not always a bad thing."

Jojo cut back in, "Happy Birthday Kat!"

"And all who sail in her," added Dave.

We all clinked glasses. Dave started bellowing, "Haaaaaaa ... pppeee" until everybody else joined in. He turned around to the other drinkers and waving his arms like a dipsomaniacal conductor, press-ganged the whole pub into singing Happy Birthday. It was both brilliant and mortifying and not the worst way to see in my last year as a thirty-something.

When our giggling had subsided Ben stood up, rattling his keys against his glass.

"If we can have your attention, please."

Bil finished his sentence, "We've also got an announcement."

"You're not gay, are you?" Dave said in mock horror,

"Oh hilarious," Ben hissed, "I can see why you're such a comedy sensation."

Before Ben and Dave could start bickering again, Bil butted in.

"Kat, we hope you don't feel like we're hijacking your birthday, but we just wanted you to know..." He paused for dramatic effect, "We're getting married!"

I jumped up from the table and hugged them both, as did Jojo while Dave sat nursing his pride and his beer.

"Amazing!" Jojo exclaimed.

"When?" I asked.

"Not for ages. At least a year," Bil gushed, "but we just couldn't keep it secret any longer."

"Naturally you're all invited," Ben said. He glanced sideways at Dave, "Even you."

Dave looked up from his beer, "Very kind of you. Where will these nuptials be taking place?"

"Martinique" said Ben.

"Ooh bloody la la," Dave goaded, "I better have my agent hire a jet."

"Hardly anywhere in the Caribbean allows same sex marriage, " Ben retorted, his anger clearly rising.

"And it's really so Ben's grandparents can attend," Bil qualified, trying to ease the tension. "They're both in their nineties and it's only a 25 minute flight from St Lucia."

Dave looked rightfully cowed. Ben had been through quite an ordeal revealing to his family that he was both gay and in love with an Asian man, and Bilal had experienced similar stigma from his own relatives.

"Yeah, 'course," Dave stammered, "I'm really happy for you both. Bit jealous actually if I'm honest."

The confession was unexpectedly sincere and there was a

moment of silence as we all looked at Dave in a new touchy-feely light. He went as far as standing up and hugging them both. Jojo and I joined in until we were all caught in an awkward rugby scrum of affection.

As we extricated ourselves I felt something brush my breast and found Dave looking at me with his hands held up in surrender, looking bashful and apologetic. It felt like an honest mistake, as opposed to the usual surreptitious pass that had earned him the moniker "Gropey".

We toasted the happy couple several times and then proceeded to get so drunk that the landlord had to lure us off the premises at closing time like the Pied Piper of Hamelin, promising us cut-price take-away booze if we agreed to go home and not stand outside the pub singing.

Chapter Three

Grating Expectations

When I woke up late the next morning I had a text from Bil, *Check your e-mail kitten, small birthday gift from us. Kisses, B&B xxx.* A little thrill ran through me; Bil and Ben had excellent taste and deep pockets. They had got into website hosting when the industry was in its infancy and now their company practically ran itself. At the very least whatever they had bought me wouldn't be from Poundland.

I rinsed the flaky bits of limescale out of the kettle, made a cup of instant coffee and opened my e-mail. In among the junk mail for a penis enlargement, a job offer of working from home licking postage stamps and several casting calls, none of which I was suitable for, was Bil and Ben's e-mail. I clicked it with glee.

Hi Kat! Welcome to GreatDate.com. I read on with diminishing glee. *Your profile is nearly complete! Romance is just a few clicks away! So log on now and start dating today!* Too many exclamation marks, too early in the day. Could something written in such bad rhyming couplets really yield true love? There was also an e-mail from Bil in my inbox.

We took the liberty of making a profile for you. Forgive any misspelling, we were quite pissed at time of going to press. The password is "MataHari." Have fun. We're expecting great things – and all the details ;-) xxx

I drained my coffee and put the kettle back on. I found two pieces of ancient bread in the bulging ice compartment of the fridge, grimacing at the post-it note that had been curling on the door since I moved in, *DEFROST ASAP.* Toast liberally smeared with peanut butter in one hand and coffee with extra sugar in the other, I sat back down and clicked on the link that took me to my dating profile.

Apparently I was five years younger than I actually was. I definitely wanted children and I fully expected a long-term, committed relationship with the man of my dreams at the very least, if not a husband. Overall I came across as a fun-loving, man-obsessed, bunny-boiling domestic goddess who was panicking that she was about to miss the baby boat. I tried not to be ungrateful. I knew that Bil and Ben only wanted the best for me and had spent a fair amount of money on a "Platinum Membership" which was supposed to guarantee my profile highly visibility on the site, the dating equivalent of a billboard advertising *LOVE FOR SALE*. Still, I felt angry and patronised. They had made me sound like a cross between the female lead of my mum's favourite film *Fatal Attraction* and a ditzy rom-com heroine; desperate, stupid and potentially dangerous.

I texted Ben, doing my best to sound grateful, *Thank u both. Such a wonderful surprise. Do you mind if I tweak it a bit? xx* He replied immediately. *Not at all. You might want to leave the age as is though ;-) xx* I stared at that response for some time. I had no idea why I found it so devastating. Perhaps because it brought home the fact that this was really the last year of my thirties. I did the dating maths; next year I would be forty, officially middle-aged, because 2x40=80, and that's *definitely* elderly. In a year's time would I be ready to succumb to elasticated slacks and loafers with arch supports? Would I be willing to exchange *Elle* for *Reader's Digest*? Would I still enjoy *Dr Who* or develop a sudden interest in *Flog It*? But lying about my age felt cheap, as if Bil and Ben were a couple of second-hand car dealers, knocking a few miles off the clock to guarantee a quick sale. What was so wrong about being thirty-nine, or forty for that matter? Surely a blatant lie wasn't the best way to start a relationship?

To add insult to ageist injury Bil and Ben had chosen a profile photo that was at least seven years old, taken onboard a narrow boat on the Norfolk Broads that Bil had hired as a surprise for Ben's birthday. Rob had made excuses not to come along and I was mortified at the snub but Bil and Ben weren't perturbed in the least. They'd started to call Rob "The Mirage" – as soon as you got close to him he disappeared. I knew exactly what they meant. I'd long since given up hope of Rob making any effort with my friends; he'd rather be playing football, or watching a game on the big screen at the pub, then catching up on the match highlights when he got home. I was resigned to being a football widow. Sometimes I wondered why Rob leaving me had come as such a surprise. We were already living separate lives a long time before we actually broke up.

I looked so young and carefree in that photo that I barely recognised my former thirty-two year old self. I was all Breton top, rolled up jeans, plimsoles and mad wispy hair in a nonchalant bun, barefaced and glowing. I wondered if I drew a line between then and now would I be able to pinpoint the exact moment when I stopped looking forward to life? Or would my graph simply reveal a slow decline that had already begun back then?

I was shaken from my dark reverie by a sickly sweet chirping. I looked back at my phone screen to see two lovebirds kissing, the kisses turning into fluttering hearts and flowers. *You've Got Male!* Great Date informed me. Unsure if this was a typo or an awful pun I clicked on the twee red postbox to retrieve my message. HorniGuy4U69 couldn't wait to meet me; *Hi sweetie. Ya up for it?x* I clicked through to his profile photo, a bathroom mirror selfie of his six pack. Pristine, skintight white boxer shorts clung to his gym-whittled hips and hovered dangerously low around his nether regions, which were bulging with excitement. His spray-tanned skin was as smooth and hairless as a baby's bottom. Across his chest was a gigantic tattoo in fancy curling script that said "DES TINY". I was confused as to why he'd had such a self-deprecating name inked on him for all eternity until I realised that the flex of his pecs was distorting the lettering and it was all in fact one word. He'd neglected to include his head in the shot giving the overall impression of a freshly waxed orange surfboard.

There was another sound effect, this time the smacking of two lips blowing a kiss and HorniGuy4U69 popped up on the instant chat feature.

So yous up for sum fun hun? he asked.

What kind of fun? I typed malevolently, *Bungee jumping? Or we could take a picnic on the Woolwich Ferry and pretend that we're on a luxury cruise? I've never been on the London Eye or would you prefer to take me up The Shard?*

He didn't pull any punches. *I usually find women 30+ are gagging for it. The closer they get to 40 the more desperate they are.*

I felt emotionally winded but I suppose Des Tiny had just illustrated Bil and Ben's point. I hit "block and delete" and sent HorniGuy4U69 into the vacuum of cyber space, where I imagined his six pack collapsing in upon itself as he was sucked into his final des-tiny, a very dense black hole. So much for the Big Bang theory.

I wondered if it was really possible to find a relationship online or if everyone was going to be like my first assailant. My mother liked to make sweeping generalisations about men, "No man wants to get married Katie, that's what feminine powers of persuasion are for," or, "No man decides to have a child, Katie, that's what timely accidents are for." She seemed to live in a world that had cobbled together its moral code from the Marquis de Sade and a Jilly Cooper sex romp. According to her all I needed was an iron will, a frilly apron and a riding crop and I could have Des Tiny and all his kind cowed into a submission of weekend trips to Homebase, wine tastings at Waitrose and arguing over Malta or Madeira for the next summer holiday.

I boiled the kettle again and poured the water straight into the empty coffee jar. I heaped in milk powder and sugar, popped the lid back on and shook vigorously. I stared at my profile as I drank the dishwater-coloured concoction straight from the jar. One thing was certain: if I was going to be entertaining gentlemen callers I would definitely need to go grocery shopping and wash up every now and then.

Chapter Four

Thunderballs

Later that afternoon I received the usual summons to birthday dinner from Mum. "I've made your absolute favourite, Katie," she enthused down the phone, like an older, suburban Nigella Lawson, "lemon meringue." It was true that lemon merengue was my all time favourite pudding – when I was nine. Back in those halcyon days of prepubescent innocence, before raging hormones gave my personality awkward corners that life then knocked off me over the next three decades, merengue was the pinnacle of culinary sophistication. These days I never went near anything lemon unless it was accompanied by gin or vodka. But far beneath the icy surface of my cynicism, an attitude of casual discontent I had been honing since I was thirteen, I was secretly glad to be going home to the familiarity of a stack of *Woman's Weekly* under the coffee table, heated electric throws on the sofa and M&S comfort food in the well-stocked fridge. I hated the overbearing smell of air freshener in the downstairs loo at Mum and Dad's and yet when I wasn't there somehow I missed it.

Mum handed me a glass of Prosecco as soon as I walked through the front door. "Happy Birthday!" she bellowed, not entirely necessary as I was standing right next to her. She clinked her own glass to mine before I even had a chance to say hello and as I took a swig she winked conspiratorially, "Don't worry. Next year it'll be a bottle of the real stuff, what with you turning the big four-o." The wine turned to acid in my mouth. "Great. I can hardly wait," I said with such an undertow of sarcasm that had I been a river my mother would have been sucked into my merciless depths immediately, never to be seen again.

I went through to the living room where Dad was sitting on the enormous chesterfield doing the *Daily Mail* crossword. I snuggled in next to him and looked over his shoulder.

"Goads," I said. He looked over the top of his reading glasses at me.

"Five down," I explained, "torments and teases."

Mum breezed in with what was left of the Prosecco. I looked at her wryly, then back at Dad. He laughed.

"Not 'Gonad' then?" he asked.

"Close," I said. "But no cigar. Without gonads probably more of a cheroot."

Dad put the paper on his lap and hugged me tight. "Happy Birthday Treacle, How's my favourite girl?"

Mum rolled her eyes, "Hardly a girl anymore."

This was our annual routine; Mum would make a big deal out of celebrating my birthday but at each opportunity remind me of my advancing years and the dwindling hope of my ever providing her with grandchildren. It was the elephant in the room that I wilfully ignored as Mum buffed it to an immaculate shine. It wasn't exactly like she was stabbing me in the back with the cake knife but she certainly knew how to blow my candles out. Dad squeezed my knee. Over the years we had developed a secret code of support between us, a kind of emotional sign language that helped us deal with Mum's prickly nature. Still, sometimes I wondered how and why he put up with her.

"Speaking of gonads," Mum said, "your father's got something to tell you." I was shocked. In my whole life I had never heard my mother refer to genitals as anything other than "downstairs" and even this was mouthed silently. For Mum to be so forthright something must definitely be up downstairs. Dad went a bit red.

"Let's not do this now, Patricia," he said, "it's Kat's birthday, for Pete's sake."

Mum huffed and disappeared into the kitchen.

"Dad, what's wrong?" I asked, mildly terrified. Mum and Dad

weren't supposed to get ill. They were supposed to be bombproof, slightly annoying and indestructible, like cockroaches in a nuclear war.

"It's nothing sweetheart," he said softly.

"That's not what the doctor said, Derek," Mum corrected from the kitchen.

I took Dad's hand. I suddenly felt shaky and sick.

My heart was thumping in my ears, my mouth dry. "Dad, please just tell me," I croaked.

"Really sweetheart, I'm fine," he said and stroked me under the chin like a cat.

"It's prostate cancer, isn't it?" I whispered tearfully.

Mum had returned now and was standing in front of me holding a fresh bottle of Prosecco.

"Don't be ridiculous, Katie," she scolded, "of course it's not cancer."

I stopped crying. "It's not? That's the best birthday present I could ever have." I burrowed my face into Dad's chest and he kissed the top of my head.

"But he does have a prostate problem," Mum continued.

I blinked into the dark cave of Dad's armpit. I loved my Dad to bits but I wasn't about to engage in a conversation *about* his bits. I pulled away from his chest. My mascara had left a damp, sooty patch on his baby blue Pringle sweater.

"It looks like a double celebration then, doesn't it?" I said cheerfully, "I've survived another year and Dad's as fit as a fiddle. Let's crack that bubbly open."

Mum handed the bottle to Dad, "Just done my nails."

Dad seemed to take an age to untwist the wire. He wiggled and prised at the cork, sucking in air through his teeth, hiding his pain.

"Bloody arthritis," he cursed under his breath.

"Dad, let me."

"I'm perfectly capable of opening a sodding bottle of sparkling wine," he growled.

Mum raised her eyebrows, "Language, Derek." She sat down on the recliner tutting while Dad continued to wrestle with the cork. Eventually he plonked the bottle in my lap.

"You've probably had more practice," he said.

"I've *definitely* had more practice," I replied and pretended to have all sorts of trouble opening the bottle. "Gosh, it *is* stiff, isn't it?"

"Oohh matron," said Dad in his best Kenneth Williams. Mum just looked annoyed.

Once I'd opened the bottle I topped Mum up until her glass almost overflowed. She would be a lot more pleasant when sedated. As I filled Dad's glass up Mum said, "Not too much. He'll be up all night weeing." This was far more information than I needed or wanted and I resented her treating Dad like a child.

"Well, it is a special occasion," I said defiantly, filling Dad's glass to the brim. Mum looked bleak.

"You're not the one who has to clean up the dribbles," she said resentfully. I glared at her.

"I'll go fetch us some canapés," she said and returned to the kitchen.

Determined to get to the bottom of Mum's pique I called after her menacingly, "I'll give you a hand."

Mum busied herself spreading pâté onto crackers and forcefully spearing baby onions with cocktail sticks as if they were enemy combatants, avoiding all eye contact with me. She bounced between the fridge, the larder and the chopping board like a bluebottle on amphetamines. Every time she opened the French country kitchen doors of the fitted units she slammed them shut again with such force that their leaded glass quivered.

"Mum, what's wrong?" I asked.

"Oh nothing," she said with forced joviality. "Let's just have a lovely birthday party, shall we?" She'd kicked up such a fuss that there was no way I could drop the subject now, however uncomfortable I found it.

"Are you worried you won't be able to go on holiday this year if Dad's having treatment?"

"It's fine, really Katherine."

I bristled. I hated anyone using my full name, especially my mother. It always sounded like an insult.

"Mum. Talk to me."

She stopped fiddling with the finger food, threw the knife down on the counter and turned to me, tight-lipped and seething.

"He can't do it anymore," she said bitterly.

"Do what?" I asked.

She glared at me. "The Sex."

I stared at her, the ticking of the kitchen clock punctuating the awkward silence at regular intervals. "Mum, I'm not sure —" I began. It was too late. She had taken my enquiry as her cue to launch a full-scale assault on Dad's shortcomings. Literally.

"He hasn't been interested for a while. I knew something was up. Or rather not up." She gave a bitter little laugh at her own joke.

I wanted the heated flagstones to open and swallow me whole. Ever since I could remember I had pretended that I was adopted, as much to distance myself from the thought of my parents ever having had sex as their other embarrassing foibles. Joking about sex *Carry On* style with Dad was one thing: a full-blown account of the actual details with my mother quite another. Oblivious to my burning shame Mum continued, having only just warmed to her topic.

"I made him see the doctor. And she said —"

"You made him see a *female* GP?" I interrupted, incredulous.

"She said it was age-related, probably something to do with his prostate. She prescribed Viagra to get things moving again. But he's just not interested."

I was mortified. Mum and I had never had a close relationship. We were never "like sisters", we had never shared clothes and while I loved her I didn't see her as a best friend, nor any kind of friend for that matter. Above all else, we never, *ever* talked about deeply personal things, least of all "The Sex". We were both at fault but I held her personally responsible for a catalogue of poor parenting choices, like not bothering to tell me the Facts of Life which led to me embarrassing myself in the last year of junior school when I authoritatively informed my entire class that women got pregnant through kissing but only if they were in love and married. During early adolescence my friends started to talk about periods and I drew a blank. All I knew was that sometimes women put padding in their pants or had to use a huge cotton bud with a string on it. I finally confronted Mum when I was twelve. She was loading the washing machine and carried on with the task as she told me about "the birds and the bees", as if focusing on the laundry somehow sanitised the messy biology of it all. I was mortified to find out that a) I had come to exist this way, b) Dad had done that to Mum, c) Someone might want to do that to me some day, and d) I was going to have an open wound once a month which, according to Mum, was "a messy pain in the bottom," and lead to a great deal of confusion on my part about how to use tampons when I did start menstruating.

And here we were now discussing The Strange Case of Mum's and Dad's Missing Sex Life. It was more than I could stand. I picked up the plate of crackers. "Shall I take these through?" I asked as if she hadn't just seared the terrible image of Dad struggling to engage in coitus onto the already warped cinema screen of my mind for the rest of my life; Mum the merciless praying mantis, Dad a helpless worker ant. She let out an exasperated sigh, "Katie, I am a woman. I have needs." Good grief, I thought, she's morphed into Erica Jong. I half expected Barbra Streisand to burst into the kitchen and start wailing "I Am A Woman In Love".

I put the plate back on the counter harder than I needed to. "You should probably discuss this with Dad."

She squared up to me, hands on her hips. "Trust you to take your father's side."

"I'm not taking sides," I said, trying not to shout though aware of my voice becoming high pitched and reedy. "This is just a bit weird, okay?" Then, even though I knew it was tantamount to pouring petrol on a fire, I added, "Perhaps you can talk to Patrick about it?" Her eyes flashed with anger.

"Why on earth would I ask your brother?" she asked.

"Well, if we're talking about favourites."

She looked extremely hurt and I felt like a total cow.

"That's not fair," she said, her voice cracking with emotion, "I love you both equally."

I was caught between wanting to hug her and the desire for revenge, to reprimand her for what felt like a lifetime of injustice; like the day Patrick got lost at the zoo because I wouldn't hold his hand – he was in the habit of constantly picking his nose and wiping it on me at the time – and it was deemed to be my fault. Or the occasion when Patrick was playing Commando and broke Mum's Art Deco umbrella and I got the blame. And the time that Patrick ate all of the Christmas fruit cake and I was held accountable because I was left in charge while Mum and Dad were gift shopping. Patrick could have been involved in human trafficking and Mum would still have defended him with something like, "Those girls had nowhere else to go. He hired that van at his own expense, you know." I could feel years of bitter resentment and jealousy towards my little brother bubbling up through my gut, oozing from every pore. The desire to spew all that bile forth now was immense. Instead I said flatly, "That's nice," picked up the plate again and returned to the living room.

I kicked what Dad called "the poof" out of the way and sat back down next to him. Mum and Dad had bought the pouffe the previous year on a trip to Turkey and Mum would consistently reference its presence as proof that she was neither racist nor homophobic.

"Everything okay, Treacle?" Dad asked doubtfully.

"Just peachy," I said, forcing a smile.

I shoved a dry cracker in my mouth. Jagged chunks of it caught in my throat. It felt appropriate, a metaphor for how wronged I felt in Mum's presence, always at the sharp end.

Mum came back in wearing her benign expression, the one that showed everybody just how much she was hurting but would somehow muddle through for our sakes. We were caught in the kind of emotional stand-off that could only be resolved by more cheap fizz. She topped us all up again, ignoring her own advice about over-hydrating Dad as a show of good will and we clinked glasses.

"Happy Birthday, Kat," Mum said. I knew how much it pained her to use my nickname, she thought it made me sound common. "Thanks, Mum," I replied, consciously softening my attitude in return for her generosity. Still, I had no doubt we'd be reaching for the emotional hammer and tongs again at some point in the very near future.

Chapter Five

First Blood

Dirty Harry, 38, London. Stable, robust, creative. Charming and adventurous male seeks female for fun times, romance and perhaps more seemed like the perfect candidate for my first online date. Judging by his profile he was reasonably attractive, gainfully employed, about the same age as me and he could spell. The fact that he hadn't asked me for a blow job or what my favourite sexual position was in any of our messages was also a big bonus.

Pre-date I spent hours on the phone to Jojo, Bil and Ben obsessively asking questions about what to wear, how to behave, whether we should split the bill (me and my overdraft were desperately hoping they'd say no, but everyone agreed on going Dutch). Even Dave had given me a little pre-date pep talk. Apart from being broke I was feeling sassy, powerful, confident, and something I hadn't felt in a long time – hopeful.

My hopes were dashed from the moment my date trundled into the restaurant. Whoever said "the camera never lies" has obviously never online dated; Dirty Harry was at least ten years older than his profile picture, ten stone heavier and ten inches shorter. It wasn't so much a value judgement on my part – I was hardly a candidate for *Love Island* myself – but rather a feeling that I'd been hood-winked.

With my heart sinking quicker than a doomed ocean liner, I watched my date plough through his meal, barely pausing for breath let alone conversation. Through a mouthful of Pad Thai, noodles hanging out of his mouth like one of the dogs in *Lady And The Tramp,* he mumbled, "How's your curry?" He rammed his fork into my food before I could answer. "Delicious," I said, as I wiped away a speck of crushed peanut that Harry had just sprayed in my face.

"Dirty Harry" was in fact Kieran from Ashford, Kent. Apparently working in London qualified as living there. Kieran's "creativity" lay in his ability to skim off stationary supplies from the sales company he worked for, and "adventurous" was all about paint-balling on the weekend and a particularly nasty bungee jumping experience during a bout of diarrhoea in Thailand. "Talk about the galloping gourmet," Kieran guffawed, thoroughly amused with himself, "I was certainly hot to trot." I tried to turn my grimace into a laugh.

"Dessert?" asked Kieran, practically throwing a menu at me.

"Oh, no thanks, I've had quite enough," I responded, barely bothering to disguise my sarcasm.

I tried to find solace in the fact that at least I was out on a date and not stuck on my own in the flat watching the entire box set of *Sex And The City* for the 299th time. Maybe, I tried to convince myself, beneath the overpowering aftershave and overbearing manner Kieran was actually a nice guy, a diamond in the rough. I shot him my best smile.

He looked confused. "Are you okay? My dad used to make that face when his piles were giving him gip."

"I'm fine," I said, deploying everything I had ever learned in Method acting class, "I'm really enjoying the food – and the company." I added a flirty, girlish giggle for good measure.

"Because if you do suffer from haemorrhoids curry's probably the worst thing you could eat," Kieran said, sucking in air for emphasis. "Very nasty indeed. Burny bum-bum."

When the bill came Kieran put on a pair of spectacles and suddenly looked exactly like my dad. He examined the receipt with all the careful attention to detail of a UN weapons inspector.

"Oh," he exclaimed gravely as if he'd just found a WMD, "service not included. Now that is a pity." He produced a calculator from his shirt pocket and began to work out his exact share.

"Don't worry," he said with a cheeky wink, "I won't charge you for my dessert. But you did polish off most of the wine by yourself so I guess we're even-stevens."

After we paid Kieran yawned exaggeratedly, stretching his arms and patting his mouth like a 1970s mime artist. He looked at his watch. "It's been lovely," he said drowsily.

"Yes," I said flatly, praying that the whole "I'm very tired" routine wasn't a precursor to get me into bed.

"But I don't think we should meet again."

"Oh," I replied, my relief immediately giving way to miscomprehension. I had no romantic interest in Kieran and yet the rejection still felt like a slap.

"I probably should have mentioned it earlier, but I've met someone special."

"Right," I stammered, "then why are you on a date with me?"

"Got to keep my hand in," he said, with another cringe-making wink, "stay in the game and all that. And you looked so gorgeous in your photos."

His use of the past tense, the merest suggestion of faded beauty, set my teeth on edge. Perhaps I shouldn't have used my acting head shots for my dating profile. I suppose the lighting and airbrushing might have oversold me somewhat. I could feel the red-hot heat of humiliation rushing into my face, a sting of tears behind my eyes.

I stood up from the table, deliberately scraping my chair as I pushed it back. Kieran grabbed my coat from the waiter and twirled it round like a matador's cape, before dumping it on my shoulders and giving me a thudding pat on the back. "It sounds like you've met your match," I said thickly, extending my hand in an attempt at good sportswomanship. Instead of shaking my hand Kieran leaned over and gave me a sloppy, bad-breath kiss on the cheek, my runner-up prize in the dating game. It was like being licked by a Labrador.

"Be lucky," he said.

"Oh I am," I said acidly, "Kat with nine lives."

I left with as much grace as I could muster. When I was sure that Kieran could no longer see me I quickened my pace, the adrenalin of first date failure propelling me forwards, faster and faster until I was running tip-tap-clatter-clatter in my killer heels which were by now murdering my feet.

The lurid fluorescent glare of an all-night shop ahead in the distance stopped me in my tracks. Now here was something robust and stable; the crispness of Chardonnay, the rich, pepperiness of Rioja, and the dirty burn of cheap vodka. I grabbed a Two-for-One offer on white wine from the fridge and made my way to the counter. The greasy man serving behind it looked me up and down with a lecherous smile. "Very nice," he leered, "very nice, indeed." Too tired to lecture him on objectification and desperate to douse my despair with wine I dropped the money on the counter and bolted out of the shop, a bottle in each hand like a pair of alcoholic maracas.

The relief lasted as far as the end the first bottle. By the time I'd reached the bottom of the second I was not in a good way at all. My expertly applied smoky-eye make-up was running down my cheeks, creating a startling resemblance to Bette Davis in *Whatever Happened To Baby Jane*. It began as a snivel, escalated into a siren-like wail and before I knew it I was on the floor, crying from the depths of my heart and soul, in an Oscar worthy performance, "Best Distraught Single Woman In An Unsupported Role."

Chapter Six

Pigs Might Fly

Bad date and not-too-bad birthday over, it was time to get back to work – I was running out of excuses to tell my landlord Mr Barrington about the well overdue rent. Fortunately for me, Mr B was a shuffler and the sound of his knackered leather slippers on the threadbare communal hallway carpet, accompanied by a hacking smokers' cough, usually alerted me to his presence long before he could corner me.

I was up long before dawn, too early even to be caught by Mr B, who was a "rise with the lark, to bed with the sunset" kind of man (although I suspected this was because he was too miserly to switch his lights on rather than any joy to greet the new day). The fee for the job was too paltry to justify a taxi, meaning a ninety minute journey on three night buses. I crept out of the flat at three a.m. clutching a fleece blanket, my Oyster card and a muesli bar. Poverty turns everything into a feat of epic proportions and being broke in London, one of the most expensive cities on earth, amplified this tenfold.

I was appearing in a television commercial for an upmarket hair styling product as "third salon head from left". After signing in at reception I went through to hair and makeup. A man with a massive white-blonde quiff, glossy black leggings and enormous crepe-soled beetle crushers was fawning over a stunning model, so thin that she was verging on two-dimensional – had she turned sideways she would have disappeared completely. She was surfing photo after photo of herself on Instagram, while Quiffy gushed about her incredible bone structure as he brushed her poker straight russet hair.

I slumped down in the chair next to the Red Queen trying to ignore my ghoulish reflection in the dramatically lit mirror. I had matching puffy hand baggage under each eye, the bulges emphasised by panda-like dark circles. The harsh lighting made the spider veins at the side of my nostrils pop so that my face resembled an ordinance survey map, my nose its Ben Nevis. Every little flaw was magnified a hundredfold, my grey skin and enlarged pores a lunar landscape of imperfections.

Quiffy stopped brushing and stared at me with a surly open mouth.

"I know what you're thinking," I said, "and you're right. I don't just get out of bed looking like this. It's taken years of abuse." Red laughed. Quiffy's lip curled into a sneer.

"I'm Kat," I said, waving to his reflection in the mirror.

"Oh, hiiiii," he replied, holding onto the last vowel, letting it float up at the end so that it sounded like a question, "I'm Richard."

I smiled, a bad move as it showed every wrinkle and with the eye bags gave me a startling resemblance to Winston Churchill.

"Sir Quiff Richard?" I asked. Quiffy looked non-plussed but Red laughed again and smiled warmly, revealing perfectly straight white teeth and zero crows feet.

"I'm Storm," she said. Another model called Storm. It never rains but it pours. What was it, I asked myself, with all the beautiful people being named after inclement weather systems?

"Cool," I said, and suddenly realised how old I must have sounded as well as looked. Nobody said "cool" any more. It was the kind of thing Beatniks drawled in the 1950s.

"Shall I just hang here until you're ready for my close up, Mr De Mille?" I asked Quiffy in my best gravelly Gloria Swanson. He sighed agitatedly, slammed down the brush he'd been ritually paddling over Red's hair and picked up a clipboard from the table.

"What a pity Kitty, I don't seem to have you down on my list," he said cattily. I started to think that I was in the wrong studio or had got my days confused when Quiffy corrected himself.

"Oh no, soz. You *are* on my list. Right at the bottom."

"That's a relief," I said with forced joviality.

"Yeah," he continued, studying the clipboard dismissively, "You're a background artist, aren't you?"

"Background artist" is a fancy way of saying "extra", the lowest of the low in film and TV land, ranked below even apprentice camera crew and sixth-formers on work experience. "You're next door, love," he sneered.

I'd already learned my lesson about being difficult with anyone on a shoot. Two years previously I was playing a lady's maid in a diabolical period TV drama, but at least I had some dialogue. My agent – back when I had an agent – had got incredibly excited about it. "Play this one right and you could be off to LA for pilot season," she'd enthused, dollar signs in her eyes. Unfortunately my sense of dignity precluded my desire to be rich and famous. The heavy-handed hairdresser, who was supposed to be the best in the business at recreating historically accuracy, had pinned an awful rat's nest so tightly to my head that I couldn't even move my eyebrows. When I yelped in agony she rammed a pin directly into my scalp. After three hours I had a pounding headache and could bear the torture no more. Filming had to be halted while I was sent back to hair and make-up where the Wicked Witch Of The Wardrobe called me a baby and told me I was unlikely to be cast in the next series. Her prediction was spookily accurate and my agent dropped me shortly afterwards.

"Silly me," I said to Quiffy as I stood up, "my eyes must be painted on. Have a great day." I heard him burst into peals of laughter as soon as I'd left the room and say, "What was *that?!*" Tiredness had left me Teflon coated and his insult slid off me like an egg from a well-oiled frying pan. Famished, I went in search of breakfast. The one good thing about these rubbish jobs was the catering.

I joined a queue of gaffers and camera guys, all wearing baseball caps, combat trousers and fleece jackets, like a micro-plastic polluting army. As I got closer to the glow of the heated display unit and its comforting aroma of high cholesterol I noticed that the man serving behind the counter looked familiar. When I got near enough to examine the chalkboard menu I realised with alarm his identity: we'd been on a date about a year previously.

I'd met him at one of Gropey's gigs, where the man had sat laughing his head off as if Dave was some kind of comedy legend. He even mouthed the punchlines. He said he went to as many of Dave's gigs as possible (which was a bit stalky) but after the gig he bought us pint after pint (and seemed far less stalky). He wasn't bad company – although that could have been the beer talking – and at the end of the night we had a drunken snog and exchanged numbers. I'd forgotten his name and put him in my contacts list as "Laughing Gas".

We went on a date. He told me his name again and I forgot it. He talked about his work as a Michelin star chef with his own chain of restaurants, only they were all called different names which explained why I'd never heard of them. He said he didn't like to brag. He sniped about the quality and presentation of the food the whole time we were eating. I tried not to be offended even though I had chosen the place because it was my favourite restaurant.

My date made a big deal of flashing his Rolex but when the time came to pay we split the bill. I noted that his credit card was bog standard like mine, not a platinum Am Ex. When he went to kiss me goodbye I swerved his embrace and I avoided going to any more of Dave's gigs for a good six months in case I bumped into him again. And now here he was at the film studio canteen, shovelling fat and carbs to the great unwashed. Clearly the swanky watch was counterfeit and his whole story of being the next Gordon Ramsey was nothing more than a figment of his imagination.

Once at the counter I ducked behind a pile of breakfast baps to avoid coming face to face. The grumpy gaffer behind me said, "You ordering food, love, or trying to hide from it? Crouching Extra, Hidden Sarnie?" He laughed loudly at his own joke and several other techies joined in at my expense. With my cover blown I had no choice but to stand up. I did so too quickly, like a slice of bread shooting out of a toaster, sending the baps rolling off the counter in all directions. I heard the gaffer curse behind me. And then I came face to face with Laughing Gas.

At first he jumped at my sudden appearance. As he began to realise who I was his jaw went slack and his face white.

"Hi Kat," he said sheepishly.

"Fancy seeing you here," I said cheerfully, desperately trying to remember his name.

I watched his Adam's apple move up and down in his throat. It looked like he was finding it hard to swallow.

"I had no idea that you also ran outside catering units too," I said, with just a whisper of early morning irony.

"Yeah. It makes sense to diversify," he stammered, turning from white to red.

"Are you actually ordering something?" demanded the gaffer, his breath hot and roll-up stinky on the back of my neck.

"I'll have your finest pulled pork on a freshly baked baguette with chipotle sauce please," I said sardonically. Laughing Gas looked lost.

"In other words, a bacon sandwich with shedloads of ketchup, thanks."

I almost felt sorry for him; a plastic sports watch had replaced the Faux-lex and the expensive cologne was now overpowered by the smell of chips. He was wearing a polo shirt with the company logo, "Porkies" and his shoulder length hair, so pristinely blow dried on our date, was scraped back into a greasy pony tail.

His boss came up behind him while he was making my sandwich saying, "Hurry up Sam. Look at this queue." There could be no doubt that Sam was a mere minion. "Great to see you again," I said, grabbing the sandwich, "and all the best with your gourmet empire."

Part of me was glad for shaming him. He was like the little

boy who cried "food chain" and I had caught him with his apron down. Non-Despicable Me, the part that had just been made to feel one life form up from an amoeba by Quiffy, felt genuinely sorry for Sam. We live in a world that measures personal worth quantitatively; bra size, car size, bank balance. Was it any surprise that Sam had fabricated a better, bigger, wealthier version of himself?

I spent the rest of the day with my head hanging over the basin of the make-believe hair salon mulling over this status-quo. The models were only expected to shoot for twenty minutes before being bundled back into fluffy white robes like baby birds at imminent risk of hypothermia. Trolls like me, with our insulating layers of blubber (or what anyone sane would call a healthy BMI) had to stay where we were for the duration, even though we were barely visible in shot and could probably have been replaced by mannequins.

Was this how it was always going to be, I wondered? Would people like Sam and I always be trapped at the bottom of the food chain? What I needed, I resolved, was a regular job. Some place where I could get to know people and have my talents appreciated. Somewhere that I could be part of a team. And mostly something that was going to give me regular pay and not expect me to work before noon.

On the next tea break I spied a copy of *The Stage,* the theatrical luvvies trade magazine, on one of the knackered easy chairs in the canteen. I sat on the paper and surreptitiously stashed it down the back of my trousers when I didn't think anyone was looking until I heard the gaffer's charming East London tones behind me.

"All that sitting down giving you haemorrhoids, love?"

"Sorry?" I asked, as sweetly and innocently as I could. He nodded at my backside.

"You got piles, or have they run out of loo roll in the Ladies?"

I wished that complete strangers would stop commenting on my anal health.

"Those chairs are like concrete," I said, with my girl-next-door grin.

"Best place for that rag, in my opinion. Wouldn't wipe my arse with it," he snorted.

I nearly said, "I doubt it would be big enough," but giggled instead, like it was the funniest thing I'd heard all day. Yes, I decided, I would meet this trashy, superficial world on its own terms.

Fired up and ready to unleash New And Improved Kat on the world I started circling auditions in the paper on the Tube journey home. I felt positively upbeat. I even marked stuff that I didn't have a chance of even being seen for – *Sixteen year old ingenue. Model looks, 5'10 minimum, catwalk build* and *Lead, all-male musical.*

I was woken up at Brixton Station, the end of the line, by one of the cleaners. He was picking up discarded newspapers with a metal grabber that made his arm look like a Bond villain's. Wiping the dribble from my mouth I caught sight of my hair reflected in the window of the Tube. The cheap shaving foam that had been applied on my head all day in imitation of shampoo lather had left my hair in a mad, dried out mess reminiscent of Albert Einstein.

I scanned the carriage for my copy of *The Stage* and realised that the cleaner had just binned my future prospects. I dived into his rubbish sack and retrieved it while he shook his head and said, "crazy lady." I smiled – my new smile. He looked alarmed and scuttled off into another carriage. Oh well, I thought, at least I'd had some impact.

Chapter Seven

Tequila Mockingbird

I was flat broke. In fact I was concave broke. I was getting to the point where my overdraft needed an overdraft. I knew the money from the advert I'd just done wouldn't arrive for at least a month and unless more work came in I would have to coast on the fumes of my credit cards – or ask my parents for a loan. Every time I had to borrow money Dad would make a joke about 200% APR interest. What he meant was "Give it back if and when you can." Mum, on the other hand, would give me a look of disappointment that said, "No wonder Rob left you." It made me feel shitty about myself but the thought of being evicted was worse. I decided that the sooner I found my mother a prospective son-in-law the better.

From Purley To Eternity, 39. Bored administration worker, would-be beat poet, seeks spirited woman with good grammar for wild but concise road trip was waiting for me outside Liverpool Street station. I spotted him instantly. He was like a character Kerouac might have created. He had red hair and a matching beard, the moustache of which was waxed and curled at its ends. He wore a pigeon fancier's flat cap, a chunky, hand-knitted sweater, a shirt with bow tie and a tweed jacket. His corduroy trousers were rolled up, revealing natty socks (odd) and golfing brogues. I wasn't sure if this was a fashion statement or because he rode a bicycle, quite possibly a penny farthing. He was very tall and thin, like an eccentrically dressed exclamation mark.

He gave me a big smile when he saw me, making the ends of his moustache snake towards his ears like Salvador Dali.

"You must be Kat," he said, extending his hand.

"And you must be from Purley," I replied, shaking his hand very firmly. I did my best to give him a manly, platonic handshake, having made my mind up in those first vital three seconds that I didn't fancy him.

"Nigel," he said, holding my hand just a little too long. "You look great," he added, "natural. Nice to meet a woman who isn't plastered in make-up."

"Normally I wear truckloads of the stuff, you caught me on a down day," I replied, trying to assure him that I wasn't his type. He thought I was being ironic and laughed.

"Do you fancy a drink?" he asked. "There's an amazing Latin bar a couple of blocks away. Live music and cocktails that'll make steam come out of your ears."

It was Saturday night so I figured I may as well enjoy myself. Linking arms in a chummy kind of way – like I did with Jojo – Purley and I strolled to Spitalfields, bantering as we walked.

The place was called *Ms Kahlo's* and there was a massive monobrow above the door. We sidled up to the bar and took a cow-hide covered stool each, side by side. "Shall we start with a shot of Tequila and a beer before moving on to the hard stuff?" he asked. I gulped. If this was his idea of easing into a night I shuddered to think what qualified as a bender. A beautiful woman behind the bar, with dark lose curls that tumbled over her shoulders and framed a perfect cleavage, lined up our shots. We winced our way through the obligatory salt and lemon before clinking the tiny glasses and downing our antiseptic in a single gulp.

"Wow," I said to Nigel, gasping through the vapour of the liquor, "she's stunning." I was hoping to divert his attention well away from me.

"Do you like women?" he asked, his curiosity clearly piqued.

"Of course," I said, "I mean no. I mean not like that. Not that I'm homophobic. Two of my best friends are gay." As the words fell out of my mouth I realised that I sounded like an absolute homophobe. Nigel didn't seem to notice.

He twirled his moustache suggestively and said, "She's okay. But you're much more interesting."

I took a swig of my beer to wash away the Tequila. "Who wants to be interesting? I want to be deadly and gorgeous. A femme fatale."

He raised an eyebrow in the direction of my drink, "Carry on like that and you'll be a femme fatality."

"May I remind you that it was you who suggested this?" I said, jabbing him in the ribs.

He raised his beer to make a toast. "Guilty. What shall we drink to?"

I examined my own bottle of craft beer and read the quote on the label. "To anything and nothing, and everything that lies between."

He looked at me dreamily. Without even trying I had tapped right into his Beatnik soul. He was the kind of guy who would have appreciated me saying, "cool".

"I couldn't have put it better myself," he said.

We bumped bottles and he stared deeply into my eyes.

"You know Kat, you're my kind of woman."

I avoided his gaze by picking at the label on the bottle. "I doubt that very much," I said drily.

"You just don't seem to care about what anyone thinks about you."

I wanted to say, "I just don't care what *you* think of me." Instead I gave him a nervous smile.

"It's so refreshing," he continued, "you shoot straight from the hip, there's no facade. You are who you are." He reached his hand out to touch my arm and I playfully slapped it away. He smiled at me and sighed, "Oh my. You're perfect."

I felt a rush of mild panic. My attempt to dissuade Nigel had had exactly the opposite effect.

"Margarita?" I suggested to Nigel, hoping to dampen his ardour with copious amounts of alcohol.

"Hell yes," he replied.

By the time we got to the bottom of the next drink I had fallen victim to my own design. The booze only made Nigel bolder in his advances but at least in my sozzled state I was less bothered by them. We had a few more beers, another cocktail, something that arrived on fire and finally one last shot of tequila. I remember dancing, slapping Nigel's face when he tried to embrace me under the auspices of showing me how to shoot pool and then a cartoonish pursuit around the bus stop when he tried to kiss me. Whatever he lacked in charm and sex appeal he certainly made up for in persistence. Breathless from swerving his advances and giddy from the booze I finally confronted him with the truth. "Nigel," I panted, "you're a great guy. I'd really like to stay in touch. But only as friends. Really. It's never going to be any more than that." He grabbed his chest as if I'd shot him and dropped to his knees. At least he took it in good humour and had an interesting flair for the dramatic.

I hugged Nigel goodnight, a firm platonic embrace, turning my face away so he couldn't get his tongue anywhere near my mouth, and tottered onto the bus. He stared at me through the bus window, doing various amusing charades representing his broken heart much to the amusement of my fellow passengers. As the bus pulled away he traced an imaginary tear down his cheek. I giggled to myself and felt a little wistful. Maybe I should have let Nigel kiss me, just to see what it was like? I wasn't attracted to him at all but what if I was in the twilight years of dating and, like the last suspicious looking turkey in the supermarket on Christmas Eve, Nigel was all that was left? Was it better to take a punt on salmonella or accept dining alone for the rest of eternity in a purgatory of my own making? What if I was in fact the turkey, rapidly approaching my sell-by date and about to be binned for good? Maybe some other desperate woman would nab Nigel off the shelf in a last-minute panic buy. Or perhaps Nigel was exactly someone else's cup of tea. Like my nana used to say, "Every pot has its lid."

I dutifully texted Bil and Ben on my way home. *It's another no from me, I'm afraid* :/ I wasn't surprised that they didn't respond since they'd popped off to Paris for a last-minute romantic weekend to celebrate their engagement. I messaged Dave, *Online dating SUCKS*, but he also failed to reply, unconscious drunk or shagging a groupie after his gig, I supposed (or quite possibly both, knowing Dave). I started to call Jojo and then realised she was probably in another time zone or otherwise tucked up in bed with jet lag so I sent a WhatsApp instead. She answered immediately. *Kat! Just landed. My place 11am tomorrow? xxx*

Chapter Eight

Ugly Sister

The next morning I sat at Jojo's tiny kitchen/desk/dining/coffee table in her minuscule but incredibly stylish studio flat with my head in my hands. She slid a freshly made latte in front of me. It was the first time I'd seen Jojo since my birthday. She'd been madly traversing the globe for her job and had just got back from Brazil. She looked a little drawn, but as usual effortlessly chic, even in sweatpants.

"That bad?" she asked, as she sat down opposite me.

"It's the noise of that bloody coffee machine. It sounds like a 747 taking off. You realise you could have bought a small car for the same price?"

Ignoring my belligerence she reached across the table and opened the fridge, retrieving a bottle of fancy sparkling water with an unpronounceable name.

"Oh dear," she soothed, "nasty hangover?"

She then leaned the other way, grabbed a tumbler from a shelf and opened the bottle, adding in an enormous vitamin tablet for good measure. The clonking of the giant pill against the glass annoyed me. The hissing of the bubbles annoyed me. The fact that I don't even like carbonated water, especially at that price, annoyed me.

"How's the dating going?" Jojo asked.

I looked up and shook my head. Jojo pulled a face. "Do you want to talk about it?"

"God, NO," I moaned.

We spent the next two hours talking about rubbish dates and bad men over very good coffee and warm flaky croissants. I regaled

Jojo of the tales of Kieran of Kent and Nigel of Purley while she groaned and laughed in the appropriate places. When I got to the part of the story where I was purging my Chardonnay-induced misery into the toilet, she opened the fridge again and produced a very decent bottle of Pinot Noir.

I balked at the thought of more alcohol, "Oh no, Jojo."

She laughed, "Nonsense. Hair of the dog."

"But it's so expensive," I protested, "wasted on a hangover."

"We must drink to forget," she said channeling Marlene Dietrich, "and we must never forget to drink". She popped the cork with the speed of a master sommelier and poured me a large glass of chilly blackcurrant-hued heaven.

Jojo never ceased to amaze me. First, I couldn't understand how she was single. "Beautiful" was a gross understatement. She was stunning. Tall, with dark brown skin, endless corkscrew curls and green eyes set in a perfectly symmetrical face. Her father, long since passed from a sudden heart attack, had been a doctor from Bermuda, her mum, now retired to the countryside, a nurse from Barnsley. Her parents had been madly in love, a love which had seen them through considerable prejudice from family and complete strangers alike. Jojo often referred to them as "Mr and Mrs Mills and Boon". Jojo's accent was a melange of her mum's broad Yorkshire, scattered with her dad's favourite Bermy sayings like, "Stop de madness" or inviting everybody round to her place for a "greeze", the Bermudan equivalent of a huge fry up, after many an all-night party.

To walk down the street next to Jojo was to sink into complete obscurity. Men and women both went weak in the presence of her physical perfection, small children gazed at her adoringly. On one occasion I witnessed a window cleaner lose all control of his squeegee as she passed him. It plopped into his bucket, splashing both Jojo and I with water. He went bright red and stammered "Sorry love." Jojo laughed while I tutted over the water stains on my brand new dress. "Bloody idiot," I hissed. "Miserable cow," he returned. Jojo looked back at the pair of us, and the window cleaner assured her, "Not you darlin', I meant your mate."

Jojo had studied fashion at St Martins before being seduced into the world of commercial retail. She was a buyer for an upmarket high street women's clothing chain and her life was a whirlwind of international flights (economy class), catwalk shows (back row), hotels (three to four star), free samples (travel size) and glossy magazines. But her high-flying career came at a price; her job was horribly low paid in relation to her expertise and the long hours had taken a crippling toll on her personal life. She was hardly in London long enough to pick up her dry cleaning, let alone date anyone.

Jojo's flat looked like a cross between something from Mary Norton's *The Borrowers* and *Elle Interiors*. She was a living doll living in a doll's house. A stint in Tokyo had given her the knack of taking the latest trend and downsizing it to fit her tiny apartment. Everything was spotlessly clean and tidy, the designer sofa bed put away each morning to turn the flat into a useable space. Rather than feeling cramped there was something incredibly Zen about the way she lived. She would often have six people or more over for dinner, made with the minimum amount of fuss in her micro-kitchen. Most bewildering of all she had mastered the art of the capsule wardrobe. By contrast, I still had days when I struggled to find a clean bra.

If Jojo wasn't the sweetest, kindest woman I'd ever met I would have positively hated her. Except that Jojo had it as hard as I did, in some ways far worse. Women often disliked her for being so gorgeous – they would automatically assume that she was vain and self-obsessed before she could open her mouth. The few who did venture beyond her looks were even more wary, either assuming that her sweetness was false, or despising her because she really had that rare combination of grace and beauty.

Straight men were often simply too in awe to even make an approach, but looking like an angel fallen to earth Jojo had no problem attracting a certain type of man. Egomaniacs, odious City trader types, second-division footballers and wide boys, literally threw themselves at her feet, impressed by the gleam of her jet-set lifestyle. The infatuation usually lasted until her first buying trip, when these men decided that they were no competition for Paris, New York or Mumbai and stopped calling. The ones who made it as far as the inner sanctum of her bijou apartment realised that she wasn't anywhere near as well-heeled as the designer clothes suggested and dumped her as a gold digger. Jojo just couldn't win, it seemed.

She once dated one of the most handsome men in the world, at least according to a popular fashion magazine's "Top Ten Hunks of The Year". Jayson Grayson was godlike in his perfection, an Adonis to her Venus. But he was so stupid. I used to ask Jojo if she could hear the sound of the ocean when she put her ear to his head. One time he tried to fix her gas boiler saying that he'd had "some training as an engineer at college" (before he was spotted on Oxford Street and shot to fame overnight as an underwear model). I had been in the flat at the time of Jason's DIY attempt and yanked the cigarette he perpetually had hanging out of his mouth (because he thought it made him look like James Dean), throwing it out of the tiny kitchen window before he had a chance to turn the gas back on. In his broad Scouse accent he protested, "What the bloody 'ell d'you do that for? I was smoking that, I was." For the duration of their relationship I acted like a social worker, making sure Jay-G, as he preferred to be known, didn't leave the handles of boiling pots sticking out over the stove, hadn't overloaded the washing machine or poisoned Widget, Jojo's pedigree Siamese (now exiled to her mum's house in Hereford because of Jojo's prolonged absences).

And that's how beautiful Jojo had taken to online dating long before I, her ugly sister, had even considered it. Despite her many talents Jojo wasn't good with the written word and once we'd demolished the first bottle of Pinot and she was opening another she asked me to have a look at her profile. I bristled at the task – the text was reassuringly dull, making me feel a little bit better about my own efforts – but the images, the thing that I knew really counted, were stunning. I half-considered photoshopping Groucho Marx glasses, nose and moustache onto her flawless face. She produced photo after photo of natural perfection but was genuinely insecure about each one, asking, "Is this okay? Too slutty? Ugh, my hair looks awful in this one." I wanted to slap the perfect bone structure of her cheek. But I couldn't hate her. It was impossible. Besides – and I'm ashamed to say it now – she was no match for my wit. Jojo may have had the face of Nefertiti but I believed that I had the smarts of a leading lady in a Shakespearian comedy. I may not have landed many dates but I'd already had a plethora of compliments on my humorous profile and I collected these like club card points in lieu of the actual object of the exercise.

Jojo made an omelette while I tinkered away at updating her profile. I hit "confirm changes" just as she put a steaming plate of fried perfection in front of me.

"I'm thinking about freezing my eggs," said Jojo as she rammed a piping hot yellow forkful into her mouth.

"Won't they go funny when you defrost them?" I asked. "I know you're away a lot, but maybe just buy less eggs?"

"My eggs, silly. These ones," she replied, using her thumbs to indicate her ovaries. "I'm seriously considering putting them on ice for later use, in case I can't get pregnant or don't meet the right guy."

"I knew that. I was being sardonic," I lied.

"I thought you were being ironic," Jojo replied munching on a piece of toast. "Sardonic would indicate a streak of cruelty and I know you only want the best for me." She grinned and continued telling me her plan. "I've already started looking into it. Every round of insemination costs a packet, but you can do a swap, donate your eggs to an infertile couple and share a freezer."

I thought the whole thing sounded awful, like a black market baby supermarket, the kind of place where you could also pick up a new kidney if you had enough cash. I imagined her IVF profile reading, "Single female seeks sperm donor for cosy monthly nights in with turkey baster."

"Plus, I've got a back-up plan," she said looking pleased with herself. "Dave."

I stopped eating. "Dave?" I dropped my fork on the plate. "Gropey Dave?"

Her eyes widened, like a child feigning innocence while caught red-handed raiding the cookie jar.

"What's wrong with that?"

"Jojo, if there was a lifeguard at the gene pool Dave wouldn't even be allowed in the changing rooms."

She pulled a face, "That's a bit harsh, isn't it?"

"A harsh, acidic environment is the best place for any reproductive effluent Dave emits." I was being rather brutal about one of my oldest friends but I was convinced that in the fatherhood stakes there was no fate worse than Gropey Dave.

"Anyway," I continued breezily, "why don't you wait and see how your all-new profile works out? I bet you'll be fighting off marriageable cock with a big stick."

"Okay," said Jojo picking up her glass, "here's to big sticks."

"And even bigger cocks," I added.

"I should think that's inevitable," she said a little glumly. We both knew she wasn't talking about size.

Chapter Nine

Say It With Carrots

All the talk of IVF had put the willies up me. I knew Jojo was just being realistic and practical but I preferred not to share her sentiments. Surely it was just a question of frequency where dating was concerned? Like Edison's thousand attempts at inventing the lightbulb, i.e. date enough men and at least one of them had to be capable of reliably and consistently turning me on? Or maybe looking for love online was a hopeless quest, like the one-in-fourteen million chance of winning the lottery? Either way I didn't have the funds to keep spinning the Wheel Of Love and allowing my dates pay for me was out of the question because a) I didn't want them to feel like they were buying their way into my knickers, and b) women had the vote and could drive cars and run multinational corporations. I decided that I could just about stretch to a coffee.

On a warm early spring Saturday afternoon I sauntered down Electric Avenue in Brixton, past market stalls selling every conceivable kind of fruit and vegetable. I ignored the catcalls of a lascivious man on an underwear stall, who reminded me of my creepy great uncle Arthur, and marvelled at the Halal butchers rhythmically chopping meat in time to hardcore grime music. I had arranged to meet my date in "The Village", an art deco covered shopping arcade where stallholders hawking giant rolls of toilet paper nestled among stores with dazzling displays of wigs and hairpieces. In turn they all jostled for space with the newcomers, painfully hip pop-up restaurants serving tapas, pulled pork, and wood-fired pizza. Impeccably trimmed, retro clad waiters slouched between tables taking orders with a distinct air of ennui: they were only there until their records came out or their work was exhibited at Tate Modern.

I waited for *Get Fresh, 37, Organic vegetable gardener and part-time pop star* by one of the entrances to the market. I pulled the neckline of my low cut T-shirt up a little higher to conceal my cleavage, and tugged my blazer down to hide my bum. I could feel my thighs chafing as I shifted nervously from side to side and wished I hadn't worn such tight jeans. Get Fresh arrived ten minutes late, cycling up to me breathlessly on his fixie, a single speed bike with a ridiculously tiny set of handlebars that wouldn't have looked out of place in a circus.

"Soz," he gasped, "I got a puncture." Despite it being a sunny day, almost warm enough for short sleeves, Get Fresh was wearing a beanie and North Face body warmer and sweat was pouring down his red face. I was flattered that he had made an effort to get to our rendezvous as quickly as possible but wondered why he hadn't just taken his hat and coat off. I supposed it was a fashion thing.

"No problem," I said breezily, "shall we grab a coffee?"

"Let's go to Fidel's," he suggested, "they only serve freshly ground fair trade Cuban beans." I tried not to laugh.

He ordered a decaf skinny soya cappuccino with carob sprinkles – if I could have sacrificed an organic milk cow on the counter there and then I probably would have just to wind him up. I asked for a full fat latte with two espresso shots, extra syrup and a triple chocolate muffin to gauge his reaction. He wasn't fazed. We sat at a table by the window and watched hipsters stroll past and the occasional elderly lady struggling by with a beaten-up shopping trolley.

"I brought you something," he said proudly. He opened his vintage Pan Am flight bag and pulled out a comic book-perfect bunch of carrots.

"Thanks," I said, trying to sound grateful.

"I grew them myself," he said a little defensively.

"That's pretty amazing." I meant it as a genuine compliment: the only thing I had ever successfully grown was foot fungus.

"All organic," he added.

"I can see," I replied, trying to brush away the dirt that had dropped on my pale blue jeans.

"What kind of music do you play?" I asked.

"A jazz funk acid house folk fusion type thing."

He paused and I felt the burden of filling the gap in the conversation fall on me. "That sounds, really, erm ... eclectic?"

"Yeah exactly. Ya dig?" I wasn't sure if we were back to discussing organic gardening or still on the subject of music.

"Like totally," I lied, adding, "cool," despite my previous misgivings on the coolness credentials of the word.

"But we're on a break at the moment," he continued nervously.

"Artistic differences?" I ventured.

"Kind of. The other guys were struggling a bit with my narcissistic personality disorder."

I was taking a slurp of my latte and nearly sprayed the window with coffee. I gulped it back, scorching my throat on the burning hot milk. At least he was honest. The only thing I could think of to say in return was "Intense." He gave me a doe-eyed smile, the kind someone gives you when they feel like you're on their wave length and are finding the fact intensely attractive.

"My therapist said it was probably for the best if we had some time away from each other." He gave me a shy smile. "Me and the band, I mean, not you and me." Get Fresh snuggled in a little closer and I squirmed. He watched me intently, and with a mournful sigh, his light blue eyes full of meaning, he asked, "Do you ever feel it's all pointless?" Now that his face had gone from beetroot red to its normal hue and the sweat had dried, he was an attractive chap, despite the fact he was dressed like a Manga character. Although I had no idea if he could actually sing or play anything, he clearly had wide and varied interests, and in the event of a complete breakdown of society he would be more useful than an investment banker (unless the zombies of the apocalypse turned out to be genetically engineered, giant mutant rabbits and raided his carrot patch). But yet again this date was turning into nothing more than another bizarre anecdote to tell my friends. Yes, I concluded, it was all beginning to feel completely pointless. However, I wasn't about to get into a discussion about the unbearable lightness of being. I needed an exit strategy.

"This is really embarrassing," I said as I stood up, "I have to go. I just remembered that I have an appointment." I might as well have told him that I liked killing kittens for fun. He looked hurt and abandoned, and in the next breath I found myself trying to save his feelings. "Maybe we can meet up again another time?" My nugget of false hope sent his mood soaring.

"Brilliant. When? Are you busy tomorrow? Or tonight? I could wait here for you or meet you at your place later?" If he'd had a tail it would have been wagging madly.

"Oooh..." I said, hanging onto the word while I came up with a plausible excuse, "I have to see my parents tonight."

"I could come with you?" he suggested hopefully. Like a terrier with its jaw locked on its prey he was clinging to the possibility of seeing me again.

"That's not a good idea" I replied.

"Why?" he asked, the desperation back in his voice.

"My mother" I said bleakly, "She's a bit..."

Before I had the chance to think what I was doing I found myself making a circle with my finger by the side of my head, the international sign for 'crazy person.' His face dropped, reminding me of Barry Smith, the boy whom I had stabbed in the leg with a compass when I was eleven because he wouldn't stop touching me up in maths class.

"You're a fucking bitch," Get Fresh spat.

"Sorry," I said as I put a fiver on the table. "That was thoughtless and clumsy of me. I have just proved your point though. I wouldn't be good for you. I think I better go."

I left the cafe quickly and glanced back over my shoulder. He sat there in the window clutching the carrots like a set of bright orange nunchaku, his mouth twisting around curses. It was like watching a cartoon with the sound down. I felt awful and unkind. When Rob left me I'd had some serious mental health issues and a stint on medication myself so I really should have been more empathetic. But as the safety card in the airplane says, "Fit own life jacket before helping others" – and given that Get Fresh had just told me he was a narcissist my sympathy was limited.

I walked calmly until I was out of his view and then I ran, descending into the warm cave of Brixton Underground station. If Get Fresh decided to follow me I figured it was better to lead him in exactly the opposite direction to my flat. He could reappear at any moment, like the psychopath who refused to die in a horror movie. I imagined myself on the loo unable to find any toilet paper and Get Fresh suddenly appearing with a fresh roll, laughing cruelly, "Looking for this?"

I boarded a Tube, and with no sign of a body warmer in pursuit I relaxed as we pulled out of the station. I slumped down in a seat opposite a couple in their early twenties. The man was reclining, legs splayed, alpha primate style. He smiled at me and his girlfriend immediately registered his roving eye. She entwined her arms and legs in his like an over-possessive octopus. I could see her sharp little eyes watching him watching me. She turned her gaze to me, a look that said "Back off bitch, this man is MINE." Good grief, I thought, aren't relationships full of enough land mines already without women throwing one another incendiary curve balls?

Chapter Ten

Paris, London

When I got home from my abortive date I found a very curt note shoved under my front door from Mr Barrington, threatening eviction if I didn't pay this month's rent immediately (plus the two months I already owed). I was still waiting for the money from the commercial and I hoped desperately that the advertising agency hadn't gone bankrupt. The telephone line seemed to be constantly engaged. I missed having an agent to deal with this for me. Reluctantly I bought another copy of *The Stage* and started circling any job which seemed remotely applicable. I was sure with some highlights and a good push-up bra I could pass as the *Buxom 25 Y.O. required for panto in Peterborough*, but instead I rang the more likely prospect, *Cabaret singer wanted, immediate start*. I was asked to come in for an interview the following day.

As usual I was running late which meant doing my hair and makeup en route to the audition. Every time the bus jarred to a stop my kohl pencil threatened to have an eye out and I didn't fare any better with my lipstick. I was aiming for a provocative pout, but the bumpy ride left me looking like I'd eaten a very messy jam sandwich. As I finished my makeup on the Tube I could feel the eyes of fellow passengers searing into me. I caught a disapproving reflection in my compact mirror, an elderly lady in tweed, wearing a crucifix. Granted, I was troweling makeup on like a plasterer trying to disguise major structural damage at one-thirty in the afternoon but still, I resented the judgement of another woman. I turned to her haughtily and said, "If you must know, I'm late for a job interview." No sooner had I spoken than I saw a white cane and realised that she was blind. She hadn't even registered that I was talking to her. A large, thick set man in a tracksuit with tattoos on his neck smirked at me. I scowled.

"At least I'm going to work and not scrounging off the State," I mumbled to no one in particular.

"I am going to work too," replied the man in an Eastern European accent, "I am chef. Later when I finish maybe we could meet for drink?"

"I have a boyfriend," I said, referring to Ewan, the imaginary other half I always used in tricky situations. I set back to finishing my face, my foundation already waxy with the heat of the Tube. To my consternation Chef plonked himself down next to me, nearly crushing my make-up bag with his buttocks, which were spilling over the top of his jeans.

"Why you not like me?" he asked with sad, bloodshot eyes. "You are racist. I am decent man. Make very good husband."

"I'm so not racist," I said to the businessman next to me, who despite having his nose buried in *The Evening Standard* was clearly listening in to the conversation. "My boyfriend's from Scotland."

Businessman briefly looked up at us both and said, "You have both confused racism with xenophobia." Then thrusting his nose back in his newspaper he added, "Very good workers, the Polish. Exceptionally brave during the war."

"I am NOT Polish," retorted Chef furiously. "I am Lithuanian."

Luscious Ludmilla was Lithuanian. I was about to ask the chef if home-wrecking and husband-stealing was a national sport in his country, when the businessman folded his paper and replied, "They're not a million miles apart, are they?"

It only served to enrage Chef even more, "How dare you? Are you Irish?"

"No," Businessman replied coldly, "I'm from Hampshire."

Without pausing for breath Chef and Businessman entered into a full blown debate concerning trade relations and the shifting allegiances between Lithuania and Poland over the last four hundred years. It was like being trapped in between two rival MPs on *Question Time*.

As we pulled into Bank station I zipped up my cosmetics bag and stood up.

"This has been lovely but I really must go."

Chef stood up too. "Is ironic. Also my stop."

Businessman got to his feet awkwardly and sighed, "And I."

Like an ad hoc comedy trio we inadvertently moved as a group, pushing our way through the crowded carriage to the doors. Just before we got off the train a tall, skinny young man in even skinnier jeans, horn rimmed glasses, and a weak attempt at a goatee said to me, "That was amazing. Such an interesting polemic. Are you guys a guerilla theatre group or something?" I imagined he was a student.

"Don't be so bloody stupid," I said and got off the train. To my annoyance Chef continued to walk by my side while Business Man disappeared up the escalator as fast as he could.

"You are not racist then?" the Lithuanian continued.

I rolled my eyes, "Of course not."

"Then why you not go on date with me?"

I was beginning to lose my temper, "I have a boyfriend."

He shook his head, "You no have boyfriend."

"How do you know?" I asked, annoyed but curious.

He smiled knowingly, "Woman with boyfriend not make this kind of effort in middle of the day."

"If you must know I'm going to a sodding job interview, okay?" I snapped and barged past the queue at the escalator, up the stairs and out of the station.

Five minutes later I came to a small doorway with a shiny awning above it bearing the logo 'Petite Paris'. A neon sign trumpeted, 'CABARET' with a flashing Eiffel Tower that had fireworks shooting out of it, in anticipation of the excitement to be found inside the club, I supposed. I sighed; a literature degree from a top university and a post-grad at one of the best drama schools in the country and my career was about to be reduced to a seedy basement club that was probably just a front for drugs and money laundering. Resigned to my fate, I rang the bell.

"Petty Pareey, 'ow can I 'elp you?" an unmistakable Essex accent crackled over the intercom.

"Hi. It's Kat Wheeler. I'm here for the audition."

"Bloody hell," came the immediate reply, "you are well late. She ain't happy."

There was a buzz and I pushed the door open. I made my way down the narrow staircase and found myself in a gleaming reception area with scarlet curtains and sparkling chandeliers. A very blonde, very orange girl of about nineteen was sitting behind an ornate glass desk.

"Awright babes," she greeted me, "I'm Britney. Mags is just fru there."

"Thanks ... babes," I replied, and pushing a beaded curtain aside I entered into the main area of the club.

A woman in a no-nonsense trouser suit walked straight towards me, thrusting her hand out and delivering such a firm handshake that I heard the bones in my own crack. "Maggie," she said in a nasal Australian accent, "Maggie Thatcher."

"The Iron Lady," I quipped.

She stared at me blankly, "Sorry?"

I got that feeling I used to have at school when I thought I was going to make my teacher laugh only to realise I'd made an absolute prat of myself in front of the class with a desperately unfunny joke.

"Mags. Short for Margaret? Margaret Thatcher... Don't worry, I'm much more entertaining on stage."

"Let's hope so," she replied, her heavy framed Gucci glasses making her blank stare all the more penetrating. She flicked through three double-sided pages of hopefuls until she found my name. "Kath?"

"Kat," I corrected trying to keep the pique out of my voice.

"You're going to sing something from Cats?" she asked. "Bit passé, isn't it?"

Before I could explain that I wouldn't be singing anything by Lloyd Webber she landed her final blow.

"Appropriate for someone of your generation, though. I saw Starlight Express when I was seven, if that's the one with people on skates pretending to be trains?"

I took a deep breath. "I think we got off on the wrong foot. My name is Kat, and I would rather gouge my own eyes out with a fork than sing anything by Andrew Lloyd Webber, or Tim Rice for that matter."

She stared at me expressionless and then suddenly broke into gales of laughter that sounded like my vacuum cleaner had done before it finally blew up.

"Kaaaat," she screeched, "You. Crack. Me. Up. Let's hear you then."

I walked onto the stage and took off my coat to reveal a red sequinned evening gown. Mags roared with delight. "Brilliant pastiche," she shouted, "You really look like a cheesy cabaret singer." I'd had no intention to parody the genre. I thought the dress made me look hot in a classy way. I cleared my throat and stepped up to the microphone.

I sang a few bars of "Maybe This Time" from *Cabaret*, which Mags cut short after the first verse. "You can sing," she shrugged. "What about the funny stuff?" The advert had asked for singers and dancers who were comfortable talking to an audience. I didn't realise that stand-up comedy was part of the remit or I'd have asked Dave for a crash course. But I and all my unpaid bills desperately needed this job. I started talking about the first subject that came into my head: the journey to the audition. Once again my prospective employer was doubled-up with laughter. "You're a freakin' pisser!" she snorted. I wasn't sure if that was a positive Antipodean expression but she beamed at me. "Our current singer is off to host a Moulin Rouge thing in Shanghai at the end of the month. Can you start then?" The situation was far from ideal but I would just have to send Mr Barrington e-mails for the next three weeks pretending that I was filming in a country where I had been warned not to conduct any financial transactions over the internet.

"Perfect," I replied.

Mags jumped up from the velvet booth. "Follow me," she said, "I'll show you around." We walked through a set of double doors into an entirely different world. Whereas the club was a sumptuous, half-lit opium den, the backstage was all industrial innards and garish fluorescent lighting. An African man and woman stood before an enormous sink, up to their elbows in suds, chatting animatedly. As we passed them Mags said sharply, "Don't forget to wash the underside. We had a complaint last week about a dirty bottom." I suppressed a laugh at Mag's unintended innuendo but it was clear that she didn't miss a trick. I was going to have to watch my back to hold on to this job. "Yes, boss," the dishwashers replied.

Next we walked by the kitchen where several chefs were busy chopping and splicing, overseen by an irate Frenchman yelling obscenities. Mags poked her head into the doorway. "Tout va bien, Pierre?" she asked in flawless French. Smiling ingratiatingly the head chef replied, "Mais bien sûr, ma chère," before turning back to harangue a young pastry cook in Spanish. At the end of the corridor there was a dress rail, a mirror, a couple of chairs and some used wine glasses on the floor.

"Voila," she said with mock grandeur, "your backstage area."

I nodded at a large metal door, "Is the dressing room through there?"

"That's the cold storage," Mags laughed, "you can get changed in there if you want but you'll freeze your tits off. This is it, I'm afraid. We're really pressed for space. On the upside it's cash on the night plus complimentary wine." The prospect of getting changed in a corridor with all the other performers and staff running between the kitchen and club floor did not thrill me. However, the twin perks of ready cash and free booze softened the blow.

"Can't wait to start," I said, trying to ignore the rodent traps placed strategically along the corridor.

"Great," said Mags, "I'll see you out."

I followed her and as we passed the kitchen again I heard singing, a haunting male baritone.

"Who's that?" I asked.

"Titas," she said, shouting into the kitchen for emphasis, "He's from Poland."

The singing stopped abruptly.

"NOT Poland. I am Lithuanian," boomed the reply.

I could see the back of a large man with tattoos on his neck and I felt my bowels loosen. Mags was oblivious to my panic. "Gaaawd! So touchy," she whispered, "people call me a Kiwi all the time and I don't get upset about being mistaken for a sheep-shagger." I feigned a laugh and shot past the kitchen entrance as quickly as I could. There was no doubt: Titas was my suitor from the Tube.

Mags saw me as far as reception. "See you in a couple of weeks, darl," she said and disappeared behind the beaded curtain like Willy Wonka magically vanishing in his chocolate factory. Britney's eyebrows were raised even further than her normal over-plucked arch, "Cor, she likes you. See ya soon, babes." She smiled warmly and I felt a pang of remorse for judging her appearance so harshly. "Totes babes," I replied and Britney broke into peals of laughter. I clomped up the stairs, pushed the buzzer to release the door when I reached the top and was spewed back into the street, feeling simultaneously chuffed that I got the job and terrified that I'd have to face Titas again.

Chapter Eleven

Two For One

Flushed with the success of landing a job I wondered if I might be on a winning streak. Perhaps, I hoped, I was about to become one of those romance success stories plastered all over adverts for dating sites I'd seen on the Tube. The problem, apart from having zero cash to go out on, was that I couldn't seem to find anyone remotely my own age that I was interested in. Nor they in me.

I was getting a lot of messages from men in their fifties, already in semi-retirement, with cash and time to spare. I tried not to be ageist – after all, I was being thwarted by exactly this kind of prejudice – but I just couldn't see myself sipping bubbly wine on a cruise with a pensioner who needed Viagra to perk him up and blood pressure pills to bring him back down. I moaned about it to Dave over a swift pint before one of his stand-up gigs (a pint that I still had to buy despite the fact that he was the one who was gainfully employed that night). He supped thoughtfully and then said, "Sauce for the goose."

"Going to finish that sentence or do I have to fill in the blank?" I asked.

"Up-date. Or do I mean down-date?" he said rubbing his stubbly chin.

"Don't ask me. It's your brain. What's left of it," I said looking at his pint glass, half-empty already.

"Obviously you're going to have to date younger men."

I blinked into an age-related dating abyss while I processed Dave's suggestion. For some reason this idea had never even crossed my mind. I had a slash and burn policy when it came to age – messages from any man under thirty were automatically deleted on the logic that if I was old enough to be his mother I probably shouldn't be dating him. What on earth would we talk about? For years I thought Nintendo was a chain of sushi bars.

When I told my fears to Dave he sighed wistfully, "Beggars and choosers, Kat. Speaking of which..." He slid his glass across the table to me indicating that further counsel would cost another pint. I started to think that there might be something in Dave's advice. Maybe it was time to embrace my inner cougar despite loathing the word. Why was it that a man who dated younger women was "one of the boys", a "Jack the lad", while a woman who did the same was the equivalent of a vicious, predatory animal? It seemed horribly unfair.

Despite my reservations when I got home I logged onto the dating site and made myself a new profile: *Mountain Kat, 39*. I dropped my bottom line for a man's age to twenty-five and I was immediately inundated. The euphemistic offers to trim my hedges and unblock my pipes came flooding in within an hour. It was like Help Yourself To The Aged. Your Local Milfman messaged me: *Are you looking for a hot, hard young stud?* I replied: *Yes. If you know someone please forward their details.* Things improved when The Swede popped up in my mailbox. I was relieved to find that he had nothing to do with hardy root vegetables; *28, Music-loving, design-obsessed male seeks aesthetically pleasing partner. Clean lines, elegant handling, beautiful simplicity (me+you).* We batted a few messages at each other and he made it clear immediately that he wasn't looking for a relationship having just broken-up with his fiancée. I didn't relish the thought of being a Band-Aid shag but reasoned that it was better than continuing to starve in my current sexual wasteland. We exchanged phone numbers. I suggested dinner. *That's a bit formal, isn't it?*, he replied. *What do you suggest?* I asked. He didn't respond.

Disappointed but undeterred I agreed to a date with The Graduate; *25, Young, reckless, skinny and skint. Goldsmith's graduate and sophisticated fop seeks his Pygmalion.* I told myself that it might be "fun", even though he sounded like every hipster cliché I despised; inner-city dwelling, pulp-fiction reading with a nonchalant "found this on my bedroom floor" thrown together style that had in fact probably taken several hours to achieve.

It was early April, mild bordering on balmy, the kind of premature summer night that makes you think global warming might not be such a bad thing after all. I had arranged to meet The Graduate in a so-dingy-it's-cool pub in a painfully trendy part of the East End. I walked in to find him sat with a pint of Guinness that positively dwarfed him. As his profile promised, he was cute, he was skinny – and he looked young enough to be the teenage pregnancy I'd never had. I had no doubt that he was twenty five but unfortunately he looked half his age. "Babyface" would have been a far more appropriate profile name. I cringed and tried to stop my face from telegraphing my feelings all over it. He smiled when he saw me and even moved his pint glass over to his side of the table, the Snapchat generation equivalent of good manners, I supposed. "Nice to meet you," he said with a cheeky grin, "You *do* look good for your age. Very good indeed."

I collapsed into the knackered banquette seat of the pub, my heart sinking too. Why couldn't he just say the "looking good" part, without adding the 'age' bit?

"Sorry I'm late," I replied, "Tube journeys aren't included in my Freedom Pass and the bus takes forever."

The Graduate looked like he'd been hit by a wave of FOMO, worried perhaps that he might not be up on the latest trend.

"Freedom Pass? Is that like a new app or something?" he asked uncertainly.

"A Freedom Pass allows free bus travel for the over sixties. I was joking."

The Graduate nodded, his foppish mop-top of rusty hair flopping in his eyes.

"Yeah right. It's funny though because I saw where you grew

up and I think you might have actually gone to school with my mum."

This experience was going to test the stress-fractures of my dating stamina to their absolute limits.

I sat for two hours drinking overpriced sour wine, wishing that the London sewers which ran beneath the pub would open up and swallow me whole, but not before I'd watched this little shit succumb to his excremental end first. The Graduate boasted about his art, his exhibition, his T-shirt making business, how he didn't care about anyone or anything. I nearly asked him if his degree was in self-obsession but I couldn't get a word in edgeways. The stale air, cheap booze and constant drone of his voice began to make me nod off. I felt my head loll a couple of times and had to drag myself back to consciousness. The Graduate caught me cat-napping and smiled patronizingly, "Sorry love, am I keeping you awake? I 'spose you're usually tucked up in bed by this time of night with a cup of Horlicks?"

I had had enough. I stood up from my seat, banging into the table as I did so, setting the glasses on it rocking precariously. I put my hands on my hips and thrust my chin up, looking down my nose at him fiercely, all the while trying not to slur or wobble.

"You, my little friend, are the most vain, self-righteous and odious creature I have come across in a very long time. I've bought you drinks and listened while you talked about yourself all night, but I draw the line at that kind of ageist crap, especially from someone who drinks an old man's drink in an old man's pub because he thinks it makes him look cool."

The Graduate stared at me, open-mouthed but nothing came out of his slack, slacker-generation jaw. I, on the other hand, was just hitting my stride. "And seeing as you're so fond of the Black Velvet why don't you take a bath in it?" I picked up his nearly-full glass and dumped the contents on his head.

The Graduate sat blinking through the tan foam running down his face. I grabbed my bag from the seat and knocked the table over in my hurry to get out of the pub as the full enormity of what I'd just done hit me. I pushed the heavy door open and let it slam behind me.

I started running down the high street towards the Tube not daring to look behind me nor pausing to catch my breath. I shot through the station barriers, high heels clang, clang, clanging down the escalator. I made it onto a train just as the doors closed. I flopped onto a seat and began to laugh.

Twenty minutes later the Tube regurgitated me at Brixton. The night air was still unseasonably warm and while the effects of the wine had worn off the bravado hadn't. With a sudden increase in my heart rate, I took out my phone and texted The Swede:

What are you doing right now?

Less than a minute later he replied, *Nothing. Why?*

Taking a deep breath I typed, *Want to come over?*

Thirty seconds later he asked, *Now?*

YES. Right now, I typed emphatically.

OK, he responded, *C U in 40 mins x*

I gulped as I put my phone back in my bag. I had just invited a complete stranger, a man with whom I had never even had a telephone conversation, over to my house for the sole purpose of having sex. I marvelled at my loucheness, how much I was behaving like a nymphette in a Serge Gainsbourg movie. I was wild. I was free. I was totally shitting myself. What if this guy was a sociopath? What if he was violent? What if he had a very, very small penis?

My flat was a mess. It looked like a football squad had had an all-nighter with the staff of a strip joint; discarded booze bottles and take-away containers mating with tubs of body lotion, lipsticks and assorted women's magazines. I grabbed a broom and swept everything under the bed. I hastily changed the sheets, squirted bleach down the loo and stacked the dirty dishes into a neat pile. I lit candles, sprayed myself and the bedroom liberally with perfume and poured myself a large glass of wine. Then I waited.

Chapter Twelve

Best Unlaid Plans

I woke up 12 hours later, groggy and unsure of where I was. I stretched my arm out across the lonely expanse of bed just to confirm that there was nobody else there. I was resolutely alone with only a smear of red lipstick and dried saliva on my pillow for company. I blinked until the room came back into focus in the grey morning light.

After ninety minutes of waiting for The Swede to arrive the previous evening I became concerned that he'd got lost or worse, been mugged. I texted him five times but he didn't reply. At midnight I opened another bottle of wine and at one a.m I conceded that for whatever reason The Swede was not coming – in any sense of the word. I'd been had. Or rather I hadn't.

I was more relieved than disappointed. I had three auditions the following afternoon, none of which requested *hungover, sexually rampant harridan* in the brief. Had the Scandinavian Casanova appeared I'm not sure I would have known what to do anyway. I could only have talked about Ikea and ABBA for so long before he would have wanted what he came for and I would have inevitably met my Waterloo. I've never been good at casual sex.

After my auditions – which were the usual whirlwind of questions, three seconds to camera, followed by "we'll be in touch" (I knew they wouldn't) – I arranged to meet Jojo at Oxford Circus. It was a sunny Friday, the kind of day when every tourist, fashion victim, and man who has been told to smarten himself up, heads to the shopping Mecca of London's West End. We were all there a day early hoping to avoid the weekend crush only to discover that we were already caught in the thick of it.

I battled my way to the exit of the Tube, buffered by the throng on the escalators. When I finally got to street level I stood scanning the crossroads and clutching onto my hand bag. Hundreds of shoppers traversed the black and white piano keys of the pedestrian crossings. I couldn't remember which corner we'd arranged to meet at. I called Jojo but her voice was an intermittent garble. I texted her instead and moments later her reply pinged back, *Regents St exit. Send Reinforcements x.*

After nearly getting run over by a taxi coming one way, a bus going the other, and a rickshaw racing to get through the gap between the two, I found Jojo pushed up against a shop window. She looked like one those sticky rubber toys that you throw against glass. It was like a scene from the sinking of The Titanic, as the crowd jostled me off course and Jojo waved and shouted, "Kat. Kat!"

"I swear this place gets busier on a weekly basis," I said as I finally made it through the deadly current of rampant consumerism.

"I know. I have no idea why we agreed to meet here," Jojo said breathlessly.

"Me neither. At least it's central."

I wasn't being entirely honest. In fact I wasn't being honest at all. The reason I had suggested Oxford Street was on the off-chance that I might bump into Jem.

According to all of my friends Jem was bad news. Even Dave warned me off, which should have been enough to tell me that Jem would never be more than a Friend With Benefits, a casual hook up that wasn't ever going to blossom into a genuine relationship. But no matter how non-committal Jem was, no matter how much he used me, I kept going back for more. Jem was the dirty little secret I didn't even like to admit to myself.

We met at a music festival about a year after Rob left me. I thought my days of mud, reeking portaloos and eardrum bursting decibels were long gone but Jojo had a spare ticket and begged me to go. It turned out to be one of the hottest weekends of the year. The weather was perfect, the bright yellow sun burning in a vivid blue sky, the fields primary green. What with the rainbow-hued banners and hippy-inspired outfits of the revellers the scene popped with colour like a psychedelic children's cartoon.

Jem and I had quite literally bumped into one another; he was carrying a cardboard tray full of plastic cups brimming with beer across the dance music field where I was whirling around on the spot. I don't know if my helicopter arms hit him or if he walked into me, but the tray flipped backwards and drenched him in beer.

"So sorry! Let me give you some money," I said, patting myself down like a drunken policewoman giving herself a body search.

"Shit," I said on finding empty pockets, "I don't have any cash on me. Do you want to come back to my tent?"

Jem smiled bashfully, "No. I mean yes. I mean don't worry about the money. But yes I'd like to come back to your tent."

It didn't come across as cheesy or creepy. He put what was left of the beers on the floor and took his sunglasses off. His eyes were dark chocolate, almost black, with the massively dilated pupils of someone who had been partying hard. The whole effect was hypnotic, a bottomless erotic whirlpool into which I fell headfirst and had been drowning in ever since – on the occasions when Jem deigned to be available, that was.

I took my own sunglasses off, doubtless revealing the kind of bloodshot that happens when you consume your own body weight in cask wine. I hoped the red veins at least made my eyes look a brighter blue.

He extended his right hand, ridiculously formal under the circumstances. I returned the gesture except I put out my left, meaning that we looked like a couple of schoolchildren ready to walk two-by-two on a field trip.

"Jem," he said, stroking my fingers gently.

"No," I shouted over the din, "Kat." He laughed again and I felt something in me thaw.

"No," he corrected with a very sexy smile. "My name's Jem. You're Kat."

For a moment I was impressed, thinking that he had psychic abilities until I realised that I had just told him my name.

We spent the afternoon together. We finished what was left of the beer. Jem flagged down a passing hawker and bought some delicious chocolate brownies that made me feel funny. We talked, we danced, we laughed. As the shadows cast by the huge banners and flags grew longer with the afternoon we found the highest spot in the festival. He put his arm around me and we watched the sun go down. I turned to him to ask him where he lived but before I could speak he engulfed me in a kiss that made me spin in and out of myself and temporarily froze the party beneath us like a Pompeian fresco. I texted Jojo, *Don't wait up xx*.

I hadn't slept with anyone since I met Rob — meaning that I hadn't made love with anyone else for more than a decade and hadn't had any sex at all for an entire year. I was practically a born-again virgin. While I was terrified that my lady parts may have gone the way of my ear piercings, closed over from lack of use, I was extremely eager to break the curse of The Vagina That Time Forgot. I'd had enough foresight to bring condoms with me and had planned to give myself a cursory going over with some baby wipes before I let Jem anywhere near me. But as soon as we got back to the tent he devoured me. I don't know what he was on but it kept him up all night, quite literally, and he focused his undivided attention and endless energy on me.

He was an amazing lover and knew exactly when to be butterfly-soft and when a little more pressure was required. He kissed me often and repeatedly and kept the little light in my tent on so he could gaze into my eyes. It was like being a teenager again, a voyage of discovery that made my heart race, one of those rare times when I finally felt like I knew what all those silly love songs were about.

Festivals have a funny way of scorching things into your memory. Those three days felt like a lifetime. Jem and I were utterly infatuated with each other, forsaking our own friends for the rest of the weekend. We weren't so much joined at the hip as surgically fused; by day we toured the festival fields hand in hand, smiling benignly on all we surveyed like a royal couple on a hospital visit. At night we wandered back to my tent, the limited space no impediment to our sexual gymkhana.

After the terrible heartbreak of my husband leaving me for another woman it felt like I might be finally getting my life back. I took some selfies of Jem and I and posted them on Facebook live from the festival. I managed to restrain myself from changing my relationship status but I hoped that Rob would see that I was moving on, that an attractive young man thought I was special even if he didn't.

At the end of the festival I walked Jem back to his VW. He didn't introduce me to any of his friends, just pecked me on the cheek and then clambered into the knackered camper van. He gave me a brief thumbs up and then started larking around with his mates as if I wasn't even there. The VW bounced off down the dried out mud track leaving me standing alone spluttering in a cloud of dust. He didn't even wave goodbye. By the time the haze cleared the van had vanished. For a moment I wondered if someone had slipped LSD into my chai latte on the first day and I'd imagined the whole thing.

I finally caught up with Jojo who had spent the weekend in the meditation field having her chakras realigned. She had the look of someone who had seen the light. She was positive and philosophical about my predicament.

"Maybe he was embarrassed in front of his mates? Or sad about saying goodbye? Sometimes people disguise loss as rejection."

I thought about Rob. His rejection was definitely not a cover for either loss or sadness. He just preferred Ludmilla to me.

"Maybe he has a girlfriend?" I said feeling the festival come-down bite me hard in the arse, "Or maybe I've just been had?"

Jojo put her arm around me. "Come on Kat," she said, "you've lifted The Curse and neither of us has come down with trench foot. I'd call that a win–win."

I forced a little laugh. But I felt used and stupid.

I pretended to be asleep for the whole train journey back to London. The memories of the festival had soured like a carton of milk in the sun. I looked around the carriage and all I could see were strung-out kids dressed in tatty, dirty clothes, hollow-cheeked and dull-eyed, their minds struggling with the serotonin crash while rain lashed the windows.

Jem and I had exchanged numbers and I knew his surname. When I got home I immediately found him on Facebook. *Jem Jackson only shares personal information with people he knows. Do you know Jem Jackson?* That made me laugh, a hollow, bitter, little laugh. "Yes," I thought to myself, "at least as well as his own mother, perhaps better." I shut my laptop. The last thing I wanted to do was appear like a desperate stalker. No, I resolved, he had my number. If he wanted to see me again he knew how to contact me.

The days turned into weeks. I pined for Jem. Jojo told me to text him. Several times I started writing upbeat, friendly messages, one time even hitting *send,* but my phone signal dropped out which I took as a sign that it was never meant to be. After nearly three weeks the festival became a dusty, distant memory. I carried on with my daily round of rubbish auditions for commercials and low-end television dramas and gave up on the idea of ever falling in love again. Then just after eleven o'clock one night my phone pinged and there it was. A text that made my stomach do somersaults as muscle memory sent a rush of blood around my body. *Hey Hep Kat. Whatcha up to? J xx*

I sprang out of bed and did a little victory dance. Jojo had been right all along. I texted back immediately. *Nothing much, in bed already. Lovely to hear from u xx*. In under thirty seconds he replied, *That sounds nice. May I join u? xx* It was like cupid had blinded me with my own mascara wand. I texted him my address and Jem arrived within the hour, breathless as if he had run the entire way from North to South London. He walked into my flat and I urgently pulled his clothes off, I actually heard his T shirt rip, while he threw my bathrobe on the floor.

It was just as good as it had been at the festival, better in some ways because of the sense of having won something back that I felt certain was lost. Even without chemical assistance Jem was insatiable, rolling straight on top of me again in the morning before he left for his something-to-do-with-music media job off Oxford Street. His casual, quirky style, the hoodie worn underneath a pinstripe jacket and vintage satchel, made him look the part. I imagined that his days were a whirlwind of pop star interviews, although he hadn't gone into much detail. He could have been the tea boy for all I knew.

He left too early to have the are-we-in-a-relationship-now-then? conversation. "Big day," he said kissing me goodbye. "Rumour has it that Dua Lipa is stopping by." I wasn't that impressed. As an actress, albeit not a terribly successful one, I'd met a few celebrities in my time and found them to be self-obsessed at best and often downright rude. But I didn't want Jem to think of me as anything other than a smart sassy woman with her finger on the pulse of contemporary popular culture.

"Dope," I replied, hoping that this word was still cool and not actually a request for drugs. I pushed my body into his at the door. I felt something move in his groin area.

He pushed me back inside my flat, laughing. "You're very naughty," he purred and planting one last delicious kiss on my mouth said, "I'll call you."

He didn't. I texted him later that evening, a chummy, *Did Dua show-up? xxx* He didn't respond until the next day, *Nah, but Stormzy popped in x* I noticed that his kiss quotient had diminished and there was no mention of meeting up again. Several days after that at around ten o'clock in the evening Jem sent me a very clear message. *Watcha up to? xx* I hovered between elation and disappointment. Obviously he liked me or he wouldn't keep coming back, but why so much time in between? He invited me over to his place, which at least felt like progress.

And so it went on. I managed to convince myself that Jem was just "taking things slowly", despite Bil, Ben, Jojo and even Dave (especially Dave) unanimously telling me that Jem was a player and would never be boyfriend material. As the affair dragged on my friends became less and less sympathetic. Jojo commiserated but pleaded with me to stop seeing Jem.

I didn't. I couldn't. I tried to justify my addiction by fetishising Jem; he was my part-time lover, my undercover assignation. I was never introduced to his friends, he didn't even enquire after mine. We – even though there was no 'we' – existed in a parallel universe. When I was with Jem I forgot that I had a life outside of him. When we were apart, which was the vast majority of the time, I missed him desperately. I pretended to be fine with the situation just as it was. Pieces of him felt better than nothing at all. Secretly I hoped that one day he would realise just how great I was, stop dicking me around and proclaim his love for me in front of the entire world.

Sometimes there would be a hiatus, no contact at all for a month or two, and during these times I conceded that Jem had probably got himself a real girlfriend and I would never see him again. But eventually, like a hungry homing pigeon, he always found his way back to me and once reunited we would retreat to his flat for entire weekends, cooking, eating and spending endless hours in bed. He would run me a candlelit bath, bring me a glass of wine and wash my hair. Despite all the overwhelming evidence I still managed to convince myself that I had a future with Jem. And I avoided having The Conversation about it in case it confirmed otherwise.

Fast-forward nearly two years and there I was meeting my best friend on the pretext of window shopping when all I really wanted was to catch a glimpse of Jem. I hadn't seen him for nearly four months and this time I was sure that he must have met his ideal woman, the one he used to talk about marrying while he soaped my back, giving me a weird sensation of goosebumps and loss.

I suggested to Jojo that we retreat to somewhere quieter for coffee since I didn't have a tranquillizer gun in the event of a stampede.

"Macchiatto's?" I proposed hopefully.

"On East Castle Street?"

I nodded.

"Perfect" said Jojo, looking relieved. "You look great by the way. Have you got a date later?"

I hoped that I hadn't coloured up with guilt. I was definitely overdressed for a shopping trip, and probably for the auditions I'd just done, too – checkout girl in a TV commercial for a cut-price supermarket, a radio voice-over warning of the dangers of smoke inhalation and a minor drug-abusing character in a gritty soap – but if I did bump into Jem I wanted to look my best.

"Nah," I said, nonchalantly, "but you never know who you might meet."

We sauntered down Oxford Street and I slowed my pace as we got to Jem's office.

"You alright?" Jojo asked.

"It's these shoes," I said, faking a limp, "blisters."

We sat at a table outside Macchiatto's and I stared hard at the building that Jem was somewhere inside of, willing him to appear. There was a little used entrance on the street where we were sat – it would be exactly like Jem to take the path less trodden, just to be different. I knew that Jem subsisted on a diet of coffee, Coke and pastries and that Macchiatto's was his regular cafe. The chance of spotting him was actually quite high.

"...so what do you think?" I heard Jojo say. I only caught the tail end of what she had been talking about for the last five minutes.

"Sorry?" I said. Jojo eyed me suspiciously. Then she looked to where my gaze had been frozen. She stared at the building, surveying it from the ground floor up. Her eyes focused on the spinning retro sign on the roof, reminiscent of the old RKO logo. As the enormous letters revolved slowly above our heads, she turned back to me.

"Oh Kat," she said unable to disguise her disappointment, "you're not still seeing that wazzock, are you?"

Chapter Thirteen

Mommy Dearest

Jojo's frustration woke me up to just how pathetic my obsession with Jem was becoming. The whole thing had been a charade. I used Jem to get over Rob, but all Jem did was make me feel even worse about myself. Rob didn't think I was good enough to be his wife and in Jem's mind I wasn't even girlfriend material.

The only question was how to attract the right kind of man. Dave's update to my dating profile had resulted in plenty of attention but entirely the wrong kind. Unwilling to trust my romantic fate to an overgrown alcoholic teenager I started looking at other women's dating profiles for clues. There seemed to be quite literally a cookie-cutter template – baking cupcakes had become a national sport and just about everyone was as happy curled up on the sofa with a bottle of wine and Netflix as they were scuba-diving or nightclubbing.

And then I came across something that made me gasp with horror; *Don'tCallMeBaby, 59. Glamorous gran seeks handsome chap for mature, adult fun. All vintages considered; fine old claret or something a little fresher off the vine ;)* There in full glorious Technicolor was my mother's dating profile. My own mother. The woman who had given birth to me and, as far as I was aware, was still very much married to my father. I kept covering my face, looking through my fingers, hoping it was my imagination. It was like a traffic accident; wrong to stare but impossible to ignore.

She had knocked five years off her age and, unless my own eyesight was prematurely ageing, she'd either had a shot of Botox in the last week or someone had airbrushed the photos. I stared aghast at image after image of her staring seductively at would-be paramours. In one she was wearing the M&S jumper I bought her the previous Christmas. I was used to seeing its low V neck teamed with a respectable blouse, but here she had gone for the full plunge, her pert breasts sculpted into a substantial cleavage thanks to a push up bra – or a boob job. In another photo she was wearing an unbuttoned man's shirt that clearly belonged to my father, teamed with her Chanel reading glasses and hair in a messy chignon while she sucked coquettishly on a fountain pen. Most of the photos seemed to be selfies taken with a phone, surprising since technology was not Mum's forte.

The photo that hurt most was a shot of her on the beach in Cornwall. She was tanned, toned and smiling, not a scrap of makeup and she looked stunning. Both my father and I had been there, it was one of our better family weekends away, helped, at least for me, by the lack of sibling squabbling thanks to Patrick's absence. Mum had ambushed a poor man minding his own business walking his dog, asking him to take the photo. We all sat down on the blanket, Dad and I either side of Mum. And now Mum had cropped us out of the picture entirely.

Enraged, I read on; *I love to keep fit, and regularly do Pilates and Yoga.* "Bullshit!" I shouted at the screen. Mum owned one yoga DVD that she got free with *The Mail on Sunday* and she'd never even watched it. For a long time she thought Pilates was a religious sect. *I have a keen interest in politics and am extremely well read.* I suppose this at least had some truth in it; Mum wore black on the day of Margaret Thatcher's funeral and had purchased every issue of *Woman's Own* since 1974. *I enjoy charity work, and get involved in my community whenever I can :)* Mum had once entered a 5 mile charity fun-run but pulled out after the first mile because her new trainers aggravated her bunions, and her "community involvement" consisted entirely of phone calls to the local police to report errant youths loitering on the pavement outside the house. And since when had she started using emojis?

The thought that Mum and Dad might still be having sex or

had ever had sex at all was bad enough, but the possibility of my mother having extra-marital relations with a complete stranger was unbearable. I dialled her mobile.

"Hello?" she said uncertainly, the concept of a telephone not attached to a physical line still confusing her.

"It's me."

"Hello Katie," she singsonged. "How are you?"

"Just fine," I said, "and how are you, Shirley Valentine?"

There was a short pause. "Oh dear," she said.

"Oh dear, indeed," I repeated.

"I suppose we better meet," she sighed.

"Yes," I said, "we better."

I was sat at a secluded table in Sweet Dreams Are Made of Cheese, Mum's favourite cafe – "such a clever name, don't you think, Katie?" she trilled every time we visited – belligerently knocking the salt and pepper cellars together while she ordered at the counter. She returned with a tray laden with cakes and pastries, a coffee for me, and pot of tea for her.

"I got you a scone," she said cheerfully, as if this was a standard mother-daughter lunch date. "Cream and jam too," she added, as she pushed a doughy lump in front of me.

"Yum yum," I sneered, refusing to look up at her and still engaging in my Battle Of The Condiments.

"Katie," she said, quietly but firmly, "please *stop* doing that."

I pushed the salt and pepper pots away and glared at her. "Why?" I asked. "Am I embarrassing you?"

She laid her hand on mine and I pulled it away like I'd been scalded.

"Katie," she began.

I cut her off, "You're a GILF, Mum!"

She looked at me blankly, "What's a Gilfmum?"

I antagonistically decoded the acronym for her, "Grandmother I'd Like to F–"

She cut me off before I could finish, her face turning white. "Do keep your voice down! We're on the Broadway!"

"I wouldn't care if we were at Buckingham Palace. You've got a lot of explaining to do."

Mum busied herself pouring lapsang souchong and buttering a scone. She very deliberately stirred the milk into the cup and then looked directly at me.

"There are a lot of things you don't know," she began.

"Evidently."

"Please," she whispered, "don't make this any harder than it already is."

"Does Dad know you're looking for 'mature, adult fun'?" I asked. "And how young are these 'fresh off the vine' ones? I can pass you some of my left-overs if you want?"

She missed my irony entirely. "That's very sweet but not necessary."

"I was joking, you stupid woman."

She slammed her butter knife down on the plate and fixed me with her piercing blue eyes, the same intense shade as Rob's. Her naughty-step stare could still make me feel like a six year old. "Don't be so bloody rude," she hissed.

She only used the "B word", as she called it, when she was hopping mad. I was glad. I wanted her to be as furious as I was. I wanted to hurt her.

"Don't be so bloody adulterous then, Mother." We sat in silence while I had a Hamlet moment, before I broke the deadlock with a litany of questions.

"Where does the 'glamorous grandmother' bit come in?" I asked.

"I'm still an attractive woman. And I could have been a grandmother if Patrick and Annabelle hadn't decided against having a family."

I might have known Mum would defend Practically Perfect Patrick and Amazing Annabelle's "conscious childlessness" despite scotching her dreams of becoming a grandparent. Annahell, as I like to call her, and I did not get on. The first time I ever visited the Docklands flat she and Patrick had just bought I felt like I was cluttering up the clean lines of their minimalist interior from the moment I sat down on the designer couch. When I kicked off my shoes and used the footstool she barked, "That's a limited edition Ligne Roset." She didn't see the funny side of my reply, "Don't open the good stuff on my account. Supermarché white will be fine." I hadn't been invited back since.

"And it doesn't look like you'll be having children either so I told a white lie," Mum continued.

"Thanks very much," I said sulkily. "Sorry I'm such a barren disappointment to you."

She looked genuinely pained. "I didn't mean it like that. I really am very..." she paused while she searched for an appropriate, non-abrasive expression, "proud of you."

"Well I'm not proud of you," I fired back. "Can you imagine how embarrassed I was when I came across your profile?" I stared at her crow's feet. "How did you manage to turn back time?"

"Your brother showed me how to use Photoshop," she said sheepishly.

"Patrick *knows* about this? He's helping you to have sex with random men behind Dad's back? Unbelievable!"

Mum casually blew on her tea. "Not behind your father's back."

"Dad *knows* about your extra-marital activities?"

"Sort of," she said, struggling.

I shook my head. "What does 'sort of' mean, exactly?"

In between sips of tea Mum finished the conversation she had started in the kitchen on my birthday. She explained how "intimate relations" had gone downhill since "the prostate thingy," and that despite forcing Dad to take a double dose of Viagra at an over fifties tantric sex weekend nothing had been able to, "lure the Mustang back out of the garage." I winced at every slice of information, each disclosure a parental confession too far. Dad had apparently adopted a "don't ask, don't tell" attitude and given Mum a licence to thrill outside of their relationship. If she was telling the truth, that was.

"How could you?" I asked.

"You don't understand," she said defensively. "Your father and I haven't had sex for nearly two years."

I smiled ruefully, "Oh no, I think you'll find I understand that all too well."

"Then you know how I feel," she said with a kindly expression, attempting to appeal to my empathy. "If you think you're randy now just wait until you get into your sixties. You'll be wanting to let the dog see the rabbit every minute of the day."

I shuddered. Not only was Mum internet cheating on Dad but she was talking like a Cockney bookie. I blamed HRT for the whole sorry turn-out and vowed to let myself desiccate gracefully when my menopause hit.

"Why don't you divorce Dad if you don't want him anymore?"

She gave a benign smile, full of self-sacrifice. "I love your father."

"You've got a funny way of showing it."

I couldn't listen to any more. I stood up too sharply, knocking my chair over and sending the glare of several pairs of bifocals in our direction. Mum blushed and shifted uncomfortably. I set the chair right with a deliberate bang and slung my bag over my shoulder. "Bye Mum," I said coldly and stormed out of the cafe.

In my blind rage I had taken what I thought was the rear exit only to find myself in the kitchen instead. Through a haze of steam and smoke one of the kitchen staff asked, "Are you from the council? Have you come about the rats?" Before I could answer the chef appeared and realising that I was a customer he started shouting that I had breached every health and safety regulation known to mankind and had better "piss off". I had no choice but to walk out the same way I came in, coming face to face again with my mother. Her eyes lit up when she saw me, thinking I'd had a change of heart. I glared at the scone she was about to put into her mouth. "I wouldn't if I were you," I said with a bitter little laugh. "it's absolutely filthy in that kitchen." There was a clatter of cutlery as the ladies who lunch stopped lunching. Then a harassed looking woman in a smart suit came towards us. "Nothing to see here," she said cheerfully to the open mouths of the other customers. "Just a little marketing stunt from our rivals at Let Them Eat Cake, ha ha ha."

The woman, who I presumed was the restaurant manager, took me firmly under the arm and led me towards the elevator. She was still smiling but her eyes were murderous. I glanced back over my shoulder at Mum who looked immensely pleased. "I didn't know you'd got a real job," she called gaily across the tables. "And in PR too. How exciting. Your father will be pleased." She waved to me excitedly. "Bye-bye, Katie. Speak soon."

Chapter Fourteen

Write and Wrong

I fumed and scowled all the way home then threw myself on the bed and sobbed. I rang Jojo but my call went straight to voice-mail. I tried Dave but his phone just kept ringing with no answer. I hung up and started to dial Bil and Ben but something stopped me: I was ashamed. I just wasn't ready to tell anyone, not my sympathetic gay friends, not my best mate, and especially not Dave (who would probably take notes and use it in his next routine) that my mum was hellbent on a sexual rampage through the Home Counties.

I did call Patrick though. He picked up straight away in a very businesslike manner. "Patrick Wheeler here. Is that you Katrine? We've been expecting your call."

"No," I said viciously, "it's your sodding sister *Katherine* calling to find out why you've been pimping out our mother on the internet."

"We seem to have a crossed line," said Patrick sounding rather alarmed. "Let's have a look at those flip charts while we try to get the right number for Katrine, shall we?"

The line went dead and I realised that Patrick must still be at work. He texted me a few moments afterwards. *Thanks v much. Was in really important meeting with company directors when you called – on speaker phone.* I knew I'd screwed up rather badly but it didn't change the fact that Patrick was helping Mum cheat on Dad. The only consolation I could find was that at least I was too old to be socially embarrassed if Mum and Dad did end up getting divorced; I would be spared the humiliation of "whose weekend is it to have the kids?" and the emotional minefield of step-siblings.

I tried to put the nightmare of Mum's dating profile out of my mind and get back to my own search for the man of my dreams. Just as I was politely declining the offer of an all-you-can-eat Korean buffet (he didn't specify whether it was North or South) with an accountant from Swindon, an altogether more appealing prospect appeared in my inbox; *Word Smith, 39, North London. Successful screenwriter (personal friend of Mr Darcy) seeks creative, complex, funny woman for war and peace.* While we text chatted via the site I scanned his profile. There was just one black and white photo of him in a doorway, trilby tilted over one eye, coat collar up. It was a great shot, very film noir, but the dark shadows made it impossible to see what he really looked like. Still, I was intrigued.

Word Smith mentioned that his first screenplay had starred some heavy hitting acting talent so naturally I Googled. I found Word Smith in a feature interview on the BBC website, photos of him sat chummily next to several high profile actors. Word Smith was handsome, talented and available. I felt like I had stumbled across the holy grail of online romance. The fact that we were the same age and in the same business seemed like a good omen. But why on earth was this calibre of man internet dating? Surely he was surrounded by beautiful young actresses eager to share his star-studded orbit?

I meticulously planned the date for three days while studiously ignoring my mother's plaintive calls and text messages. Outfit after outfit was laid out on the floor and shown to Jojo, Bil and Ben via video calls with unanimous agreement on the little black dress. I splashed out on a cut and blow dry that I couldn't afford, but reasoned it was unlikely British Gas would actually cut me off however serious the Final Demand sounded. Somehow I still ran out of time and I resorted to painting my nails on the Tube en route to the date. Just as I finished my left hand and was admiring the vampish red gleam the lady sitting next to me began to kick up a stink about the odour. I exaggeratedly replaced the cap on the nail polish and sat there waiting for one set of talons to dry, inventing ways to get through the evening one-handed.

I hadn't been able to find any clean contour pants so had to resort to my sluttiest knickers; four bits of ribbon and a gusset. As I changed Tube lines the bows came undone and the thong fell off. I tried to behave as if I'd just dropped my bank card as I picked up the rogue underwear and jammed it in my handbag.

When I walked into a disappointingly down-at-heel pub in a backstreet in Islington Word Smith was already half-way through a large glass of red. He raised his eyebrows towards me and tapped his watch. I extended my hand to him when I reached the bar, "Sorry I'm late. Signal failure on the Tube."

He ignored both my excuse and my hand and turned back to the bar, nodding at the barman to summon his attention like a bidder at an auction.

"Red okay? Something stronger?" For a writer he was a man of few words.

"Red's fine," I said, even though I would have preferred a double G&T.

He asked for another glass, neglecting to say please or thank you to the bartender. Silently he poured my wine and then pushed the glass towards me.

"So," he said, with a penetrating and not entirely warm stare.

"So," I replied. I took a sip of my wine, trying not to wince at its overripe acidity.

"Tell me all about Kat."

The date had suddenly turned into an audition. I gave him a potted history of my life and times. He nodded, raised his eyebrows at a few points, looking mildly horrified when I told him that I would soon be appearing in a cabaret club. He punctuated my sentences with "Hmm. Hmm," but offered up absolutely no information about himself. It was like being at the doctor's office.

I was grateful when Word Smith's phone rang. Without making any apology or excusing himself he answered it and began shouting, "You tell Colin that I'm the bloody writer. If Firth can't say the lines as I've written them we'll get someone else. He's not even that

popular any more. Ask McEvoy... Too young? Absolute bollocks."
Word Smith carried on bellowing down the phone, ignoring me
completely. Part of me was fascinated by his casual rudeness in
the face of mega stardom, the other part totally turned off by his
belligerence and bad manners. It was all too clear why he was
internet dating – no sane, real world woman could bear him.

I signalled to Word Smith that I was going to the Ladies. Phone
clamped to his face he looked irritably at me as if to say, "Should
I give a shit?" I walked into a cubicle and pulled out my phone.
Jojo's line was busy and Wednesday was Bil and Ben's Bikram night.
I called Dave as a last resort. "Can you climb out of a window?" he
suggested. I glanced around the putrid cubicle before realising that
he was taking the piss. "Thanks a lot," I said and hung up.

I pulled my knickers out of my bag, putting them back on in a
double knot: there was no way they were coming off again until
I got home. I put the lid down on the toilet and sat for a few
moments gathering my thoughts, staring at the graffiti on the door.
I wondered why *Barry Jones* was *Da best* and if Mark Linley really
did have a penis as massive as the one scrawled in blue marker pen.
At least I wasn't on a date with *Ian B*, who apparently had *warts,
herpes and gonorrhoea*. Looking at these prosaic messages of love
and hate I longed for the simple romantic etiquette of my youth: a
quick snog to "Careless Whisper" at the school disco and I'd have
pretty much bagged myself a boyfriend, at least until half-term.

When I could no longer stand the sight of used tampons spilling
out of the sanitary bin like bloody lollipops I left the toilet cubicle.
I hoped that by the time I returned to the bar my date would have
got so fed up waiting that he might have gone home. Sadly he was
still there, working on his laptop and munching his way through a
bag of crisps.

"You took your time," he smirked.

"Sorry" I said, no longer caring what he thought of me, "I've
got really bad diarrhoea."

I made a point of sinking my hand into his potato chips, grabbing a large serving and stuffing them in my face. I crunched noisily and then licked every single one of my fingers before thrusting my hand back into the bag. I was like a government information film for the perils of food borne infection. This didn't put him off. In fact, quite the reverse.

"I like a girl with a healthy appetite," he quipped. "Even one with the shits."

"Speaking of which," I said, and took my cue to escape to the bathroom again.

I finally got through to Jojo. "Tell him your best friend's been taken seriously ill," she advised. "Not really a lie, more of a beige truth. I've been feeling like shit lately." I bristled. Since I was a child I'd had it drummed into me that lying came with punishments and penalties, like rubbish Christmas presents or the cancellation of gifts altogether. As I grew up the potential consequences became graver and I imagined very bad things happening to very good people all because of a story I made up. Then again, this man was truly awful.

I went back to the bar clutching my phone and tried to sound breathless with worry. "I'm so sorry but my best friend's been taken seriously ill. I have to go."

His face softened with concern, making him human and extremely attractive. Why couldn't he have been like this from the beginning?

"That's terrible," he said, shutting his laptop. "Where is she? I'll drive you."

I felt awful. Maybe he wasn't such an arse after all? But I couldn't change the story now. I tried to remember the hospital where my grandad had died, the same one where Mum had her bunions removed. I drew a blank.

"Holby City," I said, in desperation.

He narrowed his eyes. "That's a fictional hospital in a television series."

"Is it?" I said innocently. "I don't have a television so I wouldn't know. She's probably confused with all the stress. I better call her back."

Word Smith had busted me. "Am I really that boring?" he asked, looking genuinely hurt.

"God, no," I blustered. "It's been lovely. Such a pity I have to go."

"At least let me drop you at the Tube," he offered.

I looked out at the grey street where the drizzle was turning into heavy rain. Tempting as it was a lift back to the station would only prolong the agony.

"I can't get in your car," I said.

"Why?" he asked, his mouth hardening once more into a poisonous postal slit. His question echoed in my skull for a few moments until a low energy light bulb came on.

"Because I get violently car sick."

He shook his head, "You're the worst liar I ever met. If you ever fancy a career change I'd give politics a miss. This does, however, explain why you might be struggling with the acting."

He was back to being Mr Nasty and his comment got me right in my achilles heel. I teetered on the edge of truth and fiction.

"What kind of upholstery do you have?" I asked.

"What?" he said, exasperatedly.

"Cloth, leather or pleather?"

"Nubuck," he replied.

"There you go," I said plainly. "My bum, your hideously expensive seats – recipe for disaster. Right, I really have to go."

He had turned quite red now. "Can I call you?" he asked hopefully.

"Sure," I said and almost sprinted out of the pub, breathing a sigh of guilty relief when I got outside.

As I was walking back to the Tube there was the beep of a text message. It was Word Smith, *When?x*. I would need to be a bit more ruthless from now on. I selected "block number" then hit DELETE.

Chapter Fifteen

Life is a Cabaret

My debut at Petite Paris was a welcome distraction from my non-existent romantic life but it also felt just like a first-date; I had no idea whether we'd like each other and want to go out again, only if this pairing didn't work out I could end up homeless. I desperately needed Petite Paris to fall in love with me or I'd be moving back to my childhood bedroom where the ghosts of boy bands long forgotten stared down from the walls waiting to pour scorn upon my spinsterhood.

After spending the entire morning creating an Everest of clothing on the floor only to chose exactly the same sequin dress I'd worn for my audition, I turned my attention to the Titas problem. I flirted with the idea of wearing a disguise and pulled out an old cherry red afro wig that had been skulking in the bottom of my wardrobe since drama school. I vetoed it, concerned about cultural appropriation. As it turned out the closest the Petite Paris audience came to PC was when they were being frisked by one after driving home from the club legless. Next I found a black bob but it made me look more Edward the Confessor than Sally Bowles. I was just going to have to apologize to Titas – in Lithuanian. I half-considered texting Rob to ask Ludmilla for a translation. Instead I Googled and then inked the phrase phonetically on the inside of my wrist, repeating it over and over as I shaved my legs, pointlessly applied anti-cellulite cream and wound my hair in hot rollers, yelping when I stabbed myself in the head with a scalding metal pin.

Mum called while I was bleaching my moustache. "Bonne chance!" she gushed, "Life is a cabaret, old chum." Being nice to

Mum under the current circumstances irritated me more than peroxide on my top lip, but I knew Dad was hovering in the background waiting to say "Good luck, Treacle," so for his sake I pretended there was nothing wrong.

Ashamed that my new colleagues might see me in my Spanx, I got dressed at home. With the control pants, push up bra, nylon tights, corset, evening gown and inch thick layer of stage makeup I was sweating like a piece of cheese in a sunny window before I even left the house. To avoid being gawped at on the Tube I covered up my glitzy dress with a rain coat. I belted the coat and felt my temperature soar even higher.

It was a warm spring evening, the kind I usually longed for but tonight I would have preferred a sharp frost. I took my time getting to the station, trying not to perspire while moisture popped on my forehead and top lip, baubles of sweat running a regular service between my breasts, navel and buttocks. I tried to sashay but the effect was more sachet – I could almost feel my fat turning to liquid inside the tube of a dress. One malfunction of my underwear and my flesh would squirt out like ketchup or something from a slasher movie, spraying everyone and everything in the carriage: fifty-seven varieties of me, everywhere.

When I arrived at Petite Paris the floor staff were busy with place settings. Mags was darting between the chairs and tables like a silver service samurai, lining up napkins and wine glasses. She jettisoned a piece of grubby cutlery at a waitress with the skill of a knife thrower, shouting "unacceptable". The knife got caught in the woodwork and reverberated, before falling to the floor with a clang. I noticed that the waitresses were wearing corsets, knickers and stockings and I wondered when they were going to put their clothes on. Mags spotted me while she was examining a dinner plate for smears. For a moment I thought she was going to launch it at me like a frisbee. "Kat," she bellowed, "nice to see you, darl," and with that she ignored me again in favour of pelting one of the waiters with a defective bread roll.

I took a deep breath and pushed open the double doors into the garishly lit nerve centre of Petite Paris. It was a hive of activity with Pierre the head chef swearing at his staff in a variety of languages and physical gestures. The African dishwashers had been replaced by a South American duo, and I wondered if the first two had been fired after leaving another dirty bottom unwiped. I passed the other side of the kitchen and saw Titas' thick neck. He was singing again, a mournful, beautiful song. He stopped abruptly when we came face to face.

"You?" he said, slightly menacingly.

"Asstiprahschauw?" I stuttered.

"What?" he asked. I repeated the phrase. Titas shrugged. I tried again.

"Yes," he said, his face softening. "I understand, but I am not in your way."

I had learned the wrong phrase. Sorry really did seem to be the hardest word.

"I'm trying to apologise," I said, "for being so rude. And calling you the P word. Anyway, I'm sorry."

Titas face suddenly lit up.

"What you said was, 'excuse me'," he explained. "Is different to 'sorry'. But your accent perfect. Is very nice of you to try learn Lithuanian. Is good you changed your mind about us."

Somehow I had made the situation worse and Titas thought I was trying to flirt with him. I backed out of the doorway slowly like an action hero facing a cobra about to strike.

"I better get ready," I said as my mouth turned to cotton wool.

"After show we get drink?" asked Titas.

I didn't want to antagonise him by raising the subject of my imaginary boyfriend again so instead mumbled something about my friends coming to see the show and then scuttled off down the corridor. Titas went back to singing, joyfully belting out "It's Not Unusual" until Pierre shouted, "Tais-toi."

The heat backstage was unbearable. I slumped against the icy metal of the freezer room, half-considering going inside and stripping to my underwear just to cool off. I scanned the changing area for water but all I could see was several bottles of wine.

Two glasses of Chardonnay later I was beginning to feel a whole lot better about my impending debut. The performers for the evening had arrived; one stick thin burlesque dancer with an impressive pair of breasts quite at odds with the rest of her petite frame, and another with Rubenesque curves. While was I trying to control my flesh with Operation Spanx, "Dangerous Delight-Full" (her stage name, she told me in a thick Liverpudlian accent) was getting ready to let it all hang out. An extremely beautiful male acrobat came breezing down the corridor, all ripped skinny jeans and neon vest top. "'Ow do, I'm Gary love," he said, sounding very *Coronation Street*. Right behind him was a belly dancer with a snake around her neck, her eyes mysterious dark kohl pools. "I'm Charm, bub," she said in a Midlands accent, waving hello with the serpent's tail.

As the performers abandoned their civilian clothes and covered their faces and bare bodies in shimmering makeup they gossiped and joked. I tried not to look as Gary stowed away his substantial genitalia in a dancer's support belt. Whispering Willow, the slighter of the burlesque artists was glueing rhinestones to her nipples with Copydex as she enquired after Gary's health. "It's so fooked up babes," he griped. "I've got no problem getting cock – I mean look at me – but I can't seem to find a bloke who wants to stick around. I'm twenty-six. If I can't find a boyfriend by the time I'm thirty it'll be too late. Who's going to want me when I'm that old?" I bristled, realising I must look like a relic to these bright young things.

"Typical, innit?" Willow laughed. Her accent was straight out of *East Enders*. "You can't get one, and I can't get rid of mine. I'm only twenty-two, I don't need a bleedin' psycho bloke in my life." Gary looked very grave, "Still having problems with Theo?" Theo, I learned, was Willow's on-again-off-again boyfriend. He was properly posh, confused about his sexuality and addicted to cocaine. "What about you, Kat?" asked Charm, draping the snake around my neck as if I was a hatstand while she adjusted the jewel in her belly-button. I was pleasantly surprised to find the snake bone dry and not slimy as I had always imagined, but still I was frozen to the spot.

"No-one special, too busy with work and all that," I said lightly, trying not to panic as the snake began to show an alarming interest in my left breast.

"You should try internet dating," suggested Delight-Full, thankfully removing the serpent from my neck and cuddling it like a puppy. "Me mum's done it. She's got a really nice boyfriend now. He's a lorry driver from Leeds. She even travels with him and everything."

Gary interjected. "Nah, babes. I've done internet dating. No bloody good. Just cock, cock and more cock. Cock-a-doodle-cock."

"All the cock you can eat?" asked Willow.

"They should offer that here," said Charm, "might get more punters in."

Despite my wine-fuzzy edges I smelled trouble. "Business bad then?" I asked, slightly terrified that the "Wilkommen" mat was about to be yanked from under my sparkly platforms.

"I got cancelled last week," grimaced Charm.

"Me too," said Delight-Full.

While I was mulling over my suddenly insecure employment prospects a man resembling Iggy Pop appeared in the hallway holding a microphone. He was a proper old-school rock and roll roadie, with a Leatherman multitool and an ashtray on his skull-and-crossbones belt, and rolls of gaffer tape stacked on his tattooed arms. He wiped the head of the microphone on his Led Zeppelin T-shirt and handed it to me. "Alright Kaz, I'm Daz. Let's get this show on the road." I followed him down the corridor and into the club. The waitresses still hadn't put any clothes on and I realised that the lingerie *was* their uniform. I could just imagine my mother's glare of disapproval as her fillet steak was delivered with a side order of buttocks. I wished I hadn't invited Dave who was bound to see the flesh on display as a boobs and bum buffet, a sexual smorgasbord to which he could help himself.

As a tinny karaoke version of "Come To The Cabaret" started up, I shimmied along a catwalk to the stage, hoping I wouldn't fall over nor forget the words to a song I'd been singing since I was seven. I received a decent enough round of applause as I hit the last note and just as I was welcoming everyone to the show a man already half-cut shouted, "Get yer tits out!" My mouth went so dry I could feel my vocal chords sticking and time spun out endlessly before me. The mic began to feedback. Then from somewhere, the gods of comedy and tragedy smiling in my favour for once, I found my comeback. "I'd love to get my tits out but they're so massive I'd never be able to put them away again. Unlike your cock. And I hope your imagination is bigger than your dick or you and your hand are in a lot trouble when you go home tonight. Alone. Again."

The audience broke into gales of laughter, cheering and clapping. I looked over to the sound-booth where Daz was giving me a big thumbs up and Mags, standing by the bar, was whistling through her fingers. Bil, Ben, Jojo and Dave, who were seated in a VIP area, were shouting, "Go Kat!" and, "That's our girl." I was going to fit into Petite Paris just fine.

After the show I went to find the gang who were waiting at the bar with a bucket of champagne, ready to toast my success.

"Kat, you were simply a-maze-ing," gushed Ben.

"Truly," said Bil. "You're a star."

Jojo hugged me and said, "Just brilliant."

Even Dave seemed impressed. "Nice come back after that heckle. Can I use that?"

I laughed. "I don't think you've got the necessary front."

He stared at my cleavage without a trace of shame. "You're probably right."

We finished off the bottle and Ben and Bil ordered another.

"Do you mind if I go?" yawned Jojo, "I'm knackered."

"You okay?" I asked, coming down to earth from my performance high. It was hard to see her properly in the dim neon glow of the bar, but she did look exhausted.

"Just need some sleep. Work's been mental."

We all hugged Jojo goodbye and as I watched her walk across the club and through the beaded curtain to the exit a shiver ran through me. She looked stunning as always but there was something different about her, not quite right. Then suddenly Titas was in front of me.

"You were very good. Good singer. We should do duet," he suggested with a serious look on his face. For a moment there was an uncomfortable silence. Bil and Ben were wearing raised eyebrows that enquired, "And you are?" and I could see a little smirk of schadenfreude on Dave's lips.

"This is Titas," I explained. "He is a great singer from Lithuania." I said Lithuania very deliberately and Titas smiled proudly.

"We have a drink now?" he asked, with big, expectant eyes. Ben had a slightly murderous expression on his face but Bil asked a waiter for another glass. Dave was enjoying my agony.

"Let me introduce you to everyone," I said as Titas took his drink. His hands were hams that dwarfed the glass, making the champagne flute look like it belonged in a doll's house. Even when smiling a big warm grin his grey eyes was still unbearably sad.

"This is Bil and Ben. And this," I said pointing very deliberately to Dave, "Is my boyfriend, Ewan." Titas' face dropped with disappointment. I felt awful.

"Actually, Kat," said Dave/Ewan. "There's something I've been meaning to ask you." He dropped dramatically to one knee. Punters and staff were now beginning to pay attention. I could see what was coming and was powerless to stop it.

"Will you marry me, Katherine Wheeler?"

Bil and Ben were smiling. They were no fans of Dave but had clearly worked out what was going on with Titas and they were finding the whole scene highly amusing. I looked at Titas and hoped that he couldn't tell the difference between a broad Welsh and Scottish accent. He seemed to be holding his breath, looking at me hopefully and willing me to say no. There was only one solution. "Of course I'll marry you, Ewan!" I gushed. Dave stood up beaming and took me in his arms. He then planted a kiss on my lips that seemed to go on forever. I wasn't very happy to find his tongue in my mouth but after my horror subsided I found him to be a very nice kisser – great in fact. When I began to feel a tingle I pushed him away. Dave was my mate, an absolute mess of a man. I was *not* supposed to fancy him.

By the time I unhooked myself from the clinch everyone was clapping and cheering. The DJ was playing "Love Is In The Air" and a complimentary bottle of champagne appeared on the bar in front of us. Mags came up and hugged me. She looked at Dave and said, "Needs a haircut but he'll do," then she went off to shout at a member of staff about a puddle of sick in the Ladies. Crestfallen, Titas shook Dave's hand, refusing to meet my gaze.

"Congratulations," he said as magnanimously as he could under the circumstances.

"Thanks, mate," said Dave, shaking Titas' hand a little too enthusiastically.

Titas put his glass on the bar. "I must go," he said and disappeared back into the kitchen.

I felt incredibly mean. This was the kind of game that I was often victim to when I was at school. I knew how it felt to be on the other end and I hated myself for it.

"Why did you do that?" I shouted at Dave over the music.

"You looked like you needed help," he bellowed in my ear.

Ben sneered at Dave and Bil just shook his head.

"What's wrong?" Dave asked with wide-eyed innocence. "You had a problem. I solved it." He picked up Titas' unfinished champagne and drank the whole glass as if it was a shot of tequila to congratulate himself, "Simples."

Chapter Sixteen

The Scream

Determined to avoid a dating fate worse than Dave I ploughed on with my online search for love and a suitable baby father. Give Us A Clooney, 42 sounded like a catch; *Silver fox seeks vixen. Willing to leave cub-rearing and suburban bins behind for big city night time adventures.* True, it wasn't ideal that he was already a father and by the sounds of his profile he didn't want any more offspring, but at least his equipment was in working order.

We arranged a late supper in the West End after one of my shows – asking Clooney to meet me at Petite Paris wasn't an option since everyone who worked there was now under the impression that I was engaged. Two weeks on and staff and performers were still asking, "When's the big day?" I'd force a smile and say, "We haven't set a date yet," cursing Dave under my breath.

It had been a difficult night at the club. When I arrived backstage there was a noticeable gloom. "Why is everyone so sad?" I asked Mags as she came whizzing through the corridor, "and where's Titas?"

"Gone," she said sadly.

"He's left Petite Paris?" I asked, hoping I wasn't the reason for his departure.

"Left the country, darl," Mags replied. "Home Office wouldn't renew his visa. Bastards said he wasn't a 'skilled worker'. Unskilled? They never tasted his crème brulée."

"Visa? Isn't Lithuania in the EU? Even with Brexit surely he's allowed to stay?" I asked

"Yep Lithuania's in the EU," said Mags picking up some empty glasses. "But his parents and his passport are Russian. What can you do?" she shrugged and disappeared down the corridor.

Titas had built a new life for himself in London and now it had been stripped away from him because of a geopolitical anomaly. And I thought I had it hard.

There were two enormous hen parties in the club that night, gaggles of drunken women festooned with brightly coloured feather boas, the cheap kind from party shops that shed everywhere. By the end of the night the place looked like a chicken coop that had been raided by a starving fox. I'd been on several hen-dos myself over the years and behaved extremely badly (like the time I got stuck up a lamp post in Southend and the Police could only coax me down with the threat of an ASBO), but being on the receiving end somewhat changed my perspective. By the time the curtain came down I was tired and cranky.

My heart sank even further as I walked into the restaurant in China Town. I spotted my date immediately, his grey, grizzled head resting despairingly in his hands, poring over a menu with a look of angst as if reading an apocalyptic prophesy. In his profile photo he was attractive in a mature, Carey Grant kind of way – in person he was fifty shades of beige, like the tortured soul from Munch's most famous painting come to life. There would be no silver fox lining to this rubbish evening.

I half considered simply turning around and walking away but he'd already spotted me and was on his feet to greet me. I took a deep breath and consoled myself that if nothing else he had good manners.

"Hello," I said, forcing a smile, "I'm Kat."

He shook my hand firmly as if we were having a business meeting. "Simon, pleased to meet you."

I sat down at the grubby formica table and immediately stopped a passing waitress to order pork ribs, duck pancakes and a beer.

"Don't mean to be rude but I'm starving," I said, trying to sound jovial.

"I can't eat most of this stuff," he said ruefully. "I'm paleo. And I don't drink." It was the final nail in the evening's coffin.

He ordered boiled chicken and vegetables and we made the requisite small talk about work, family and friends while we waited for our food, both of us skirting the nasty issue of divorce. Simon said that he was something to do with the music business and had just had a late meeting in town. I told him that I was a singer at a club and had just had a late gig in town. It should have given us common ground. It didn't.

"What kind of men do you like?" he asked.

It was a pertinent question and it completely blind-sided me. All I knew was that this beige fox wasn't one of them. "Funny guys, I guess? What kind of women do you like?"

"Natural women with simple, elegant taste," he said eyeing my stage makeup and sparkling cleavage disparagingly.

"Ever considered dating a nun?" I asked.

"No," he said blankly.

I quickly drank the rest of my beer and ordered another, intercepting a waiter who looked like he was going for some kind of plate-stacking world record.

Simon looked at me searchingly with his sorrowful grey eyes, "What do you *really* want?"

What I wanted was not to be on another awful bloody date. But again, it was a penetrating question and something I hadn't really thought about until now. What *did* I want? I'd been so preoccupied my whole life with delivering what other people expected of me – onstage and in front of the camera, as a wife and lover – that I'd never really stopped to consider my own needs. "The same as everyone else," I replied, stumped for a better answer, "I just want to be happy." It came out hollow. Simon took it as a cue to launch into statements about "our time of life". It was hard to believe that he was only three years older than me and his supposed camaraderie and grating epithets about middle age made me fidget irritably on the rickety chair. As he droned on and on I drank more and more.

Eventually I excused myself and went to the bathroom. I texted Jem: *Are you awake?* In less than a minute he replied: *Yeh, coming over?* Why Jem couldn't use "yes" I'll never know. I put it down to too much junk food and abusively loud music through his ear pods. I returned to the table, we finished our food and then I wobbled to standing on my tipsy legs. I tried to pay my share of the bill but Simon insisted it was his treat. He also insisted on walking me to the bus stop.

"Don't you live South?" he asked, "surely you want the other side of the road?"

I found myself spinning another yarn. "I'm staying with a girlfriend in Archway. I've let my place on Air B&B for the weekend. The extra cash is really handy."

"I admire your ingenuity," said Simon.

"Thanks," I replied, certain that I must be turning pillar box red with the guilt of the whopping lie I'd just told.

I was getting a little too good at telling stories and it worried me, but being a decent person hadn't really worked out for me so far. All my life I had paid my own way, told the truth, put my partner's needs before my own. And where had it got me? Humming Bert Bacharach's "I'm Never Gonna Fall In Love Again" all alone in the pouring rain at the bus stop of life while everyone else barged in front of me. It was a shame that the beige fox was on the receiving end of my worm turning bitter. He was a decent man.

Simon saw me onto the bus, holding me underneath the elbow as if I was an elderly lady. He waved as the bus shunted out into the West End traffic, cars still bumper to bumper even though it was well past midnight. I waved back and breathed a sigh of relief: dating was becoming something to be got through, like tax returns and smear tests. I reasoned, as best I could in my sozzled state, that there had to be a better way and a plan started to percolate in my booze-soaked brain. Maybe expecting everything to show up in one package was unrealistic? Maybe my dream man – smart, funny, caring, handsome – was destined to stay just that because men like that didn't exist in the real world. Maybe 'The One' never really existed at all, except in the movies? Maybe to get what you really wanted you had to go for a multipack; The One For Sex, The One For Financial Advice, The One For Dining In A Restaurant With Real Napkins?

No point in throwing the bastard out with the bathwater, I decided as I stumbled up the narrow stairs to Jem's flat. Why not keep Jem for pleasure until a decent man showed up? Simples.

The fundamental flaw in my genius new dating plan became apparent as soon as I woke up the next day. I left Jem to sleep off his hangover and as I stumbled to the bathroom I tried to remember what had happened the night before. I'd been so blind drunk that I wasn't sure if Jem had used a condom – and if not had he pulled out of the danger zone in time? I flipped the lid on the bathroom bin gagging as I rummaged through the contents of discarded tissues, dental floss and disposable razors. There was no condom but I did come across an empty box from a Clinique women's face cream. I swallowed hard. Jem liked to take care of himself but even by his standards this was a metrosexual step too far. I checked his bathroom cabinets to see if there was a corresponding jar but all I could find was a can of Lynx, a nasal hair trimmer and some Nivea For Men products. There had definitely been another woman in Jem's flat.

Jem snored while I continued my bizarre treasure hunt. He moaned at me when I moved the duvet to see if there might be a condom under it. All I could see was a tell-tale white crust on the sheets. I had to concede that we had probably had unprotected sex – and that Jem was sleeping with at least one other woman. It wasn't that this possibility hadn't crossed my mind, I saw him so rarely and we weren't even dating, but it was only now, in the stark grey light of the morning after that it had any significance.

I gently shook Jem awake. He growled at me and mummified himself in the duvet. I lost my temper and yanked it off of him.

"What the fuck are you doing?" he snapped.

"Did you use a condom last night?" I said, more accusation than question.

"Dunno," he said agitatedly. "Don't think so," and rewound himself up in the bedding like a human sausage roll.

I felt the blood drain from my face. "Why not?" I asked, staring at his hairy toes sticking out at the end of the bed.

"I thought you were on the pill," came his muffled, casual reply.

It was as if I'd woken him up to tell him that there wasn't any milk.

I left without saying goodbye, immediately Googled the nearest STD clinic and made an emergency appointment, receiving a good telling-off followed by a prescription for the morning after pill and profuse bleeding over the next week. Jem probably spent the rest of the day in bed eating pizza and watching motor racing on TV. I could blame him all I wanted but I was the one who had let this happen. Continually.

Chapter Seventeen

Who's Your Daddy?

Bil and Ben invited me over for dinner, eager for news of my dating success. I had no intention of telling them how my latest scheme had just blown up in my face. I dutifully showed up at their stunning Kennington town house at the appointed time. They were full of excitement about their wedding plans.

"We're both wearing white!" Bil squealed. "Isn't that hilarious? A couple of filthy queens masquerading as choir boys. Butter wouldn't melt."

I was happy for them, despite the fact that they had stolen my dream wedding of a boho barefoot beach ceremony. I flopped down onto their buttery soft leather couch and kicked my shoes off. Bil and Ben had the finest of everything but they were generous with it and always made me feel at home. Bil bought a bucket of champagne and three glasses over to the coffee table, while Ben clutched something to his chest.

"There's something else we want to ask you," he said mysteriously.

I glanced from one to the other. "I'll do it," I replied with a big grin.

They looked blankly at each other.

"Matron of Dishonour, right?" I qualified.

"Oh *that*? Of course. Goes without saying," said Bil.

"This is Nahla," said Ben, passing me a framed photo.

I looked at the beautiful young Indian woman smiling back at me. Bil and Ben watched me expectantly.

"Is this your sister?" I asked Bil.

"No relation," he replied.

"Oh right. Are you sponsoring her then?" I was confused.

Ben sat next to me. "Kind of."

Bil finished his sentence, "She's going to have our daughter."

I wasn't sure if I had heard correctly. "A baby? You two?"

Ben looked a little offended. "Yes, Kat, we're going to have a baby. Aren't you excited for us?"

"It's wonderful," I stuttered, "it's just such a surprise. But I'm *so* happy for you both. Really."

I stood up and hugged Bil, then Ben stood up and hugged us both. Their joy was quite literally suffocating. Eventually we all sat back down, Bil and Ben either side of me delivering a barrage of baby news in stereo.

"Nahla's a total sweetheart," enthused Ben. "She's twenty-two, lives in California and she's going to use the surrogacy money to fund her medical degree. Isn't that amazing?"

I nodded and echoed, "Amazing," asking myself why Nahla had to have someone else's baby to see her way through college.

"It's a little girl," Bil said proudly

"We thought we'd call her Betsey," Ben chimed in.

"You can't call her that," I laughed. "Bil, Ben and Betsey. Sounds like a bad sitcom from the eighties."

"What about Lotus Lily, in honour of her Indian heritage?" offered Bil.

"Not unless you want your daughter to sound like a porn star."

They both laughed. I began to wonder if it was Bil and Ben who had planted the IVF seed in Jojo's mind.

"So was it your idea for Jojo to freeze her eggs?" I asked archly.

"That's your problem right there," Ben said a little sourly.

"What's that supposed to mean?" I asked, taken aback by the sudden drop in the social temperature.

"Not you specifically, but women your age in general, ignoring the ticking time bomb of their ovaries."

"Oh good," I replied tartly, "as long as it wasn't an attack on my personal life choices."

"He doesn't mean it like that," said Bil, stepping in to defuse the ticking time-bomb of the conversation. "He's just talking biological reality. That's something we do understand."

"So you're suggesting I find myself a sperminator?"

"FYI," said Ben defensively, "we had no idea about Jojo. But maybe she's got the right idea. Have you thought about putting your eggs on ice?"

"No," I replied flatly. "I can't even shut my freezer door – let alone stock it with potential children."

"Then what about letting us help you?" Bil asked calmly.

"Thanks. But a spatula and a hairdryer normally does the job."

"We want to have another child," said Ben, ignoring my sarcasm. "We could pay for the treatment if you let us have your eggs."

I was stunned. What had started out as a quiet evening with two of my closest friends had turned into womb raiding. The dinner invitation suddenly felt like a ruse.

"Why don't you ask Jojo? Two birds, one stone?"

"Jojo's gorgeous..." replied Ben, the pause inferring I wasn't quite as stunning, "but you're wittier."

"Thanks," I said without a trace of gratitude.

"And you're practically family," continued Bil. "We thought we could offer you a child of your own – or at least the chance to be a special Aunty. We want Betsey or Lily or whatever we call her to have a sibling."

They had it all planned out. Their unborn baby was probably already on the waiting list for the best independent school in the area and enrolled in a gifted child program.

"You want to turn me into FrankenMom?" I asked in disbelief. "My egg, my womb, your sperm, I give birth then you take it away? Why don't you just put a bolt through my neck?"

"A bolt through that gob of yours might be an improvement." Ben's attempt at humour fell flat. I stared at the bubbles in my champagne glass.

"It doesn't have to be your womb," Bil said gently, "We could use a surrogate."

"Yes," Ben added, "you could just give us your eggs."

"Now my womb's not good enough?" I snapped.

"I've seen the way you look after your cookware," Ben replied. "Who knows how you'd cope with gestating a baby for nine months."

Bil tried to explain, "You'd only carry it if it was your child. We'd use a surrogate for our baby. That way there would be less risk of bonding issues."

"Are you having a kid or a tube of super glue?" I asked, aghast.

Bil refilled my glass. I laughed bitterly, "Is that wise? The quality of my eggs is already pretty rubbish at my age. Isn't alcohol very damaging to fertility?"

Bil put his arm round me. "I'm sorry if we didn't put things the right way. We just thought it might be mutually beneficial." He squeezed me firmly.

"We're not saying you're not getting any younger," continued Ben, "but you're thirty-nine, Kat. This might be your last chance. If you do want a baby you need to do something. Sooner rather than later."

I hadn't really faced up to the fertility question until that moment. I was still in reasonable physical shape, I didn't smoke, I didn't drink excessively (not every night, anyway) and I was still getting my periods. I just assumed that a man whom I could tolerate would show up eventually and we would breed. This conversation had shaken me to my marrow. The champagne now tasted flat and bitter. I could feel tears pricking behind my eyes. I hated and loved Bil and Ben at that moment in equal measure; hated their affluence, the way they could snap their fingers and have a ready-made family as easily as doing their weekly online grocery shop, loved them for caring enough to offer me a procedure that I could never afford in a million years so I didn't miss the baby boat.

"Just going for a pee," I said hoarsely and clomped up the

reclaimed rainforest spiral staircase, noting it as a potential total death trap for a toddler. I bolted the bathroom door behind me and stared at my reflection. I noticed how my crow's feet were deepening into rivulets and my chin looked as if it was heading towards the plural. What if Bil and Ben were right? What if the accident with Jem had been my last chance? What if it was already too late?

Chapter Eighteen

Desperation and Dave

Just when it looked like I might have enough regular income to really apply myself to the dating marathon which seemed to be required to find somebody to love messages from potential partners all but dried up. The conversation with Bil and Ben had sent me into panic mode but my dating inbox was emptier than a catwalk model's stomach at Fashion Week. I needed help. Jojo was off in the developing world somewhere bulk buying questionably produced clothes for an upmarket womenswear chain and, with Bil and Ben more interested in my womb than my emotional well-being, Gropey Dave was the last resort. He may have been unsuitable, unstable and unethical but at least he was available.

Dave had never actually been convicted of groping or any other sexual offence and despite having the sartorial elegance of a grubby student he was a nice-looking bloke and extremely funny. He was also a chronic 'social drinker' – officially he was an alcoholic but since his boozing mostly took place in public settings he flatly denied having a problem. Like a good sale women found him irresistible and he was apt to take advantage of those who threw themselves at his feet. He wasn't particularly choosy: whether the shoe fit or not, Dave would wear it. He was incapable of window shopping. Female fans at Dave's comedy gigs would buy him many post-show drinks and then take him back to their flats for a night of bilious sex and a cooked breakfast the morning after. Dave's parting promise of "I'll call you" would never materialise. Part clown, part gigolo – definitely *not* boyfriend material.

Dave didn't really deserve my caustic judgement. He'd been a very good friend to me since we met many years previously when we were both working at a call centre. I'd just finished my degree and Dave had recently qualified as a civil engineer, a career he never embarked upon but said that learning to judge distances had come in handy for avoiding missiles launched at him while onstage, ranging from beer bottles to stilettos and on one occasion a breast pump. We bonded at the office Christmas party when we both bowed out of the festivities at the same time that several of our co-workers started photocopying their genitals.

I realised early on that Dave and I would be better off as just good friends and soon after that I met Rob. Rob wasn't keen on Dave, and the feeling was mutual, so I hardly ever saw Dave once I was married. As soon as Rob dumped me Dave was there to catch my fall. Throughout my post-Rob woes Dave always joked, "If you ever need a bit of cock and a cuddle you know where I am." He listened patiently to my stories, although I discovered that this was not entirely selfless; one night I turned up at one of Dave's gigs unannounced just as he was regaling the audience with a tale that sounded very much like my last date. He had at least protected my anonymity by changing my name to "Kate".

I sat opposite Dave in the gastro-pub, heaving with weekend brunch parties, and pushed a packet of pork scratchings, a pint of lager and a double whiskey towards him. It was the price of his counsel but still cheaper than professional therapy. I sucked on a straw, drinking a very plastic tasting Diet Coke.

"Not boozin'?" he asked incredulously, in his best Chas 'n' Dave cockney, so incongruous with his native Welsh lilt.

"Dave, it's eleven a.m."

"So?" he shrugged. "It's Sunday." He downed the whiskey the way desperadoes do in movies and then started on his pint. "Right then, Love's Young-ish Dream," he said licking lager foam off his lips, "tell me about your latest victim."

I jabbed the straw in my drink, "That's just it. There aren't any."

Dave blinked at me. "No cock at all?"

I rolled my eyes, "I'm not looking for cock. Well, not specifically for cock. I really do want to find someone. Right now I couldn't even land a pen pal on Death Row."

"Well that's a new spin on life partner," he replied, chuckling at his own joke before taking another swig of beer. He clapped the pork scratchings between his paws, opening the bag with a loud bang that made half the punters in the pub turn and stare at him. A shaggy-haired, beanie-wearing man lowered his *Independent On Sunday* and glowered at us. Dave glared back like a stroppy teenager, and Mr Independent disappeared behind his paper again.

"I fucking hate hippies," said Dave dispassionately. "I bet he's a vegan. Unlike your Death Row pals, who have a disproportionate amount of necrophiliacs and cannibals among their population."

"You disgust me," I responded.

"Show me your dating profile," Dave continued, "and I'll tell you how you've cocked it up."

Against my better judgement I pulled my phone out, logged onto the site and pushed it across the table to him. "Do your worst."

"I'm sure it's not that bad," he said generously. "Another pint please. And a packet of cheese and onion crisps. The baked not fried ones." He patted his stomach, "Have to keep an eye on my girlish figure."

He winked at me with his slightly bloodshot eye, an endearing habit that also made me want to punch him in the face. I returned to the table to find Dave wearing the same expression I'd seen last on my bank manager.

"Kat, Kat, Kat," he said as if my very name were designed specifically to express exasperation.

"Here we go," I said, sitting down sulkily.

"Your dating profile is Mother Mary meets Tonya Harding."

I looked at him blankly, "Who's Tonya Harding?"

He laughed. "I forgot, you're *so* much younger than me." Unperturbed by my flaring nostrils he explained, "She's the ice skater who allegedly had a rival competitor's knees smashed with a truncheon."

I folded my arms crossly. "Thanks very much. I asked for some feedback, not a character assassination."

He looked at me, his hazel eyes warm and sympathetic through messy dark blonde curls. "Look, all I'm saying is that it's a bit ... full on."

I grabbed the bag of crisps and opened them with such force that they spilled out all over the grubby table. "Full on?" I mumbled through a full mouth, "how so?"

Dave picked up stray crisps and shoved them in his mouth as he talked.

"The stuff about how whacky you are 'I sing and talk to myself on the street late at night so weirdos will leave me alone'."

I shrugged, "Yes?"

"It makes you seem a bit ... well, mental."

I crunched menacingly on an ice cube. "I'm just trying to be honest," I said through frozen teeth, "Are you suggesting I lie about who I am? Or is there something wrong with who I am?" I looked away from him, taken off-guard by my own question.

Dave kicked me softly under the table. "Don't be silly. You know I think you're ace. But you asked for an honest opinion and I'm giving you one. If it's sympathy you're after talk to Jojo or The Gays."

"Don't be homophobic," I reprimanded.

"Sorry," he shrugged, "Bil and Ben, The Flowerpot Men."

But I had to admit he was right. Dave may have been a womanising drunk but there was no malice in him. He was far less likely to roll the turd in glitter than the rest of my friends.

"Then what do you suggest?" I asked.

He pushed his empty glass towards me as if it was a chess piece. "Let me write your profile."

I balked. "What?"

"I'm serious. Let me have a go."

I was about to flatly reject the idea when he continued, "What you've written here is funny. Properly. But most men don't want funny. They feel threatened by it."

"What am I supposed to do?" I said, feeling my voice oscillate between tears and anger. "Pretend to be someone I'm not? I am what I am. And what I am is bloody well brilliant."

I was trying desperately hard not to cry. Dave took my hand and looked at me with genuine tenderness.

"Kat, there's nothing wrong with you. You're great. Unique."

I suddenly felt hot all over and distinctly tingly in certain places. I snatched my hand back and set my features into outrage again.

"But I'm an acquired taste?"

He exhaled deeply. "Try to see me as your window dresser. I'll hook them, you can reel them in."

I shook my head, "I don't think that's a good idea. Do you remember when I let you sell my exercise bike on eBay and the buyer hit the roof because it didn't come with wheels?"

"That was your fault, you didn't give me all the relevant information."

I grabbed my phone back. "Dave, it was a stationary exercise bike."

He winked at me again. "Go on, Kat. Let me have a go. If you don't like it you can just delete it."

I searched my brain for reasons why it was a terrible idea to let Dave write my dating profile. They were few and far between, I really didn't have a lot to lose. And who better to understand what a man wants than another man – even if that man was pissed on a daily basis? I pushed the phone back towards Dave.

"Okay. Do it. But don't you dare upload anything until I've read it."

He pushed his hair out of his eyes and looked at me earnestly, "Trust me."

I was considering the implications of that statement when he tapped his empty pint glass. "Same again, thanks sweetheart."

Chapter Nineteen

Rebel Without Applause

Dubious of Dave's skill as a matchmaker, more doubtful still that he'd even remember to write me a new and improved profile, I ploughed on across the glacial seas of online romance alone. On a chilly Saturday afternoon, when late spring had decided to turn into winter again, I made my way to a brasserie by the South Bank to meet the sole prospect in my dating inbox; *Rebel, 33. Born in the USA – made in Singapore. Property developer by day, stand-up comic by night, seeks partner in crime for laughing in the face of adversity.* Funny and solvent. On paper he sounded more than perfect.

Rebel was waiting outside for me when I arrived. Even without the profile photo I would have spotted him immediately, people on first dates stick out like sore thumbs; we're the ones on our own, fiddling with our hair and clothes and frantically scanning texts to make sure we're in the right place, looking hopefully at every passing stranger that bears the merest resemblance to the person we're meeting, all the while trying to appear relaxed (and failing abysmally). As I walked towards Rebel he gave me a big smile, flashing a set of perfect teeth so white they made my eyes hurt. He had jet black, glossy, fifties style hair and I thought how much fun it would be to run my fingers through it and give it a firm tug.

"Sorry I'm bit late. Tubes are messed up," I said, my standard excuse for my pathological tardiness.

"No problem," he said, in one of those shiny, mid-Atlantic American accents favoured by newsreaders on CNN that make the most tragic world event sound not so bad after all. "This is for you," he said proudly.

He pulled something out from his black leather bomber jacket and handed it to me. It was a postcard of Damien Hurst's *Piss Christ*. I figured he must have been to The Tate Modern before meeting me and he'd gone to some considerable effort to personalise his gift. Over the top of Hurst's work Rebel had drawn a cartoon of himself wearing flippers, goggles and a snorkel, toting an open umbrella which was being rained upon, the tip of a penis just visible in the corner making the rain. I was touched by this unique if rather odd memento of our first date. I wondered if this was the kind of thing he went in for with his stand-up. It explained the need for a day job.

"Wow," I said, forcing a smile as I put the postcard in my handbag, "you've created a masterpiss."

"Thank fuck!" he exclaimed. "A sense of humour. Drink?"

We went into the brasserie and approached the bar. Without asking what I'd like Rebel ordered two Singapore Slings, and then shot me a filthy grin, "Something from the motherland." The bartender, who looked about twelve and clearly had no idea how to mix a cocktail, shuffled nervously. "How exactly would Sir like that?" Rebel pulled out his iPhone, flashed the recipe at the red-faced bartender, and then strode off towards the tables. I found myself mouthing "sorry" to the barman.

Rebel picked a cosy corner booth and slid in. Being somewhat broader of hip I clumsily jostled in next to him, making the table rattle and bang.

"Mountain Kat," he said, "Short for Kat?" His eyes drifted towards my cleavage, clearly more interested in the "Mountain" part.

"Rebel," I said, trying to return his repartee, "as in James or Marlon?"

"Norman, actually," he said.

I bit back a laugh. I was not expecting this cool cat to have the same name as the elderly man with the comb-over hair who ran the hardware store near my parents house. The drinks arrived and

I took a swig. I felt the air evaporate in my lungs as forty percent proof neat alcohol hit the back of my throat.

"Shit the bed!" I gasped.

"One part Cointreau, eight parts Gin," he said wickedly.

"You do stand-up comedy, then?" I asked after the burning in my gullet had subsided enough to permit speech.

He nodded proudly, "Sure do. Haven't been doing it long, but I love it."

"Do you know Dave Rees?" I asked.

Norman pulled a face, "I've seen him. Not my style. Bit obvious." I felt offended on Gropey's behalf.

"He's one of my best friends," I said, trying to drink the cocktail without actually tasting it.

"My condolences," Norman said.

Bristling against his arrogance I asked, "What do you do to pay the bills?"

"Property developing," he replied, as if it was of no concern.

"What a coincidence," I chirped, "I live in a flat. We have so much in common."

"Actually," he said, gravely, "I've been going through a very nasty divorce and all my property is tied up. My ex-wife's intent on ass fucking me as hard as she can."

"Right," I said, taking a long slurp of my drink and unsure why he thought that painting his wife in such a poor light might engender my sympathy. Feeling the date drifting towards a dangerous conversational weir I changed the subject, "When can I see you do a gig?"

"More to the point," he returned, "when can I see you do a gig?"

"Any time you want," I said, "but I'm not sure if it's your sort of thing."

He smiled mischievously, "Aren't there strippers where you work?"

I was so tired of this question that I was half considering putting 'cashier' as my profession on my dating profile. Men seemed to imagine that I was an all-singing, all-lap-dancing modern day Nell Gwynn with a sex toy stuffed in every orifice. It felt especially unfair seeing as I was only the monkey on the bumping and grinding organ of Petite Paris. The only time I had done any burlesque was by accident when my corset burst open during a particularly heartfelt rendition of "I Will Always Love You".

"Yes," I replied wearily, "there are burlesque dancers."

He interrupted, "Burlesque. Stripping. Same difference."

"It's all a question of perception," I replied, noticing that the table of young women next to us had inclined their heads towards our conversation.

"Let me get this straight," Norman said with forced disbelief, "these girls take their clothes off? These girls do it onstage? These girls do it for money? Sounds like stripping to me." Every time he said the word 'girls' it fizzed across my brain, a flash of hot pink neon. Why was it, I asked myself, that when a man wanted to make a disparaging point about the female gender he used the word 'girl'? It was literally belittling. He took a sip of his drink staring at me sharply, as if daring me to challenge him. What had initially seemed like casual confidence was clearly macho arrogance. I could feel my cheeks flushing with indignation and gin. Norman's knee had been brushing my leg the whole time, a fact I was now finding intensely irritating.

"I wouldn't know," I said caustically as I shuffled away from him, "I've never been to a strip joint."

"Do you want to go to one?" he asked, sliding his hand under the table and grabbing my thigh.

I peeled his clammy fingers off of my leg and stared directly at him, "No thanks. Not my kind of thing."

"Really? I would have thought a wild girl like you would have been up for anything."

I wriggled out of the booth and stood up, holding my clutch bag like a cosh. "As well as not understanding the difference between lap dancing and cabaret, you also seem to have confused online dating for prostitution." I reached inside my bag and pulled out a crumpled tenner. "Not that I have a problem with the latter, it's an honest living. But just to clarify, here's the money for my drink." I pushed the note into the waistband of his jeans. "And by the way, grown-up men date women. Only little boys or paedophiles are interested in girls." I stomped towards the door and the table of women burst into applause. I turned around as one whooped, "You go girl!" Her friend prodded her and she corrected herself, "I mean woman!"

The whole group were convulsed in fits of laughter. Norman stood up, his jaw twitching; if looks could kill I would have needed an ambulance. He pulled the ten pound note out of his waistband and threw it on the table, serving a filthy glare to the women as he headed towards the toilets. I took a little bow for my feminist fan club, who applauded again, and then I hightailed it back to the Tube in case Norman decided to follow me. As I ran under Waterloo Bridge my laughter bounced off of the walls and echoed all around me, the pure, joyful sound of someone not giving a single shit and refusing to be beaten.

My new lust for life was demolished as soon as I got home and checked my email. I saw Rob's address and the subject "URGENT" and suddenly my heart was in my mouth. Was he sick? Did he need me? Or had he finally realised his error, dumped Ludmilla and was ready to give us another chance? My finger hovered over the "read" button and I thought I might be one step closer to understanding Schrödinger's cat – all the love I ever had for Rob was both simultaneously alive and dead until I opened that message.

Kat, he began. Not a whisper of affection. I felt my stomach plummet through my feet. I read on in utter despair. *Do you have a copy of the divorce certificate? Lud's preggers and we're getting married in Vilnius ASAP before she's too big to fly.* Once more the fault line in my heart was ripped wide open.

Chapter Twenty

Seven Year Glitch

Finding out that my husband was unfaithful one fine summer morning three years earlier was the worst day of my life. I wanted to die. I was in complete and utter despair. The emotional pain immediately manifested itself physically and attacked my body. The hurt twisted my guts so tightly that I couldn't eat. The lies and regrets ricocheted around my brain so loud I had to be completely pissed before I could even contemplate trying to sleep. I'd put all my time, effort and energy into Rob, devoted an entire decade of my life to him, and he'd turned on me, thrown it back in my face, stabbed me in the heart with my own love. I couldn't breathe. I didn't want to any more.

I had just refurbished the flat when it happened. It was supposed to be a seventh wedding anniversary surprise for Rob when he returned from a business trip. But even as I hand-stitched cushion covers and framed photographs of us (when I should have been learning lines for an audition), I knew that something was wrong. When he got back late from the airport he barely acknowledged all the effort I'd made. He hardly spoke, turned his back on the candlelit Mediterranean platter on the table I'd painstakingly assembled and went straight to bed. I sat up drinking wine on my own and pushing olives around on a lonely side plate.

When I eventually went to bed Rob was fast asleep. I reached over him to turn the light off and he suddenly looked like a stranger to me. The Rob I knew, the one who said he'd never leave me, who promised to love me in sickness and in health in front of over a hundred people, was gone. I lay on my back staring into the darkness with only the buzz saw of Rob's snore for company. Then

116

there was a flash on his phone as a message came in. I leant over him again and saw the name 'Ludmilla'. And I just knew.

The next day I pretended to be asleep until Rob went to work. Then I opened his laptop and searched 'Ludmilla'. I found a deluge of e-mails, poems, and photos. He was even making her a website, something I'd begged him to do for me for months. I hoped that with a name like Ludmilla she might look like a Soviet shot putter, but she was absolutely stunning; slim-hipped, large-chested with bright blue eyes and white-blonde hair straight out of a shampoo commercial. I felt like Dolly Parton when she sang "Jolene" – I didn't come close to this icy goddess.

Rob hadn't deleted anything, as if every single e-mail, however banal, was precious, whereas he binned birthday and Christmas cards from me as soon as he'd read them. In one particularly dull message Ludmilla told him about her new casserole dish. Granted it was Le Creuset, but why was she talking about cookware if they were in the first throws of passion? Rob replied that she was his "dream girl" – an angel in the kitchen and a whore in the bedroom, I supposed. It was like a bad soap opera. I was surprised that Rob hadn't tried to hide the affair, no secretly coded folders, no password on his laptop. I could only conclude that he wanted me to find out.

By the time JoJo arrived later that morning I was lying face down on the street crying, two laundry bags of random stuff at my side, while people stepped over me as if I was a chalk outline left behind at a crime scene. Jojo called Dave, who turned up an hour later with a reeking hangover and a driver called Alexi in a beaten-up transit van. Jojo and Dave peeled me off the street. I imagined that I must have looked like a cartoon character who'd been flattened by a steam roller. Jojo and Dave walked me back to the flat, holding me under the elbows to steady my wobbly legs. I felt like a widow. They grabbed my stuff, jamming it into bin liners while I just stood there limply saying, "Maybe I read too much into it? Maybe it's a joke? Maybe he'll change his mind?" Jojo, tears in her eyes, just shook her head and hugged me. "Your husband's a total bastard," Dave said.

We threw the bags into the back of the van and I could hear fragile, precious things breaking but it was like it was happening to somebody else. We all squashed in the front, me sandwiched in between Jojo and Dave. Alexi took one look at me and reached into the glove box, producing a bottle of vodka which he thrust into my hands. "I am sorry your husband is such a cipa," he said. I had no idea what a "cipa" was but, like Dave, he was probably right.

Alexi offered to store my stuff in his garage. He and Dave went to drop it off, leaving Jojo and I outside her flat. A single tattered bin bag of my belongings hung lifelessly in my hand. I didn't realise that the bag had split until I got to the front door. The remnants of my married life littered the street, as if Hansel and Gretel had gone on a bender and left a trail of bizarre markers to find their way home; a pink sequin boob tube that Rob said made me look like a glamorous sausage lay forlornly next to some acid yellow running shorts, bought in an effort to keep up with my sports-mad husband and never worn. Wrapped around a gaudy but expensive table lamp, a wedding present from my parents, was a suspender belt. It had been my attempt a couple of years earlier to spice things up. I had strutted into the living room like a porn star only for Rob to laugh and ask me to move out of the way of the television so he could read the football results.

In the debris I spotted a photo of Rob and I on our first ever holiday together. We looked tanned, windswept and carefree, amazing considering that we were staying in a caravan park in North Wales. We were so young and full of love that I hardly recognised the two dreamy figures clinging to each other. I marched over to the photo. "You fucking arse!" I screamed at Rob's lovely face and then bought my foot down on it. My heel made a bullet wound in the middle of his forehead. It was immensely satisfying – for about ten seconds.

Next I was on my hands and knees scooping up the photo, cradling it in my arms and kissing the puncture wound in Rob's head. "Why?" I whispered, "why?" Jojo coaxed me up off the pavement and gently pried the photo out of my hands, "Let's get you inside, Kat."

I sat in Jojo's tiny kitchen, downing glass after glass of red wine, staring at my phone. Jojo offered to call in sick but I insisted that she go back to work. I wanted to be alone with my misery, to turn my bitter grief over and over like a jagged rock in my palm. I wanted to make my pain concrete. I wanted to gouge myself with it again and again until I'd caused myself so much damage that I would be numb. Most of all I wanted to wake up to find that this was all a terrible nightmare. I wanted Rob to come and get me right now, take me home and make me tea. I wanted him to tell me that there was no affair, that it was just my imagination run wild. I wanted him to hold me, kiss my eyelids and tell me not to be so silly, to say how much he loved me.

I was looking into an abyss, a bottomless black hole where my life used to be. I remembered a postcard I once saw of a house on a cliff after there had been a sudden landslide. A whole wall had fallen away but the rooms inside – kitchen, bedroom and bathroom – were all perfectly intact. The breakfast things were still on the table, the beds unmade. A ribbon of toilet paper was blowing gaily in the breeze like bunting. I could almost picture myself in the postcard now because that was exactly how I felt; a massive chunk of my life had been ripped away and I had been caught short with my knickers around my ankles, my arse swinging in a bitter and unforgiving breeze.

I jumped when a text came through but it was just Mum inviting Rob and I over to Sunday lunch. She adored Rob and I was sure she'd be more upset about losing her son-in-law than the fact that he had left me for another woman. I deleted the text. A couple of hours and much wine later the phone buzzed again. This time it was a text from Rob. My heart raced. I was sure he was going to tell me that he'd made a terrible mistake, that in a moment of madness he'd shagged Ludmilla but that it was me he really loved.

Of course I would make him suffer for his crime but there not a whisper of doubt in my mind that we'd get back together. I remembered an article I'd read about couples who managed to overcome infidelity and were stronger than ever. If regular waxing was what it was going to take to keep my man faithful I would do it, despite breaking out into an awful rash after every session. I took a deep breath and read his message: *Working late, then swift pint. Can u record Match Of Day?* He hadn't even used my name, let alone signed off with a 'x'. I texted back, *WHO IS LUDMILLA?*

When there was no reply after ten minutes I called his office and told the receptionist it was an emergency. Rob sounded nervous when he said hello.

"WHO THE FUCK IS LUDMILLA?" I shouted. He was silent.

"ROB?" I harangued, "you better start talking or I'll come there right now." I meant it, even though I could barely stand up by that point.

"Let's talk about it when I get home," he said coldly.

"Home?" I said spitefully, "I'm at Jojo's. Come here straight after work. Don't fuck me around – not any more than you already have."

I hung up. I felt momentarily good, powerful; a strong, independent woman, part Beyoncé, part Germaine Greer. In the next instant I'd flung myself on the kitchen floor and sobbed so loudly that the next door neighbour banged on the party wall and shouted, "Knock it on the head Scarlett, Rhett's not coming back, you silly bitch."

I woke several hours later to find Jojo standing over me flanked by a stony-faced Rob. Good, I thought to myself, he can see how much he's hurt me. In retrospect I realise that I must have looked like a pathetic, puffy-faced mess and he was probably happier than ever that he'd left me for lovely Ludmilla. "I'm popping out to meet Dave for a drink," Jojo said tactfully and disappeared. Rob sat down opposite me, hands resting calmly on the table like he was about to conduct a job interview with a candidate who he'd already decided was desperately unsuitable.

"Well?" I asked, more an accusation than a question. He shrugged. I wanted to smack him over the head with the empty wine bottle. I also wanted to fall into his arms, bury my face in his neck and pretend this wasn't happening.

"How long?" I demanded.

He paused and then said, "A couple of months."

"A couple of *months*? When were you going to tell me? Were you going to tell me?"

He shrugged again.

"Rob. I'm your wife. Your WIFE."

He took a deep breath, then sighed deliberately as if I was a rather stupid child that needed something explaining yet again. He reached across the table to take my hand. I snatched it away. "Things haven't been good for a while, have they?" he began. What was he talking about? The salad days of our relationship may have passed, but we weren't on dry crackers and water just yet. Sure we argued, but no more than other couples and we still had sex, sometimes every week. At this thought I brought my hand up to my mouth in horror.

"Oh God. You've been fucking both of us. Do I need to get tested?"

Rob laughed, making me even more angry, "Ludmilla's a chartered surveyor, not a heroin addict." Brilliant. My rival also had a proper grown-up, well-paid job.

"That's right," I said acrimoniously, "chartered surveyors are immune to HIV. Who knew the cure to a global pandemic would be wearing a hard hat and touting a tape measure?"

"Lud's been tested, and so have I. We're fine. Unless you've been sleeping around?"

Just like that he was already in another "we" that didn't include me. And how was it, I wondered, that my cheating arsehole of a husband was sitting here as bold as brass talking about his sex life with his lover and somehow managing to make it sound as if *I* was the guilty party?

"Of course I haven't been sleeping around you cock. I haven't even kissed anyone else in the last decade. And NO," I shouted, "I AM NOT fine. How could you do this to me? Ten years. Doesn't that mean anything to you?"

Rob just stared at me. The answer was rhetorical: he'd left 'us' behind two months ago and I had been clinging to a ghost. That made me gasp and clutch my stomach. I felt like I might pass out from shock. My own husband had been mercy fucking me because he didn't have the heart or balls to tell me that he'd fallen out of love with me and head over heels for someone else.

I started to cry uncontrollably. I smacked my head on the table as hard as I could. I wanted to knock myself out and wake up with amnesia – or not wake up at all. Rob stood up alarmed and came around to my side of the table. He tried to restrain me but instead I turned on him like a wild animal and started thumping his chest with my fists screaming, "How could you? How could you?" over and over again.

"Kat *please*," he said, with genuine concern. I melted and fell against him. I wanted to disappear inside him. He held me close and I sobbed into his shoulder. But I could feel resistance in him, his chest was a brick wall and I was now banished from his feelings.

"Please Rob," I begged, "don't leave me. Whatever I've done I'll fix it. I'll be better, I promise."

He patted my back and soothed me, "You haven't done anything wrong."

"Then why are you doing this?" I sniffled. "You're my world, Rob. I'm not going to be able to cope without you."

He stroked my hair. "You'll be fine, Nine Lives."

He used the pet name my Grandpa gave me and it made me sob even louder.

"And we can still be friends," he added brightly.

I stopped crying as what he was saying sank in. My whole world was collapsing, imploding like a burnt out star. But he was behaving as if nothing serious was occurring, as if we were a couple of young adults off to university, outgrowing a childhood romance. I backed away from him.

"Friends?" I repeated.

"Yes, of course," he said, matter-of-factly.

"You're out of your fucking mind," I screamed, "If you really are leaving me then fuck off right now. I never want to see you again."

"If that's what you want," he said, rolling his eyes as if we were having a disagreement about floor tiles.

He turned his back on me and went to walk away. It was more than I could stand. I launched myself across the table and jumped on him like a demented monkey. "You can't just walk out like this!" He shook me off and I stumbled into the table. He didn't look back and continued to the door. Propelled forward by blind panic and fury I ran full tilt, jump-kicking him in the arse like a very pissed martial artist. Without a word he turned back towards me, his face purple with anger. I had never seen him so mad and I knew the reprisal would be bad. We had never had a physical fight, but Rob was verbally aggressive in an argument and always won. Still he didn't speak. Just as I was about to apologise he kicked me back, booting me squarely between my legs. He used to play football, semi-pro, and he hadn't lost his touch. There was a hollow thud, the sound of his shiny work shoe thumping against my vagina.

I crumpled to my knees, gasping in pain unable to catch my breath. But I was glad for the throbbing in my pubic bone because it distracted me from the agony in my chest. Somehow physical pain was infinitely better than emotional loss. Rob hovered over me for a few moments. Eventually he said, "It's a pity it had to end like this. I never meant to hurt you. Goodbye Kat."

He closed the door quietly behind himself and I sat on the floor, clutching my crotch as the initial pounding gave way to a sharp sting. Inside I was calmly numb. The hysteria was subsiding and I could finally take it all in. It was real. Rob had left me for someone else and he wasn't coming back. He hadn't even said sorry. In fact I couldn't remember him having ever apologised to me while my sentences had been bookended by contrition throughout our relationship; "Sorry the lasagne's a bit burned," or "I'm such an idiot, can you change the plug please?" and "I'm rubbish at Grand Theft Auto, aren't I?" All that self-deprecation and where had it got me? A single ticket to the End Of The Line on the Mad Old Cat Lady Express.

I took a long, hot shower and watched the water run off my limbs. I imagined my old life draining down the plug hole. I wanted to believe that the gaping space left by Rob's sudden departure would eventually be filled by someone else, someone nicer, who wouldn't run off with an exotic chartered surveyor nor bid me farewell with a kick in the crotch. I rubbed the steam off the bathroom mirror and stared at myself. I was pink and bloated, my eyes swollen shut from crying. I cleaned my teeth on autopilot and pulled out the sofa bed, Jojo's living room area disappearing beneath it. When all the wine had gone I helped myself to the only other alcohol I could find, a bottle of Frangelico, so old that I had to prise the crusted lid off with a knife.

I fell asleep before Jojo came home and didn't wake up until late the next morning. I rolled over half-expecting to see Rob's broad, slightly hairy shoulders. Temples throbbing and confused by my surroundings and the sticky, sweet stuff matted in my hair, I sat up slowly. The room zoomed back into focus and I realised I was in Jojo's tiny flat, alone. My marriage was well and truly over.

Chapter Twenty-One

Norwegian Wood

"It's so unfair," I moaned to Jojo as I told her all about Ludmilla's pregnancy and Rob's impending remarriage. She looked at me, her big green eyes full of understanding. "I know exactly where you're coming from, which is why I'm taking steps," she said as she pushed her phone towards me across the tiny kitchen table. "What do you think?" she asked, trying to keep her tone neutral. I read the profile on a rather antiseptic looking webpage, "Oslo-born male, 42. 195cm tall, strong, athletic build, blue eyes, blonde hair. Tech company CEO, avid cyclist, plays violin. Hobbies include running, hiking, reading and writing poetry and fiction." The man sounded like a Norse god and a perfect match for Jojo, if a little cold and lacking in personality.

"Why no photo?" I asked.

"It's to protect anonymity," she replied.

"How are you supposed to know if you want to date someone if you can't see their face? Is this a new kind of site?

Jojo laughed. "It's not a dating site. He's a potential sperm donor."

"What?" I asked, flabbergasted.

"I've already started the process of harvesting my eggs. The next thing is to get them fertilised," she continued as she attempted to tame her endless curls into a pony tail. I felt panicky and I had no idea why.

"Whoa Nelly," I said. "Hold your well-hung Nordic horses. You've already done the egg bit and now you're looking for Mr Inseminator?" She nodded, as I scrolled through her shortlist of candidates: a Colombian classical music conductor, a Ghanaian doctor, and an Australian geologist. It seemed that without the sticky issue of romance the world really could be your oyster. "I don't want a baby right now," she explained, "but it's a back-up, in case I don't meet the right guy or I can't get pregnant later on."

I was dumbfounded and I had a barrage of urgent questions, "Wasn't it really bloody painful? Like months of hormones and needles and stuff?"

"Not months exactly, but yes it did sting a bit."

"And isn't it really bloody expensive?" I continued.

"If you donate your eggs to someone else you get your own collected for free," she said, chewing a pain au chocolat. It sounded like a bizarre Easter egg hunt.

"Should I be thinking about this?" I asked, feeling like I'd missed a trick. Jojo's jaw twitched.

"What?" I asked.

She coughed nervously, "The cut-off age for donating your eggs is thirty-four."

"So I'm already past it?" Turning forty just got a whole lot worse.

"Not necessarily," Jojo said, trying to sound positive. "You can probably still do it the natural way, or IVF as a last resort."

"But if the NHS won't fund it that costs thousands each round, right?"

Jojo nodded and made an immediate attempt to change the subject, "More coffee?"

I nodded glumly and picked at one of the slightly-stale pastries I had bought, which just like me was past its sell-by date. I wondered if I'd been a too hasty in dismissing Bil and Ben's "sperm for eggs" offer. But despite all the odds stacked against me I wasn't ready to give up on having a family the old-fashioned way. Not just yet.

"Fancy some pancakes?" Jojo asked, trying to lighten the mood, "I've still got a couple of eggs left." I laughed. There wasn't much else I could do.

Later that afternoon I met Dave in the pub. He pushed a notepad over to me with a self-satisfied smile. "Voila," he said, "your all-new dating profile. They'll be flocking around you like bees to a hive. Or flies on–"

I cut him off, "Yep, I get the picture, thanks."

We both fell silent while I read his work; *Go Go Girl, 35. Fun, funny female seeks male equivalent for banter, boozing and bonding. Loves crooning, cooking & cuddling. Equally at home in a gourmet restaurant or with nice bottle of red and box-set. Your couch or mine?*

I threw the notepad back on the table and glared at him. He looked disappointed.

"Don't you like it?" he asked, sounding genuinely hurt.

"Where shall I begin?" I said. "With the fact that you've started the whole thing with a complete lie?"

He sniggered. "The age thing? I thought you might get upset about that. I think you can get away with it. Just."

I banged my fist on the notepad for emphasis, "NO. I will not start a relationship off with a blatant lie."

"White lie," Dave replied, attempting to placate me.

I folded my arms, "How is taking five years off my actual age – as written on my birth certificate, passport and driving licence – a 'white lie'? And what's with all the alliteration? You've turned me into a tabloid headline."

Dave grinned. "I thought you didn't mind a bit of assonance?" he said, hanging on the "ass" part far longer than necessary.

"Then there's the 'bottle of red and box-set' bollocks. And I hardly think being able to defrost a ready-meal counts as 'cooking'. You've made me sound like every other woman on the site."

Dave smiled triumphantly. "Exactly. Like every other woman – who's going on a date every night this week and will probably be loved up by the end of the month."

"But this isn't who I am," I groaned.

Dave wagged his finger at me, "It's not who you are now."

"It's not who I'm ever going to be," I said, slapping my hands on the table in frustration and making the glasses wobble.

"It's a game, babe," he said, tapping my phone for emphasis. "If you want to win you have to play by the rules. Keep Crazy Kat under wraps until at least the third date. The same goes for sex. No man wants to marry a girl he can shag after a few pints."

I looked at him in utter disbelief. "You've got to be kidding? You're selling me The Three Date Rule?"

He looked up at the ceiling as if in direct communication with God. "Finally she gets it."

"Utter sexist bullshit!" I said, shaking my head so violently that my neck clicked. "So what if I sleep with someone on the first date?"

Dave held up his hands in a don't-shoot-the-messenger kind of way. "It's a question of respect, babe. Maybe I'd want to see some of the birds I've shagged again — if I hadn't shagged them."

I challenged him. "Let me get this straight — if a woman, sorry, bird, refused to have sex with you, you'd pursue a relationship simply because you couldn't have her?"

I saw panic in his face. "I wouldn't go that far. But if I was in the market for a relationship it wouldn't be with someone I'd shagged on a first date."

I sucked on a wedge of lemon, its sharpness complementing my mood perfectly.

"Because women who have sex on a first date are slags?"

Dave looked worried. "Not exactly, but–"

I cut him off, "Brilliant. I've just bought you a pint and now you're calling me a slag?" Dave's eyes darted nervously from side to side, his face turning white.

"You're not a slag, okay? I DO NOT think you're a slag. All I'm saying is that if a bird, sorry, woman, sleeps with me when we've just met it gives the impression that she's the town bike."

I folded my arms and huffed, "You just called me a slag. Again."

Poor Dave. He was trapped in a 1950s moral cul-de-sac of his own making with me blocking the exit like a feminist guard dog. He stood up and grabbed both of our glasses. "Same again?" he asked rhetorically, and ploughed through the punters crowding the bar. I took full advantage of the situation. "Make it a double," I shouted at the back of his head, "and a pint of Magner's."

I sat steeping in my own anger until he returned from the bar. Dave sat down and pushed my drinks across the table. I looked at him contemptuously and downed the double vodka in one, instantly regretting it.

"Jesus," he laughed, "You *are* pissed off."

I punctuated my response while I necked my pint, "Yes (slurp). Yes, I am (slurp)."

"Okay," he said, deliberately and slowly, "say you were in the market for a house."

I laughed bitterly, "Chance would be a fine thing. I can barely make my rent."

He raised his hand as if asking for permission to speak, "Humour me?"

I shrugged my shoulders and supped the cider. I didn't even know why I'd ordered it other than the fact that Dave liked it. The last time I drunk cider I was fifteen and had thrown up in my treehouse.

"Say you were driving along the M1 late at night," Dave continued, "and you were knackered. You'd pull over at the first place you found, right?" I seethed in silence. Dave pressed on. "Any bed will do. But if you're looking to buy a house you wouldn't only go to one, would you? If it was too cheap, you'd be suspicious – not that I'm saying you're cheap. You wouldn't just move in straight away though, would you?"

I pushed my half-finished drink over to his side of the table, "I hate cider."

He finished his point as he finished my pint, "It's all a question of value. If something's given away so freely, how much is it worth? How many previous owners has it had? I'm not being sexist. I'm well aware that I am indeed a slag. A total tart. But then I'm not looking for a relationship, am I?"

My head was swimming from too much booze on an empty stomach. Most worrying was that Dave was actually starting to make sense. I knew he wasn't making a moral judgement, but rather giving me a pep talk, a pop psychology of dating that was sad but probably true. I could rail against the ways of the world all I wanted. Or I could play along.

"I'll cut you a deal," he said waving the empty pint glass at me. "You put that profile up, just as I've written it. I guarantee men will be beating your door down. If you don't get at least three dates with three decent blokes in the next fortnight you decide my forfeit."

I narrowed my eyes. "And if I do get three dates, with three good men – decent by my standards, not yours – what then?" His shoulders moved back into a relaxed position, the first time they weren't scrunched up defensively around his ears in the last hour.

He pushed an empty pint glass back to me, "Then the beef wellington's on the other foot. You owe me a meal, and I don't mind if it's the liquid kind. Speaking of which..." he winked, "same again, thanks."

Chapter Twenty-Two

Feast and Famine

It was nothing short of miraculous. Within minutes of putting up Dave's version of my profile I was inundated with messages. From men I actually liked. It was exciting and deeply frustrating. Could it be that Dave knew me better than I knew myself? Or had he presented a version of me that I couldn't possibly live up to? Was I about to become the online dating equivalent of the PPI scandal?

FunnyBoyFourO was the first to pop up on the instant chat feature. *Hello Kat, How's things with you?* Hardly original, but at least there was no dick pic – in fact there was no profile picture at all, just a portrait of a couple wearing tracksuits and kissing in front of some bins with the tagline, "We'll always have Plaistow". Mildly amusing. I replied immediately, *Your profile says you love banter? I want you to know you don't have to be banal for fear of offending me.* I sat waiting for a response that seemed like it would never come. I was convincing myself that I'd simply come across as rude rather than a modern-day Katherine Heburn when there was the ping of a new message.

Take the "b" out of "banal" and you get?

It was appalling, but I laughed in spite of myself.

Ha ha. What's your name?

David.

Eek.

What's wrong with that?

Nothing. It's just I have a very good but defective friend with the same name. What's your middle name?

St John. Pronounced "Singeon".

Let's stick with David.

Cheeky cow.

Just as I was about to ask him the dating equivalent of Twenty Questions – where do you live, what do you do, what are you looking for? – he disappeared from my screen.

But I had plenty of other candidates vying for my attention, including *JackTheLad, 35. Single Dad seeks fun, together woman for all the usual stuff. MUST HAVE SENSE OF HUMOUR.* I replied and he responded immediately asking if I was free later that evening. I hoped that this change of fortune wasn't purely down to Dave's influence otherwise I was going to have to start wearing an earpiece and have him coach me through dates like a player trying to cheat the house at poker.

I arrived at Leicester Square just before five pm. Groups of early evening revellers crowded the entrance to the station, disoriented by the bright lights and bustle of the gaudy heart of Soho. "S'cuse me, s'cuse me, S'CUSE ME," I barked as I pushed my way through the throng of bodies. Jack The Lad hadn't specified a Tube exit so once I'd wiggled my way into the street I called him. I heard the sound of an old-fashioned mobile phone melodically ringing beside me, the same jingle my dad's made.

"Hi," Jack said, "Where are you?" I was about to reply when I realised that we were standing next to each other. He turned to me and smiled and I felt something flutter inside me.

"Nice ring tone," I said.

"I'm a total Luddite," he replied. "I don't know how to change it. Can't even put it on silent." What a contrast to tech-mad Rob. I liked him already.

"I know we've only just met," he said, "but can we go to dinner? I'm ravenous. Chinese okay?"

"Bloody marvellous," I replied. I could have married him there and then.

We headed towards the glorious kitsch of China Town. Painted cats waved to us cheerfully from shop windows, racks of glistening glazed ducks beneath them steaming up the glass. The streets were festooned with bright red paper lanterns, like Christmas three hundred and sixty-five days a year.

"Do you have any preference where we eat?" he asked just as we were passing the restaurant where I'd devoured a mountain of food while the beige fox ate boiled cabbage. I couldn't even begin to work out what the odds were of finding Simon still moping over the same Formica table in the same restaurant, but given the bizarre nature of my dates so far I wasn't about to leave anything to chance. I took Jack The Lad's arm firmly, the same way I used to with my nana when she lingered too long over the underwear section in Marks & Spencers, and steered him away from the scene of my previous disaster.

"I hear that one up there is supposed to be quite good," I said briskly.

"Which one?" he asked peering into the distance where the famous Golden Arches of a fast food joint were illuminating the night sky.

He laughed. "You're shitting me?"

"Yes, I am." I decided to tell the truth for a change. "But I had a really bad date in the restaurant we just passed."

He looked at me incredulously, "No way. Me too. The staff forgot to tell us that there was sesame paste in the food and I had to epi-pen my date. And they still had the gall to add a service charge."

"You've trumped mine completely," I said. "My date was just dull and opinionated. Anaphylactic shock would have been a vast improvement."

He laughed again and gave me such a warm, sincere smile that I felt my stomach tilt just ever so slightly. It felt like welcoming back an old friend I thought I might never see again.

We stopped outside a restaurant with a headless rubber chicken dancing in the window, which we both found amusing. We walked inside, sat at the first available table and ordered a banquet of food. I was relieved to find that like me, my date was a committed omnivore. We chatted about everything and nothing. He was actually called Jack but said he was thinking of changing his profile name because "The Lad" bit seemed to be attracting the wrong kind of attention. As I watched him push his hands though his greying dark curls, the twinkle in his blue eyes when he talked, and the impressive way his plaid shirt stretched over his muscular chest I was definitely guilty of giving him the wrong kind of attention. It seemed that he had no idea how attractive he was, which only added to his appeal.

Jack told me that he was amicably separated with a three-year-old son and had been single for just over a year. I filled him in on Rob and we talked over the pros and cons of having/not having children.

"I wouldn't change it for the world," Jack said wistfully. "Now, that is. Louie was unplanned, and to be honest I don't know if I'd do it again. It's so much work." Jack no longer seemed quite so perfect. "Did you never want kids?" he asked. Suddenly I felt like I'd been slapped in the face. Just as a pregnant woman's bump is patted by complete strangers like a Buddha's belly is rubbed for luck, my fertility was up for public debate once again. Only the week before an older lady at the bus stop had showed me a photo of her grandson. When I said I didn't have kids she looked sad. "Maybe it's not too late? There's always IMF," she said consolingly. I wasn't quite sure how the World Bank was supposed to help my child deficit.

"I was ready to have a baby when I was twenty-eight," I told Jack, "but Rob said we didn't have enough money, even though I told him I would make it myself." Jack laughed again. "Just when it seemed like he was coming round to the idea," I continued, "I stopped taking the pill and he met someone else. Typical, eh?"

Jack had a pained expression in his eyes, my irony landing flat.

"So you're a social worker?" I said, changing the subject and hoping I hadn't jinxed the date. "What's your area?"

"I work with children and young adults at risk. Violence, drugs, sexual abuse, that kind of thing."

"Blimey," I said, not sure how to steer us back to levity.

Jack smiled sympathetically, "It's hard work but I love it. Your job sounds rather more glamorous and fun than mine," he continued.

I snorted. "Smoke and mirrors. Front of house it's all sequins, feathers and feminine mystique. Backstage it's discarded C strings and fluorescent lighting."

Jack looked confused. "What's a C string?"

I leaned in confidentially, "Trade secret. It's like a spangly panty pad with double-sided tape on the inside. The dancer sticks it to her undercarriage and it just about conceals her bits."

He picked up a long curly prawn cracker. "Does it look anything like this?"

The cracker bore a striking resemblance. "Pretty much. I think you might have a new angle on edible underwear there."

He popped it in his mouth and gave me a wink, reminding me of Dave but far less irritating.

I was trying to stay grounded but I could imagine myself falling head-over-heels for Jack. As for not wanting any more children, I reasoned that he might change his mind. Maybe he'd fall madly in love with me, throw common sense to the wind and sign up for another two years of dirty nappies and sleepless nights. Or maybe it was time to let the baby thing go? I was beginning to realise that being so single-minded about what I wanted might be the very thing that was keeping me single. Perhaps I was missing out on great guys like Jack because of the ridiculous promise I made to myself on my thirty-ninth birthday. Something had to give.

I glanced at my phone and realised that it was seven thirty, I was onstage in an hour. "I have to go," I sighed.

"Pity," said Jack flirtatiously, "I was hoping for a lesson in edible underwear eating etiquette."

"You wouldn't want to bite off more than you can chew," I replied, delighted that he clearly found me attractive but mindful of Dave's warning about being too sexually available. "Another time?" I asked hopefully.

"Call me," he said, with a grin that could have charmed me right out of my non-edible knickers there and then.

I went to pull out my purse but Jack dismissed the gesture, "You get the next one." I beamed at the confirmation of a second date.

"Well, goodbye then," I said when we got outside the restaurant, rocking from foot to foot and unsure what to do with my hands. He laughed softly at my awkwardness. It sounded like brandy crackling over ice and I found myself pining for Rob, for that easy emotional shorthand you have when you're in a rock-solid relationship. Jack pulled me towards him and kissed me briefly but squarely right on the mouth, just long enough for a shot of electricity to run through my body, thrilling me from my head to my toes, its epicentre a scorching tingle between my thighs.

"Better go," I stammered clumsily.

"Bye Kat," he purred.

I ran to the tube, but it felt more like dancing as I glided effortlessly in and out of the crowd, a figure skater high on oxytocin. When I boarded the Tube at Leicester square I dropped into the tatty velvet seat as if I was reclining into the most sumptuous wing-backed chair. My face was aching from smiling so broadly. I had finally met someone who was ringing my bell. I surfaced at Bank Tube and before I descended into the bowels of Petite Paris I texted Dave, *1-0 to you :) x*

Chapter Twenty-Three

Jacked Off

I woke up early the next day, full of anticipation as I scanned through the six new texts on my phone. One from Jojo, asking what time we should meet for Bil and Ben's Big Bank Holiday Barbecue, another two from Bil and Ben respectively, wanting to know what time they could expect us, and a reply from Dave, *Reckon I'll be cashing in by next week ;) x*. The fifth was from my mother, a shameless attempt to get back on speaking terms, *Can we please talk? Love Mummy xxx*, and the last, my final morning kick in the teeth, was a message was from Rob, *Don't need certificate now, found my copy*. Not so much as a thank you. The whole world had texted me. Except Jack. My disappointment was immense.

I started making excuses for Jack, sure that he must be looking after his son, or maintaining that six pack at the gym, or helping his elderly neighbours, because that's exactly the kind of guy he seemed, like my childhood hero Michael Landis from *Little House On The Prairie*. But I had a sinking feeling that I wasn't going to hear from him again, no olive branch of friendship, let alone the fig leaf of something more intimate. Had I come across as having too much emotional baggage? Or did I give off a last-loaf-on-the-shelf whiff? Maybe he just wasn't into me. I wondered if it still counted as being ghosted if you'd only been on one date.

My despondency dissipated a little when Funny Boy popped up on Instant Chat again. Still no proper photo on his profile, though.

What do you do for a living? I asked, trying to get back on the dating horse that had just unceremoniously bucked me off.

Oh not much. Normal 9 to 5. You'd be really bored.

Boring is good. Normal is good. In fact normal is fantastic.

I'm a stock controller.

You're right, that is excruciatingly dull.

You're funny.

Funny weird or funny "haha"?

Not sure yet, I'll let you know.

With that Funny Boy dematerialised into thin, online air. I felt myself falling off the cliff again, into a very dark place called I'm-Going-To-Be-Single-Forever. Even Funny Boy, the Man Without A Face, wasn't into me.

My phone rang and my mood soared, sure it was Jack. "Pub?" Dave asked without even bothering to say hello.

"You can tell me all about lover boy."

My mood plummeted again. "Can't," I said irritably.

"Why?" asked Dave.

"Barbecue."

"I forgot about that," said Dave, "Shall I meet you there?"

This was going to be awkward. Bil and Ben hadn't invited Dave; Jojo and I were under explicit instructions not to let him tag along.

"I don't know how to tell you this, but you can't come." There was another pause.

"No, I can. Scarlett Johansson cancelled. I'm free all day."

"You can't come because you haven't been invited," I said.

"Not invited? Some mistake, surely?"

I pictured him doing that thing that dogs do when they don't understand, head on one side, eyes blinking.

"You're barred."

"Barred," he repeated dumbly.

"It means 'to prevent or prohibit'. Google 'restraining order' if you're confused." I could almost hear the rusty cogs of his brain turning over.

"But why? How could they do this to me? We're a group. Without me it would be like *Friends* without Joey. I'm part of the furniture"

"I think you'll find that's why you've been banned."

"What?"

Sometimes I had to remind myself that Dave was an alcoholic – rarely in charge of his own actions when under the influence, and even less likely to remember them.

"Last year, when you rained on their parade?" More silence. "When you pissed on the barbecue?"

"The bloody thing was on fire!"

"They were flame grilling. It was supposed to be on fire."

Dave had claimed that the barbecue was getting out of control, that the flames were about to catch the wooden fence alight at any moment, a fence shared with a neighbour whose child was playing in the garden at the time.

"It could have been another Pudding Lane," he said defensively, "I was performing a community service."

"You're lucky you didn't end up doing community service. Next door wanted to have you charged with indecent exposure."

The barbecue had ended rather abruptly after the neighbour called the Police. Bil didn't see the funny side of Dave's joke about "golden showers", Ben ended up screaming hysterically and Dave was banned from coming within fifty yards of the house ever again. The couple still suffered his company in a social setting, just as long as he wasn't in *their* back yard.

"Can't you ask for me?" he whined.

"I'll give it a go but I don't think they're going to budge. That was a brand new barbecue and they had to bin it after your little water display. I'll text you, okay?"

"Whatever," Dave said sullenly and hung up on me.

I met Jojo just after midday outside Kennington Tube station. She smiled and waved madly when she saw me. "You okay?" I asked as I pecked her on the cheek. "You look a bit peaky."

"I'm fine," she said, a little crabbily. "Just tired." Jojo had got back from New York and was being sent to China the following week. The trips consisted of twelve-hour days meeting suppliers in sweat shops after disembarking red-eye flights. It made me quite thankful that I didn't have a successful career.

"You still look better than me," I said, desperately back-peddling.

She softened, "Sorry, didn't mean to snap."

I linked my arm through hers. "No apology necessary. Shall we go and get drunk with the boys?"

"Absobloodylutely," replied Jojo.

I squeezed her arm and she drew a sharp intake of breath. Before I could ask she said, "It's nothing. Those bloody clothing samples weigh a tonne."

When we arrived Bil and Ben met us on the doorstep. They were wearing matching tennis outfits and there was rainbow-coloured Union Jack bunting throughout the ground floor leading out to the patio where the new barbecue had pride of place. It looked like an alien spaceship, with a lid that could be pulled down over the grill to protect it from rain and other hazards. Nodding at the barbecue I said "You've thought of everything this year."

"Hopefully it won't come to that without Captain Caveman here," said Ben.

I felt sorry for Dave – his exclusion seemed a little excessive.

"He called this morning," I said, trying to keep my tone neutral.

"NO," said Bil and Ben in unison.

"You don't even know what I'm going to ask yet."

Ben raised his eyebrows. "We discussed it last night. Lifetime ban."

I looked to Bil. He nodded, pulling a "sorry, can't help" face.

Jojo stepped in as chief negotiator, "What if something happened to Dave? Something really bad and you never saw him again?"

"If something happened to Dave I doubt if he'd even know about it," said Ben angrily prodding a fat uncooked sausage for emphasis.

"That's really harsh," said Jojo, "And horribly judgmental". I'd never heard her be so forthright.

"We just don't want a repeat of last year sweetheart," said Bil, gently but firmly.

"You're being unnecessarily tough. Life's too short." There was something odd in her expression, like a shadow passing over the sun and it made me shudder.

"How do we know he won't ruin everything again?" Ben asked skeptically.

"Because lightning never strikes in the same place twice," Jojo replied.

I knew for a fact this wasn't true. In physics class at school we had learned about Roy Sullivan, a US National Park ranger who had been struck by lightning seven times, one time so severely that he lost his eyebrows.

"I'll vouch for Dave personally. I won't leave his side. Promise," Jojo said with her pretty, winning smile.

Bil looked at Ben for a reaction. "Okay," Ben sighed reluctantly. "But let this be a warning to you," he waggled the sausage ominously. "Any trouble and he'll find himself on the end of this fork."

I was impressed and slightly jealous of Jojo's powers of persuasion. Everything seemed to be so much easier when you were beautiful. I pulled out my phone to tell Dave the good news. "Tell him to come alone," Ben added, "NO guests."

A light drizzle made the barbecue fizz, but Ben soldiered on, grilling his way through what looked like the entire supply of grass fed, organic meat from their local independent butcher. Bil made sure that the drinks flowed as Jojo and I jigged around on the narrow patio to *Wham! Greatest Hits* blaring out from the tiny but powerful speakers. I furtively checked my phone while I took photos of us in case there was a text from Jack. Every time there wasn't I refilled my glass with Pimms. When I felt my phone vibrate in my jeans pocket I fizzed with excitement, my mood dampened again when I realised it was only Dave. "What the bloody hell's going on?" he said, amping up his Valleys accent, "I've been ringing the bell for ten minutes. I can hear the racket from out here."

I resisted the temptation to lecture Dave that he was lucky to have been reinstated at all and went to open the door, wherein Dave immediately pushed past me, leaving a very young, dishevelled looking woman of no more than twenty-five in his wake. I nearly shut the door in her face, thinking she was some kind of addict chancing her luck until Dave bellowed over his shoulder, "That's Angie." Trust Dave to do what he had been expressly asked not to and turn up with a wasted groupie straight out of a Rolling Stones song.

I was about to explain to Angie that she couldn't come in when she said "Hi" in a husky American voice and breezed passed me. She reminded me of young Alannis Morissette. "Why, good day to you too, madam," I said to the door as I closed it, "please do come in." I returned to the garden to find Dave smiling broadly, his hand draped around Angie's shoulder. Ben was glaring at him.

"Sorry," said Ben cattily, "we weren't expecting two. I don't have enough meat to go round."

Dave looked at the spread of choice cuts next to the barbecue. "That's not what I hear. Legend has it you have *all* the meat."

I saw Ben's knuckles go white as he gripped the spatula tighter.

"I never touch meat anyway," said Angie, "not with all the shit they pump into it. I'd rather die than eat a sausage."

"That's a shame, isn't it Dave?" I said with a knowing glance.

"I'd love a beer though" said Angie, oblivious to my joke at Dave's expense.

"Why don't you come into the kitchen and we'll see what we can find," said Bil, like a parent coaxing a toddler with the promise of chocolate.

Once Angie and Bil were out of earshot Ben slammed the spatula down on the barbecue. "Unbelievable," he said, then turned on me. "I told you he wasn't to bring anyone with him."

"I *did* tell him. It's not my fault he never listens."

Ben tutted. Suddenly I felt fourteen years old again.

Jojo jumped to my defence. "She did. I heard her."

"I am standing here, you know," Dave said drily.

Ben gave him a withering glance, "More's the pity."

I don't know which one of us noticed first. There had probably been a smell of burning plastic hanging in the background for some time but we were too busy arguing to pay any attention. The "whoosh" as the spatula finally combusted made us all spin towards the barbecue in horror. Ben, Jojo and I stared open-mouthed as an Aberdeen Angus burger cross bred itself with the kitchen utensil, a blue-green flame from the plastic giving way to bright yellow licks as the meat fat popped and spat menacingly, fire breaching the boundary of the barbecue's protective lid. The barbecue looked even more like a space ship now, one that had crash landed and was about to explode at any moment, taking innocent bystanders with it.

Ben grabbed the nearest liquid he could find to douse the flames – failing to notice that it was a bottle of vodka. Dave yelled "No!" and tackled Ben to the ground. Lightning quick Jojo grabbed the bottle from Ben and ran inside the house to find Bil. Dave began to unzip his fly. "Don't even think about it," Ben screamed. "For fuck's sake!" Dave shouted. He zipped his jeans back up and then grabbed the spatu-burger off of the barbecue with his bare hands.

Swearing profusely Dave threw the flaming hybrid on the ground and stamped on it until the fire subsided and all that remained was a bizarre smoking carcass of mangled plastic and charred meat. The small pile of blackened remains hissed and squeaked in the rain as Dave blew on his blistering fingers. Without a word Ben stood up and stomped into the kitchen like a diva storming off a film set. Jojo reappeared moments later. She looked at the debris and then she doubled over, clutching at her stomach. I laid my hand on her hunched over spine.

"Jojo," I said, alarmed, "are you okay?" Slowly she raised her head to me, and I saw that her face was quite red, not from smoke inhalation but rather with suppressed laughter. She could contain herself no longer and broke into a laughing fit. Dave was white with shock. "It's not fucking funny," he said, his voice an octave higher than usual, "I could have been seriously hurt." Jojo just carried on giggling helplessly and pointing at the smouldering pile on the patio. Dave stared for a moment, his face taut. Then I saw the corners of his mouth curl, and he began laughing too. Angie returned, and stared at the smouldering mess. "Jeez," she said, without a trace of humour, "I'm glad I'm vegan." This tipped me over the edge and I collapsed into laughter too. Dave, Jojo and I rolled around on the floor as the rain poured down, holding out aching sides. Just when we thought it would stop one of us would start giggling again, setting the other two off, like the laughing gas scene from *Mary Poppins*.

Angie just stood in the rain blinking at us. Bil and Ben appeared in the doorway. They stared at their ruined barbecue. Ben's lip quivered and without a word he went back into the house.

Bil shook his head. "I think you all better leave."

We stopped laughing. Dave began to apologise. "Sorry, mate. I really didn't—"

"Just fuck off, Dave. This is all your fault. Again. It's why we didn't invite you in the first place. When are you going to grow up?"

"Come on," Dave said, "it was a genuine accident this time – in no way my fault."

"Leave. Now. All of you," Bil said, a vein twitching under his eye.

He disappeared back into the house and we stood in silence. The rain made hollow noises as it bounced off of the wrecked barbecue, which now resembled a burnt out nuclear reactor, the pile of remains on the floor like the Chernobyl elephant's foot. "That went well," said Dave. "Pub, anyone? You can tell me how the dating's going, Kat."

Chapter Twenty-Four

Tits Up

After the second BBQ Gate I didn't hear from Bil and Ben for nearly a fortnight, having been sent to the doghouse with Dave. Jojo was rushed off her feet with work but diplomatically fed me tidbits of information in calls and texts, keeping me updated as Bil and Ben's anger slowly cooled. I seethed at the injustice but knew calling them would only make it worse. In turn I excommunicated Dave as punishment for taking me down with him. Since I still hadn't made up with Mum my only company was the cast at Petite Paris and my dating inbox.

I noticed that Funny Boy had finally added a personal profile picture. He was sporting a bowl cut, acne and a shiny nylon tracksuit. I guessed it was taken when he was about twelve years old. As I was staring at the photo trying to picture his face as it was now, like a police artist creating an image of what a long lost child might look like in adult form, there was the ping of a message.

Hey Kat, how's the dating going?

It was Funny Boy.

Pffft. Up and down I guess. And not in a good way.

You know you could save yourself a lot of trouble by just going on a date with me?

I'm not going on a date with an adolescent – I presume that photo is you, btw?

Yes it's me in my Smash Hits period.

Upload a proper profile pic FFS. I won't meet you until you do.

But what if I am indeed THE ONE?

Unlikely.

You'll never ever know if you never ever go.

Where have I heard that before?
The Hoseason's Holidays brochure circa 1984.
Sorry, too young to remember that. I'm a millennial.
Well technically you're two years too old to qualify.

I felt myself bristle with irritation. There it was again. The age thing. Men were falling over themselves to point it out.

Gotta go I typed dismissively.
Was it something I said?
Yes.

I felt the old familiar stab of disappointment. Even a disingenuous, faceless stranger on the internet seemed intent on bringing me down. I logged off without saying goodbye. Everything felt pointless.

I had no idea if Mum was still looking for "discreet adult fun" though she had at least taken down her dating profile. The thought of Mum being unfaithful to Dad, with or without his knowledge, continued to gnaw at me. I still hadn't been able to confront Patrick about it, he was always conveniently busy when I called. I couldn't keep the secret to myself any longer.

It was early June now and the weather had at last stopped raining long enough for it to feel like summer. Jojo finally had a day off and we agreed to meet up at Borough Market. We weaved our way in and out of the artisanal market stalls while tourists posed for photos, pulling silly faces as they held up weird produce from around the world.

"I've got something to tell you," I said stroking a dark brown breadfruit.

"Me too," said Jojo. "You go first."

"Age after beauty," I insisted. "You, then me." I was still mortified by what I was about to say.

"I've got breast cancer," she said, sniffing a pair of cantaloupes for their freshness.

I picked up a banana and two kiwi fruit for my witty retort, "I've got prostate *and* testicular cancer."

She turned to face me, expressionless. "Kat. I have cancer. Really."

I dropped the fruit on the floor feeling like I might wet myself. "Fuck me," I whispered.

Jojo gave a funny strangled laugh and then she burst into tears. I pulled her into my arms and squeezed tightly, she in turn clung to me. We were both shaking. Sobbing into her shoulder I said, "I'm sorry. So sorry."

I heard the stall holder clearing his throat, "That'll be ninety pence, please."

I let go of Jojo and stared at him, "What?"

"For the fruit," he explained.

"Not for your skills as a counsellor then?" I reached into my bag and threw a handful of coins at him, "Keep the change. Have a great day and a wonderful sodding life."

I linked arms with Jojo and frog-marched her away. It was only when we emerged from gloom of the covered market that I realised that Jojo had shoved the two melons up her sweatshirt.

"I might be needing a replacement pair," she said, "And I always fancied an upgrade."

We found a quiet cafe, I got us some coffee and Jojo chose an empty booth by the window. I stared at her, biting my lip, trying not to cry and desperately searching for something appropriate to say other than "How long have you got left?". Suddenly her emergency egg harvesting all made sense.

I grabbed her hand. "Why didn't you tell me?"

She smiled, "I just did."

"You know what I mean. Like when you were having the tests. Or when you found the lump."

She shrugged, "I don't know. I didn't want to worry you. It seemed pointless until I knew for sure."

I felt awful. I had been so obsessed by with my stupid dating that I failed to spot the tornado on the horizon hurtling towards my best friend. She looked at me sympathetically. Anyone would have thought I was the one with the life-threatening diagnosis.

"It's okay, Kat. We can talk about this. I *need* to talk about this. I thought we could start with a spot of turban shopping this afternoon?" I choked back my tears and gave her the biggest smile I could summon, but I felt guilty that Jojo had cancer and I didn't, like somehow it might be my fault.

"You don't think it was the chicken fillets, do you?" I asked, full of angst.

"What?!" she laughed, confused by my non-sequitur.

"Those silicone bra boosters I got you. Maybe they leaked when you got sweaty, and were all toxic and stuff?"

She was really laughing now, "I thought I was the dim one?"

"Oh God," I gasped bringing my hand up to my face. "And I told that awful date that you were in hospital. Bad karma."

"Kat, I was already ill by then. It's not your fault. It's just bad luck − really bad, really shitty luck."

I hugged her again and I felt her chest heaving with emotion. "I wish my dad was still here," she whispered. I was hit suddenly with a surge of remorse for all the times I'd treated my own father like an inconvenience.

We spent the rest of the afternoon drinking tea and eating cake. As we forked great clumps of cream and chocolate into our faces she very calmly told me how she had found the lump and named it "Bastard". The lady at the counter stopped reading her copy of *The Sun* and glared at us. "I'm sorry," I said with mock sincerity, "My friend here has Tourette's. I say friend. I'm actually her carer. She doesn't have any friends left because she told them all to fuck off." Jojo laughed so hard that she sprayed the table with cream, sending Counter Lady into a litany of tuts and much angry rustling of her newspaper.

"What were you going to tell me, anyway?" asked Jojo, her mouth gummed up with chocolate brownie.

"Nothing," I shrugged. "Not important."

"Tell me. I could do with something to take my mind off Bastard."

"I think Mum's having an affair."

"Kat, no. Really? Are you sure? Who with?" Jojo asked, wide-eyed with shock.

"Everyone – potentially. She's online dating."

It was all too much, I started crying again. Jojo listened and commiserated, rubbing my back and thrusting shiny paper napkins into my hands when snot threatened to bubble out of my nose. They were woefully non-absorbent and all I succeeded in doing was moving cake, makeup and mucus from one part of my face to another. Jojo said all the things I needed to hear, "it's probably just a phase," and, "I doubt if she's even been on a date". In turn I apologised profusely for bothering her with what was nonsense in the light of her own situation. "That's what friends are for. Come on," she said mischievously, "I fancy getting a hair cut."

I settled the bill and Jojo dragged me out into the milky afternoon sunlight. I expected that we'd be jumping on the Tube into the West End but instead we carried walking along Borough High Street. Seeing the spinning candy stripe pole of an old fashioned gents' barbers Jojo said, "This'll do." She bounded into the shop and plonked herself down on the nearest chair.

"Jojo, what are you doing?" I asked apprehensively, even though I already knew what was on her mind.

She smiled bravely. "No time like the present."

An old Italian barber approached. "Bongiorno, beautiful lady. What can I do for you today?" he asked, making no effort to disguise his attraction.

Jojo beamed at him, "All off, please."

The barber looked worried, "A trim, si?"

Jojo shook her head, the shiny spirals of her beautiful curls glistening amber in the fluorescent light of the shop.

"Just shave the whole lot. A number three."

I gasped. "Jojo, you're not serious?"

She stopped smiling and looked at me. "Kat, I have surgery next week. Then chemo. I'll probably lose my hair. Better this than it falling out all over the place, it was bad enough when the cat used to moult."

I fought back tears as Jojo's glorious mane fell onto the floor. The buzzing clippers revealing more and more of her skull until all that was left was fuzz. She looked stunning, her green eyes even larger, reminding me of Sinead O'Connor in that video that we all cried over as teenagers. I felt an urgent need to show as much solidarity as possible.

I sat down in the chair beside Jojo, nodding at the barber, "Now me."

"Kat," Jojo said, looking concerned, "you don't have to."

Reeling on the inside, I tried to sound unconcerned. "Think of all the money I'll save on hair products. I fancy a change anyway."

The barber came and stood behind me. He hesitated. "Make it so, Number One," I said, like a Star Trek captain. Unfortunately the barber missed my reference and whereas Jojo was left with a gamine crop, my hair was shorn on the clippers' most brutal setting, leaving only a Desperate Dan five o'clock shadow. With each movement of the clippers the dull canvas of my face became more apparent. My cheekbones seemed flatter than usual and the lack of hair framing my face merely highlighted the bags under my eyes. I looked like the one with cancer. "Thank you," I said drily to the barber, avoiding eye contact and my own reflection. I pulled out my purse and as I was reaching for a twenty pound note the barber cleared his throat, "I hope you don't mind that I say, but this haircut is no good for you. Your friend she can wear it, but you, no." I was about to tell him what he could do with his clippers when Jojo jumped to my defence, "Signor, *I* mind, actually. That's my best friend you're talking to. Vaffanculo, cretino!"

I had no idea what she had said, unlike the barber. At first he turned red then started shouting in Italian, gesturing wildly with his free hand. "Oh shit," I said as Jojo laughed gleefully and opened the shop door. "Kat," she shouted, "Let's make a run for it!" We shot out of the shop followed by the barber, swinging his clippers by the cable like a mace. He gave up after about two blocks but we carried on sprinting until we turned a corner. Breathless and in hysterics we rested against a wall, ignoring the stunned passers-by.

"We're Bonnie and Clyde," I gasped. "That's our second robbery of the day."

"Shall we go to Selfridges and lift some decent stuff then?" wheezed Jojo.

I'd never felt more alive in my life. For a moment I almost forgot that Jojo had cancer.

Chapter Twenty-Five

Shorn of the Dead

I don't remember much after the buzz cut. Jojo wanted to go straight to the nearest pub. I was concerned that getting steaming drunk wasn't the best thing for her health but she stressed that she wanted to have a "bloody good time", because she didn't know how long it would be before she would be able to resume normal service. I didn't take much persuading.

According to Jojo after the pub we ended up in a club in Soho where I insisted that the DJ play every song ever recorded by Annie Lennox, Jimmy Somerville, Right Said Fred, and climaxing in my rousing finale of "Nothing Compares To You" – basically anything by anyone who didn't have much in the way of hair. Jojo said that when "How Deep Is Your Love" by the Bee Gees came on, I started shouting at the hirsute DJ, accusing him of a lack of compassion and tugging at his beard and shoulder length hair so hard that I had to be restrained by the bartender. I didn't remember any of it.

When I got up the next day I scared the living shit out of myself. At first I thought I'd got so drunk that I'd taken a Millwall supporter home until I realised that the skinhead in the bathroom mirror was me. It was truly horrific. There was nothing good about this hairstyle. In fact it wasn't a hairstyle at all. With my long, highlighted locks gone all that remained was a mousy stubble. I had more hair on my bikini line than I did on my head. I started to cry bitterly, immediately regretting my rash show of support.

I went into the bedroom and rifled through a draw, pulling out several head scarfs, a few hats and the two rubbish wigs I had already vetoed for my debut at Petite Paris. Both wigs were completely unsuitable for anything other than the stage but the bob was the most natural looking option. I pulled it on and brushed down the flyaway strands. It did nothing for me but it was better than being bald. I would just have to wear false eyelashes and vampish lipstick until my hair grew back. Passing for a drag queen seemed preferable to looking like an egghead. Or someone with cancer.

This thought stopped me dead in tracks. My hair would grow back. Eventually. My best friend, on the other hand, was facing surgery and chemotherapy. A wave of guilt washed over me. I grabbed my phone and called Jojo. My call went through to voice-mail and I began to feel panicky. Normally I wouldn't call Jojo after a heavy night out until well after midday but her diagnosis had changed everything. I frantically Googled "Effects, cancer and alcohol". All I could find online was an article in *The Lancet* about sterilising radiography equipment. I tried Jojo a few more times with no success. Frightened and impatient I texted her then made myself a cup of tea and waited. After a few agonising minutes my phone rang.

"Kat," Jojo croaked. "What's wrong? You okay?"

"I'm fine," I said. "Although I thought I'd had a one night stand with Humpty Dumpty when I looked in the mirror this morning." She laughed. I was glad.

"Just wondering how you are?" I asked.

"I feel terrible," she groaned.

Once more a surge of panic raced through me. "Shall I come over? Do you need me to call a doctor?"

"It's just a hangover, Kat. I'll be fine," she said yawning.

"Well, if you're sure. Is there anything you need?"

"More sleep would be amazing. I was out for the count but some idiot kept calling me."

"That might have been me," I admitted. "Sorry." If she was annoyed she didn't show it.

"I'm going back to sleep. And try not to worry," Jojo soothed. "Everything's going to be fine."

I pulled the itchy wig off and crawled back into bed, pulling the duvet over my head. I wished that I had a time machine, that I could wake up in a year's time when my best friend was cancer free and my hair had grown back. My mother put paid to that when my phone rang again. I made a mental note to give Mum her own ringtone; "The Funeral March" or Darth Vader's theme from *Star Wars*.

"Hello," I said, making sure I sounded as aggrieved as possible.

"What time can we expect you?" she chirped.

I had totally forgotten I was supposed to be going over to my parents for Sunday lunch. Having put them off since my birthday I knew I couldn't possibly extend my stay of execution any longer. Besides, I was feeling shaken to my core. The world as I knew it yesterday was gone. However shocking Mum's foray into internet dating was and however weird Dad's apparent acquiescence, my family home was the closest thing I had to stability at that moment. A hug from Dad and a withering glance from Mum seemed like just the tonic.

"What time do you want me there?" I asked, making it sound like I was doing her a massive favour.

"No rush at all. When you're ready," she said sweetly. "Within the hour? Don't be late. I've made Duck a l'Orange. We don't want it turning to marmalade, do we?"

Dad called out in the background, "That would be quackers." Good old Dad and his rubbish jokes.

"See you soon," I said, "and Mum..." I paused.

"Yes?"

"Nothing. Tell you when I see you."

Two hours later I arrived at my parents' house. Mum opened the door wearing her "you've ruined everything" face. "Sorry I'm late," I said. She would not be pacified with a simple apology. "It's all baked into the pan now. Your father and I have already had ours." I nearly told Mum to go duck herself with the orange, she was still on probation after all, but instead raw emotion and panic overtook me. I grabbed her, clinging to her like a terrified clam, the way I used to when I was little after waking from nightmare. She was taken aback. Mum and I rarely demonstrated our affection physically. She held me at arms length and looked doubtfully at the wig. "Oh no, Katherine," she said in a frightened whisper. "I knew something wasn't right. Is it cancer?"

I was momentarily confused, wondering how she already knew about Jojo. Dad appeared behind Mum in the hallway. With worry etched on their faces Mum and Dad both suddenly seemed so small and fragile. My parents had aged and I hadn't even noticed. When did they become old people?

"No, I'm fine," I said. "Never better." She missed the sarcasm completely.

"Thank God," she said, her body sagging with relief. She was still staring at my head. "Bad hair day then?" I pulled off the wig. Dad gasped. Mum's eyes filled with tears. "You're a lesbian, aren't you?" she sobbed. "It explains so much. I can't pretend I'm happy but I still love you." This remark cut me to the core, not because Mum thought I was gay but because finally she had a tangible reason for the failure of my marriage and why Rob had dumped me. And yet again it was my fault. "Don't be ridiculous," I said, feeling my blood rise. Mum carried on staring at my head, Dad's eyes were still wide with shock. "Cuppa?" he asked, eager to avert a family row on the doorstep. I nodded gratefully.

Mum continued with the hallway inquisition. I would not be permitted into the inner sanctum of the living room until she got to the bottom of my radical new look. "Have you gone back to college then? Is it a student thing?" I started giggling. "I hardly think it's a laughing matter," she continued, putting her hands on her hips. "You look awful. You're struggling for acting jobs as it is. Who's going to employ a woman who looks like a crack addict? There are only so many television crime dramas, you know." That wiped the smile off my face.

The enormous shock of Jojo's revelation had made me forget I needed hair to be employable. Being the very wrong side of thirty in the entertainment business was bad enough, but without my former lustrous locks I was screwed unless someone was shooting a remake of *Aliens* in the UK.

"Jojo has breast cancer," I said quietly.

"Jojo?" she asked.

"My best friend." Mum's face brightened a little. Not quite the reaction I was expecting.

"It was very considerate of you to do a charity thing for her. But a little foolhardy. What will you do until your hair grows back?"

"I don't know," I shrugged. At Petite Paris bizarre hairdos were par for the course. I doubted if anyone would even notice.

"Anyway," Mum said over her shoulder as she bustled down the hallway into the living room, "we may as well give you some money." I was touched by her generosity.

"I've got enough to cover the rent this month," I called after her, "but it's really nice of you to offer." Mum had already retrieved her handbag from the side of the sofa and was fishing out her purse.

"I don't suppose a fifty pence fix does it anymore," she laughed. It was only then that I realised that she was offering to sponsor my buzz cut, not help me with my expenses until my hair grew back.

"There you go," she said, presenting me with a five pound note as if it was one of those enormous cheques you see competition winners receiving. I didn't have the heart to tell her that I hadn't been smart enough to shave my head for charity. Tired, hungover, and broke, I took the money.

"Thanks Mum, that's very kind." She gave me a magnanimous smile, the sort employed by celebrities when gazing at orphaned babies in the developing world.

"It's the least we can do," she said benevolently.

Dad came in with the tea and sat next to me on the sofa. He stroked the top of my head.

"Feels nice," he said. "Like Fuzzy Felts. Remember those?"

I did; pieces of stiff, brightly coloured felt cut into all sorts of shapes, each set themed. I had the farm and the circus. I would have given my eye teeth at that moment to be five years old again, yelping as Mum dragged a brush through my tangled ponytail while Dad amused himself with the Fuzzy Felts, making a ballerina ride a cow or running a clown over with a tractor.

"I've got some old hairpieces somewhere," Mum said. Before I could stop her she jumped up from her chair and was on her way to the spare bedroom, where all the relics of forty years of family life had been consigned to. She was still incredibly spritely, especially when she had a plan in mind. While Mum was rummaging upstairs it gave me chance to check in with Dad to see how he was doing downstairs. So to speak.

I cleared my throat. "Everything okay with...um... you?"

"I'm fine, Treacle. Apart from the fact that my only daughter's turned into a soccer hooligan." He ruffled my head. "I'm sorry to hear about Jojo, love." I put my head on Dad's shoulder and he kissed my fuzz.

"It's so bloody unfair, Dad," I said, trying not to cry.

"I know, sweetheart. Unfortunately, life often is."

I was glad that Mum returned with a dusty cardboard box full of tat from the nineteen seventies before I had a chance to collapse into floods of tears.

"Found them!" she said enthusiastically. She opened the box and pulled out an ash blonde wig, mid-length, with long flicked layers, the kind of hairdo that Farah Fawcett had sported at the height of her fame. When he was a teenager Patrick had a poster of Farah in a swimsuit on his bedroom wall (along with the girl in the tennis skirt scratching her bum). Mum retrieved a mahogany-coloured bowl cut from the box and a shoulder length copper bob. It unnerved me that I couldn't remember ever seeing her in any of these wigs. It felt as if a vital piece of my childhood jigsaw puzzle was missing.

"I only ever wore them for best," she said. "I used to love a bit of disco but your father was never much one for going out.

They seemed a bit excessive for trips to Sainsbury's." I should have known it would be Dad's fault.

"No point in them going to waste," she sighed.

"Perfect," I said. "I'll be able to be an Abba tribute act all by myself."

"What an excellent idea," she said enthusiastically. "That's the kind of thing they go for at the club isn't it? See, every cloud has a silver lining."

When I got home after lunch with Mum and Dad I opened the dating app, vowing to delete my profile or at least hide it from public view until my hair grew back. As my finger hovered over the "are you sure button?" Funny Boy appeared in Instant Chat.

What's up Kat? You've been quiet lately.

Where do you want me to start? My best friend got breast cancer, my mum's online dating more than I am and Dave has disappeared without a trace.

I'm so sorry, Kat x

It's ok. Not your fault, is it? I just feel abandoned.

By Dave?

By everyone, everything. And yes, especially Dave.

Well, you know men and feelings. But this David's right here for you x

I thought about that statement for quite some time after I logged off. It seemed I knew the feelings of a complete stranger far better than those of a very close friend. I felt doomed to only ever have fragments of people, from my own mother living a very private life from which I was totally excluded, to Jem being more than happy to share his bed but never his heart. And I hadn't had a single message from Dave since Jojo's diagnosis. I was feeling shortchanged by life and thoroughly fed up. And then shame crashed over me. Jojo had cancer and by comparison I had very minor first world problems.

Chapter Twenty-Six

Bedside Manners

I was dreading my first hospital visit to Jojo wondering how I was going to keep my emotional biscuits in their tin, while at the same time desperate to give her as much support as I could. She was having surgery today, which would be followed by long rounds of chemotherapy. I was in such a state of anxiety that I had to go into the toilet twice to compose myself before I could face seeing Jojo on the ward.

Whoever was running the place had done their utmost to make it not look like a hospital. The foyer had a large bright atrium, several shops including a W.H. Smith and the ever present Costa. Civil war could break out but there would always be the nerve-jangling comfort of a coffee chain to soften the blow. Despite the mini shopping mall, abundant plants and mood lighting the hospital still had that smell you only find in public buildings, as if there was a fragrance called "Institution", a combination of boiled cabbage and disinfectant.

I found the wing where Jojo was being treated. The receptionist was busy thumbing through a file, phone glued to her ear and there were two people ahead of me at the desk. I browsed the leaflet rack while I waited. "Living With Cancer" terrified more than it informed, so instead I weighed myself on the digital scale. As I was trying to work out its BMI function the receptionist gave me one of those "ahem, excuse me" type coughs. "Those scales are for patient use only. Are you a patient?" she asked, staring at my crop. Red-faced I walked back to the desk. "I'm here to see Josephine Baker." The receptionist did a double-take to see if I was winding her up and looked even more put out when she found Jojo's name on the patient list.

"Do you have any coughs or colds at the moment?" the receptionist asked.

"Just a hangover." She gave me a withering stare.

"It's no laughing matter," she snapped. "The patients here are seriously ill. A simple cold virus could kill them." It was a verbal slap that woke me up to just how serious things were; Jojo really did have cancer, she really was in hospital and her treatment really was starting today.

"I didn't mean to be flippant," I said full of remorse and feeling tearful.

The receptionist's face softened, "She's in room five, love. Give your hands a squirt." She indicated a huge bottle of sanitiser on the counter that looked like the sauce dispenser in a burger van. I dutifully pumped the antiseptic into my hands and rubbed it in. I took a deep breath and looked at the receptionist, half hoping she would give me a detailed set of further instructions that would take at least an hour. She nodded in the direction of Jojo's room. "Off you pop then," she said. "Right," I replied through gritted teeth, "Pop, pop, pop."

I could just about make out Jojo's waif like silhouette through the Venetian blinds. I knocked gently on the door. "Room service," I said, trying to sound as jovial as possible. "Kaaat!" Jojo yelled, "Come on in." She was sitting on the bed, hooked up to a serious looking IV. I didn't know whether I should hug her, but Jojo gestured with her free arm and I squeezed her as gently as I could. I nodded at the drip, "That better be vodka."

She looked a lot better than I'd expected. Apart from the lack of hair and plethora of medical equipment there were no immediate signs that Jojo was ill. Then again, watching *Beaches* was my only prior experience of something like this. I had been obsessively Googling "breast cancer" ever since Jojo's diagnosis and probably knew at least as much as the nurse on reception. Of course I didn't breath a word to Jojo about hair loss, eyebrow loss, eyelash loss, rashes, brittle nails, nausea, tremors or any of the other nasty side effects associated with chemotherapy. Somehow I managed to convince myself that Jojo would sail through her treatment. The worst side effect so far was timing. Jojo loved the music festival season and cancer had really fucked up her happy glamping plans for the summer. If cancer was a man I would have kicked him straight in the balls for that. Bastard, indeed.

I stood awkwardly for a few moments, worried that all sorts of germs were lurking on my clothes and could be transferred to Jojo. "Sit down," she said laughing, "I'm not going to break." I sat on the edge of the bed and opened my bag, tipping a plethora of guilty pleasures into Jojo's lap; *Grazia* and *Look* magazines, Minstrels, Maltesers and a giant bar of Toblerone, and some travel size toiletries from The Body Shop.

"Thanks," said Jojo, scooping up the booty from her lap.

"Nice pyjamas," I said looking at the beautiful silk camisole and shorts she was wearing.

"Gift from Bil and Ben. You just missed them." I still hadn't heard from the couple but now was not the time to bring up my exile.

"How is it?" I asked.

She shrugged. She smiled. "It's okay. Early days. Won't know about the side effects immediately, but I've come prepared." She furtively unzipped the pocket of her laptop sleeve, revealing a small plastic bag full of dark green buds.

"Where did you get that?" I asked.

Jojo giggled. "Dave, of course. Little going away gift. Posted it along with a lovely Easter card. Only two months late." She nodded to the nightstand. Dave had turned the egg on the front of the card into a massive bald head with the body of a stick figure girl.

"When was the last time you saw him?" I asked

"Not since the barbecue. Guess he's busy." She was doing her best not to look bothered about it.

"Busy?" I snorted. "With a stand-up gig twice a month? Or

scrounging pints in the pub every night?" I realised I was being extremely hard on Dave but for him not to show up at a time like this was beyond careless. He was definitely avoiding us, and more especially Jojo, and I couldn't work out why.

"It's no big deal," Jojo said lightly. "He'd probably just steal the towels anyway. And he'd definitely get high on his own supply. I'm not sharing. I'm a sick woman." She had a valid point.

I walked across to the window, looking down at the tiny pedestrians on the street below. Hundreds of cancer-free people going about their everyday cancer-free business, getting upset over inconsequential bullshit, each precious minute of their cancer-free lives ticking by, unused or unnoticed.

"How does a girl get her kicks around here?" I asked turning back to Jojo.

"There's bingo on Tuesday and Pilates on Wednesday. It's a bit quiet at the weekends though." Her last quip made me uneasy. I'd heard a statistic that patients were more likely to die over the weekend while the consultants were getting pissed on Cotes du Rhone at their second homes.

"They're going to see how I go with the first session chemo session. Depending on the side effects they'll do me as an outpatient." I could have jumped for joy.

"That's brilliant. Although this room is bigger than your entire flat. You could have made a fortune subletting your place while you were in here." She laughed again.

"How's the dating going?" asked Jojo. I pointed to my head and sighed.

"You haven't stopped have you?" she said, sounding genuinely disappointed.

"In case you haven't noticed," I said framing my head like Madonna in the "Vogue" video, "I'm bald."

"What was it Monroe said?" Jojo asked thoughtfully.

"Can you feel the breeze from the subway?" I replied breathily.

"No, silly," Jojo giggled.

"Men don't make passes at girls who wear glasses?" I said, even breathier.

"No," said Jojo emphatically, "about being worthy, 'If you can't handle me at my worst you sure as hell don't deserve me at my best'."

I was about to say I was sure that I looked my absolute worst right now but thought better of it.

"Maybe it's the perfect time to meet someone?" Jojo continued. "It's easy to find a man when you're on top of the world. But a guy that will pick you up when you're rock bottom is a keeper."

As I was contemplating if there was any way I could go on a date while practically bald, a nurse entered the room. She was large, matronly and efficient, and something about her made me wish she was my mum. She started changing the bag which was feeding drugs into Jojo. I swallowed hard.

"Shall I leave?" I asked.

"No need," the nurse said over her shoulder. "We encourage friends and family to be here for the whole process. If Jojo starts having chemo at home she might need help."

I baulked. It wasn't that I didn't want to look after Jojo, but rather that I didn't trust myself not to kill my best friend by hooking her up to a camping shower instead of an IV bag. I made myself watch the nurse studiously and tried not to wince as she replaced the tubing into the port in a bulging vein in Jojo's arm. Seeing my alarm the nurse said, "Don't worry, it's only pills at home, not all this paraphernalia," then she bustled out of the room.

Jojo yawned and sank back into her pillows. The colour drained suddenly from her face and she closed her eyes, "I think I might be starting to come up on this shit." She was dwarfed by the bed and the medical equipment surrounding it. She looked relaxed and peaceful but the afternoon sun flooding into the room highlighted how thin and pale she was, like a shadow. "I better go anyway," I said, standing up and pecking her on the cheek. She smiled softly, squeezing my hand, letting me know she was okay. I crept out of the room as if I was playing Grandma's Footsteps. I was cautiously closing the door when I heard someone gasp my name. It was Jojo's mother.

"Hello Francine," I said. Francine grabbed me. I could feel her shaking. She smelled of panic and parma violets.

"Is she okay?" she whispered, her breath hot with fear.

"Absolutely fine. Having a snooze."

"She only called me this morning. Said she didn't want to worry me."

Francine was 74 years old. Jojo was an only child, a late, unplanned and much-wanted baby after years of apparent infertility. Poor Francine. She must have gone to the station as soon as she heard the news and arrived from Herefordshire just that moment.

"She'll be okay," I tried to soothe. "They caught it really early." Francine looked at me doubtfully, her face creased with worry. She let me out of her embrace and I took both her hands in mine. "She'll be fine. I guarantee it." I hoped that I hadn't made a promise I couldn't keep. I couldn't live without Jojo either.

"She's a fighter," I said, trying to smile.

"Just like her Dad," replied Francine.

I gave Francine my number and told her to call me any time, day or night. I watched as she slipped silently into the room and slumped down in the easy chair opposite the bed, staring at her sleeping daughter. Francine fumbled inside her ancient handbag and produced a ragged tissue. She dabbed her eyes and then balled the tissue up in her fist, bringing it to her mouth in an act of defiance and despair. It was heart-breaking.

I summoned Dave to the pub later that night. I hadn't seen him since I'd shaved my head. He sat open-mouthed as I marched towards him.

"Bloody hell," he said. "What happened to you?"

I looked at him squarely. "My best friend got cancer."

"And there's me thinking I was about to cash in on our deal," he said, shifting uncomfortably.

"Fuck the stupid online-dating and fuck your stupid bet. Jojo, my best friend, one of *your* best friends, has cancer." I shook my head at him in disgust and went to the bar.

I bought him half a pint to make my point, sliding it menacingly across the dented, sticky table.

"Half-rations?" he said blinking at the glass in disbelief. "You seem to have mistaken me for a hobbit." I wondered if this is what it would be like to have a prepubescent son.

"When are you going to see Jojo?" I demanded.

He gulped at his drink, "I've been really busy."

"Dave, she hasn't seen you since her diagnosis. What's going on?"

"Stuff kept coming up. I will go though," he said. He finished the rest of his beer, his hand shaking – had he held the glass any tighter it would have shattered. Then he stood up, wiping his lips on the sleeve of his sweatshirt. "I need another drink."

"Sit," I said sharply, sounding like my mother used to at the dinner table whenever Patrick or I left our chairs without permission. Dave sat back down reluctantly and took a deep breath.

"This is difficult," he began slowly.

"Try me," I said harshly.

"My mum died of cancer a few years ago."

Dave stopped talking, struck dumb by his pain. He looked like a lost little boy, shell-shocked with grief. I felt awful for emotionally ambushing him. I had no idea that his Mum was even dead. I counted Dave as one of my closest friends and I realised how little I actually knew about him. There was a brittle silence. It was my turn to stand up.

"Pint?" I asked gently. He nodded. His eyes were shiny with sadness and I could see his Adam's apple moving up and down in his throat. I had never known Dave to be lost for words.

By the time I returned to the table he had regained some of

his composure. I put a whiskey chaser in front of him which he downed in one, before clinging to his beer like a toddler to its comfort blanket.

"I was fifteen. It was all very sudden. She went to the doctor's about a stomach upset. She was dead two months later."

I put my hand on his. "I'm so sorry."

"My dad was a wreck, my two brothers had moved out already, there was no one to talk to. It was like our lives came to a full stop."

It struck me as odd that he said his mum had died "a few years ago". Dave was forty now, so his mum had passed away twenty-five years previously. It was like the clock in his heart had stopped the day she died. He was emotionally stunted, remaining a teenager while the rest of the world grew up and moved on without him. It dawned on me that Dave wasn't so much commitment phobic as just completely confused by the whole concept of anything that might resemble an adult relationship. He simply hadn't developed that far.

"No wonder you're such an arse when it comes to women," I said patting his back gently, as if I was burping a baby,

"You're right. I've been a total twat. I need to go and see Jojo now." He knocked back his entire pint and then stood up. He let out a loud belch, looking very satisfied with himself. Same old Dave.

"Royal London?" he asked.

"Charing Cross," I corrected.

"Thanks Kat," he said and pecked me on the cheek. He stroked my head with surprising tenderness.

"It really suits you," he said.

"Shut up," I replied smiling.

He touched my face softly for a brief moment, as if he was about to say something really important but thought better of it. Then he walked out of the pub with purpose leaving me alone with only an untouched glass of white wine and the dust motes for company.

Chapter Twenty-Seven

Plastic Fantastic

"Kaaaat," Mags bellowed down the phone as excitedly as her Australian drawl would allow. "How are ya, darl?"

It was just after ten a.m. and I was barely awake. "I'm great," I lied.

"How's Dave?" she asked. I balked. I'd been working at Petite Paris for more than two months and still didn't have the balls to tell anyone that I didn't really have a boyfriend let alone a fiancé. It was time to come clean. Ish.

"Actually Mags, we've called it off." I couldn't resist embellishing, "I caught him with a total trollop."

"If I see him I'll rip his balls off," she growled. I couldn't wait to repeat that to Dave.

"Are you free tonight?" she asked, straight back to business,

"Hang on," I said rustling a magazine pretending to shuffle through the pages of a bursting-at-the-seams-with-bookings diary. It didn't pay to be too available. "I am as it happens."

"Bonzer," Mags said, ignorant of my pantomime. "Bit left field but it's three hundred quid in your hand."

"Left field? Just call me Lenin and spank me with a copy of *Das Kapital*." She could have been offering me a job jelly-wrestling in a bikini and I would have considered it at half that price.

"Hotel in Mayfair, private party," Mags continued. "You just need to sing a few numbers, introduce the acts and be your lovely bubbly self."

It was a good job Mags couldn't see me. I had gobs of yesterday's mascara in the corners of my eyes and what appeared to be a piece of pizza stuck in what was left of my hair. I was about as bubbly as a stale bottle of Asti Spumante with dog ends floating in it.

She hung up before I had the chance to say goodbye. I put the kettle on and while it creaked into life like a dormant volcano deciding whether it could be bothered to erupt or not I checked my phone. Mags had already sent the e-mail: *Wear your best gear. V generous client, will tip on top if happy. 8 pm call, 9 pm start. If finish late client pays taxi.* A taxi. Not quite a limousine but to me a mini cab was luxury, even if the interior did smell of ear wax and stale vomit.

I regretted not taking the box of wigs from Mum and called her immediately. "Goodness," she exclaimed, "I've just put them out for the bin men." The line went dead and I had images of Mum diving into the garbage truck to rescue the wigs. Just as I got to the part where Mum was about to be crushed flat by the jaws of the waste compressor my phone rang.

"It's your lucky day," Mum said breathlessly. "Mind you, smells like the foxes have been at them."

"Thanks Mum," I said with a twinge of guilt for the way I'd treated her lately. Jojo was probably right; it was highly unlikely that Mum was getting up to anything, just a spot of lunch and a smooch on a park bench at the very most. All very *Brief Encounter*, nothing more.

"I'll be over at about one then," I said.

"Today?" she asked, sounding nervous.

"Yes. I need the wigs for a job tonight," I explained, sensing her disquiet.

She paused and then said, "I won't be here."

"Why not?" I asked. She paused again. Mum was normally a gusher when it came to information, telling everyone everything she was doing whether they wanted to know or not. If Mum had worked for British Intelligence in the Second World War we would have all ended up speaking German. I had never known her to be so tight-lipped.

"I'm going out," she said stiffly.

"I know that, you just told me." I could feel the nasty creeping into my voice, "where?"

"Shopping," she blustered. I could tell she was lying.

"I don't have a key," I lied, in return. Of course I had a key. But Monday was Dad's golf day so he wouldn't be home. I was trying to stop her from leaving the house and getting up to whatever it was she had planned.

"Oh Katherine, you've not lost it again, have you?" she said, exasperated. "Someone could start a scrap metal yard with all the keys you've misplaced."

"Sorry," I said, sounding anything but.

"I'm not leaving keys out," she said bluntly. "Neighbourhood Watch warns against it. Besides, there's a Romanian moved in at 42."

I hit my forehead with the phone in despair. "He's from *Roma*, Mum. As in Italy. He's opened a cafe on the High Street according to Dad." I restrained myself from adding, "You remember Dad, don't you? The one you married and had two kids with? The one you're probably cheating on this afternoon?"

"I'll leave the wigs in the garage," she said sounding flustered. "The key's still under the flowerpot. Watch the garage door. Your father smacked himself in the nose getting the Rover out last week. Must dash." Like Mags she hung up without saying goodbye.

What a bizarre paradox the whole situation was. Two years ago, Mum and Dad's neighbour "Sandra from across the road" divorced her husband and found a boyfriend several years younger than herself. Mum and Sandra had until that point been what you might call "close"; in the 1970s they had loaned each other Tupperware, in the 80s they puffed their way through Jane Fonda workouts together and in the 90s they both got a "Rachel from Friends" haircut from "Teri with one R", the hairdresser who used to do home visits.

Mum put the divorce down to a "selfish mid-life crisis" rather than Sandra's husband's continuous extra-marital affairs, and as soon as Mum got her trifle dish back she barely spoke to Sandra any more.

"Disgusting," Mum had said. "Leaving those kiddies fatherless so she can gad about with her fancy man." When I pointed out that Sandra's youngest son Henry was thirty-two Mum said, "It doesn't matter, that boy's still living at home. What kind of message is she sending him?"

"I don't know," I said. "Move out?"

And now here we were, roles reversed; Mum was potentially off to meet her fancy man and I was judging her with a sense of outraged moral decency worthy of Mary Whitehouse. The last I heard of Sandra she'd chucked her boyfriend and found Jesus.

I grabbed the key to Mum and Dad's. It was attached to a photo fob that Mum had given to all of us a few Christmases ago. The photo was taken at a donkey sanctuary in Dorset when Patrick and I were little. Mum and Dad had their arms wrapped around one another and I was perched smugly on a donkey as if I was the star member of the Pony Club, while Patrick was poking the poor creature with a stick. I slung the keys into my bag with a bitter sigh.

When I got to Mum and Dad's I rang the doorbell several times on the off chance that they were at home. I stood for some moments listening to the birds chirp, staring through the stained glass of the front door at the distorted image of the deserted hallway. I turned my key in the lock gingerly. What if Mum was at home after all and had hired a male escort? What if found her in the living room, greased up in front of the living flame effect fire with a ball gag in her mouth, like a pig ready for a spit roast?

I inched along the hallway, trying not to knock down the ornamental plates and barely daring to breath. Once I had convinced myself that I was alone I set to work. I crept up the stairs and started in the master bedroom where my parents' laptop was sat on the dressing table. The computer had been a gift from

Patrick for their fortieth wedding anniversary the previous year. At the time I'd joked that it was going to be the most expensive door stop ever purchased, but Dad had been having a whale of a time playing online poker and now it seemed that Mum was making extensive use of the laptop too. Bloody Patrick. If he hadn't been so desperate to introduce them to the internet none of this would have happened.

My ears fizzed with guilt as I opened the laptop. The screen asked me for a password. I typed in my name. Nothing. I tried Dad's name. Zero. I typed in "Patrick" and the patronising start-up tune of Windows chimed forth: my brother appeared to hold the key to all Mum's dirty secrets. She had left her e-mail open. I swallowed hard, my throat suddenly dry from the fear of what I might find. There was nothing of any interest, although I was alarmed to see that Mum had labelled a message offering her a million pounds from the estate of a deceased government minister in a country that probably didn't exist as "not spam". As I shut the laptop and I noticed a yellow post-it note on its lid written in Mum's neat, florid script: *Hamilton, 3 Portland Mews 2.15pm*. I swallowed hard, my heart was thumping in my ears and I had the sudden urge to vomit. I doubted very much that Mum was going to see a musical, if she was it was more likely to be *Phantom of the Opera*. I could only conclude that she was meeting someone.

I stuffed the note in my jeans pocket and bolted down the stairs, slamming the front door behind me so hard that the mock Tudor beams and leaded windows rattled. I got to the end of the drive before I remembered that I'd forgotten the wigs. After locating the key to the garage underneath a terracotta plant pot furry at the edges with bright green moss I yanked the stiff sliding door. Without warning the hinges suddenly yielded and the garage door flew open smacking me squarely under the jaw. My teeth sank into my tongue and I felt the salty warm flow of blood fill my mouth as I remembered Mum's warning. Wincing with pain I grabbed the box of wigs and kicked the garage door closed. I looked at my phone. One fifteen. I might just be able to get back into Central London in time to find out what the hell Mum was up to.

I sat down on the train and I caught sight of my reflection in the carriage window; bald, dried blood at the corners of my mouth, clutching a cardboard box full of wigs. An elderly woman looked at me with kindly, sorrowful eyes. I made the mistake of smiling at her and she looked away, doubtless horrified by my bloodstained teeth. I must have looked like an overgrown feral child who'd just eaten her collection of prize guinea pigs.

When I got to Portland Mews I found number three and with my legs feeling like jelly I climbed the elegant Georgian steps. Outside the smart black door was a brass name plate, and there was my answer: *The Hamilton Group, Gynaecology, Urology & Aesthetic Plastic Surgery*. I shuddered. The thought of Mum waxing her bikini line was bad enough but the possibility that she was getting her lady garden completely excavated and remodelled was too much to bear. I succumbed to a terrifying daydream wherein Mum was having an ornamental fountain installed that turned her into the human equivalent of a sexual Soda Stream. Then I heard voices in the hallway.

I shot down the stairs and out of the mews, running into the communal garden in the centre of the road. I hid in a bush from where I could just about see the entrance to The Hamilton Group. I became aware of a noise behind me and turned around to see a very drunk man. "Oi!" he said angrily, breathing Special Brew finished off with top notes of woodbine and stale urine straight in my face, "This is my spot." I bared my bloody teeth at him, "Not today, it's not. Now piss off." Even though his face was encrusted with dirt I could see him turn white. He didn't say a word, backing away and then breaking into a run. I had a moment of remorse, realising that I'd probably just made a homeless man even more homeless, but I had to find out what my mother was doing.

I turned my attention back to the entrance of the clinic. The door opened and I saw my mother appear, with a debonair, perma-tanned charmer behind her. His hand rested lightly on her elbow and she was fawning all over him. "Bloody hypocrite," I hissed. Mum wouldn't shop in her local convenience store because it was run by "foreigners" but a creosote brown boyfriend was fine as long as he was British. He looked like a freshly painted garden fence in a blazer.

I watched Mum descend the stairs, dressed to the nines and smiling. She could have passed for Ivana Trump. Since she still had facial expressions I guessed she hadn't done lunchtime Botox. She turned back to the doctor and gave him a girlish wave and then disappeared from view.

I found an automatic toilet in the gardens and once I was safely locked in the spaceship-like pod I cleaned my face under the erratic sensor tap. I pulled on the Farrah Fawcett wig and fluffed it around my face. I slicked on lipstick, eye liner and mascara but with my puffy jaw I looked like the victim in a 1970s crime drama. I put my giant Jackie O sunglasses on and my celebrity-in-rehab make-over was complete.

I left the toilet, stashing the wig box behind an ornamental hedge, and made my way back over to the clinic. I cleared my throat and pressed the buzzer. A hoity toity South African female voice answered.

"Do you have an appointment ma'am?"

"Indeed I absolutely do," I over-compensated.

"With whom?"

"Dr Hamilton," I said, trying to sound confident and well-heeled.

"Which one?" Hoity Toity asked. Oh God. There was more than one Dr Hamilton. What if they were from a massive family of child prodigies and there were eleven doctor Hamiltons at the clinic?

I took a chance. "The one who deals with ladies of a certain age?"

"That'll be George," Hoity informed me. I nearly wet myself

laughing because the object of my mother's affection was a dead ringer for his Hollywood namesake.

"And your name is?" she asked suspiciously.

I was stumped. I touched my wig. "Farrah" I said. Struggling for a surname I looked at the shiny brass lock on the door, "Chubb. Farrah Chubb."

"We don't have you on the list Ms Chubb."

I tried not to sound panicked. "There must have been an oversight. I've come all the way from Royal Tunbridge Wells."

"You better come in," Hoity said with aggravated politeness.

There was a buzz, the door opened automatically and I walked into a cosmetic surgery wonderland. In the grand hallway stood a statue of Aphrodite, dipping one dainty foot into an ornamental pond. She was bearing a jar on her shoulder from which flowed yet more water. The tinkling made me want to wee. On closer inspection Aphrodite had a tiny button mushroom nose, trout pout lips, large and perfectly round breasts, a stomach so flat it was almost concave and legs that seemed to go all the way from Athens to LA. It was like Mattel had got hold of the rights to ancient mythology and turned the goddess of love and beauty into an alabaster soft porn star. Underneath the statue was an inscription in Greek style lettering, *The Hamilton Group: Improving on Mother Nature since 1988.*

I walked through to reception which by contrast was all sleek modern lines, polished reflective surfaces and white clinical lighting, clearly designed to make visitors realise just how much they needed the services of the Doctors Hamilton. I could see my dreadful reflection everywhere. Hoity Toity was sat behind the space age desk, illuminated to perfection with one manicured eyebrow raised above bronzed, gravity defying breasts which reminded me of those balls that used to hang outside of pawn brokers shops.

"Miss Chubb?" she asked, staring down her slender nose at me. "But I think it's Lewis you want. He's the maxillofacial specialist." I wasn't quite sure what one of those was but I guessed it was something to do with the jawline because she was staring at my chin which was now so swollen that I could have passed for Jay Leno.

"No, no," I insisted in a clipped Home Counties accent, the kind my mother used with telesales people, "It's George I want."

To emphasise the fact I pointed towards my lady parts. Hoity shrugged and said under her breath, "It's your money."

"Yes," I said with the air of a disgruntled television licence fee payer, "it is."

"Take a seat. Dr Hamilton will be with you shortly."

I sat down in the waiting room and helped myself to the extensive tea and biscuit selection and the glossy fashion journals that were stacked on the coffee tables. I opened one of the magazines and holding it in front of my face I covertly surveyed the other women in the waiting room. One lady in a white bathrobe and turban was clearly mid-consultation. Her face was etched in magic marker with dotted lines and notes, "LIFT HERE/CUT HERE/ PULL BACK", like the wing of an aircraft. A few seats along was a stunning young woman of about twenty-six. She was achingly beautiful and there was no reason for her to be here. I thought perhaps she needed a psychiatrist, not a plastic surgeon.

Sitting opposite her was another woman, at the most eighteen years old. She wore a hijab and her face and hands were terribly scarred. I felt guilty for staring and when she raised her eyes to mine I immersed myself in a *Vogue* article about cruise fashion even though the closest I had ever come to a yacht was a pedalo in Hyde Park. I thought about Jojo. Luckily she'd had a small lumpectomy, and the visible damage was negligible – but so many women having radical mastectomies relied on breast reconstruction to get their lives back on track. I realised that I had judged The Hamilton Group far too harshly.

Then Dr George Hamilton suddenly appeared before me, as if out of thin air. Up close his handsome face reminded me of Barbie's husband Ken, classically attractive in a completely unnatural way.

His perfectly smooth, waxy features made him look like an escapee from Madame Tussaud's. It was impossible to say how old he was, all very Dorian Gray.

"Miss Chubb?" he asked. His voice was seven figure posh but so soft that he was barely audible. I nodded, too stunned by his over-stretched features to say anything. "Do come through," he whispered.

His office walls were festooned with thank you cards and before and after pictures. On his desk was a Newton's Cradle, one of those desk toys with chrome balls, and on the floor was a black metal cage that looked like a small medieval torture device but was in fact an "ab rocker". It seemed that time in Dr Hamilton's office, and indeed his face, had stopped somewhere in the mid 1980s.

Breast implants of various shapes and sizes sat in a bowl on the desk like bizarre party favours. I picked one up and started playing with it. They reminded me of the slime toys Patrick used to put down the back of my trousers when we were kids.

"Amazing, don't you think?" asked Dr Hamilton. "So natural. Only better. They'll never sag and last ten years, maybe fifteen without too many long-haul flights." Nodding at my cleavage he added, "Not that you need volume. Is it an uplift you're after?" His voice was jovial but the only thing that moved on his face were his mouth and eyelids. He reminded me of a perfectly coiffured turtle.

"Well, actually," I said leaning in conspiratorially, "I've come on the recommendation of a friend. Patricia Wheeler."

Turtle Face tried to smile again. "You ladies," he chuckled, "so competitive with your one-up-man-ship. Or should I say 'nip and tuck man-ship'?" Delighted by his own joke he carried on laughing until I interrupted him.

"I want whatever she's having." Dr Hamilton stopped laughing.

"Miss Chubb," Turtle Face began calmly, "I understand the need to look as good as your peers, and in your case we have extensive work to do, but I can't possibly disclose the details of Mrs Wheeler's business here."

"Why not?" I asked bluntly. "I'll pay you."

"Miss Chubb, I am a member of the BMA and BAAPS." I tried not to laugh when he said "baps". He caught me smirking and I felt like I was back in the head-master's office after I got caught smoking behind the bike sheds. Turtle Face looked angry, although he couldn't frown so I wasn't absolutely sure.

"I don't take bribes," he said sharply, "nor breach patient confidentiality."

"What if I were to tell you that I am Mrs Wheeler's daughter?"

He looked at me closely. "I sincerely doubt that."

"But I am," I said agitatedly pulling off my sunglasses.

"If that really is the case I advise you to talk to your mother. Perhaps family therapy might be a better use of your resources than plastic surgery?"

He wasn't being clever or spiteful. The limited expression that he was able to make changed. He seemed to soften, looking at me kindly. He patted my hand gently, his fingers smooth but the knuckles gnarled with age. The skin on the back of his hands was dotted with liver spots. He was very old, perhaps the same age as my grandpa had been when he passed away. I could feel tears welling up in my eyes and I wanted to jump into Dr Hamilton's lap for a hug and a Werther's Original.

"I'm sorry," I said standing up. Dr Hamilton handed me a tissue.

"Not at all my dear. We can do amazing things for the face and body these days, but the heart and mind remain a mystery." I blew my nose and became aware of my aching jaw and the fact that I had a show tonight.

"Thank you, Dr Hamilton," I said gratefully shaking his hand. He pressed his business card into my palm.

"You know where we are if you need us. Come back when you've sorted out all this business with your mother. I'll give you a ten percent family discount. I could take years off you."

Chapter Twenty-Eight

Harem Scarem

Worrying about what Mum may or may not be getting up to was beginning to consume me, as the demented jaunt to Harley Street had just proven, but I was going to have to park my obsession for the time being and get back to work. When I got home I gave the wigs a quick shampoo and left them drip-drying out of my kitchen window. From the street my flat must have looked like a budget Traitor's Gate, the scalps of the executed on display as warning. I blow-dried the Farah Fawcett wig and patched up my bruised chin with pan stick. I found an ancient Biba halter-neck dress lurking at the bottom of my wardrobe and retrieved a pair of platform sandals from under the bed. I added a gold rope pendant that dangled enticingly between my boobs, distracting attention away from my jaw and threw on a wide-brimmed, floppy felt hat and a faux-fur Afghan gilet. Very Kate Moss at a festival, I thought.

By the time I got to the Tube my ears were burning, as much from the sniggers of fellow travellers as from the insulation of wearing a wig and hat in June. A middle-aged man in a pastel pink polo shirt and deck shoes jumped on at Brixton as the doors closed and sat opposite me. "Fancy dress party?" he smirked. "Something like that," I replied. "What's your excuse? Forgotten where you left your catamaran?" He went a bit red and looked away. At Stockwell I spied a mob of lads getting on at the end of the carriage and tried to stay calm as they came towards me. Their leader, so huge he looked like he was wearing American football shoulder pads under his rugby shirt, started chanting, "Stevie, Stevie, Stevie," to which his minions bookended, "Nicks, Nicks, Nicks!" Then all at once they launched into "Tell me lies, tell me sweet little lies, tell me lie-ies, tell me, tell me lies", more of a hooligans anthem than an homage to Fleetwood Mac. I shrank in embarrassment as every single passenger turned their attention to me, and the ringleader capped my humiliation with, "Nice tits, shame about the hat."

I arrived at Bond Street feeling like a melted wax voodoo doll, soaked with sweat and tearful. The street was full of couples strolling hand in hand enjoying the balmy night, the girls laughing softly and shaking their lustrous hair in slow motion like the love interest in a music video. I felt sad and envious, my jealousy turning immediately to shame when I thought about Jojo.

When I arrived at the hotel I was ushered straight up to the penthouse. The entire top floor had been reserved for the party. What Mag's had made sound like a low key affair was in fact an entertainment extravaganza, with preparing performers spilling out of three rooms. In one bedroom a pole dancer was warming up on the floor, her spangled crotch twinkling beneath the chandelier as she scissor-kicked. Two burlesque artists whom I knew from Petite Paris were having a face-off. Due to clerical error they had both been booked to do a Jessica Rabbit striptease and now they were standing either side of the bed, purple gloved hands defiantly on sequinned hips, flicking their red nylon hair like agitated ponies.

Feeling claustrophobic I walked back towards the hallway to find my way blocked by a four piece boy band. They were rehearsing, bare-chested and singing vaguely in tune as they jigged frenetically from side to side. I ducked into another slightly less hectic bedroom but still the only place to sit was on the safe inside the fitted wardrobe. I entered the tiny Narnia of cool and quiet, and shut the door. Nobody even noticed. Moments later there was a polite knocking and a bubbly American woman popped her head in.

"Kat?" she asked, not remotely perturbed that the person who would be hosting the whole show was sat in the closet.

"Gillian?" I asked, jumping out of my hiding place.

"Dilli-Anne," she corrected. No sooner had I left my dark sanctuary than we were walking down the corridor towards the penthouse while Dilli-Anne briefed me. It was like an episode of *The West Wing*.

"It'll just be the sheik and eight ladies, very relaxed. Normally they'd go off to a night club but they want something a little more intimate. Just do your thing and have fun. Mags says you're the best there is."

"That's, er, nice of her," I replied uncertainly. As we got closer to the ornate double doors leading into the penthouse Dilli-Anne glanced over her shoulder.

"By the way, the big guy is... Well, big. Try not to make any reference to his size, he's very sensitive about it." I suddenly felt a ripple of fear rush up from my bum hole, making my throat dry and sticky. I was opening with "Big Spender" but it was too late now. I would just have to edit *in situ*.

I had been expecting the usual set up of a stage with tables and chairs arranged around it. What greeted me was a couple of square metres of carpet flanked by sofas on two sides and a few footstools lined up as a makeshift front row. I was about to do a show in someone's living room and I felt a surge of nostalgia; when I was seven and discovered that I could do impressions Mum and Dad used to wheel me out whenever they had guests over, whether I wanted to perform or not.

Eight immaculate Arab women of various ages were dotted around the room, all dressed in expensive western clothes, some very young, others my own age, some middle-aged. They were all stunning and each one of them was sucking on a shisha pipe. At first I didn't notice Mr Big Stuff. The room was dimly lit and thick with smoke and it didn't help that the colour and texture of his outfit matched the sofa so perfectly that his head appeared to be suspended in mid-air like the Cheshire Cat. When I did finally manage to connect his head to his body I was disappointed. I expected a dashing Lawrence of Arabia type, but instead, Mr

Big Stuff was wearing a fleece and a pair of stonewashed jeans. I mentally slapped myself for being sizeist and ethnocentric. I tried to focus on the money. It made me feel even worse.

As I walked to the centre of the room the buckle on my sandal got caught in the hem of my dress. I tumbled forward, falling flat on my face, landing on the same part of my jaw that had impacted with the garage door earlier that day. There was a loud thud as the microphone hit the floor, then a squeal of feedback. Like a bug trying to get itself out of trouble I flipped over onto my side. I raised one hand above my head, showgirl style, while frantically trying to free the sandal from the dress with the other. The buckle refused to come undone so I wriggled my foot out of the shoe. I stood up and tried to look confident while my halter neck dress swayed precariously with the weight of the shoe which was still attached to the hem, like a terrier locked onto its prey. There was a polite ripple of applause for my impromptu display of slapstick before we launched into the smorgasbord of talent; two pole dancers, one snake charmer, a magician, a ventriloquist, the boy band, a contortionist double act, an acrobat of restricted growth, another vocalist, a ballroom dancing couple who nearly fox trotted into the coffee table, a hula hooper, a juggler, a tap dancer, a small dog act, a ballerina, an impressionist, all bookended by the two feuding Jessica Rabbits.

During one of the longer acts I slipped into one of the bedrooms to extricate my shoe. The room was full of shopping bags from designer stores; Prada, Gucci, Max Mara, Louis Vuitton. Feeling simultaneously envious and disgusted at such rampant consumerism, I closed the door. I imagined that the sheik was probably an oil magnate but I couldn't work out what the women were to him. Wives and daughters or hired escorts? Either way they were being very well looked after. As my grandma used to say, "money can't buy you love, Katherine, but it can definitely make the misery sweeter."

When I returned to the party a mime was giving the ladies

imaginary flowers. Once he got to the sheik he mimed the flower going limp. Dilli-Anne who had been hanging in the shadows looked at me, her face suddenly becoming whiter than the mime's. I encouraged a hasty round of applause while Dilli-Anne pantomimed pulling the performer offstage with an invisible rope, he in turn slashing his own throat with his finger.

I had been specifically asked to sing "Diamonds Are A Girl's Best Friend" and this seemed like an appropriate moment. It was the only point that I saw the sheik smile during the entire evening. His eyes lit up and from the side of his chair he picked up a Cartier gift bag. The women clapped their hands with delight and made their way over to Saudi Claus, perching on the edge of the sofa or at his feet. One by one they were each given a beautiful diamond necklace. They lifted their hair seductively and the sheik did up the clasp, his chubby fingers surprisingly nimble. I could almost feel myself turning green. I wasn't particularly a fan of precious jewels – even before I watched *Blood Diamond* – but I estimated that I could have bought a small studio flat in a shabby London suburb with one of the necklaces alone. As I carried on singing about louses and spouses, getting older and the cold shoulder, I wondered what Marilyn would have made of all this.

After the gift-giving the juggernaut of entertainment continued. The audience was largely unmoved, sucking on their shishas as dispassionately as if they were watching a National Geographic documentary about an extinct Northern European tribe, but the diminutive acrobat was a big hit. As he took his bow the sheik grinned at me.

"How much?" asked the sheik.

"Dilli-Anne will organise artist payments," I said politely.

"No, how much for the little one. We want to take him home"

I gulped. I looked at Dilli-Anne. The panic was back in her eyes.

"Yes," the sheik continued, "We will make a special hat with a glass top and use him as a table." I was appalled and about to deliver a lecture on human rights when the Sheik started laughing. He leaned forward and winked.

"Ya see what I did there?" he said, in perfect American-English, like a Middle Eastern Danny De Vito.

All of the ladies started giggling. His sense of humour was drier than the Wahhabi desert. I heard Dilli-Anne exhale, as if she had narrowly avoided an international public relations crisis.

I sang my final number, there was polite applause. The sheik shook my hand and pressed something into my palm. My heart leapt with excitement at the thought of a generous tip. It sank again as I opened my palm to find a squashed After Eight mint, sticky white fondant oozing out from the paper wrapper. The Sheik did that drumming thing with both of his index fingers at me, as if I was the sidekick in his buddy movie. "See what I did there," he said again. "Yes," I said, as I scraped melting chocolate off my palm, "you should take up comedy."

We finished before midnight so there was no carriage ride home, just the pumpkin of the Tube. As I hurried to the station I pondered how a man with all the charisma of a traffic warden could have eight gorgeous women fawning over him, while I had absolutely no-one? Obviously his obscene wealth accounted for part of his appeal – and if this was the only reason he had a cohort of adoring women the poor guy was even worse off than me. At least I knew who my friends were, and on the remote chance that a man was interested in me, it was wasn't my bank balance that was attracting him.

I passed a pub with smokers outside chuffing on cigarettes underneath the hanging baskets. On a corner table a couple were smooching, their ardor for one another literally illuminated by the sodium glow of the street lights. Once more I felt a stab of loneliness and loss. As I got closer the man looked familiar, something about his dark curly hair got me right in the gut. I realised with horror that it was Jem, snuggling up to a woman of about twenty-five. I watched him stroke her caramel curls, a lot like my own hair used to be before I went *GI Jane*. He toyed with her fingers, just as he had done mine. I had a sudden, bitter revelation: it wasn't that Jem didn't find me attractive, he had simply made a rational choice and I had been vetoed on the basis of age. He had opted for the younger model, the one with a bigger stock of better quality eggs, thinner thighs and firmer breasts. He had chosen a girlfriend using the same criteria he might have applied to buying a car; faster, shinier, less miles on the clock, fewer previous owners.

My misery complete, I pulled off the wig. I heard someone behind me yelp in shock. I crossed the road and bowed my head as I passed the pub. I needn't have bothered, Jem only had eyes for Younger Me, and I was just another faded notch on his bedpost.

Chapter Twenty-Nine

King Dong

By the time July rolled around my hair had grown back to a pixie crop and so had Jojo's, despite her chemotherapy being in full swing. Jojo's hair looked like a chic 1920s finger wave, mine like the sensible short style of someone accepting the inevitability of middle age. I visited Jojo whenever I could during her sessions, mostly to help her alleviate the grinding boredom of three long hours attached to a drip. She tried to keep herself busy, researching fashion trends and staying in contact with her work online. Miraculously Mercedes, Jojo's hard-bitten boss, hadn't fired her, although that probably had more to do with statutory sick regulations than heart-felt concern. The woman hadn't even sent her a get-well card.

Jojo was making up her face when I arrived. She was applying Touche Éclat like it was going out of fashion and had gone full *Geordie Shore* with the bronzer. "How do I look?" she asked. She looked awful. Like a very ill person wearing a lot of makeup. "You look great," I said, hugging her. She was still exquisitely beautiful, hauntingly so now, the dark circles making her green her eyes all the more vivid, the afternoon sunshine spilling into the room creating a halo effect around her.

I sat down on the chair next to the bed and shoved my hand into a box of Milk Tray on the nightstand.

"What cheapskate bought you these?" I asked as I stuffed a caramel keg in my mouth.

Jojo smiled. "My grandma."

"Sorry," I said colouring up.

She laughed, "At least it was chocolate this time. Last week she presented me with a gift wrapped bag of scourers."

"Is she worried about MRSI?" I asked.

"No, she thought they were marshmallows. I think she's losing her marbles. She is ninety-six after all."

It struck me as terribly unfair that Jojo's grandmother, almost a centenarian, was very much alive, whereas my friend might not even make it to her fortieth birthday. It made me feel sad and panicky.

"Everything okay?" Jojo asked.

"Fine. Apart from the anonymous text," I said, eager to lighten the mood.

She wrinkled her nose mischievously, "Show and tell."

I located the message and threw the phone on the bed. A few days earlier I had received an unsolicited photo of a penis from a number that wasn't in my contacts. Jojo examined it squealing with delighted shock and zooming in for a closer look.

"Do you know who it's from?"

I shook my head, "I only have a phone number."

"Doesn't look familiar then?"

"Not without seeing who it's attached to," I said, "I mean they all look the same, don't they?"

"All men are *not* created equal," said Jojo marvelling at the photo. "This is a whopper."

"Yes, and I'm sure I'd remember that prize marrow," I said, the prospect both fascinating and terrifying.

With a naughty glint in her eye, Jojo asked, "Have you replied yet?"

"Yes. We're going to dinner next week."

Jojo squealed with excitement once more, "Really?"

It was reassuring that she was her old, sweetly naive self, as if her current state of health was just a blip and very soon we would be out on the town again, downing tequila slammers and commiserating with each other on our rubbish love lives.

"Of course," I continued, "Just me and the penis though. I'll see how we get on and then next time I might invite its owner."

Jojo poked her tongue out. "Well, I think that you should respond."

"You can't be serious?"

"Why not?" she shrugged, "What have you got to lose? Carpe diem."

I pulled a face.

"What?" Jojo asked innocently.

"I'm guessing it wasn't intended for me. And this guy is *definitely* a player. There's enough there to service an entire cheerleading squad."

"Could just be the angle. Or Photoshop," she said, matter-of-factly.

"True," I said acidly, "my brother managed to make Mum look like Joanna Lumley."

Jojo looked concerned. "How is all that?"

I shrugged. "Okay. I guess. Mum's deleted her profile, although she could be on any of the other gazillion geriatric dating websites aimed at parting the blue rinse brigade from their money."

"And their knickers," Jojo said. I laughed. "What about Patrick?" she asked.

I paused. "We haven't discussed it yet."

Jojo withheld comment but looked exasperated.

"I know, I know. But we never seem to catch each other." I had just offered her the same weak excuse that Dave had given me when I confronted him about not visiting Jojo.

She fidgeted with frustration, "Kat, you need to sort this out. Life's too short."

Her words trailed off and I was overcome with a massive wave of guilt for continuing a childish feud with my only sibling and bothering my very sick best friend with it.

I was thankful that Jojo quickly returned to the subject of the Unidentified Flying Penis. "Back to more important matters, your mystery admirer."

"Hardly an admirer," I said rolling my eyes.

"Maybe he's really nice?" she suggested. "Maybe it's fate? Maybe—"

I cut her off and retrieved my phone. "Maybe he's a pervert?"

She grabbed the phone again. "What if," she said slowly and deliberately, "he's The One?"

"Nah," I said flatly, "I don't believe in that anymore."

Jojo began frantically typing on my phone.

"Jojo!" I begged, "Please don't send him a text!"

She was adamant, "Sorry Kat, I'm doing this for your own good."

Resigned to her will I slumped further in the chair and shoved my hand back into the Milk Tray; my best friend had cancer, and if it made her happy I was willing to suffer the humiliation. And secretly I was as curious to locate the owner of the unknown willy as she was.

Jojo looked very pleased with herself. "And send. That ought to do the trick."

"Hang on a minute," I said mildly alarmed, "I thought you were going to show me what you'd written before you started sexting on my behalf?"

I was about to reclaim my phone when there was a "ping".

"See, Jojo knows best," she said smugly. Then she frowned as she read the reply.

"What did he say?" I asked, trying to keep the disappointment out of my voice.

"Nothing. It's your Mum. She's just made Rick Stein's apple tart."

"She probably is Rick Stein's apple tart," I said glumly.

The phoned pinged a second time and Jojo handed it back to me. "I wish she'd never got a mobile," I groaned, "she treats mine like an electronic ankle tag."

The message was from the owner of the willy. *Oops, wrong Kat. Or perhaps a happy accident? ;-) xx*

I gave Jojo a big smile and once more she grabbed the phone

and texted a reply at break-neck speed. There was the ping of another incoming message.

Jojo grinned wickedly. "Right, that's your Tuesday night s orted."

"Not possible," I said dismissively

"Why?"

"Apart from the fact I have no idea who the guy is, we do pizza at yours on Tuesdays."

"Well," she said plumping her pillow, "I'm giving you the night off." I protested but she cut me off, "You see me all the time. It's almost like *we're* in a relationship."

I felt a little stung, as if she was somehow rejecting me, but I knew Jojo was right. I was using her condition as a reason to avoid dating and now that I had some hair I was running out of excuses not to get back in the game.

Jojo put her hand on mine, "Kat, I'm the one with cancer. Life goes on. Promise me that you'll go on this date?"

"What if it turns out to be a disaster," I whined.

"What if it doesn't?" she responded reasonably.

"Okay," I sighed, "But if I end up in hospital with a prolapsed uterus I'm holding you personally responsible."

She laughed. "Perfect. We could be roommates."

"Slight problem though," I said scrolling through the messages, "I have no idea what his name is."

Jojo giggled. "Just give him a code name for now."

I created a new contact in my phone, *Random Cock Man*.

Secretly I hoped that it might be David The Stock Controller, although by the Rules According to Gropey no man genuinely interested in getting to know a woman would send an unsolicited photo of his genitalia as a prelude to a lifetime of love and commitment. As soon as I left Jojo I logged onto the dating site and sent Funny Boy an instant message, just to be sure.

I didn't happen to give you my phone number did I?

He responded immediately. *No! I wish you would! I was about to give up on you, thought you might have got it together with Defective Dave?*

God NO. ONLY a friend.

Well you know that song about friends turning into lovers...

NOT in this case. NEVER going to happen.

Well, that's good news for me. But I have to ask, if he cares about you enough to write you a profile maybe he fancies you?

I don't normally use acronyms, far too old, but LOLZ.

No spark?

If there was a spark it would be put out immediately by Dave spilling his pint. Or pissing on it.

Ah I see.

Not to mention his womanising.

Right...

And then there's the fact that he doesn't have a proper job.

What does he do?

Supposedly he's a stand up comedian.

Sounds more exciting than stock controlling. Any good?

He's okay. Doesn't really apply himself. I sometimes think the only reason he does it is because most of the gigs take place in pubs. Easier for him to indulge his binge-drinking addiction without ever admitting to having it.

Maybe we could go and see him perform together some time?

Going on a date to see Dave perform was just about the worst thing I could think of. But I didn't want to seem too stand offish.

Maybe. But not until you post a proper profile photo.

He logged off.

Chapter Thirty

Free Willy

I finally had a name to go with the penis – *Truly, Madly, Bradley 36. Graphics creator seeks gaming partner. Once bitten, twice shy – third time lucky? Or let's just enjoy the ride ;-)* Brad, as he liked to be called, turned out to be one of the respondents to Dave's version of my dating profile. I'd forgotten that we had even exchanged numbers; what with Jojo's diagnosis, Mum's extra marital activity, my hugely unsociable working hours, not to mention lack of hair, romance was the last thing on my mind. I had taken to deleting messages from the dating site without even reading them and was on the point of cancelling my subscription altogether. It was hard to believe how much life had changed in two short months.

I texted Dave, *Back in the game,* and I could almost hear him rubbing his hands with glee. *Two more and your ass is mine,* he replied.

Brad asked me if I wouldn't mind meeting near his flat in Crouch End as he worked from home and was facing a deadline. I offered to reschedule but he replied *You should always make time for fun ;-) xx* He suggested a neighbourhood bar that served organic finger food. I almost asked him if if we were actually meeting in a crèche, but kept a lid on my sarcasm. I chose a relaxed outfit; skinny jeans, fitted T shirt, navy blazer, which I thought was chic in a casual kind of way. I probably looked more like a second division footballer on a night out (even with the stilettos and clutch bag). Still, I'd had a blow dry to make the most of my short hair and was confident that if the place was lit dimly enough I could pull this off.

For once I was early. I installed myself at the bar and perused the menu while my credit cards panicked in chorus in my handbag.

191

"Bloody hell!" Visa gasped, "Bacalau sticks with tomato chutney, £9.50?!" Mastercard agreed, "Ten quid for three fish fingers and a dollop of ketchup. Priceless". American Express just whimpered and ordered a small white wine. I waited for nearly twenty minutes, trying not to look at my phone but checking it every ninety seconds or so anyway. No call, no text. How very rude, I thought as I finished my thimble-sized serving of wine. I tried not to let my disappointment show lest the staff work out that I had been stood up. As I was easing my buttocks off the bar stool and preparing to make a head-held-high exit Brad finally arrived. He looked frantic. And very hot indeed, both in that he had clearly been running and that he was scorchingly attractive in person. He rushed over to me, kissed me on the cheek and apologised profusely.

"Sorry," he gasped, "I get so caught up when I'm designing. I completely lost track of time." The idea of becoming consumed in the creative process was both attractive and familiar – I once got so involved in making a costume that I superglued it to my leg. We both quickly realised that we were pretty much wearing the same ensemble, though Brad's version was teamed with Oxfords and a satchel rather than heels and a clutch bag. My hair was almost the same colour and length as Brad's delightful sandy mop. We smirked at each other and I felt that killer combination of attraction, serendipity and humour.

"Nice outfit," he said.

"You have excellent taste yourself," I replied.

He laughed, a rich, hot chocolate kind of laugh.

"You're gorgeous," he said, undressing me with his big green twinkling eyes.

I felt myself blush with pleasure. "Stop it, you charmer."

He laughed again and I had to stop myself from slipping off the bar stool with delight.

"What do you want, babe?" he asked picking up the menu. "My treat."

My stomach did a little somersault when he called me "babe." It

192

had been a long time since anyone had called me that, except Dave and he didn't count.

"I don't want to take advantage," I protested briefly before selecting a smorgasbord of snacks. Brad insisted on ordering mojitos.

"Passé," he said as he sucked on a straw, "but bloody delicious."

I smiled through the brain freeze brought on by the crushed ice and agreed even though I had no idea that Latin American cocktails were now old hat. We laughed and talked and drank and fingered the organic finger food for about two hours. Noticing the clock above the bar Brad sighed.

"I could chat with you all night but I have to get back to work."

"A pity," I said, rather tipsy and swaying somewhat, "s'been lovely."

Brad's eyes danced mischievously. "It could go on being lovely for a bit longer if you like?"

I made a weak attempt at resistance. "Oh, no, I should probably let you get on."

"Sure you won't come back just for a bit?" he asked, stroking the nape of my neck, "I'd like to show you what I'm working on. And I've just decorated my flat. Let's see how similar our tastes are."

Was it my imagination or did he just say he wanted to see how compatible we were? My mind skipped off into a fantasy land where we were filling out our gift register, laughing when we simultaneously agreed on a Vera Wang for Wedgwood dinner service. I was wearing nothing but an Aran knit sweater (miraculously non-itchy) and a pair of plain-but-sexy white cotton knickers on my super-toned, tanned thighs. My hair was perfectly "un-done" in a top knot secured by a pencil, geek-chic glasses balanced on the end of my nose. He looked sublime in a grey marl sweatshirt and loose ripped jeans. Just when we were about to throw aside the to-do list and have pre-wedding sex for the tenth time that day I was shaken from my reverie, "Katie? Are you still with us?" I shook myself back to the present moment. Did he just call me Katie? My head was fuzzy and I felt a bit off balance. "My place then?" Brad asked.

Moments later we were walking along the street hand in hand. The cooler air was a welcome relief from the stuffy bar – and sobering enough for me to start asking myself exactly what I was doing. I was about to say I really ought to catch the last Tube when Brad kissed me. It was one of those grab-your-face-sweep-you-off-your-feet kind and I just melted. I threw the tipsy remnants of my conscience to the wind.

His flat was interiors-blog perfect, all hardwood floors and limited edition prints. I arranged myself on the sofa while he banged around in the kitchen. He returned with a bottle of champagne, strawberries and chocolate fondue that he just happened to have lying around. I began to feel sick, not so much from the booze but the realisation that this had all the trappings of a well-rehearsed one-night stand. Brad's sense of sexual entitlement galled me.

He was about to open the champagne (clearly not the only cork he intended popping) when I stopped him, using the "busy day tomorrow" line. Undeterred he said, "Okay babe. But you must try one of these." He dipped an enormous strawberry in the sticky fondue, somehow managing not to spill a drop of dark brown liquor on the white goatskin rug. He fed it to me and before I could get the whole thing in my mouth he began to nibble the other end, and then slurped the bits I had already chewed right out of my mouth. It turned me off more quickly than the fire brigade shutting down a condemned gas appliance.

"Everything okay babe?" he asked with bedroom eyes. "Babe" was really beginning to grate now. "Er, yeah," I replied slowly, trying to fill the vacant speech bubble hanging over my head with a plausible excuse, "I'm just not that keen on strawberries." I found myself telling an outrageous lie about my brother being allergic to strawberries as a child and breaking out into terrible, weeping hives. It worked a treat. "Jesus," he said pushing the bowl away, "Horrible. How come you didn't mention it sooner?" Before I knew it I was fabricating a whole swag of family allergies, according to which it was a miracle that we weren't confined to sterile biospheres like the boy in the bubble. Judging by the visible swelling in Brad's jeans I would be telling him about a latex allergy momentarily.

He pulled me towards him again and kissed the top of my head, "Bless you, babe," he said in a syrupy voice, "you need someone to take care of you." Good grief, I thought, this guy would promise the moon on a stick dipped in chocolate fondue if he thought it would get him laid. "You'd never guess you were so fragile looking at you," he added, making me feel like a heifer about to be inseminated by a prize bull. The bulge in his trousers was getting even larger and he started to undo his belt. "Hope you don't mind?" he said rhetorically, "It's just that I get so uncomfortable."

"I think I'm going to need that champagne after all," I said, unable to avert my eyes away from Brad's enormous bulge. It was beyond gigantic. He assumed a comic strip super-villain status to me now, no longer Brad but his evil alter-ego, "Anaconda Man." I wanted to ask if he had planning permission for such a large erection, I felt like I should be filling out a risk assessment and wearing a high vis jacket before I was allowed to go anywhere near it. At the very least it was a tripping hazard. Like a proud boy presenting his mummy with a drawing on the first day of school Anaconda Man showed me his condoms. "Super King, XL," he said puffing out his chest. Why did he have condoms in an ornamental dish in his living room? Couldn't he keep them out of sight gathering dust in a bedroom drawer like any other normal, sexually inadequate British person? Brad smiled at me and indicating his weapon of mass distraction he asked, "Do you want to touch it?" I did indeed, but only for purposes of scientific research. It had the same kind of attraction for me that live electric wires held when I was a kid; I knew that I was chancing certain death by going anywhere near it, but my curiosity was piqued. I had never seen such a massive todger in my whole life and I felt the need to verify that it was genuine in case the *Guinness Book of World Records* should ever get in touch.

Gingerly I stretched my hand towards the penile python. "Don't be shy," Anaconda Man cooed, "it doesn't bite, and neither do I –

unless you want me to?" I tried to echo his laugh but just sounded awkward. I reached my hand inside his pants and took hold of his penis at its base. I couldn't actually close my hand, so wide was the girth. He looked down admiringly at his equipment and kissed me. It was a nice kiss but entirely ruined when he opened his mouth, "Yeah, c'mon baby," he whispered breathlessly, sounding like the voice-break in a Nineties dance hit, "touch me. Slide your hand up and down my shaft." His penis became even harder, stood up even straighter, reminding me of one of those giant inflatable banana rides on the Med.

Maybe it was the unnecessary dialogue or the indulgent delight he was experiencing in viewing his own equipment, but I started to feel like an extra in a porn movie. Still, I couldn't quite get over my fascination with the sheer size of his underpants monster. It tapered away from a massive base to a smaller but still enormous end, the foreskin and head of it reminding me a of a roll-on deodorant bottle, although more traffic bollard in scale.

"So babe," he said, licking my lips as if they were an ice cream sandwich, "can we fuck now?"

I pulled my hand out of his pants immediately. "I don't think so."

"Jesus," he said, both confused and annoyed that I had declined the offer, "A blow-job then?"

"Absolutely not," I said as if he was trying to sell me double-glazing. Brad pulled away from me, anger in his face, disappointment in his pants, the anaconda shrinking to normal size.

"What the fuck?" he shouted. "You're not going to have sex with me at all?"

I backed away from him coolly and tried not to let my fear show.

"We were having a bit of sex, weren't we? We've kissed, I've held your ... thing"

He wasn't going to be dissuaded, "You fancy me, though?"

"You're gorgeous," I assured him, "and ... big?"

What was supposed to be an ego-boosting compliment came out as a question. He was not impressed.

"At least give me a wank?" he whined.

"No!" I snapped. It was starting to feel like a childhood argument with my little brother, which made things even weirder.

To my relief he pulled his jeans back on, huffing with frustration. While he undertook the genital equivalent of origami, folding and prodding his penis and scrotum back into his trousers I questioned his choice of skinny jeans. It was like he was trying to squeeze a sausage back into its skin. "Fucking prick tease," he said under his breath as he started zipping his jeans up. I was about to tell him that he shouldn't automatically expect my legs to part like the tomb doors in *Raiders Of The Lost Ark* just because he had a massive cock when he yelped in agony. He had miscalculated the trajectory of the zip and the re-stowage of his penis and scrotum. I once accidentally trod on a lap dog in a cafe in Paris and Brad's agonised squeal was eerily similar.

I stifled a laugh that his zipper had shown allegiance to me by sinking its teeth into his most treasured possession. I think I finally understood what Shakespeare was going on about. Brad had literally been hoisted by his own petard.

"Arghhh!" Brad cried in agony as I hovered in front of him not knowing what to do. His face was very red and he had tears in his eyes.

"Don't just stand there," he bellowed. "Do something!"

"What do you want me to do, exactly?" I asked.

Clutching onto the arm of the couch he gasped, "Scissors."

I repeated the word slowly as I imagined him freeing himself in the same manner as that rock climber who got his arm caught in a boulder in Colorado. Did he seriously intend to cut off his own penis?

"Where are they?" I asked hopelessly.

He looked like he was about to thump me. "Fucking bathroom fucking cabinet."

I went to the bathroom and was momentarily distracted by the cabinet's contents, full of high end face creams, from La Prairie gold serum (containing actual gold) to La Mer eye masks. I did a quick tally and worked out that the contents of his medicine chest cost more than my month's rent (which I still wasn't entirely caught up with).

A tortured yell came from the living room, "Have you fucking well found them yet?" screamed Brad. I opened a drawer and was met with an impressive array of hair brushes, tweezers and clippers neatly laid out as if for major surgery. I grabbed the first pair of scissors I could see and ran back into the living room.

"Not those," he screeched, "they're thinning blades."

I can only imagine the kind of pain he was in but his attitude was bringing out the Lorena Bobbitt in me.

"Which blades would you like, exactly?" I said with flaring nostrils.

Still clutching the arm of the sofa he gasped, "Nail scissors."

I went back into the bathroom and found the correct instruments. Holding them out like a surgical assistant I said, "Scissors. Nail cutting variety."

He looked at me in disbelief. "Well I can't do it."

I stared at him dumbly, "What do you mean?"

"Cut me out, for fuck's sake!'

I gulped. Although no longer drunk I would still have more than failed a breathalyser test, which suggested I should not be going anywhere near a fragile human appendage with a sharp object. Once more he groaned, "Karen, please!" On hearing that my disposition changed entirely. "My name is Kat. KAT. Now stand up," I hissed before cutting the entire crotch area out of his Givenchy jeans, the remnants falling limply around his ankles. "Sit down," I barked, and left him whimpering on the couch while I went into the kitchen in search of lubrication.

I returned with a jar of goose fat and wearing a pair of Marigolds. "What the fuck?" Brad shrieked. I ignored him and got to work greasing the zipper and his penis where I could. Then I began moving the zipper very slowly while at the same time easing the skin out of its metal teeth. He said "Jesus fucking Christ" a lot, but slowly and surely I freed willy.

"Should I go to A&E?" he asked, cupping his injured member.

Peeling the gloves off I said, "I really don't know. When was the last time you had a tetanus jab?"

"I have no idea," he replied regretfully.

I tossed the Marigolds on the floor. "Better to be safe than sorry. I'll call you a cab."

He now looked like his feelings as well as his crotch were very hurt indeed, "Aren't you coming with me?"

"I've had more than enough excitement for one evening," I said with an ironic little laugh. " Besides, I hear Casualty is an excellent place to pick-up, even midweek."

When the cab company finally answered the operator asked, "Any baggage?" Looking at my patient nursing his penis, I replied, "only emotional". Brad glared at me again. I went back to the kitchen in search of frozen peas but all I could find in the freezer was a bottle of Grey Goose vodka, so I wrapped it in a tea towel and dropped it in his lap.

"That should help with the swelling."

"It might numb the pain at least," he said unscrewing the top and taking a swig.

"I meant put the cold bottle on your cock, you cock."

I couldn't resist adding, "You could also pour some on the cut. Vodka's antiseptic."

He looked at me uncertainly, "Won't that sting?"

"Just a bit," I said soothingly, "but better than having your knob rot and drop off."

He poured vodka liberally onto his crotch and instantaneously let out a strangulated, "Mother fucker!" I watched the alcohol fizz white in the wound and I almost felt like blowing cooling air on it to calm the sting. Instead I picked up my clutch bag. "Your taxi will be here in five minutes. It's been... Interesting? Good luck."

Chapter Thirty-One

Plummy Mummy

The next morning I was sitting huddled in bed with an ancient copy of *Marie-Clare* and a cup of coffee, trying not to think about the previous night's disaster when Mum called to let me know that my cousin Wendy had just had another baby. "Isn't it marvellous,?" she gushed. "A little sister for Jake!" I bristled with irritation. I hadn't entirely forgiven Mum her online indiscretion and I certainly hadn't forgotten about her visit to the Palace of Plastic Perfection. Patrick still hadn't returned my calls, leaving me feeling like I didn't know the whole story.

"Great," I said with no enthusiasm at all. "Not the same as having my own grandchildren of course," she continued in a wistfully sad voice, "but nice to have some babies in the family, nonetheless." The last thing I needed at 9 a.m. after a particularly bizarre and rubbish date was to be made to feel even more inadequate by my libertine mother.

"Thanks a bunch," I said bitterly.

"I know you're doing your best," she replied mournfully. "Things just haven't worked out, have they?" If there was one thing my mother was adept at it was obvious understatements.

"Anyway, Mum," I said hastily, "gotta go. Busy day."

It wasn't a total lie. I was contemplating finally defrosting the fridge and was definitely going to change the duvet cover at some point. "Okay. But do call Wendy. She'd like to ask you something. Bye now."

She rang off before I could say goodbye. I wondered what Wendy, my glamorous, successful, slightly-older-but-suspiciously-younger-looking, cousin could possibly want from me?

Wendy and I had spent a lot of time together when we were children, farmed out to our grandparents during the long summer holidays. While Grandad pottered in his shed and Nana watched her daytime quiz shows Wendy and I were sent into the spare bedroom to play together. Wendy would construct elaborate make-believe games and I was expected to strictly comply. Any failure on my part would result in a spiteful twist to my ears or nose. Most of the scenarios consisted of playing house along the lines of a soap opera or rom com. Depending on Wendy's mood we would either be Julia Roberts and Richard Gere, or if she was feeling particularly vicious a warring couple from *Dallas*. I was always expected to take the male role, while Wendy swanned around in outfits raided from Nana's wardrobe. Invariably I would disappoint Wendy with my poor acting skills and lack of commitment to my role. One time she got so mad because I wouldn't slap her face and then kiss her that she threw one of Nana's shoes at the wall. Both flock wall paper and shoe were damaged beyond repair and somehow I was blamed for it all.

When Wendy hit puberty she delighted in showing me her padded bras and which pop stars she fancied in *Just Seventeen*. One Saturday afternoon when she was going through a Lenny Kravitz phase she decided to pierce my nose using a sewing needle and an ice cube. On hearing my ear piercing scream Grandpa walked into the bathroom to find blood trickling down my face and dripping onto the fluffy pink candlewick pedestal mat that always reminded me of a giant marshmallow. Once more it was my fault, having apparently begged Wendy to do it. I still carry the pockmark of Wendy's aggression to this day.

Wendy and I saw considerably less of each other after Nose Dive, save for the usual family gatherings of weddings, birthdays, Christmas and funerals. Every time I visited Nana and Grandad I would be updated on Wendy's progress, from her selection for the Junior England swim squad to the Double First in applied mathematics from Oxford. Photos of a determined Wendy in swim cap and goggles or looking particularly smug while receiving her degree crowded the shelves of my grandparents' wall unit. The only photo of me was as a seven year old hugging the Honey Monster.

Wendy had gone on to become the CEO of something or other and then married Giles, a stockbroker from a wealthy family with a minor title. They lived in a rambling Victorian villa in Clapham overlooking the Common, exactly the kind of house that I thought I ought to have ended up in. Wendy had impeccable taste – although she did hire one of the most exclusive designers in London to decorate her home, ensuring that it featured in *Tatler*. At their wedding I couldn't help noticing that our lot were somewhat further from the top table than the groom's clan, although I got the feeling this was more to do with Wendy than Giles. Try as she might, no amount of pedigree chumming could cleanse Wendy of her suburban beginnings.

I logged onto Facebook to snoop on Wendy's progress, forewarned being forearmed. There she was, lying in a hospital bed looking like she'd just had a blow dry and facial on a spa break, with a brand new baby in her arms. I felt an appalling stab of jealousy at her perfect life. More photos showed her four year old son Jake holding his sister, the expression on his face like Damien from *The Omen*. Then a shot of the whole family, Giles the handsome patriarch with his arms wrapped protectively around his wife and offspring.

Reluctantly I messaged. *Hi WenWen!*, I wrote, knowing how irritating she found her childhood nickname. *Congrats! It's a girl :) x*. She called me immediately.

"Thanks Katty," she purred, using her pet name for me, which I also hated. "Come and meet baby ASAP. There's something we need to ask you." I sensed unreasonable requests to babysit in the offing, which was extraordinarily bloody cheeky considering she hadn't been in touch for nearly a year. If I wasn't going to have kids of my own I was damned if I'd get lumbered with somebody else's.

"Kat?" she asked into the silence.

"Sorry. Shitty phone reception in my flat."

"Isn't it appalling?" she groaned. "Can't wait for 5G on The Common. Can you make lunch?"

"Erm, maybe. When?"

I heard her shout out to Giles. "Sunday?"

"*This* coming Sunday?" I asked, as if it was going to be a major inconvenience.

"I know it's short notice but there's nothing like seeing a baby straight out of the box."

"Er okay," I replied before I could think of a reasonable excuse to avoid perusing Wendy's freshly laid produce.

"Brilliant," Wendy said, "Shall we say two-thirty for three? Will you drive?"

"I don't have a car." She knew that.

"Never mind, G will pick you up."

I had no intention of letting Giles anywhere near the ghetto where my flat was located.

"No need. See you Sunday at three."

"Two-thirty for three," she corrected.

Why was I about to subject myself to this?

When I arrived at Wendy's one week later I was greeted by a miniature Buzz Lightyear at the door.

"What do you want?" he said displaying the impeccable manners taught by his £6000 a term prep school.

"Hello Jake," I said with all the emotion of HAL in *2001*, "is Mummy there please? I've come to see your sister."

He screwed his nose up as if I'd offered him a muffin made of dog poo.

"Muuuu-uuum," he bellowed, "there's a bald old lady at the door to see *her*."

Wendy appeared in the hallway, looking more super model than postpartum, flanked by Marie-Claude the au-pair who ushered Jake away. The child protested his impending exile in perfect French like a miniature Napoleon.

"Katty!" Wendy yelled as she flung her arms around me. "*Sooo* good to see you."

She held me at arms length and studied me for a few seconds. "Something's different about you. Have you lost weight?"

"Only on my head," I replied.

"Right. Hair cut. Of course. Teensy bit severe but actually really suits you. Easier to deal with than this unruly mop," she said, swinging her perfectly kept mane. "It's *such* a disaster."

My hand tingled with the desire to drag her onto the driveway by her lustrous locks.

"Come in and see the princess," she said, pulling me over the threshold. I felt like a hostage being yanked into a besieged bank.

I tripped over an assortment of cars and plastic weapons on the way into the drawing room where I discovered Giles holding the baby, feeding her from a bottle. He looked like a man head over heels in love. There it was again, that stab of disappointment and bitter envy in the hollow of my stomach, the feeling of emptiness for all the things I currently lacked and felt like I would never have. Not so much FOMO as AMO – Actually Missing Out.

"Not breast-feeding, then?" I asked as I sat down on the reconditioned antique couch. The question was directed as a joke to Giles. It went straight over Wendy's expensively highlighted head.

"I know, total slummy mummy," Wendy said, indicating her voluminous breasts, "but I only got these done last year."

"Well, you look amazing. No one would guess you'd just had a baby."

She winked, "Elective C Section. So much more convenient than leaving it up to Mother Nature."

Giles, who was burping the baby on his shoulder, glanced over the top of her tiny bald head at me, rolling his eyes, "Too posh to push," he said. I laughed. Despite being terribly plummy in a *Jeeves & Wooster* kind of way he was a genuinely nice guy. How Wendy landed him I will never know.

Wendy plucked the baby from Giles' shoulder and came towards me. I froze.

"Would Aunty Katty like a cuddle?"

Jake, who had been busy crayoning on the coffee table, sans paper, glared at me, "She's not my Aunty."

I saw Marie-Claude smirk at her clever ward, who already knew his genealogy.

"No Jakey, not officially," said Wendy – she was an only child, and Giles one of four brothers. "But Katty's the nearest thing you've got"

Wendy thrust the baby onto my chest before I could protest. The baby nuzzled my neck and I immediately relaxed. She smelled absolutely divine, a bundle of warm, pure new life demanding nothing but love and care. I could feel my eyes welling up. I gently stroked the baby's back and cleared my throat.

"What's her name?"

"Lulu," Wendy announced proudly. "We were thinking of Fifi, but Giles vetoed that because his grandmother had a Yorkie of the same name." I stifled a smirk at Wendy's pomposity.

We invited you here today," began Wendy grandly and adding a dramatic pause for effect, "because there's something we'd like to ask you."

I froze again. Wendy mistook it for delighted anticipation.

"Giles and I think it would be amazing for you to be an important part of our little girl's life and it's *such* a shame you missed out on children of your own. Katty, would you do us the honour of being Lulu's godmother?"

I could feel my mouth gaping while I processed the all-in-one insult and favour I had just been treated to.

"I don't know what to say," I lied. I stopped myself from adding, "*other than fuck off.*"

"Just say yes," Wendy said with a very insistent smile.

I swallowed. "Okay." Giles grinned. "Er, yes, I guess?"

Lulu toasted my acceptance by vomiting down the back of the only cashmere sweater I owned.

Chapter Thirty-Two

What's Up, Doc?

"I can't do it any more," I announced to Jojo one afternoon while I watched the drip, drip, drip of the chemotherapy slowly empty from the bag into her arm. It was August now; the weather was rubbish, I couldn't afford to take a holiday and Petite Paris was still full of uncontrollable stag and hen parties. If getting married was so great why did they all need to get so blind drunk in the lead up? I was losing my faith in everything.

"Do you mean The Sex?" Jojo asked, trying not to laugh.

"Chance would be a fine thing," I said bleakly. "My lady garden's gone total Gethsemane. It's going to take a miracle to remove the rock wedged in front of the cave. No, the online dating. I'm giving up."

"Noooooooooh," said Jojo, just like Charlton Heston on the beach in *Planet Of The Apes*. "You can't stop. You have to keep going for both of us. I'm dating by proxy."

"Poxy, more like. No one wants to come near me," I sighed, "and Mags needs me on five nights a week at the club. I won't have time, anyway."

"Then let me be your Svengali," Jojo said, opening her arms expansively so that the drip swung backwards and forwards at alarming angles.

"What?"

"Let me be your matchmaker," she explained.

"I really don't think that's a good idea after Anaconda man – not that I'm blaming you." She pulled her sad face, the one I couldn't say no to even before she got sick.

"Think of it as a team effort," she said thoughtfully. "Dave's written your profile, I'll do your admin. I'll preselect some guys and if you fancy them you go on a date, if not, what have you lost?" She had a point, but the whole idea seemed ludicrous. Jojo saw me wavering and pulled the sad face again.

"Come on," she cajoled, "I'm going out of my brains with boredom here. It'll give me something to do. You can be my pet project." I wasn't sure I liked the sound of that either, it made me feel like the school hamster about to be taken home for the holidays. But Jojo was right. I literally had nothing to lose. Except perhaps my dignity, and the presence of that had never been certain in the first place.

"Okay. On one condition."

"Name it," Jojo replied seriously.

"You let me vet all potential candidates before setting up any dates."

"I promise," she said holding out her little finger. We did a pinky shake and then Jojo whipped out her iPad and extracted all my personal dating data in under sixty seconds. She was wasted in fashion; counter intelligence would have been far more suitable. Thirty minutes later she had organised a date for me with a doctor.

I was surprised and delighted to find that my heart skipped a beat as Dr Dream Boat sailed across the tapas bar towards me a few days later. *What's Up Doc, 38. Medicine man seeks patient woman for nights at the theatre (non-surgical)* was literally tall, dark and handsome with a sparkle in his eye. I was already imagining what his bedside manner might be like and how beautiful our children would be. As soon as he saw me he waved and smiled in a friendly and ever so slightly flirty manner. I felt myself blush a little. He gave me a peck on the cheek and said warmly, "Hello you." And that was when it hit me. His halitosis was by far the worst I had ever experienced – it made Kieran of Kent seem minty-fresh by comparison.

Dr Death Breath was achingly attractive. He had thick, dark hair, slightly curly and greying at the sides and the darkest brown eyes

I'd ever seen, even darker than Jem's. His teeth were immaculate, straight and toothpaste commercial white. I definitely felt as if I was punching way above my weight – until he opened his mouth to speak. How had no one ever mentioned it to him? I had to concentrate hard to stop myself from physically recoiling.

I considered the possibility that it was my imagination and he didn't have bad breath at all. In which case I was having a major olfactory hallucination suggestive of a brain tumour. I wondered if he had a dental abscess that had somehow gone undetected in his otherwise perfect mouth? Or maybe he ate something very fragrant for lunch, like those people in Greenland who bury a dead gull and then dig it up to eat eighteen months later? "What would you like?" asked Dr Death Breath as we sat at the bar. I nearly said "surgical mask" but opted instead for a glass of white wine, extra large. In this situation it seemed like the only solution.

I was served at least a third of a bottle in an enormous balloon-shaped glass which dwarfed me. I disappeared up to my eyes in the enormous vessel, desperate to anaesthetize my sense of smell. When I resurfaced Dr Death Breath was stifling a laugh, smiling at me warmly. I felt my stomach flip over, this time in a good way. This beautiful man with horrendous breath was looking at me with something that resembled affection. I could feel myself warming at the edges. How, I asked myself, could my stomach be churning and back-flipping all at the same time? I quaffed the wine in one go.

"Hard day?" he asked nodding at the empty glass.

"Just thirsty," I said. He ordered a whole bottle of wine, topping me up and pouring himself a large glass.

"Great to meet you, Kat," he said tapping my glass with his.

I flushed and recoiled all over again. We asked for some menus and I broke my first-date rule of never ordering stinky food. I went straight for the chilli and garlic prawns with aioli.

"A brave choice," he said, stealing a prawn and dunking it in the pungent dip. Under the circumstances the only choice, I thought.

Dr Death Breath, real name Damien, was genuinely funny, regaling me with tale after tale of life in emergency medicine. I managed to cope with his stench by breathing through my mouth and gulping wine at regular intervals. Every time the bottle was empty Damien ordered another. The conversation and alcohol flowed and, breath aside, I was really enjoying myself – until the room began to spin and I suddenly felt violently sick.

Damien took my hand. "Are you okay?" he asked, looking closely at my pupils and breathing right in my face. I nearly fell off my bar stool.

"I'm sorry," I said slurring and feeling embarrassed, "I think I might be drunk."

"You're still lovely," he said, stroking my arms and sending shivers of pleasure through my body, in spite of the feeling of acid rising in my gut.

"The patient appears to be intoxicated and in need of resuscitation," Damien said looking at his watch. "Time twenty-two fifteen. Commencing kiss of life."

All I remembered was the suffocating waft of his breath, swaying to and fro, and then blackness. I had flashbacks of being picked up from the floor, bundled into a taxi, and then tucked up on a sofa with a large glass of water swimming on the coffee table before me. When I woke up the next morning Damien had left me a note on the table under a vase full of fresh flowers. It was written in an elegant, grown-up script, not the block capitals I was used to from Rob: *Didn't want to wake you. You looked so … "peaceful"?! Coffee on stove, food in fridge, spare key in cookie jar. Come and go as you please – or stay :) Damien xxx*

I blinked at the note and felt a monumental shift within myself, my heart lifting like a hot air balloon. It had been a long time since I had got totally wasted in the presence of a straight, single man and he hadn't tried to get into my pants. And it had been even longer since anyone with a romantic interest in me had put three kisses and genuinely meant it. At the bottom of the note he had added:

PS. You'll meet She Who Must Be Obeyed. Don't take it personally if she's a bit offish, she's really very sweet when you get to know her xxx. I was a little concerned about this new development. Did Damien have a flatmate? Or even worse did he live with his mother? I was sure he hadn't mentioned it the night before – although I had been so blind drunk I didn't remember very much at all.

I heard something rattle and my heart leap into my mouth as I realised that I was not alone in Damien's flat. I unfroze a few moments later when a blue-grey Siamese cat appeared and jumped up onto the sofa. She meowed, nuzzling her chin on my hand and stared at me hypnotically with freakishly blue eyes. For a moment I thought it was Jojo's cat Widget. I looked at the tag hanging from her diamanté collar. "Sheba," I said out loud, "Queen Of Everything, no doubt." She looked at me regally, stretched and then put her arse straight in my face before slinking out of the room as if I didn't even exist. I heard the cat flap swing and bang shut. It felt like a judgement.

I dragged myself up, catching sight of myself in the mirror above the fireplace. My hair was matted and flat on one side, sticking up madly on the other and my eye makeup was now mostly on my cheeks. A white trail of dry saliva outlined my mouth. I was still wearing my underwear but my clothes had been replaced by a man's T shirt. I momentarily wondered if Damien and I had sex, but quickly dismissed the thought. There was definitely nothing sinister about him, save for his breath, and I was more concerned that he had seen me in such an awful state – and knew that I wore tummy control pants.

With my head pounding and a feeling of battery acid in the back of my throat I went in search of the bathroom. No sooner had I pulled my pants down to pee than I was on my hands and knees bidding farewell to the remainder of last night's prawns. I panicked when I realised that I had managed to spray the pristine white bath mat with vomit. I heard a padding behind me and Sheba reappeared in the doorway, sniffing the air. "And you can sod off," I said, as I vomited once more. Sheba sidled up to me and then started licking up my vomit from the bathmat, purring contentedly. I looked at her in utter disgust. At least the bath mat was being cleaned in an environmentally sustainable manner. Sheba rolled onto her back, looking at me expectantly. Despite still feeling bilious I tickled her belly and she jabbed at me playfully. Then without warning she sank two sets of razor sharp claws into my hand and bit me. "Fucking cat!" I yelped in pain and she shot off again. "When I get pregnant you'll have to go," I shouted after her, "toxoplasmosis risk."

I grabbed a fluffy White Company robe from the bathroom door, and turned on the taps of the enormous claw foot tub. Everything was so serene and uncluttered. On a shelf above the sink I found some hideously expensive Jo Malone bath soak which I glugged liberally into the tub. There was nothing with which to remove my stale makeup so I found my way to the kitchen in search of oil, lard or any non-abrasive cleaning product.

Damien's cupboards were packed with jars from Fortnum and Masons. There was a box of real truffles, the kind that cost a week's wages and can only be found by specially trained pigs. I found a bottle of sesame oil and rubbed a palmful into my skin. The pleasantly warm sensation quickly became unbearable and my eyes began to stream. I grabbed the bottle and through my tears read *Contains Scotch Bonnet chilli*. I felt as if someone had barbecued my face. Half-blinded I stumbled around the kitchen until I found the sink. I ran the cold tap at full pelt, cool water bringing sweet relief and wiped off the remaining grease with a tea towel.

I was on my way back to the bathroom but I couldn't resist the lure of the door ajar to my right. I reasoned that Damien would have shut it properly if it was truly private. I pushed the door open to find Sheba sitting centre-stage in the middle of the bed, licking her fur. She stopped dead when she saw me, narrowed her eyes, and then went back to cleaning her vulva, hind legs behind her ears like a feline centrefold. I don't know why I felt the need to explain myself to a cat. "Just looking for something, thought it might be in here," I said. I opened the wardrobe doors to find a neat display of colour coded shirts, suits and ties. All of his footwear, even trainers, uniformly blossomed on shoe trees, his belts coiled tight like a nest of black and brown cobras in their wicker basket. On the shelves above the rails were precisely stacked file boxes, all clearly labelled. I made a mental note of their order and then took the boxes down one by one and set them next to the bed.

Sheba stopped preening herself and looked at me accusingly. "What?" I said. She stood up, arching her back and flicking her tail at me, then jumped off the bed and sloped out of the bedroom. Undeterred, I picked up a box labelled UNI DAYS. Inside I found Damien's degree certificates, assorted knickknacks and lots of photographs. Many featured a stunning, ice cool blonde. For a moment I thought it was Ludmilla, they could have more than passed for sisters. I guessed that this ice queen was Sheba's former mistress, there was something familiar in the piercing blue eyes and look of absolute superiority that they both shared, an attitude of genetic superiority that only the truly beautiful can pull off convincingly.

I found nothing to set my alarm bells ringing. In fact it was all rather normal, sane and charming. There were childhood pictures of Damien playing sport, winning competitions, in fancy dress and photos taken with friends, elderly relatives and a stylish, elegant lady I presumed must be his mother. The only thing missing seemed to be his dad. I found myself daydreaming about my new mother-in-law, shopping for my wedding dress, a fantasy that my imagination then ruined by having my own mother show up, unannounced and uninvited, with a long-haired internet lover in tow. sporting leather pants and a gold tooth.

I was re-stowing the boxes, conscientiously lining up the edges of each as precisely as I had found them, when I became aware of the sound of running water. I smiled, thinking that there must be a patio somewhere with a water feature. I imagined some kind of

Buddha sat on a lotus flower, spiritual and tasteful, in the garden. I realised with horror that the delightful trickling noise was in fact coming from the bathroom. I had left the taps running.

I sprinted into the bathroom like Gene Hackman in *The Poseidon Adventure*. I had left the cap off of the Jo Malone and the cat had knocked it over. The entire thing was empty. But wasting fifty quid's worth of bath oil was the least of my problems. The tub was overflowing, the rug was soaking wet, so was the rest of the floor. I turned off the taps as quickly as I could. And that's when I saw it, floating in the bathwater like a thin black enemy submarine – a long stick of poop. I heard the cat flap bang again as my nemesis made her escape. We were now officially at war.

Chapter Thirty-Three

Friends

I cleaned up the flood damage as best I could. After chasing Sheba's little gift around with a pair of barbecue tongs and a soup ladle I finally admitted defeat and plunged my bare hands into the bath, gagging as I fished out the cat crap. I wrung out the bath mats and then screwed the lid back on the Jo Malone, hoping that Damien somehow wouldn't notice a completely empty bottle.

The cat flap clunked again. I walked into the kitchen to find Sheba face down in her food bowl. When she had cleared it she prowled over to me, curling herself around my legs and purring. She stood up on her hind legs and paddled my shins with her front paws, not a claw in sight, like the perfectly behaved pussy in a cat food commercial. I rifled through the cupboards until I found a box of Cat Crunchies. I shook the box temptingly and Sheba began to purr loudly, madly rubbing her chin on my leg, then a table leg and a chair leg. When the table and chair proved unresponsive she came back to me.

Sheba shoved her head into the bowl while I was still pouring the food and one of the little fish-shaped snacks got stuck in her ear. She shook her head irritably and then resumed her gorging. I stroked her neck and she flicked her tail. I should have known to stop right then. Instead I ran my hand along her sleek back, determined that she would a) love me, and b) know that I was her new mistress. Sheba had other ideas. She ducked her head and lashed out, scratching my hand once more. "Little bitch," I yelped. The cat completely ignored me and went back to munching and crunching. It was painfully clear who had the upper paw.

Sheba aside, it was tempting to stay in Damien's beautiful flat all day but I had absolutely nothing with me; no clean underwear and it would take more than the dab of concealer and slick of lipgloss I had in my handbag to repair my face. I began to write Damien a note. *Thanks so much. Had slight accident in bathroom. Sorry. See you later?* My hand hovered over the paper. Should I write, *From Kat*? That seemed a bit stand-offish. Or *Love Kat*? No, that was a Cure song. *Love from Kat*? Too much like a Birthday card. Eventually I settled on an affectionate but unassuming *Kat x*.

When I got halfway down the road I began to regret the question mark after *See you later?* Did it sound too pushy, a bit clingy? Then again, maybe only one 'x' after my name seemed chummy rather than romantic? Since I hadn't taken the spare key it was too late to change the note and besides, once Damien discovered his sopping wet bathroom, depleted luxury bath soak and over-fed cat I doubted that I'd ever hear from him again.

I went home. I texted JoJo, *Definitely maybe :) xx*. I texted Dave, *Possibly 2-0 to you xx*. I shoved dirty pieces of costume into the washing machine, wilfully ignoring the "DRY CLEAN ONLY" labels. I made a cup of tea. I looked at my grubby windows and thought that I really must get around to doing them some time. I knew I never would. I checked my e-mails.

There were notifications of messages from the dating site. I could only retrieve them by logging back in. But if Damien logged on he would see that I'd signed in too and what kind of message would that send? Then again, if he had signed in did it mean he was already checking on me (worryingly controlling) or was he still hedging his bets with other prospects (disappointing)? I was in that no-woman's land, the early days of a relationship when you're not sure if you're even in a relationship. Just as I was wondering if Damien was going to be my boyfriend, my phone pinged, *How are u KitKat? Busy tonight? Few friends over for dinner. Please join us if u can. D xxx* My heart leapt for joy. Three kisses was good. And he wanted to see me again. Tonight. And he wanted me to meet his friends. I'd deal with the breath issue later.

I spent all afternoon trying to find the perfect "casual dinner party" outfit. A dress seemed too dressy, but jeans felt too underdressed. I tried on a crisp white shirt with a pair of plain black trousers and realised I looked like a waiter. I swapped the shirt for a different colour but this gave the impression that I was about to give a Power Point presentation. I went back to my go-to outfit; dark skinny jeans, blouse and blazer. Smart, casual, boring and inoffensive, something to please everyone: the pressure of a second date and being introduced to Damien's circle was immense.

When Damien opened the door later that evening he was holding the soup ladle that I had used as a pooper scoop earlier that day. With his free hand he reached around me, gently pressing into the small of my back as he pulled me towards him, and kissed me on the lips. He was handsome. He was sexy. His breath was still awful.

I followed him through to the kitchen where all sorts of pots and pans were bubbling on the stove.

"I hope you don't mind Japanese," he said.

"I can't stand Japanese. What they do to whales is appalling." Damien looked worried.

"I'm kidding," I said tickling his ribs for emphasis, "I love Japanese." Damien nodded, as if he was getting the measure of me. I looked at the table where a dazzling array of sushi and sashimi had already been prepared. Damien retrieved the ladle from the soup pot. A long dark sliver of shiitake mushroom glistened on it, the exact colour and dimensions of Sheba's poo.

"Tell me what you think," he said pushing the slimy offering towards my mouth.

"Mmmm, delicious," I said trying not to gag.

Feeling compelled to confess I began, "Erm, we had a little accident earlier.."

Damien gave a wry smile. "Sheba?"

"How did you guess?"

"Happens all the time," he replied. "Basically this is Sheba's house and she lets me live here."

"You really are a cat person," I said, trying not to be peeved.

He pulled me towards him and kissed my nose, "I am now."

I cringed at the comment. I had no idea why. Apart from his breath he was perfect. The voice of reason, which sounded eerily like my mother, told me I was being ridiculous. I ought to at least give him a chance. I ran my hands down his muscular back and pressed into him.

"I guess that makes me a doc person," I said. He looked deep into my eyes and I felt my pulse quicken. Maybe it was all going to be okay, and with Damien weak at the knees I saw an opportunity to have one over on Sheba.

"I shouldn't have left the lid off the bottle, but I only turned my back for a minute. I'll replace it, of course." I was desperately hoping he wouldn't take me up on the offer. I barely had enough to buy a bar of Imperial Leather.

"Don't worry about it. Reminds me of my ex anyway. I prefer Radox to be honest." I was delighted.

"You had me at Alpine Meadow," I said, channelling my best rom com heroine.

He put his hands on my shoulders and pulled me into him and this time he kissed me properly, a full on oral assault complete with tongue. To my great relief once our mouths were connected I couldn't smell his breath. He was amazing kisser and I definitely got the tingle.

Just as we were hitting our stride the doorbell rang. "Bugger," Damien said. "Shall I send them away?"

"Yes," I replied, "unless they really are your friends?"

"Well one of them is my sister, so I guess I better not," and off he went to open the door.

I froze on the spot, trying to process what Damien had just told me. Moments later Damien returned with a very pretty, female version of himself.

"Kat, this is my big sister, Nat. Nat, meet Kat. Blimey, that's going to get confusing." Nat extended her hand to me with a big smile. The doorbell rang again and then everyone seemed to arrive at once. There was Simon, an architect and Damien's best friend from childhood, whom I recognised from the photos, and his wife, "Jennyfer, with a 'Y'", an interior designer. Raj, Damien's squash partner and fellow consultant at the hospital, showed up moments later. This was going to be awkward. How was Damien going to introduce me? Was he going to tell everyone how we met? And what the hell was I going to talk to these proper adults about for the next three hours? I doubted very much that any of them shared my Netflix addiction.

As it turned out nobody pried into how I came to be there. Everyone was warm and funny, especially Nat, who made sure my glass was topped up all night. It felt like she was oiling me so I'd let slip how I met her brother but I liked her anyway. I discovered that she had run her own political consultancy but two kids and one divorce later she was a happily single stay-at-home mum who did all her own baking and grew organic vegetables. She was a fair bit older than Damien, but one of those women who make wrinkles look sexy. She was effortlessly stylish; barefaced apart from a flick of cat-eye liner and lipgloss, expensively torn jeans and Chanel loafers, without a trace of garden dirt under her perfectly manicured beige nails, a cross between Anna Wintour and Barbara from *The Good Life*.

Raj was also single and divorced with two kids. When Nat and I cleared the table and were alone in the kitchen she expressed her disgruntlement while I loaded the dishwasher.

"Damien's such a busy body, trying to set me up with Raj."

"Not interested in his Taj?" I asked. Nat laughed.

"Don't get me wrong, Raj is gorgeous. But I don't need my little brother to sort out my love life. He has enough trouble with his own."

I did my best not to take her remark personally and carried on stacking bowls, trying not to lose chopsticks in the bottom of the dishwasher.

"Sorry, that came out wrong. It's just that Damien's ex was a bit of a psycho. Have you met Sheba?" I nodded grimly.

"Sheba was Saffron's cat," Nat continued, "a birthday present from Damien. When they broke up Saf moved out and left the cat, saying Damien could have custody. Like mother, like daughter, you could say."

It was beginning to make perfect sense. The cat was her mistress' succubus, preying on all Damien's future girlfriends, hellbent on making their lives miserable. It felt like whatever happened between Damien and I the spectre of Saffron would hang over our relationship as long as Sheba was alive. I wondered if the day would come when I would have to make him choose between this Kat or that cat.

"I hope I haven't spoken out of turn?" Nat said, looking worried, "Because I reckon you're just what the doctor ordered for my brother." I felt a little flush of pride and acceptance.

We went back to the dining room. I took the plates and forks, followed by Nat carrying an enormous tiramisu she had made that afternoon. "I even baked my own lady fingers," she said with a naughty wink as she put the dessert on the table. Easy laughter rippled warmly around the table. As we dug into dessert Simon suggested a game of "Truth Or Bollocks". Jennyfer with a "Y" groaned. Apparently it was a tradition for everyone to tell an after-dinner story and the other guests had to guess if it was true or false. Nat told the tale of a former client, a well-known politician who had a penchant for ladies underwear, despite having consistently voted against LGBTQ+ rights. When it came to true or false she said that she couldn't possibly divulge that information. I described how I had been peed on by an elephant at a safari park when I was ten. Damien guessed that it was true. He then related the sad event of a man who arrived at A&E cupping his penis after it had got caught in his fly. "The poor sod poured vodka on it," Damien said, "because his girlfriend said that it would sterilise the wound. What a cock!" Everyone agreed that the man was a total cock and said the story was too ridiculous to be anything other than true. Except me. I said I couldn't possibly imagine his "girlfriend" being so stupid or cruel.

Chapter Thirty-Four

Actual Boyfriend

After everybody left Damien and I cuddled up on the sofa. I snuggled into his armpit, which smelled surprisingly good (better than his breath, anyway).

"They really liked you," he said, kissing the top of my head.

"Do you think so?" I asked trying to sound humble but glowing with girlfriend-material pride. He held me tighter and stroked the back of my neck.

"Yep I do. It's important. My friends are everything to me. I don't have much in the way of family."

I prayed that my cheeks were not flushing from the guilt of my earlier snooping but fortunately from his vantage point all Damien could see was my cleavage – ample distraction. He proceeded to tell me about his childhood. He didn't have any siblings and Simon had always been like a brother to him, having met at nursery school. Damien's Dad had died when he was six and his mother never remarried.

"He was the love of her life," said Damien, longingly. "She never found anyone else to come close." It was tragic and romantic and I wondered if Damien took after his mother. I gave him a brief outline of my family and friends, omitting Jojo's illness. It all seemed too weird, telling my new boyfriend the doctor, about my best friend, the cancer patient. I was terrified that he might start talking about prognoses and "possible outcomes". I wanted a night's respite from worrying if my best friend was still going to be here next Christmas. I wanted to forget all the other stuff too; my ex-husband, my sexually rampant mother, and the fact that I was never going to be a star of stage and screen. I wasn't lusting after a fairy tale – I'd outgrown those dreams after Rob bought me a wet 'n' dry vacuum cleaner for our first anniversary and he failed to notice the single tear of disappointment roll down my cheek as he demonstrated the machine's turbo suction – but just for a moment I wanted to feel young and full of potential again, hopeful and unjaded.

"Penny Forman?" asked Damien.

"Who's that?" I asked.

"Penny for them?" he repeated, laughing. "I know doctors are renowned for shocking handwriting but I didn't realise it extended to our diction."

"From where I'm sitting your diction seems to be in perfect working order," I said, and instantly regretted making such a cheap crack. Damien didn't notice. His hand strayed to my collar bone, pausing at the clavicle from where it was perfectly poised to launch a full-scale assault on my breasts. Annoyingly Dave's face appeared in my mind, disembodied like one of the heads in Queen's "Bohemian Rhapsody" video. "Three dates, Kat," he said, shaking all four of his heads disparagingly before fading to black.

This was going to be awkward. I'd just given Damien an obvious come-on and now I was going to have to pull my metaphorical knickers back up. I pushed the Three Date Rule Emergency Panic Button.

"It's getting late," I said, wriggling away, "better go."

"Or you could just stay the night?" Damien murmured into my hair. Dave popped into my head again, waving his arms madly as if trying to stop me from running into the path of an oncoming locomotive in a silent movie.

"That's sweet," I said, "but I have an early start tomorrow." It was almost true – I had eighteenth months worth of receipts stuffed into two shoe boxes that desperately needed sorting before I got another fine for filing my tax return late.

Damien didn't press me any further. "Can I walk you to the station?"

"You can definitely do that," I said as I stood up and grabbed my bag.

It was a beautiful summer's night. Damien slipped his hand into mine as we strolled and my stomach flipped. He paused by a particularly lovely brick wall, down which tumbled white dog roses. He pulled me into a bower made by the overhanging flowers and pressed me up against the wall, the bricks still warm from the day's sun, adding to the sensation of heat rising in my body. It was as if we were disappearing into an erotic, secret garden, the scent of jasmine banishing that of his breath. Until I became aware of something in my hair. I felt it tiptoe across my forehead and disappear down the back of my blouse. Flailing madly I barged past Damien, taking half the roses with me. I jumped up and down as if undergoing exorcism. When I thought I'd managed to shake the spider out of my blouse I felt it crawl into my bum cleavage. Damien just stared at me.

"I'm really sorry," I said, unzipping my jeans. I was mortified that this was how Damien would be seeing my bottom for the first time. I bitterly regretted wearing a thong to avoid visible panty line in my skinny jeans because now anyone who happened to be in the vicinity was treated to my full moon. "I'm terrified of spiders," I gasped while I shook my buttocks. A car honked its approval at my impromptu twerking display, and then something plopped onto the pavement. I pulled up my jeans and breathed a sigh of relief. Damien was literally agog.

I smiled bashfully. "I've been like this ever since I watched a documentary called *The World's Most Dangerous Creepy Crawlies*. One woman was loofahing in the shower and hundreds of baby spiders crawled out of her shoulder."

"Well then," Damien said bending over and picking up the offending insect, "lucky for you this is a twig." I hadn't been this embarrassed since I unexpectedly got my period while wearing white shorts on a flight home from Majorca. I wiggled back into my jeans, my cheeks burning with embarrassment. Damien put the twig thoughtfully in his pocket and pulled me towards him, a huge grin on his face.

"You are absolutely one in a million," he said, and kissed me again, a big *Love Actually* style show-stopper right in the middle of the street. "And the quirkiest woman I've ever met," he added.

"Bloody hell," I said, trying to recover my composure, "didn't you say you worked in the psychiatric wing of a maximum security prison for a while?"

He laughed again, so warm and genuine. "Don't change. I love it." He hadn't said he loved me. But he had used the "L" word in connection with my personality and the way he looked at me left no doubt that his interest was more than purely physical. It was unexpected, exhilarating and absolutely terrifying.

Chapter Thirty-Five

D–Day

I dropped in on Jojo during her chemo session at the hospital the next day. It had become something of a ritual; once we used to discuss our latest personal disasters over a bottle of wine, now we did it over a cocktail of chemicals. "Tell me *all* about it," she said eagerly. I told her about Sheba, Nat, Damien's flat, the sparkling friends, the terrifying coincidence with Anaconda Man, I talked about everything – except Damien himself.

"What's wrong?" Jojo asked.

"Nothing," I said. I wasn't being cagey or evasive. Nothing was wrong, really. I felt uneasy, and it wasn't Damien's breath making me uncomfortable. It was something altogether more subtle and harder to identify.

"Maybe I'm a bit nervous," I shrugged. "We're coming up to date three."

"Ah," Jojo said with gravitas. "The big one."

"Let's hope so," I replied, "But am I supposed to have sex on this date or *after* the third date?"

"I wouldn't worry about the detail too much. Do what feels right."

Jojo had struck the nail on the head. Something wasn't quite right. But Damien was the first decent man I had met in such a long time, perhaps ever. Jojo put it down to "opening night nerves". I desperately wanted her to be right and when I got home from the hospital I texted Damien immediately inviting him to my flat for dinner. If the mould in the bathroom, the mess under the bed and my woeful cooking skills didn't put him off, nothing would.

When Damien arrived ten minutes early later that evening both me and the kitchen were in a state of thermo nuclear meltdown. The chocolate soufflé had collapsed, the pasta sauce was burnt to the pan and the green salad had wilted to a warm sludge after I had put it on the stovetop and forgot about it. This, I thought, is why the universe won't allow me to have children.

"Who are we having for dinner?" Damien asked as I opened the front door. He wiped a streak of blood-red sauce from my forehead, checking its consistency and then pulled me towards him for a kiss. I backed away, hot and irritated.

"Hey," he said calmly, "everything okay?"

"Yep," I said, flustered, "Come through to the kitchen. Steel yourself. It's like *Come Die With Me* through there."

For a moment Damien stood in stunned silence looking at the mess like he was surveying a war zone, assessing whom to triage first. Then he smiled and wrapped his arms around me.

"Oh Kit-Kat," he said looking deep into my eyes and making me melt. "Maybe leave the cooking to me in future? And the cleaning?" I boxed him with an oven glove but I was delighted. He said "future". Then he kissed me again and it all got very passionate very quickly in a European Art House movie kind of way, like the montage from *Delicatessen*; we pulled each other's clothes off in between hugely passionate kisses, he popped on a condom and slipped inside me and the kitchen table rocked and banged against the wall, as the pasta bubbled on the stove. We were just hitting our stride when the oven timer went off.

"Hadn't you better check that?" he panted, and manoeuvred our beast with two backs over to the stove. Oven glove in one hand, his buttock in the other, I took a cursory glance at the soufflé. It now resembled a meteor crash site.

"Not ready yet," I panted. "So close. Keep going."

But the magic of the moment had gone. I felt him go soft inside me and then his penis slid out of me like a shy garden worm.

"Sorry," he said.

I smiled and kissed him, "There are other ways to have fun." I pulled off the condom and it flew out of my hands, sticking to the tiles above the hob like a piece of cooked spaghetti.

"Well, at least that seems to be done," he laughed.

I dropped to my knees in front of him. "Let's see how al dente you are," I said, feeling like Kim Basinger in *Nine And A Half Weeks*. I was about to put him in my mouth when he stepped back, horrified. "Terribly unhygienic. Let me freshen up," and he disappeared into the bathroom.

It was like someone had flicked the "off" switch between my legs. Admittedly latex-flavoured willy was not the most appetising entree to a night of erotic pleasure but I was willing to suck it and see. And I found the implication that my vagina was somehow tainted rather offensive. I had spent ages manicuring my ornamental border and spritzed what was left of my bush with Chanel No5 and Damien was turning his nose up at it. Literally. By the time he came back from the bathroom I had put on my pyjamas and was scraping the smouldering remnants of dinner into the bin. "Never mind," he said pulling out his phone. "I have Deliveroo on speed-dial."

We ate pizza and drank beer while watching *When Harry Met Sally* in bed, his suggestion. When Meg Ryan started faking an orgasm in a New York deli I thought "I'll have what she's having, too." After we turned the lights out I wrapped myself languidly around Damien, eager for a second attempt.

"Sorry," he said yawning, "early shift tomorrow. It's the school holidays, which means no end of kids will have superglued toys to various parts of their anatomy. Can we just cuddle?"

"Of course we can," I said, trying to disguise the disappointment in my voice while wondering where I'd hidden my vibrator. Damien insisted on holding me all night. I felt like a Jack Russell trapped under the paw of an overly affectionate Great Dane, Damien's breath hot, damp and doggy in my hair. I spent a long time staring into the darkness trying to convince myself that this was better than sleeping alone.

Damien woke early the next morning and I was full of anticipation. He stroked my limbs giving me multiple goosebumps. I turned to kiss him but he rolled me over on my front instead and gave me a full body massage. He told me I had impressive gluteal folds which I think this was a nice way of saying I have a fat arse. I shuddered at the way my cellulite must have looked as he kneaded my thighs. I waited expectantly for the physiotherapy to become more sensual, but it never happened. He kissed my forehead and then jumped in the shower. "Call you later Kit-Kat," he shouted as he left. He already had a pet name for me. It made my skin crawl.

Later that morning Damien texted, *Had a lovely evening. Are you busy tonight? xxx* The message filled me with dread. Our failure to make successful sexual union had magnified all the niggling doubts that had been whirring in my mind since the beginning. I left it for a couple of hours before replying, *Would love to but have to work :(x.* I needed some time out.

Chapter Thirty-Six

Stick or Twist

I was completely confused. Damien was a great guy, but it felt like everything was moving way too fast. I barely knew him and already he was introducing me to his nearest and dearest. Then there was the intimacy issue – or lack of. I wasn't a nymphomaniac by any stretch of the imagination but it seemed to me that sex ought to be one of the easiest things at the start of a romance and already we were having a problem. If sex is the glue in a relationship we were prematurely coming unstuck and I'd only just seen his Pritt Stick.

I explained all this to Jojo while microwaving a lasagne, having promised her a "home-cooked meal" in the comfort of her own flat. While we waited for the molten hot food to return to solid form Jojo wrestled with my problem.

"Intervention," she said plainly.

"What?" I asked, balking at her American psycho babble.

"We've created the situation collectively – Bil and Ben bought you the website subscription, Dave wrote the profile, I set up the date – shouldn't we resolve it the same way?"

It was both a terrible and brilliant idea; terrible because I didn't like the thought of having such a personal decision made on my behalf, brilliant because it meant that I didn't have to come to a verdict by myself. Whenever the juggernaut of Choice appeared in my life I had always stood helpless in its path, a startled bunny in the oncoming headlights of Change. For some reason I preferred to be roadkill rather than risk taking the wrong path. That way I could blame Fate for the whole thing.

Jojo called Bil and Ben on WhatsApp. She then used my phone to get Dave on his mobile, insisting that he go outside of the noisy bar he was in so he could hear properly. She put him on speaker-phone and with Bil and Ben on her screen, Jojo started the ad hoc conference call.

Ben was adamantly positive. "It's just teething troubles, kitten. Give the guy a chance."

Bil nodded in agreement, "He's right. When we first got together the sex was simply awful."

Ben looked like he'd just been slapped. "What do you mean?" he asked sharply.

I saw Bil's features tighten under the strain of having said something he really shouldn't. He back-pedalled at Olympic speed.

"We were both drunk for a start, I'd only just come out. I was a mess. Thank God you showed up." Bil squeezed Ben's hand. Realising that Bil was talking about himself as the poor lover, Ben gave him an adoring smile. It was so interesting to observe their relationship like this, the negotiations, the supplications. It made me realise all the fundamental things that had been missing from my marriage. Any whiff of discord and Rob would have been straight off down the pub or out for a run.

"How bad is it?" asked Dave without emotion, like an action hero assessing a deadly sniper situation.

"All you need to know is that neither of us have had an orgasm yet."

Nobody responded. Bil and Ben stared at each other, Jojo looked sad on my behalf.

Dave broke the silence. "That's no bloody good, is it?" It was hard to believe that Gropey was the only one who seemed to understand my dilemma. Me not having an orgasm was standard with a new partner – it took a while for me to get comfortable enough for that. I was usually so worried about positioning my legs so that my thighs didn't look massive that climaxing was the last thing on my mind. But this was my first experience of a guy failing to finish on fireworks. Either my touchpaper was too damp or his equipment was misfiring. Or maybe we just didn't fit.

"Has it ever happened to you, Dave?" I asked.

"Of course. Once. I·was so blind drunk that I forgot my own name. And to be honest I still had a boner. Just couldn't work out how to unzip my jeans. Maybe it's your technique?" Dave suggested.

"What?" I replied, slightly offended.

"Maybe it's the way you're broiling his hot dog, dipping his wick, tickling his swizzle stick?"

I folded my arms. "Yes, I get the point, thanks. Believe me, I tried every possible technique known to womankind. That thing was dead in the water before we even–"

"This isn't the time for an action replay," interrupted Ben with a dour look. "We just ate supper and this is doing nothing for my digestion. I can feel my foie gras repeating."

"I'd call that karma, mate. Wouldn't you?" Dave said.

Bil stepped in before Dave and Ben could reignite the feud, "I think we should vote."

"And we vote that you stick with Damien" said Ben. "A four week trial."

The way things were going I wasn't sure if I even wanted to spend another four hours with Damien, let alone an entire month.

"Dave?" I asked hopefully.

"I say wave goodbye to Mr Floppy. Cut your losses. The only way is up."

Jojo ran her hands through her short curls thoughtfully. "If you can cope with bad sex or no sex then stick with it. But you've got us for that kind of relationship, haven't you?" Dave laughed like a drain on the crackly speaker.

"One thing I've learned these last few months," Jojo continued, "is that life's too short to waste time with shit flats, shit jobs or shit men. Not that I'm saying Damien's shitty. At all. But maybe he's just not right for you. Why settle?"

There wasn't a lot that anyone could say to that.

"It's two for, two against," said Bil.

"You have the deciding vote, Kat," said Jojo.

"Stick or twist?" asked Dave.

I was even more lost than when we started.

I ruminated over the problem all weekend, so lost in my thoughts that I missed back-announcing one of the acts at the club. My music played but the stage remained empty. The audience started booing and Mag's shouted, "Kat, onstage NOW." I told her I'd had a wardrobe malfunction rather than admit that I'd taken my eye off the glitter-ball. It was a tough weekend at Petite Paris, with a lot of coked-up City yobs. They heckled the circus boys, "Get off faggots and bring back the tits!" while I tried to hold the show together. Dave sent me amusing text messages of support throughout, *What about sending a burning Boris Bike through the club? xxx* It was nice to have somebody genuinely care about me, even if it was only Dave.

I decided to give it one more try with Damien. On Tuesday we met at the cinema. I could see him looking longingly at the posters for the latest shoot 'em up blockbuster but he insisted on letting me choose. In turn I insisted on paying, even though my finances were still far from healthy, but at least it was half-price. I didn't want to feel like I owed Damien anything, and I paid for him because I felt guilty. I wondered if he'd found his ears were inexplicably burning on the night of The Great Damien Debate. I'd discussed his most intimate details with people he'd never even met. It seemed like a cheap way to treat a very nice person.

The movie was instantly forgettable but it was nice to snuggle into Damien, munching popcorn like all of the other happy couples around us. I felt like I'd been reinitiated into an exclusive club that had black-balled me since Rob's departure. I was fitting back into the world again and its expectations of me; I was a woman with a career, a successful boyfriend and the potential for a family of my own. But all the time the nagging doubts remained at the back of my mind, making me fidget in my seat. I just couldn't get comfortable.

We went back to Damien's place and I ran a bath. I hoped that he might join me or at least scrub my back. He didn't. By the time I towelled myself off and padded to the bedroom Damien was fast asleep. I snuggled into him, spooning myself around him and then craftily reached my hand to his groin. There was no reaction. Not a sausage. I felt a thud and heard a loud purring as Sheba arrived to stake her claim. I could just about see her outline, grey fur ghostly in the green light of the alarm clock. She started clawing at the duvet near my head and when I pushed her away, she put her bum hole right in my face. She crawled over to Damien, nuzzling his head. He wrapped his arm around her and soon man and beast were snoring in tandem.

When I awoke the next morning Damien was already up despite not having to work until the evening, sitting in the garden. He was reading *The Guardian*, with Sheba curled up on his lap. There was a cafetière, crusty bread and fresh fig compote on the table. Sunlight bounced off of the gleaming white plates and I caught a glimpse of a butterfly on the wisteria that scaled the garden walls. Damien looked cool and handsome in sweat pants and an old Kinks T shirt. His dark hair was gorgeously tousled and he had a fine stubble that made him look extra masculine. It was such a charming scene. I should have been happy.

"Morning," I said, sitting opposite him.

"Hi," he said, putting the newspaper on the table. He looked concerned. "Are you okay?" he asked.

"Great, thanks," I replied with more formality than I intended. "Are you okay?"

He pushed his hair back and leaned forwards. His eyes caught the sun. I hadn't noticed those exquisite gold flecks before.

"Kat, I think you're an amazing woman," he began. I sensed a "but" coming. "You really fit in," he continued. "Everyone loves you, especially Nat." He ruffled his hair again, struggling to get the words out. "And I don't know why. But it's not working, is it?"

He put his hand on mine. I shook it off and folded my arms defensively against my chest. Everything he'd said was right. I should have felt relieved. Yet all I felt was the familiar bitter stab of rejection. I stood up.

"Don't go," Damien said softly, "at least have some breakfast."

"No thanks," I said bluntly, "lost my appetite."

"Please, Kat," Damien said earnestly, "If I could have made things different I would. You're hot and funny and smart. I don't know what the hell is wrong with me. You're more than girlfriend material. Any man would be crazy to not rush you down the aisle ASAP. But the chemistry's just not there for us. Is it?"

"Fine. If that's the way you want it," I said, like a spoiled child sulking because a toy she no longer played with had been given to someone else.

I went back to the bedroom, legs wobbling, heart racing, and dressed as quickly as I could. I left without even saying goodbye and the emotional dwarf inside me rubbed her hands with glee. I was back in the familiar territory of abject misery, the rejection drowning out all rationality. I was shit. No one wanted me. I was going to be alone for the rest of my life and I didn't even have a cat to mourn my loss or eat my lonely, ugly face.

Chapter Thirty-Seven

Wheels On Fire

I made my way to Mum and Dad's for Sunday lunch a few days later, still seething from the break-up. I sat on the train like an antagonistic teenager, feet on the seats, playing with my iPhone and scowling at anyone who dared to look like they might challenge my lack of manners. Logging onto the dating site had become an unsatisfying addiction, I wasn't remotely enjoying it any more, all I was doing was feeding a sick and pointless obsession, but like a deliciously painful scab I just couldn't stop picking.

Funny Boy saw me online and instant messaged immediately.

I've missed you x

I actually had a boyfriend. For a very short while. I replied.

What happened?

Didn't work out.

Sorry :'(

Don't be. Didn't fancy him.

So I'm still in with a chance?

Here we go again, I stab-typed.

What does that mean?

This is pointless. You won't post a proper photo and sorry to be shallow but I won't meet you without a recent mugshot. I wanted to throw my phone out of the window.

Can't you just have faith?

Are you kidding me? Here's what I think: you're married, probably with kids and a labradoodle. At the very least you've got a girlfriend.

Nothing could be further from the truth.

It's been great talking with you but something's not right here. Bye David.

I removed him from "favourites" and decided to delete all further messages from him without reading them, but I didn't go as far as blocking him, leaving the door slightly ajar in case he ever did post a proper photo.

When I arrived at my parents house I stood aghast at Dad in the driveway, bent over his new obsession. He was caressing her curves, admiring her form. She was polished perfection, gleaming from top to toe. I was embarrassed by this ridiculous cliché, the classic scenario of an elderly man trying to make himself look and feel better by association with youth and beauty. He was even wearing jeans. I had never seen him wear jeans in my entire life.

"Hello Treacle," said Dad giving me a firm hug. "How are you? How's Jojo doing?"

"I'm okay, and she's fine," I replied distractedly. "Whose car is that?"

He beamed and twirled the chamois leather like a male stripper about to wang his thong into a crowd of braying women. He winked.

"Dad, you didn't?"

"You only live once, Treacle."

"Where's the Rover?"

"Traded her in for this little lady," Dad replied, wiping a smear off the bumper.

I gawped at him, "I thought you'd *hired* this?"

Dad beamed at me proudly. "Oh no, she's mine, Kat, *all* mine."

I looked at the two-seater sports car in dismay. "Where are Patrick and I supposed to sit? Not really a family car, is it?"

Dad shrugged. "There's a little shelf in the back if you really need a lift. But we're not really a growing family any more, are we sweetheart? You're the youngest – and you're thirty-nine." I grimaced at the unnecessary reminder.

"Where's Mum?" I asked.

"She's in the kitchen stuffing a bird. Your brother bought ever such a nice one, beautiful fat breast."

"Thanks," I said, refusing to engage with the innuendo. I crunched off down the driveway towards the house, cursing the damage the gravel was inflicting on my heels.

I walked into the kitchen and was confronted with the abhorrent image of my mother in spray-on black skinny jeans, shiny patent stiletto heels and her arm shoved up to the elbow in the most enormous chicken I'd ever seen. She seemed thinner somehow, as if she might have had lunchtime liposuction at the Hamilton Clinic. If not I needed to find out where she bought those jeans. Mum retracted her arm from the bird and hugged me with her elbows, gooey, stuffing-encrusted hands either side of my head.

"Hello," she singsonged.

"Do you think that'll be enough meat to go round?" I quipped.

"I should think so, don't you?" she said, missing my sarcasm entirely. I left her surgically enhancing the bird and went into the living room.

I found Patrick sprawled on Dad's leather recliner, shoes off, can of beer in hand, shouting profanities at the rugby on television. The volume was up full blast. Patrick returned to student mode at Mum and Dad's. His hair was matted and greasy and there was three days stubble on his normally clean-shaven chin. Annabelle would never let him watch the rugby, let alone drink straight from the tin. I sat down on the sofa and glared at him. We still hadn't spoken since I had called him at his office.

"No Annahell?" I asked spitefully.

Without taking his bright blue eyes, so much like Mum's, off of the screen he said, "'Hi Patrick and how are you? I'm fine Kat, thank you. And may I inquire as to your health?' Nice hair, by the way."

I grunted crossly and thrust myself back into the sofa in anger, only to disappear into the Laura Ashley cushions. It was impossible to express rage through the medium of printed soft furnishings.

"We need to talk," I said. Patrick ignored me. I stood up, yanked the remote control out of his hand and switched the television off.

"Oi!" he objected. "I was watching that." Patrick sprung up out of the chair, grabbed the remote and switched the television back on. He sat down again and put the remote control down his tracksuit pants, just like he did when he was twelve and we used to fight over which channel to watch.

"Don't be so immature," I growled and switched the television off at the wall.

"You cow," he retorted. Then he actually shouted, "Mu-uuuum! Kat won't let me watch TV."

"Meet me in the treehouse in five minutes," I demanded. "No arguments."

It was late August, the fag-end of summer. Mum and Dad's suburban garden was waterlogged, the bird bath was overflowing and little puddles had collected on the lawn. I strode over to the treehouse cursing Patrick under my breath.

The ancient rope ladder up to the treehouse was frayed and covered in green slime and as I stepped on the first rung my foot slipped through. I grabbed at the ladder but it swung out from underneath me and I fell backwards on the grass, winding myself and smacking my head hard enough to send a fizzy blackness through my skull. When I stood up I had two green stains on the bum of my brand new white capri pants. Cursing I kicked my shoes off and made my way slowly up the ladder wishing I'd chosen a different spot for the showdown.

The entrance to the treehouse was criss-crossed by cobwebs which caught in my hair as I climbed inside. I hadn't been up there for at least twenty years. The tattered remains of teenage heart throbs were peeling on one wall, and on the other Patrick's football posters and a curling Pamela Anderson calendar. In one corner I found a decapitated Action Man, a one-legged Barbie and a few broken pieces of a doll's china tea set. For some reason these childhood relics made me want to cry. Life was simpler and more secure back then. Patrick was going to be a pilot and I was going to be a nurse, then a ballet dancer before I finally settled on actress in the early nineties. Mum and Dad were an indestructible unit, who while deeply annoying and embarrassing, could always be guaranteed to pick me up from the school disco and tactfully ignore a neck full of love bites.

I was shaken from my sentimental reverie by the troll-like thumping of Patrick climbing up the ladder. He popped his head inside, "Trust you to take the moral high ground so bloody literally." He had to squeeze himself through the door. I stifled a laugh. He glared at me and sat down in the opposite corner. "Christ," he said, "I haven't been up here for years." I shuddered. When I was fifteen and Patrick was thirteen I had caught him fingering my best friend in the tree house. After what I regarded as her betrayal of our friendship I didn't talk to her for the rest of the school year.

"What's wrong?" Patrick asked.

"Nothing much," I said casually, "I just brought you up here to talk about Jesus. And there was something else, now what was it? Oh yes, WHY DID YOU PIMP OUR MOTHER OUT ON THE INTERNET?"

Patrick rolled his eyes, "I didn't pimp Mum out."

"Mum told me you showed her how to use Photoshop."

He shrugged, "She told me it was for Facebook."

"Mum's on *Facebook*?"

"Yeah, aren't you friends?" he said, sounding surprised.

"We're barely speaking in the real world, let alone online. Did you know about the dating?"

Patrick looked sheepish, "Sort of."

I glowered at him, "Sort of? How could you? Poor Dad."

"Kat, it's not like that."

I pursed my lips. "What's it like then? Enlighten me."

"They have an agreement." My mouth dropped open. "Dad just isn't bothered about sex any more and Mum's got... needs." Patrick seemed oblivious to my pain.

"Mum's tried everything," he continued, "She even went to see a Harley Street surgeon about getting him a vacuum thingy." I cringed as my mind conjured an image of one of those toy spiders that jump when you squeeze the little pump. Patrick's admission did at least explain what Mum had been doing that day at The Hamilton Clinic.

"You might be happy to let Mum cheat on Dad," I said haughtily, "but I'm not." I stood up to make a dramatic exit and smacked my head on the roof sending me crashing to the floor, landing on my arse. Patrick started giggling, just like when he was nine and went through a phase of snatching my chair away as I was about to sit down at the dinner table. I fell for it every time, quite literally, and Mum only made him stop when I landed so hard one time that I bruised my tailbone.

"I'm glad you find our family falling apart so amusing," I spat as I threw a mildewed Smurf in his face.

He laughed again. "Don't be so dramatic. Can't you see the funny side?"

"No," I said flatly. He shrugged as if I was making a mountain out of a molehill. I crawled over to the doorway. "I don't care if we never speak again. You're a childish prick, Patrick. You were always Mum's favourite. I might have known you'd stick together."

I climbed down the rope ladder, kicking the tree in anger when I got to the bottom, then cursing my own stupidity as my toes began to throb. I put my shoes on and hobbled off across the lawn, shaking. I hadn't had an argument this intense for a very long time, and even when we were kids, Patrick and I had never fought so bitterly. Things seemed worse than ever.

Chapter Thirty-Eight

The Man Who Fell To Earth

I was stopped dead in my tracks by the sound of creaking wood behind me, followed by a loud crack, like an enormous bone snapping. I turned around just in time to see the tree house flip forty-five degrees as the boughs supporting it fell away. There was a whoosh of leaves as the tiny house sailed towards the ground, then a bang so loud that my ears popped. The tree house collapsed on impact, the sides falling away like something from a Buster Keaton movie. I tried to shout, but shock rendered me silent and I just stood looking at the wreckage, my mouth forming the word P-A-T-R-I-C-K soundlessly.

Mum came running out of the kitchen followed by Dad. Through his asthmatic wheeze he gasped, "What happened?"

"Where's Patrick?" Mum asked with wide, terrified eyes. All I could do was point at the wreckage. Dad's hand looked like it was moving in slow motion as it came to his face and rested on his slack, open mouth. Mum howled like a wounded animal and screamed, "My boy, not my boy!!!" as she rushed towards the debris. Dad followed and together they shouted Patrick's name repeatedly, dragging planks of shattered wood from the pile of chaos.

Suddenly a bloodied hand was sticking up. I felt my legs buckle, and then it was as if someone had thrown a black bag over my head. The next thing I knew I was lying on the damp earth, my clothes sticking to me from the wet lawn. Blades of grass tickled my face and my eyes came back into focus on three figures humped together by what was left of the treehouse. Woozily I sat up and stumbled towards Patrick. His face was covered in blood and his nose seemed to have moved over to his left ear. He was clutching the one-legged Barbie doll, her blonde hair clotted with his blood. They looked like a bizarre pair of serial killers and when I studied Patrick's injuries more closely I could see two indentations in his forehead, made by Barbie's breasts.

"She broke my nose," he said mechanically.

"Katherine!" Mum admonished. "How could you?"

Patrick immediately came to my defence, "No Mum. Not Kat. Barbie. Barbie broke my nose."

Without any suggestion that she may have falsely accused me Mum snapped, "Don't just stand there, girl. Call an ambulance."

Dad interjected, "We'll be here all bloody afternoon if we have to rely on the NHS."

Mum scowled, "Don't swear, Derek."

"He's just trying to help. He's only ever trying to help," I hissed. "Besides, Dad's right. The car will be faster."

I realised at that moment that Mum and Dad had been marinating themselves in booze since at least eleven a.m. having succumbed to that alcoholism peculiar to the suburban middle classes, wherein copious wine consumption signifies cultural appreciation rather than substance abuse.

"You better give me the keys, Dad," I said bleakly.

Mum snatched them from his hands, "Don't be ridiculous, I'll drive."

I yanked the keys from her gaudy maroon talons, "That would be fine if our intended destination was the back of someone else's car."

"But you never drive," she said dismissively.

It was true, and I could feel my bowels loosen at the prospect of getting behind the wheel, but of the four of us I was the only one who was sober and fully conscious. "Dad, let's get him up," I said, ignoring my mother's concerns.

We pulled Patrick to his feet and tucking our heads under his armpits we half-walked, half-dragged him to the car. He looked back to the debris of the treehouse and said tearfully, "I want Barbie.

Where's Barbie?" Mum ran behind us waving a scrunched up tissue, while Patrick bled profusely down my new pink t-shirt and Dad's pastel yellow polo shirt. When we got to the car we did a clumsy do-si-do trying to negotiate Patrick's punch-drunk body on the slippery gravel.

"Mum," I said, "open the car door."

"I don't have the keys," she protested.

Dad, panted from beneath Patrick's armpit, "It's open, Patricia."

She tutted. "I'm surprised you left it unlocked, Derek. You know the Milford's hybrid was broken into last week."

"Just get in," I barked, and she wriggled onto the tiny backseat. We inserted Patrick head first and his face brushed against the interior, leaving a jam-like smear across the pristine white leather.

"Honestly," Mum sighed, "your father's just bought this car."

Dad, a man so patient he made Gandhi look like Genghis Khan, had had enough. It was as if forty years of henpecking had built up and led to one almighty Krakatoa. His face had gone quite red and I was worried that he was having some kind of aneurism. "Jesus Christ Patricia, will you BELT UP. I couldn't give a monkey's about the bloody interior. Keep your mouth shut or get out." To my amazement Mum said, "Sorry Didi." It was her pet name for Dad and I hadn't heard her use it for years.

Dad paused for a moment, bewildered by Mum's rare apology, and then pulled the passenger seat as far forward as he could. His chin was practically resting on the dashboard. I glanced in the rear-view mirror. Mum was stroking Patrick's hair and kissing his forehead. "There, there, Pat-Pat, it's going to be okay."

I couldn't remember the last time I'd driven. I had a vague recollection of a thirtieth birthday party in Blackpool. I was on antibiotics at the time and couldn't drink so had been nominated as the driver. It had not gone well, with several pieces of the rental car incurring damage en route to the Paris of the North, and the rear bumper falling off before I returned the vehicle to the hire company. I glanced around at the post-apocalyptic vision of my family and gritted my teeth. "Put your seat belts on." I ground the gearbox until I found reverse, and then took my foot off of the brake too quickly, sending the car flying backwards out of the driveway. I gripped the steering wheel even tighter and shunted into first gear, creating a screech and burning smell as we sling-shotted out onto the road. Dad was clinging so hard to the dashboard his knuckles were white.

As we sped along the leafy, suburban roads Patrick asked woozily, "Is Barbie driving?" I relaxed enough to unclench my buttocks and loosen my grip a little on the steering wheel. It might been a pleasant Sunday afternoon jaunt if it hadn't been for my little brother haemorrhaging on the back seat. Patrick went very quiet. I checked the rear-view mirror again. His eyes were rolling in the back of his head, either from shock or concussion.

"Mum," I said, "talk to Patrick."

Mum looked lost, "About what?"

"Anything. Just keep him awake. Don't let him sleep."

Mum launched into a full rendition of every children's song ever written from nineteen-fifty onwards. When she got to "Baby Shark" Dad made her stop and I put my foot harder to the floor. Dad kept glancing between the speedometer and the back seat but didn't say a word. As I ignored a Give Way sign and tore around a corner in third gear, a blue flash in the wing mirror caught my eye. The light got brighter, accompanied by the increasingly loud wail of a police siren.

"Shit," I said. I pulled over and turned the engine off. Dad remained silent and Mum whispered, "Should I keep talking to Patrick?" Before I could answer the menacing shadow of a policeman was looming over the car. He rapped on the window and I dutifully rolled it down.

"Good afternoon, Madam," he said with practised exasperation.

"Hello, Officer," Mum sang out from the back seat.

"He's talking to me," I said grimly.

Mum was undeterred. "I'm terribly sorry, Officer, but as you can see we have a teensy emergency on our hands." The policeman popped his head inside the car and turned rather pale at the sight of Patrick's bloodied face.

"Family feud?" he asked.

"Oh no," Mum replied without a trace of guile, "he was playing in the treehouse and the whole thing just collapsed."

The policeman eyed our dysfunctional family unit and then spoke into the radio on his lapel.

"Follow me, I'll escort you to the nearest A&E."

I breathed a massive sigh of relief, "You're not going to arrest me then?"

"Of course not. We're here to serve and protect."

"Thank God!" I said, "I mean, thank you, Officer."

He looked bemused, "That's quite alright madam. I'll be dealing with you once the injured party has been admitted to hospital." He turned sharply on his heels and got back in the squad car. Looking in the rear view mirror I could see him sizing me up.

"A police escort," Mum said. "I feel like Lady Di. Did you hear that Patrick, my little prince?"

Dad squeezed my arm sympathetically, "Don't worry, Treacle. They might let you off with a warning."

Through a lump in my throat I said, "I'm so sorry, Dad."

"No apology necessary, sweetheart. I'm proud of you. I never knew you could drive like this. Maybe we should take up banger racing?"

When we arrived at A&E the policeman pulled up outside the main entrance and I behind him. Dad ran into the hospital, appearing moments later with a wheelchair. The policeman helped me prise Patrick from the car, and once Dad had whisked Patrick away, Mum went on an all-out charm offensive.

"I say, Officer," she said, batting her eyelashes furiously from the back seat, "could you possibly give me a hand?" Mum lent on him a little longer than was necessary but he didn't seem to mind. I could see why she liked him, he looked like a young Michael

Parkinson. "Thank you so much," she said and began to sob. "Please excuse me. It's all been such a shock. Patrick's my only son." The policeman pulled out a small pack of tissues from his jacket pocket. "I love my children, Officer," she sniffed, "Katherine's such a good girl. She was so worried about her little brother. And of course her father's not well." She mouthed the word 'prostate' while pointing to her nether regions. The woman was utterly shameless but I was impressed. The policeman let out a deep sigh.

"Okay Miss Wheeler," he said turning to me sternly, "I'll let you off with a warning. But if we catch you doing your impression of Ayrton Senna again there will be serious consequences. Do you understand?"

I could barely speak for gratitude, "Yes Officer, absolutely Officer, thank you."

Mum had a flirtatious smile on her lips, "Katherine, is single, by the way."

"Could that be anything to do with her driving, perhaps?" He doffed his cap to my mother, gave me one last withering stare and returned to his squad car just as Dad came tearing back towards us.

"I'll park the car. You two sort Patrick out," he said breathlessly.

We found Patrick in the waiting room, still bloody and barely conscious. A small boy with an Arts and Crafts bowl stuck on his head was crying. It was like a very weird edition of the *Antiques Roadshow*. When Patrick's name was called we were directed to a curtained off area, where two nurses lifted Patrick out of the wheelchair onto the bed.

"You're pretty," Patrick said to the younger nurse, his voice sounding like it did when he was seven, "Nice boobies."

"Patrick!" Mum scolded. The nurse laughed. Patrick looked at the other nurse, who was rather older and heavier-set. "You're not though. You're ugly."

"Patrick, that's enough now," snapped Mum. "Please forgive my son, he's in shock."

Po-faced, the older nurse disappeared from the cubicle to return a few moments later. I saw the flash of a white coat out of the corner of my eye.

"This is Doctor Carver," said Patrick's favourite nurse, "He's going to take care of you." Carver, I thought, that name sounds familiar.

"Hello Patrick. How are you feeling?" I slowly turned my face in the direction of the voice. It was like watching the accident all over again, everything in slow motion and no way to avoid it. Doctor Carver was Damien.

"Kat," he said, taken aback.

"Damien," I replied, my voice a high-pitched exclamation mark. Mum looked back and forth between us, trying to sum up the situation. I saw a smile playing on her lips.

"I'll leave you two alone for a moment," she said, beaming at Damien having decided already that he was her next son-in-law.

"Yes," I said, nodding at Patrick and Damien, "I'll leave you two alone too." I stepped out of the cubicle, closing the curtain so quickly behind me that I practically yanked it off the rail. Mum was gesturing madly to the cubicle. She tried to push me back inside.

"Get off me," I growled under my breath. Then, loud enough so Damien could hear, I added, "Let's just let the very nice doctor do his job, shall we?" I steered her across the squeaky floor in search of Dad and coffee. We found Dad at reception frantically trying to locate Patrick.

"It's okay. Patrick's being taken care of by a dashing young doctor, a friend of Kat's," Mum said loudly, trying to see if anyone in the waiting area was impressed. No one was. A&E had descended into a mid-afternoon lull. Even the boy with bowl on his head was having a nap.

"Is Patrick okay?" asked Dad, still wheezing with stress. Mum took Dad's hand in hers tenderly, "He's fine absolutely fine, Didi." Dad's body sagged with relief as Mum embraced him. Silently Mum led him to a quiet corner and they sat down. She snuggled into his shoulder and I watched as he kissed her the top of her head and stroked her cheek. Whatever all the internet dating and spray-on jeans had been about seemed to have been a passing phase that was well and truly over.

I was so overcome with the events of the day – the argument, the accident, bumping into Damien, my parents' apparent reconciliation – that I had to go to the Ladies for a bloody good weep. My emotional outpouring was cut short when the cleaner banged on the door and asked if I could go and cry in the second floor toilets so she could finish up.

After sitting in the waiting area for two hours feeling like a gooseberry while Mum and Dad canoodled, Damien finally called us back into the cubicle. Patrick was sitting up on the bed and looked much better, apart from the massive plaster across his nose and bug-like, swollen eyes. Mum and Dad thanked Damien profusely, and wheeled Patrick back out of the cubicle. I mumbled my thanks and turned to leave as quickly as I could. Just as I pulled the curtain back Damien said, "Kat, I really am sorry about the way things turned out."

I stopped and turned to face him. "Actually, I owe you an apology. Everything you said was true. No hard feelings."

"Really?" he asked looking surprised by my sudden emotional maturity.

"Really," I replied.

"So we can be friends then?" he asked hopefully.

I thought about how every single one of my relationships had ended in drama and disaster. Damien didn't deserve the catch-all label, "Bastard".

"Of course," I said.

Damien's face brightened, "Maybe we can hang out some time?"

"Don't push your luck," I replied. We both laughed. I shook his hand properly, like a grown-up, and walked out into the hospital car park with my head held high.

Mum was waiting for me. Dad had already left in the car with

Patrick. "Shall we go home?" she asked, linking her arm in mine affectionately. "Yes. I think the bus stop's this way," I said, craning my neck past the ambulances. "Bus?" she said derisively, "Don't be ridiculous. We'll take a taxi. Follow me," and off she minced in her tight black jeans and spiky heels, tip-tapping across the car park like a glamorous spider while a couple of paramedics gave her the eye.

Chapter Thirty-Nine

Slummy Mummy

August became September, and the day of Lulu's christening arrived. I woke up with a knot in my stomach; Wendy and Giles had asked me to read at the church service and I was woefully underprepared. I stared into the chaos of my wardrobe and panicked as I realised that I had absolutely nothing suitable to wear. I doubted that sequins and corsets would be appreciated despite the church flying a rainbow banner outside that trumpeted, "Jesus Saves. ALL of us".

I didn't even own a plain knee length skirt, so had to make do with a mini. I pulled it down low around my hips until it reached my knees and then found an inoffensive cream top long enough to hide the whale tail of my thong. In among the fishnets and hold-up stockings (doubtless named after the brutal elastic that held the wearer's thighs to ransom) I discovered a pair of plain tights. I stopped the minor ladder from ripping any further with a blob of nail varnish and dabbed a spot of marker pen on my leg where the skin peeped through the hole. It was more of a struggle to find a pair of shoes that didn't make me look like a pole dancer. I settled on black Mary Janes, hoping that the sensible T-bar strap would divert attention away from the six-inch heel. My hair was now page-boy length so I parted it neatly and gelled it back. It looked fresh and chic and I wondered why I'd hidden my face behind long layers all these years. I dug out the twee little fascinator that Mum had bought me last Christmas and appraised the outfit in the mirror. I looked like a slutty secretary who'd forgotten to tuck in her shirt after a lunchtime tryst with her boss. It would have to do.

Wendy had asked if I wanted to take a date to the christening. I half-considered asking Damien, just to turn Wendy green with envy – the more I insisted that the doctor and I were just good friends the more her suspicious little mind would have gone into overdrive. I decided against it. I already had friends. Unfortunately only Dave was available. I sent him an e-mail prior to the ceremony, outlining strict codes of behaviour; he was not to try and chat anyone up, especially Wendy, nor was he to use the open bar as a licence to get pissed, or hoard food from the buffet for later consumption. Above all he was not to start entertaining the guests nor use the christening as future material.

Dave was waiting outside the church for me and for a moment I didn't recognise him. In fact I gave him the eye and walked straight past. It was only when I heard the unmistakable Welsh twang that I realised it was Dave. "Very funny," he said, thinking I was taking the piss. It pained me to admit it, but Dave scrubbed up okay. He'd got rid of his patchy beard that I so often mocked as "design-less stubble", revealing a twinset of deep dimples. He'd had a haircut, his dark blonde mop that I was so used to seeing hanging in his hazel eyes now neatly swept back, and he was wearing a rather nice suit. Without the voluminous, ironic slogan T-shirts and shapeless jeans he was broad-shouldered, flat-stomached and firm-buttocked, no longer the perennial student but a grown-up, rather handsome man. And was that cologne he was wearing? I remembered the night that he kissed me at the club and a little thrill ran through me. I mentally slapped myself. Dave was never going to be boyfriend material.

When we walked into the church my mother gave Dave a flirty smile. She'd either forgiven or forgotten the time when he vomited on her lawn at a garden party two summers previously. Even Wendy nudged Giles approvingly. We sat down at our appointed pew and Dave picked up the christening programme examining it like a takeaway menu. When he didn't find anything that took his fancy he threw it on the bench in front of us. I jabbed him in the ribs, his

"Ow!" echoing around the walls and drawing several disapproving looks. "What d'ya do that for?" he whispered, rubbing his side. "In case you haven't noticed this is a church not a kebab shop," I hissed. "That's a pita," he said, laughing at his own rubbish joke. I tutted, but I was glad he was with me.

Moments later the church doors closed with a clang. Wendy and Giles took Lulu up to the font where the vicar was beaming at the flock before him. I imagined he would be extremely pleased to have a full house, even if most of us were only there under duress. Thank God for births, deaths and marriages. He spoke about new life and family ties while Dave drew an invisible penis on my thigh with his finger. I slapped his hand away, trying desperately hard not to snigger – and ignore the warmth rising in my body. It felt like school assembly.

When it was my turn to exalt the child I stood up and took a deep breath. As I wobbled towards the font on my way-too-high heels I heard Dave cough. I glanced over my shoulder at him. "What?" I mouthed. He nodded towards my bum. I ran my hands across my lower back. My top was no longer making up for the shortfall in my skirt and my knickers were on display to the entire congregation. I yanked at the top, pulling it down until it concealed my backside again. I looked back at Dave, who was red-faced with suppressed laughter.

Once I got to the font I scanned the audience. Mum had her lips pursed, Dad was smiling sympathetically. It was exactly the same reaction they had when I was nine and fell off of the stage after an overzealous split leap during an amateur production of *Cats*. Patrick, whose nose was still bandaged and had been expressly instructed by Mum to tell everyone that he'd had an accident playing rugby, was smirking. With the white tape on his nose and black bruises under his eyes he looked like a belligerent panda. Annahell was noticeably absent. Mum had said they were having a "relationship sabbatical". I looked over to Giles who gave me a thumbs-up and Wendy smiled encouragingly. Maybe she wasn't so bad after all – although I don't think she was aware that everybody else had just seen my underwear.

My heart was thudding in my ears and my mouth was dry. It was one of the worst episodes of stage fright I'd had in a very long time. I shuffled the poem on the lectern nervously and cleared my throat. In an effort to relax I used the theatrical technique of imagining the audience naked; a grave mistake since the average age of the congregation was sixty-five. I shuddered. I looked at Lulu, so sweet and entirely untainted, sleeping soundly in Wendy's arms. The least I could do was say a few words and genuinely mean them, however cheesy the sentiment.

It was a grey and blustery day but as I started to recite the Zuni Native American Prayer the cloud outside the church lifted enough to illuminate the gloom within. When I got to the line, *Our child, it is your day*, sunlight came shooting through the windows casting multi-coloured beams across the altar. The pastel hats of the ladies bobbed like flowers in the dancing light, nodding approvingly at my magic trick. The vicar looked impressed and for the first time in my life I could see how it might have been cool to be Jesus. Dave was smiling at me in a manner I'd never seen before and it made me feel funny in a nice way.

After group photos on the steps of the church, where the baby was handed around to various relatives I didn't even know existed, we went back to Wendy and Giles' house for the reception. Marie-Claude, the au pair, was standing in front of a table laden with hors d'oeuvres on sticks as we arrived, looking very much like a waitress in her white blouse and black skirt. I edged away from her, realising that I was wearing practically the same outfit, save for the meringue on my head. I watched Marie-Claude weaving in and out of the guests with a full tray of champagne flutes and thought it must be hell to work for Wendy.

"You did really well back there," Dave said.

"Is that an actual compliment?" I said in mock astonishment.

"You looked really good too."

I blushed.

He grinned. "You could start your own religious sect. What about calling it 'The Mooners'?"

I punched his arm. "Nice one, knob jockey."

I noticed my mother threading her way towards us, smiling beatifically at everyone like a cross between the Virgin Mary and Joan Collins. Anyone would think that she'd had the baby. I could feel Dave tense up as she got closer. "Katherine," she enthused, "that was simply marvellous." There was a pause while she stared at Dave.

"Aren't you going to introduce me?" She clearly didn't recognise him.

"This is Lucien, Mother." She extended her hand to Dave. Realising he was off the hook, he kissed it.

"Impeccable manners," she gushed.

"That's the gays for you," I said.

She withdrew her hand quickly, "I best go see what your father wants," and off she glided, surreptitiously wiping her hand with a napkin as Dave called after her, "Nice to meet you, Mrs Wheeler. Your hair looks *fabulous*."

"Funny but deeply offensive," I scolded.

"Oh, and I suppose you were doing sociopolitical satire?" he responded. It was definitely flirtatious rather than critical.

To my surprise, I was rather enjoying myself and Dave was proving to be great company. The only person providing any cause for concern was Wendy, who had been knocking back wine all afternoon and was now attacking the gin. She was looking rather windswept, her normally perfect hair sticking to her forehead.

I sidled up to her as she poured herself a quadruple measure. "Lovely do," I said, trying to distract her from the bottle. She stopped pouring momentarily and glared into the party, her eyes searing into Giles' back; had his sweater been synthetic he would have spontaneously combusted from the penetrating heat of her stare. She looked back at me, struggling to focus. "Is it?" she asked, negatively.

There was an uncomfortable pause. Then Wendy took a huge slug of her drink and blurted, "I think Giles is having an affair." I had no way to know if it was the booze talking or if she had a genuine reason to doubt her husband. More than anything I was struggling with the concept of a) Wendy being anything other than superficial, and b) Wendy having a genuine problem.

I couldn't resist the intrigue. "Who with?"

She looked like she was going to cry, "I don't know."

I put my arm around her, which felt odd but she leaned into me immediately. Things must be very bad indeed.

"I'm sure Giles isn't cheating," I said, reassuringly.

Her lower lip was trembling, "S'just a feeling ... maybe Marie-Claude? Or someone from work. Something's changed."

Giles looked over, slightly alarmed. He came towards us and Wendy let out a single sob, picked up the gin bottle and disappeared. "Sorry about that," Giles said breezily, "she's put herself under so much pressure with this christening." I gave him my left eyebrow arch. Wendy may have been a bitch to me for most of my life, but I was beginning to see Giles in a whole new light.

"Have you seen Dave?" I asked coldly. Giles twitched. It was the uncomfortable reflex of someone who knows they've been caught out. "Have you tried upstairs?" he replied pointedly. "Thanks," I said and left him standing there, a single bead of sweat trickling down his temple.

When I got to the top of the stairs I poked my head into all five of the bedrooms and found nobody except Lulu, sound asleep in her cot, unaware that her parents' marriage seemed to be descending into crisis. Looking around the pristine nursery reminded me of how deceptive appearances can be. My flat may have been a mouldering grotto decked out with all the panache of a youth hostel, but at least there weren't any nasty surprises lurking (apart from the dead mouse I found in the kitchen one morning after playing Cher full volume on repeat the night before). I heard a muffled noise in the bathroom. I flung open the door expecting to find Wendy and was more than a little surprised to discover Dave sitting on the edge of the bath tub with Marie-Claude on her knees busily engaged between his legs. Dave looked up at me and said, "Oops."

Marie-Claude seemed oblivious to my presence – or maybe she just didn't care. Dave put his hand on her head and reluctantly she stopped. "How could you?" I said glancing between Dave and Marie-Claude accusingly. Dave went bright red. He stuffed himself back inside his underpants and zipped up his flies, saying nothing. Marie-Claude turned around and stared at me imperiously like the cat that got the cream. She reminded me a lot of Sheba. I picked up a loo roll and threw it at her, "You've got something on your chin, love. And the baby's crying." She stood up and flounced out of the bathroom as if she was Bridget Bardot. Dave was staring at his feet.

"What have you got to say for yourself?" I said, mortified that I sounded exactly like my mother.

"At least I'm not pissed?" he asked hopefully. My pride was hurting more than my sense of propriety. I didn't care what our gracious hosts thought of me or Dave, especially since Wendy had turned into a character from *Desperate House Wives*.

The simple truth of the matter was that I'd actually started fancying Dave – and had done since the mock proposal and kiss at the club. He seemed to be giving me the same signals and that afternoon my mind gone into rom-com fantasy mode. I had cast Dave as 'Rubbish-But-Hot-Dad', attempting to feed our toddler and getting most of the mushy meal flicked in his eye, while I stood shaking my head in the doorway of our retro kitchen. The last thing he was supposed to be doing was getting a blow job from the babysitter. I hadn't even written her into the script.

"Kat?" Dave asked, bringing me back from my reverie. "At least you've put your cock away," I sighed. "Thank heavens for small mercies."

"It's not that small," he said with a big grin. There was no point in getting annoyed. Getting upset with Dave would be like having a go at Jeremy Clarkson for liking fast cars. Shagging anything that moved was just what Dave did, womanising, it seemed, was part of his DNA.

"Do me a favour mate," I said good-naturedly, "piss off for now and I'll see you down the pub later, okay?"

"You're not mad, then?" He asked, cautiously.

"It's my own fault – I let the dog see the rabbit," I said. "Tacky though, mate, even by your standards."

He laughed and stood up. "You're one in a million, you know that?" and then leaned forward to kiss me. I recoiled.

"No thanks. I know where you've been."

He nodded sagely, "Understood. See you later, then."

Once Dave had gone I splashed my face with cold water – I'd made a good display of adulting but I still felt a smart of embarrassment that left my cheeks warm and blotchy. As I reached for the hand towel I peered over the frosted parapet of the bathroom window and out into the garden. The first shock was seeing Giles smoking. He had never looked so human and interesting. The second and far greater surprise was the heated debate he was having with a woman who had been introduced to me earlier as one of Giles' colleagues. I wondered if they were talking shop, and briefly fantasised that Giles had embezzled millions and she was about to blow the whistle on him. What was really going on was far more intimate than that. She was gesticulating wildly and he was running his hands through his hair in frustration. She shouted something and began to walk away. He lunged for her, grabbing her wrist and pulling him to her, trying to kiss her while she writhed out of his grasp. I swallowed hard. Wendy had been right all along.

I decided that I'd be joining Dave in the pub a lot sooner than expected. I crept out of the bathroom but as I was heading down the stairs I heard a low moan. I froze, holding my breath, hoping that Lulu wasn't having some kind of respiratory problem. I glanced into the nursery where she was gurgling contentedly and blowing raspberries at the multi-coloured mobile whirring above her cot. I heard the moan again. Cautiously I pushed open the door to Wendy and Giles' bedroom. There was no one there. I felt the hairs prickle on the back of my neck. Then I heard an anguished wail and the sound of something thumping on wood. It seemed to be coming from the wardrobe. Heart racing I crept towards it and knocked gingerly on the door. "Wendy?"

The wardrobe door creaked haunted house style as I slowly opened it, revealing the apparition of a very drunk middle-aged woman in her bra and knickers. Wendy was clutching the gin bottle and her eyes were swollen and full of tears. I bent down and prised the bottle from her hands. "Oh Wendy," I said, "you can't stay in there." She was shaking. "Please just let me be," she sobbed and closed the door on herself.

I padded back to the bathroom, filled the tooth mug with water and grabbed her bathrobe from the back of the door. Then I extracted Wendy from the wardrobe, guiding her to the bed. She whimpered softly while I put her into the bathrobe and then handed her the mug of water. "More gin," she said, like a petulant toddler. "No Wendy, drink some water."

She glugged the entire mugful and then looked at me in panic, "Don't let them come up here, Kat. Especially not Giles." I plumped up the pillows and laid her on her side, in case she vomited. "Don't worry," I said, "I'll just tell them you've got Covid again". She managed a weak little laugh, and then fell asleep, snoring immediately. Despite the fact that she was a pretentious, pompous cow I couldn't help feeling sorry for her. I shut the bedroom door behind me and walked calmly down the stairs and straight out of the front door, feeling a massive weight lift off my shoulders when I reached the pavement. I sent Giles a text: *Wendy passed out upstairs. Tell guests she has migraine. Saw u in garden. BE NICE 2 YR WIFE, asshole.* Just the right amount of *Fatal Attraction*, I thought.

Chapter Forty

Hope, Fading

My hair was finally getting long enough to tong in some beachy waves just as summer was ending. I'd stopped dating, I didn't have the heart for it after the way things had turned out with Damien – I didn't have the time either, since I only had one or two nights a week off from Petite Paris now. It had turned into a real job. I saw very little of my parents and when I did I felt like I was intruding on their intimacy. It was like they were on permanent honeymoon. One Sunday afternoon when I turned up unannounced they had the living room curtains drawn and seemed very flustered indeed by my surprise appearance, Mum with her sweater on back to front and Dad's shirt tail poking out of his fly.

I didn't see much of my friends either, except for Jojo. I dropped in on her every few days, either at her tiny flat or the hospital. She was coming to the end of her chemo and was thoroughly exhausted. I had no idea how she'd managed to keep working through it, mostly virtually but occasionally she still had to go into the office. She'd become so thin that even a size six was too big and she asked me to pick up some leggings and a couple of T shirts from H&M Children's department. We both laughed about the VAT break she was getting but it broke my heart. I was finally shopping for kids clothes but they were for my grown-up friend with cancer.

I called Wendy a few times to see how she was doing but I always got her voice-mail. The one time I did manage to get through she behaved as if nothing untoward had happened at the christening. I started to think that perhaps I'd imagined seeing Giles in the garden and finding Wendy in the wardrobe. But I could understand the denial: glossing over the whole thing was probably easier than walking away. I would have done the same, if it had ever been an option.

I'd stopped hanging out with Dave, unwilling to be told where my dating technique was lacking by an ageing, alcoholic Lothario who refused to grow up. He kept texting, asking when we could hang out but I was sure that all he really wanted was for me to buy him pints. Still, I missed him. Bil and Ben kept cancelling our plans to meet due to workload. Secretly I was glad; I was in no mood for another Spanish Inquisition regarding my fertility. But when a solid dinner invitation arrived via text I yelped with delight; *Come and meet your new god daughter xxx* I was overjoyed that the much anticipated child had finally arrived, even if I was sceptical about how that end had been achieved. *Glad she didn't get lost in post*, I replied, *I'm still waiting on a set of kitchen knives I ordered 7 months ago xxx*

When I turned up Ben opened the door cradling the most gorgeous baby I have ever seen. Her skin was dark cinnamon and she had a punkish crest of thick, wavy black hair. He thrust the baby at me and with caustic affection and said, "Meet your Aunty Kat, Hope. She'll be your role model for what not to wear." Hope yawned, and opened her eyes revealing huge, dark brown irises, so dark they merged with the pupil making her look otherworldly. I knew that she was too young to form real expressions, most probably it was wind, but I could swear she smiled at me. "I never thought I'd see the day," Ben said. "Cat got your tongue, Kat?"

"She's utterly gorgeous," I said, holding back the tears.

Ben plucked the baby from my arms and disappeared into the house.

"Hope is gone," I said glibly as I stepped into the hallway to be greeted by Bil wearing an apron.

"Do you like it?" Bil asked.

"It's lovely," I replied, "not too frilly."

Bil laughed, "The name I mean?"

"It's perfect," I said, "but swerve Faith and Charity if you have any more girls?"

"You bitch," he retorted with a grin. It was just like old times.

I followed Bil into the kitchen, warm as a nest, perfumed by the smells of something delicious in the oven and the best aromatherapy candles money could buy.

I was slightly taken aback to see an extremely well-dressed man sat at the dinner table. The mystery guest stood up and extended a manicured hand towards me, "Hi, I'm Blake." His hand was smooth, far more than my own, with only the slightest pressure. "Blake is Hope's godfather," Bil explained. I felt like my special status had been slightly demoted but the evening passed pleasantly enough. Bil and Ben were drinking spritzers and after we'd finished the second bottle of wine a third was not produced. I was going to ask if the abstention was because they were both breast feeding but then thought better of it. As decaf coffee was served in lieu of a nightcap Blake raised an eyebrow at me across the table. "I know," I mouthed back at him in mock consternation. Clearly Bil and Ben were taking child-rearing extremely seriously and were expecting Blake and I to do the same as godparents. After much passing around of the baby she was installed in a Maxi-Cosi on the table, a living centrepiece. I made a mental note to start writing a film script, *Three Gay Men And A Surrogate Baby*.

When Blake excused himself to go to the toilet Bil and Ben slid along the reclaimed Scandinavian church bench, sandwiching me in between them. They smiled conspiratorially as they caught me in a friendship pincer movement.

"Well?" Ben said.

"Well what?" I replied with genuine innocence.

"What do you think of Blake?" asked Bil.

"Good job, clean nails, decent chap. Perfect godfather."

Ben let out an exasperated sigh, "But handsome, right? And charming?"

"And gay?" I suggested.

Ben pursed his mouth reminding momentarily of Sheba's bum hole. "We don't just hang out with other gays."

"I know that," I said, back-pedalling. "He's just so stylish. Straight men aren't usually that well-groomed. Or interesting." Ben relaxed.

"He's single you know, looking to settle down and have kids," said Bil.

Ben cut in, "And absolutely loaded. You could be a stay-at-home mum."

I glanced from one to the other. They were looking very pleased with themselves.

"Brilliant," I said with maximum mockery, "Maybe we can all go on a family holiday together. If you guys can wait a bit longer we could even have a double ceremony."

Ben tipped his head to one side and narrowed his eyes. "Are you taking the piss?"

"I hate to point out the blindingly obvious," I replied plainly, "but have you considered the fact that he might not fancy me – or that I might not like him?"

"We already know that he likes you," Ben said smiling.

"How could he possibly like me? We only just met."

Bil had an omnipotent look on his face. "He's your number one fan."

"What?" I asked, agog.

"He's seen you perform. Twice," said Ben, "thinks you're brilliant."

I threw my hands up in the air. "Great. You managed to set me up with a stalker *and* made him your daughter's godfather. What a coup."

Ben folded his arms, his face hardening. Bil was kinder. "Kat, he's a great guy. Really. We've known him for years. He was married, she ran off..." His voice trailed away as he saw the expression on my face.

"Right. You thought that because we're both single losers you'd pair us up?" I said indignantly.

Hope began whimpering and Ben whisked her out of the Maxi-Cosi, holding her across his chest defensively. "We're just trying to help. I don't want to offend you sweetheart, but don't you think you're being a bit too picky?"

I folded my arms. "Too picky? For someone of my age, looks and net worth?"

Ben tossed his head, "Don't put words into my mouth."

"All we're saying is that you and Blake want the same things. Just have a chat with him," soothed Bil.

I was irrationally angry, the same way I felt when I was eight and wasn't allowed in the school swim squad because I was a rubbish swimmer. Ben started clearing the table, avoiding further eye contact with me.

"It's only cos we care about you Kat," said Bil softly. "We just want to see you happy with someone who's worthy of you."

"I'm sorry," I said, feeling justifiably ungrateful, "I don't fancy him."

Ben made a point of looking at me as he blew a candle out. Bil squeezed my arm, "Get to know him. If nothing else you'll have a new friend."

"Okay. Just don't go buying a new hat."

Poor Blake, I thought, wondering how much of the conversation he'd heard when he returned to the table as we all madly over-compensated to make it look like we hadn't been talking about him at all. "I have an announcement of my own to make," Blake said, pulling out his iPhone. He showed us a photo of a pretty, toned woman, in her mid-thirties, I guessed. "This is Zara," he said glowing, "my Zumba teacher. We've been dating for about six weeks." There was an uncomfortable pause, which Bil and Ben broke by speaking in clumsy, collective sentences, "Ooh, lovely, so fit, just your type." Blake stuffed his phone back into his pocket and looked at Bil and Ben bashfully, avoiding eye contact with me completely, "I know it's going to sound crazy, a bit sudden and far too soon, but ... we're getting married."

It was as if we had been playing a game of Old Maid all night and I was left with the losing hand. I felt the routine hollowing in my stomach, an empty space in which my feelings ricocheted every time friends announced a new partner or baby. I did my best not to look like a sore loser, "Congratulations. I think this calls for another drink." I looked at Ben expectantly.

"Absolutely," he agreed, as he quickly returned Hope to the Maxi-Cosi and bolted for the fridge.

"I'll grab the flutes," I said and joined him in the kitchen area. With our backs turned on the table Ben whispered a heartfelt, "Sorry."

"Don't be," I whispered back. "Have you seen his shoes? Hush Puppies."

Ben clutched his chest in pantomime distress at this crime against fashion.

We drank a glass of champagne rather hurriedly, toasting Blake's engagement. Blake enthused about my performance and I found myself offering to put him and Zara on the guest list at Petite Paris. In return he said he would like to hire me to sing at their wedding. We said goodbye, he gave me a flimsy platonic hug and left. Bil and Ben saw him to the door while I stayed at the table with what remained of my dignity and the rest of the champagne. I refilled my glass and looked at Hope. I took a few unsatisfying gulps. "Would you say this glass is half full or half empty?" I asked the sleeping baby. I downed the entire thing in one and topped it up again as fast as I could. Ben had been right when he said I'd make a terrible mother. Perhaps it really was just as well that I would never get the chance.

Chapter Forty-One

Welsh Rare Bit

"What about this one?" Jojo asked, showing me a dating profile on her iPad. "He sounds right up your street." It was a sunny late September afternoon, a breath of Indian summer, and we were lounging on a blanket in Hyde Park after Jojo's latest hospital appointment. Although she was getting close to ringing the bell that would signal the end of her chemo she looked thinner and more tired than ever. It was hard not to be concerned but nothing could dampen her generous and persistent spirit: she was more determined than ever to find me a mate.

"I'm done with the whole dating thing," I said decapitating daisies to make my point.

Jojo took her iPad back and carried on scanning as if she hadn't heard me.

"*This* one is perfect," she said tapping the screen, "*Welsh Rare Bit.* Cheese on toast? My favourite. He's gorgeous and in the same business as you. That'll make dating easier."

"Jojo," I snapped, "you're not listening." Her eyes were suddenly full of sadness. You could see exactly what she must have looked like as a child.

"We can't give up now," she pleaded, "I've got a really good feeling about this one." She pushed the iPad towards me, holding her breath.

"Okay," I sighed, wondering why I was about to put myself through this yet again, "but it's absolutely the last time."

"Promise," she said smiling as she sent Welsh Rare Bit a message immediately.

A few days later on a wet Monday night, biting with sudden

autumn chill, I found myself in a West End wine bar sitting opposite Welsh Rare Bit. He was exceptionally good-looking and there was something incredibly familiar about him but I couldn't place him. I hoped that this was some kind of karmic good omen, maybe we were lovers from another life? Then he hopped off the bar stool to greet me and my heart sank. The top of his head came to just below my chin. I was already chalking this date up to experience as I surveyed the array of spirits behind the bar, considering trying all of them.

"My name's Dylan, darling," he said with a warm, firm handshake.

"As in Thomas, like the poet?"

He shook his head. "No, as in Dylan, like the rock star." He made the sign of the horns with his fingers and pulled a brilliantly stupid face that genuinely made me laugh.

He looked like the front man for a boy band; white jeans, pink T-shirt, white shirt (undone) and lemon espadrilles. I couldn't figure out how he could wear this outfit in the rain and remain perfectly dry. While Dylan tried to catch the bar tender's eye I excused myself on the pretext of using the bathroom. I texted Jojo. *He's tiny. And stuck in the nineties. Looks like a Westlife figurine xx* She replied just as I was returning to my place at the bar, *At least he won't have any dangerous moving parts xx* I sniggered out loud and Dylan looked quizzical.

"It's my best friend," I told him, "making a joke at your expense."

"Sick sense of humour, has she?" he said, in a thick Welsh accent that sounded exactly like Dave's.

"Very. She has cancer," I said blankly.

"My brother died of cancer last year," Dylan said. I thought about Jojo and Dave's mum and I wanted to cry.

"We really should have gone to Beachy Head for this," replied Dylan, the tone flippant but his eyes full of pain.

"Imagine a pub there," I said. "No one would ever pay their bill. Talk about dying for a drink."

Dylan laughed. "So we have some shared experience. But I'm hardly going to charm you out of your knickers with my knowledge of tumours, am I?"

"You won't be charming me out of my knickers full stop. I wouldn't mind that drink though," I said, "the service in here is terrible."

"I've got a better idea," he said. "Bar around the corner. Loads of fun. You up for it?"

"We're on – as long as you keep your hands to yourself?"

He hopped off of his bar stool again and caught me appraising his lack of stature.

"Great things come in small packages, you know."

I slid off my own bar stool, wagging my finger, "Not interested in your package."

"Let's just have a bloody good time then, shall we?" he said with a bright, charming smile.

We walked out of the bistro towards a smart saloon car. A man in a suit stepped out and opened the door for us and we slid into the plush leather interior of the back seat. That explained the dry clothing.

"Where to, Mr Jones?" asked the driver though the intercom.

"Rock-aoke, Mayfair, please Brian," Dylan replied.

"What?" I asked in disbelief.

"I thought a spot of karaoke would be fun," he replied, "you like a sing song, don' you?"

I shook my head, "Not that. Your name. Jones. You're like a walking advertisement for Visit Wales. And what's with the chauffeur?" I knew from Dylan's profile that he performed in musical theatre. I assumed he was one of fifty spinning umbrellas in *Singin' In The Rain*. I felt myself wobble inside as I began to realise who he was.

"Perk of the job," he said lightly. "Easier than falling out of taxis at 3 a.m."

"What show are you in at the moment?" I asked, even though

I was beginning to realise exactly who he was and which show he was in.

"*Riders On The Storm*. It's about The Doors," he added in case I hadn't heard of it.

"Which Door are you?"

He thought I was being funny. "The set of louvres in Act Two. I been havin' terrible trouble with my hinges." *Riders On The Storm* had blown every other musical out of the water since it exploded onto the West End six weeks earlier. I was in no doubt that the diminutive hunk I was sat next to now was the same man I had drooled over last week in a Sunday supplement, wearing nothing but very tight Levis and a cheeky grin in a feature article called, "Six Tipped For The Top".

"How come you're on a date with me, and not some model or celebrity?" I asked, wondering if this was in fact a dream (in which case the dampness of my clothes probably meant I'd wet the bed).

Dylan paused. "Kerry thought you were a good bet."

"Who's Kerry?" I asked, raising my eyebrows. Dylan squirmed as the windscreen wipers squeaked and thudded on the glass.

"She does my PR," he said sheepishly.

"Funny – my best friend set me up with you," I confessed.

"I must thank her personally some time," he said relaxing and smiling.

"She would love that."

A few minutes later we pulled up outside Rock-aoke in Mayfair. A man in a camel hair coat and ear piece opened the car door and we stepped out onto a red carpet that was made to look like the floor of a three-day old festival; ticket stubs, cigarette butts, crushed cans and what may have been used condoms were printed on it. There were a couple of photographers milling around, but it was hard to tell if they were real paparazzi or drama students laid on by the club to give wealthy merchant bankers and poor little rich kids the full rock star experience. Dylan took my hand as we walked into the club, a few flash bulbs going off behind us. He took it all in his short stride, but I was giddy with excitement.

The interior of the club was a regrettable blend of Tiki Lodge and Eighties Disco; coloured squares pulsated on the dance floor while very pretty, very thin cocktails waitresses, decked out in metallic hot pants or grass skirts and not much else, weaved in and out of the throng. On one tray alone I spotted a smoking skull, an inflatable parrot and a mirror ball on a stick.

A tanned, honey-blonde in an implant revealing bikini top came jiggling towards us. "Dylan! Aloha!" she said in an annoying baby voice as she put a string of flowers around his neck. "Kat, this is Shadow," Dylan boomed over the music, "she's a model." Shadow looked me up and down. I could see her doing the maths, calculating how much my shoes cost, where I bought my bag, my hip-to-waist-to-breast ratio, my age. "Sorry," she said cattily, "I don't have any garlands left." Her over-inflated chest was sporting at least seven wreaths of brightly coloured plastic flowers. She looked like a walking bouncy castle. "That's okay, Shallow," I said. She flicked her hair extensions at me and wiggled off in search of higher status.

"Why are we here?" I shouted at Dylan over the din. "It's Studio 54 meets Hawaiian Barbie." Dylan tapped his nose confidentially and dragged me across the flashing dance floor and up a spiral staircase to the R.I.P. – "Really Important People" – area. The bouncer unclipped the black velvet rope and corralled us towards a series of rooms with tinted glass. I could just about make out the people inside and flashes of video screen. Dylan found the first available booth and dragged me in. The room had its very own VJ. She walked towards us, her legs impossibly long in hotpants, kneehigh socks and Converse boots. "What's happening man?" she said in a Bronx accent, embracing Dylan.

"This is Charlie," Dylan said. Charlie fist-bumped me and re-installed herself behind her booth. She fired up the "Videoke" program on her laptop, whacked a record onto the turntable and started annihilating fresh fruit in the blender while mixing spirits in a cocktail shaker at the same time, all with bewildering speed, a modern day Kali. Using a ring she was wearing, she popped the cap off a beer bottle and slid it to Dylan.

"Time to pick your poison," she said.

"Hardcore rock solo or retro duet, Kat?" asked Dylan.

Charlie scanned through her playlists like a cyborg. "Let me see if I can find something from the late eighties." I winced. Surely it didn't count as "retro" if you remembered it the first time round? Dylan chose "Living On A Prayer" and Charlie handed us two diamanté encrusted microphones. Dylan took the first verse and I joined in on the chorus, feeling like an *X Factor* contestant. Dylan stopped singing momentarily.

"Do I suck?!" I bellowed into the microphone.

"No," he laughed, "you've got a great voice. And you're bloody lovely."

I was glowing with cocktails and pride. "Bloody well done me then," I shouted back.

We ran the gamut from Sonny and Cher to TLC and Eminem, each song bookended by another drink. Charlie went off to replenish the bar and Dylan and I collapsed onto the squishy fun fur sofa in fits of laughter. "She's so cool – and genuinely nice too," I said, slurping at what was left of my Mai Tai. Dylan looked at me with slightly pissed but still alluring puppy dog eyes. "Yeah she is. But you're nicer." He leaned forwards and kissed me. He had lovely soft, plump lips and there wasn't too much tongue, a perfect kiss. But I felt absolutely nothing. It was like snogging a ghost.

Charlie reappeared moments later and I soon lost track of how much I was drinking. When I dropped the mic leaving a trail of smashed crystals on the floor I knew it was time to go home.

"Dylan," I said wobbling to my feet like a baby giraffe, "don't feel sho good."

I stumbled out of the booth and in my daze I didn't even notice the black velvet rope. I charged forwards like I had just won the hundred metres, sending the heavy metal stands at either end crashing to the floor. Dylan grabbed me just in time, preventing me from plummeting head first down the staircase. He threaded me through the crowd on the dance floor which was now so packed that only the odd glimpse of flashing tile was visible. I swayed dangerously, bumping into people and knocking drinks over expensive designer outfits. When we reached the street I sucked in big gulps of cool night air as if I'd just escaped from a burning building. It was still raining and Dylan pulled me into a portico while he called his driver, propping me up against the wall with his spare hand. The street was quiet apart from the odd bicycle rickshaw grinding past with its cargo of shrieking party girls.

"Shlooow shorry," I slurred. He held me closer. "Don't be silly. I hope you don't think I was trying to get you legless for a quick shag?" he said looking at me intently. He kissed me again. All I could think of was not throwing up in his mouth. I still felt nothing – except nausea. Determined not to let a good thing slip by I decided that maybe all I needed to was commit to the role. Resisting the urge to belch I linked my hands around the back of Dylan's neck and dragged him further into the doorway, my body pressing firmly into his. I felt something stirring below his waist. He reached into his pocket to retrieve his phone. "It's on vibrate," he said and I giggled. "We're just outside the club," Dylan told the chauffeur. He put the phone into his back pocket and pressed up against me. This time the bulge was definitely organic.

I tried to concentrate on not swaying and delivering a technically proficient seduction. Dylan whispered his approval into my ear, "You're smashing, Kat." I wasn't feeling the attraction at all but I pressed on, trying to convince myself as much as Dylan. "You're not so bad yourself, Mr Jones," I slurred. I ran my hands through his thick hair and as the kiss grew more passionate I tugged at it more firmly. Until I heard a ripping noise. We both froze – our lips still connected but both of us staring into each other's eyes, so close that Dylan's eyes merged into one, like a cyclops. He looked shocked.

"Oops" he said, and backed away from me ever so slightly. In the delay that the alcohol had created between my brain and my reflexes I failed to let go of Dylan's hair. When he moved away his hair remained in my hand.

Suddenly there were a series of flashes. At first I thought it was lightning but then I realised that it was the glare of cameras. We were being papped, while I stood in the doorway clutching Dylan's toupee. The lights bounced off of his shiny head, the shutter bugs shouting, "Dylan, this way love!" I put my hands to my mouth in horror, realising that I was still holding the wig just as the cameras turned to focus on me. One photographer shouted, "Who's your bearded lady, Dylan?" which was followed by much guffawing from the rest of the tabloid scum now jockeying for space in front of the doorway. I panicked. "I'm so shorry," I said, staggering through the wall of photographers and ignoring the calls of, "What's your name love?"

I stood dumbly in the rain-shiny street, dazzled by the camera flashes and neon lights bouncing in the puddles around me. I heard Dylan shout at the crowd, "Why don't you all fuck off? I might be as bald as a coot but it's better than behaving like a total c–" His last word was cut off by the thwack of a blow being landed. It sounded just like the foley in a cartoon. There was some scuffling and then the mob moved down the street en masse, like a swarm of furious killer bees. One photographer fell into the gutter smashing his camera. He stood up and glared at the man he thought responsible for his tumble. He took a running leap at him, kicking him straight in the crotch. The injured man grabbed himself in agony and crumpled to the ground, like a controlled building demolition. And then it was a free for all.

Dylan stood on the other side of the fracas, staring at the chaos. He caught sight of me and started to move around the mob. "Kat. Kat!" he shouted. It felt like a very bad episode of *EastEnders*. I had inadvertently created a tabloid free-for-all with one tug, toppling a megastar in five minutes flat. I tried to shout back but the words dried up in my throat. The rain was falling heavier as great salty gobs of tears rolled down my face. I turned away and started running while Dylan called after me, "Kat, please! Don't leave me this way."

I ran and ran until I saw a black cab, waving the toupee madly to flag it down. The cab driver was big, jolly – and bald as a newborn baby. "You alright love?" he asked as I slammed the door shut. I looked at his kind, gentle eyes in the rear view mirror and began bawling uncontrollably. The driver pushed a handy pack of tissues through the partition. "Come on, love," he said softly, "it can't be that bad, surely?"

Chapter Forty-Two

Damage Control

I woke up with a dry, sandpapery mouth and a thumping head. My mobile was ringing and had been repeatedly, as well as emitting the "ping" of incoming texts every few minutes. I rolled over with the intention of throwing the phone at the wall but an errant beam of sunlight caught me, burning into my retinas and making me yelp with pain like a vampire trapped on a pool lounger at high noon. I grabbed my phone and was about to switch it off when it rang again. It was my mother. "Well done," she said acerbically, "you're in *all* the papers."

I had no idea what she was talking about. All I knew was that last night had started out very well and ended very badly. As Mum rabbited on about *The Daily Mail* it all came back to me in slow, disassociated fragments; yellow espadrilles, karaoke, a dance floor that lit up like a television game show set, cocktails, a girl called Charlie, a kiss in a doorway, flashes of flashes. A creeping dread began to fill me before the whole sorry affair zoomed back into sharp focus. "I hope you're at least going to see him again after you've wrecked his career?" she asked accusingly. "Sorry," I croaked, "someone else is trying to get through. I think it's work. I'll ring you later." I hung up with no intention of calling her back.

I made my way to the kitchen and jumped out of my skin when I was greeted by a giant rat laying motionless on the floor. I realised within two seconds that the rodent was in fact a toupee, and my initial relief subsided immediately – last night hadn't been a bad dream, it was a living nightmare.

My kidneys felt as if they had been freeze dried. I downed two pint glasses of water and then tried to find something to fry. I blinked numbly into the fridge, empty apart from one mouldering grape. I was going to have to go out and face the world, at least as far as the corner shop. I shuffled back to the bedroom, my body aching with stale toxins. I scrabbled on the floor for something to wear and found a pair of half-fresh tracksuit bottoms, a hooded sweatshirt and a solitary sock. I scanned through my text messages as I dressed. Most were from numbers I didn't recognise but there were three from Jojo, her most recent a confusing shorthand, *Call me if you need me. Don't panic, it'll blow over xxx* I backtracked through her earlier texts, which like my mother's phone call mentioned, "all the papers". There was also a text from Dave, *3-0 to me?*

I grabbed my handbag and eventually found my keys nesting in a pair of knickers. The jangle of the metal made my head throb. As I stepped outside the front door and slammed it behind me I saw movement in the bushes. My first thought was that I'd caught a burglar. I tried to shout out but my vocal chords shrank with fear. I was frozen to the spot. The bush trembled again and something jumped in front of me. I lashed out at the shape with my handbag before realising that it was a photographer. Despite landing several blows to his greasy, dandruff-flecked head he still managed to fire off several shots. He continued snapping while I swung my bag and shouted, "Fuck off! Fuck right off!"

Suddenly a svelte woman in sunglasses and a power suit came running up the path towards us. "You heard her," she shouted, "FUCK OFF RIGHT NOW. Leveson's a personal friend of mine." The "L" word stopped the photographer in his tracks. He slung his camera back in his battered holdall. "Sad pair of bitches," he spat as he barged past her. He jumped into a knackered shit-brown Mini and I saw my downstairs neighbour's curtains twitch as the banger backfired and farted away down the street. "Well, that got rid of him," Power Suit said chummily. I rummaged frantically inside my bag for my keys and tried to stop my hands shaking as I reached for the lock. I turned to her and said, "Thanks for the back-up. But you can fuck off too." I opened the front door as quickly as I could, ducking inside and slamming it in her face behind me.

My heart was thumping in my ears as Power Suit beat out an insistent tattoo against the peeling paintwork. I pressed my back to the door, slid slowly down it and then sat hunched on the floor. "Kat!" she yelled through the letter box. "Talk to me. I'm here to help." I slid to one side of the door where I wouldn't be visible. She was so close I could smell her perfume. I considered poking her in the eyes through the letter box, Bruce Lee style.

"Dylan sent me. He's not angry," she continued, employing a reassuring tone I imagined favoured by The Samaritans. "He feels just as bad about this as you do. Worse in fact."

"Tell him I'm sorry," I said, wiping away tears. "It was an accident. I hope I haven't ruined his career. Now please leave me alone." I pushed the letterbox closed. She pushed it open again, jamming it with her umbrella so I couldn't close it.

"Just piss off or I'll call the police," I said as I grabbed violently at the umbrella.

"I am the police," she replied.

"Bullshit" I shouted. There was a pause.

"Okay. I'm not. But I can help you." This was like the day I got trapped in the flat by two Jehovah's Witnesses. They only left when I dangled my phone out of the letterbox, playing Black Sabbath on full blast.

"I don't need your help," I snarled.

"I think you do," she replied as she pushed something through the letterbox.

A few tabloids and some broadsheets plopped on the floor. It was horrific. Photo after photo of Dylan and I, a play-by-play of the disaster, like a comic strip romance gone very badly wrong. In one photo my pupils were so wide with shock that Dylan's shiny head was reflected in them. The headline was "Stars In Her Eyes". In another I was clutching the toupee to my face. I looked like Rasputin. The rest of the headlines were just as awful; "Heads,

You Lose", "Hair Today, Gone Tomorrow", with the broadsheets offering the only slightly better "Bye-Bye Mein Liebe Hair" and "The Curious Incident Of The Toupee In The Night-Time". Power Suit was right – I couldn't even find a pair of socks today let alone handle a media storm.

"How do I know you work for Dylan?" I said to the letterbox.

"Because it's my fault you went on the date in the first place. I'm Kerry, I handle Dylan's PR." I stood up, still shaking and opened the door.

Kerry thrust a baseball cap and sunglasses at me, "Put these on and come with me." I followed her to a chauffeur-driven car.

"Where are we going?" I asked as I slid in next to her.

"A quiet cafe," she said. She opened her laptop and began briefing me. "I'll need contact details for your immediate family, friends and colleagues. It's vital I get to them before the press do."

"Bit extreme, isn't it?" I said.

Kerry took off her own sunglasses to emphasize her point. "Make no mistake. The press are utter bastards. Even the literate end. In fact they're often worse. They think they're God just because they can write 'defamation' without spellcheck. They can make or break careers – and ruin lives." Still, it all seemed a bit over the top.

Somewhere in Chelsea we pulled up outside a cafe. I was a little disappointed that it wasn't swankier but I was desperate for something to soak up the bile swilling around in my stomach. The driver sped off and we walked into the cafe. Kerry greeted the owner, "Hi Mario. Usual table please." He led us through an inconspicuous door into a small room with only a few tables and chairs. It was like a secret den from a gangland movie, away from the prying eyes of other diners.

I ordered a vast full English breakfast and a vat of coffee. Kerry ordered an espresso and a glass of mineral water. I tucked into the pile of food and ordered an extra round of toast as Kerry reeled off a checklist of "Dos and Don'ts". It all sounded more complicated than the Atkins Diet; I wasn't to answer my phone unless I recognised the number, I was to be careful what I said in conversations and e-mails, I was to stay off Facebook and Twitter, and no online dating for the time being. I laughed bitterly at the last instruction, "Think I'm done with that for good." Her face softened. "Don't say that. This'll blow over in a couple of weeks." I was beginning to warm to her until she added, "Then you'll be back to your old tricks."

"Don't take any of this personally," she said, sensing my mood, "you need to toughen up if you're going to be in the spotlight." As I dunked fried bread in baked beans Kerry sipped her miniature coffee and explained the fame game. "Dylan's at a pivotal point in his career. We're aiming for major TV next, followed of course by film. And there's talk of the next Dr Who." My eyes widened behind the sunglasses, which I took off realising how utterly ridiculous they were. "This little blip can be turned around," she said archly, "There's no such thing as bad publicity – if handled properly." I felt like an inconvenient piece of furniture getting in the way of Dylan's career trajectory.

"This could be good for you too," she added with a sly grin. I failed to see how publicly scalping a rising star would help my career. "I've got some auditions for you next week, in fact."

"Why would you help me?" I asked suspiciously.

"To say thank you," she said moistening her lips.

"For what?"

Kerry smiled, her perfect teeth a deflector shield, "For helping us keep a lid on this."

"We barely even kissed," I said sharply, resenting the implication.

Kerry jerked her perfectly coiffed head dismissively. "Some women will turn a peck on the cheek into a sexual assault before you can say 'Weinstein'. Where there's muck there's ass. Anyway, how have you found it so far?" she asked, softening again.

"I think you've told me everything I need to know," I replied.

"No. I mean the whole online dating thing?"

"Oh," I said, taken off-guard by her sudden geniality. "Mostly utter bollocks, as this episode demonstrates." But it was an opportunity to ask her why she'd chosen me for Dylan.

"Easy," she said, stealing a piece of toast and ramming it in my fried egg, "You're smart, funny, talented, definitely *not* a money-grabbing, fame-seeking bimbo. And you're hot." I was flattered and was it my imagination or was she flirting as she licked the bright yellow wax of egg from her lips? She held my gaze for a moment and then looked at her watch. "Got to get back to the office. Brian will take you home." I thought the car and driver looked familiar.

As we were leaving the cafe Kerry drilled me once more. "Don't call or text Dylan for a bit. Don't worry, he's fine. Breezed into the office this morning singing 'I've Got You Under My Skin', and doffed his toupee like a cap. Good job he has a spare, eh? He said you can keep the other one as a trophy." I laughed. With a belly full of food things were looking much brighter.

"Best put the cap and glasses back on though," she said.

"Why? Are there paps outside?"

"No," she replied sardonically, "you just look like shit."

"Thanks a million," I laughed.

"One last thing," I asked as I got into the car, "my best friend's in and out of hospital. Can I go and see her?"

"Jojo?" Kerry asked.

"Yes," I replied, feeling deeply uncomfortable that Kerry knew so much about my private life.

"Absolutely," she said. "The hospital staff have already been briefed. Here's my card. Any probs call me. Twenty-four seven. I have no life."

She saw me into the car and then disappeared without a trace, like something from a Cold War spy movie.

Chapter Forty-Three

The Forgotten

"Toupee Away," was rarely mentioned again in the papers after that first morning, although a few radio DJs and a topical satire show on television continued to go over the details with a fine tooth comb for another week. I got a round of applause from the staff the next time I went into Petite Paris and the club seemed fuller than usual. "Well done, darl," Mags said, slapping me on the back, "keep this up and you'll get a pay rise." Dave had his fair share of fun at my expense. He came out with a plethora of hair-related puns, each worse than the next. I told him he was wasted in stand-up and should apply to be a *Sun* reporter. He said if his gigs kept going the way they were he might consider it.

I hadn't heard from Dylan, and despite Kerry's posturing about my silence being rewarded with a slew of auditions, nothing materialised. I felt used on both counts, forgotten and a little bit sad. I went get back to my routine of singing for my supper, hanging out with Jojo, and missing having someone to love. I rarely logged onto the dating site, although Funny Boy was still messaging me with amusing and outlandish first date suggestions, like dressing up as pirates and commandeering a Thames Clipper or abseiling into Kew Gardens so we didn't have to pay admission. When he suggested a trip on The London Eye I came very close to agreeing to meet him. I'd always wanted to go on it but it was one of those things that as a native of the city you never seem to get around to doing. However, Funny Boy's continued failure to post a proper photo meant I had to stick to my promise of ignoring him.

I got the fright of my life when I next visited Jojo at the hospital and found an empty treatment chair. I rushed to the reception desk in a panic where the nurse rolled her eyes. "She's downstairs in the shop. Stop worrying. All indications are she's going into full remission." I nearly collapsed from the relief and rushed out of the ward to find Jojo. I scanned the main hospital thoroughfare until I spotted her. She was wearing a Pink Panther onesie, tail dragging on the floor, browsing a two-for-one deal on fiction near the entrance to WH Smith. I watched as she surreptitiously dropped two books inside her suit and then picked up another. By the time I caught up with her she had moved onto the magazine section and was fingering a *Gardener's Weekly*. "Making a honey trap for Alan Titchmarsh?" I asked over her shoulder. She spun around and beamed at me. For the first time in months she had a glow in her cheeks. Her eyes were bright and clear, sparkling with mischief. I gave her a hug and whispered into her ear, "You do realise that offer means *buy* one get one free?"

"If I get caught I'll tell them that kleptomania is a side effect of chemo."

I laughed, "In that case let's do Harrods."

"Upside to cancer my friend. There's a lot of stuff that you just don't give a shit about any more. Forgot my bank card and didn't have enough cash in my purse. Couldn't be arsed to make two trips."

After Jojo stocked up on sweets, chocolate and assorted magazines we walked back to the ward arm in arm.

"What's with the gardening mag?" I asked, "Is it for your mum?"

"I dunno," she said distantly, "I've been feeling the need to get back to nature. Do you know what I mean?" I didn't. I couldn't even keep a box of cress alive.

"One small problem," I pointed out, "you don't have a garden. Unless you're going to plant things in your wellies?"

She looked worried. My heart sank, "What is it Jojo?"

I hoped she wasn't going to start talking about creating a living legacy. I wasn't ready to lose my best friend and have her replaced by a memorial pear tree. She stopped walking.

"I've been meaning to tell you for a while," she said slowly. I held my breath. "I didn't know how you'd take it —"

I squeezed her shoulder gently, as if a little friendly pressure might release the information quicker.

"They've warned me that I might be tired and weak for a few months once I'm discharged. So I'm going back home for a while."

For a moment I couldn't quite grasp it. "To your mum's?"

"Yep. I'll probably be bored out of my brains but I could do without paying that exorbitant rent. I'm quitting my job. I've had it with fashion. It's been like pushing a big leaky bucket of glamorous poo uphill."

The announcement blindsided me completely. Ever since I'd known Jojo we had only been a few Tube stops from each other. Emotionally and geographically there was no one I was closer to. But it would have been selfish of me in the extreme to try and keep her in London.

"It's only Hereford, not Honduras," I said, forcing cheer into my voice. "I'll visit whenever I can, and you're always welcome at mine."

"Are you sure you're not upset?" she asked, still looking concerned.

I choked back the tears and grabbed her, "You're the love of my life Jojo, do you know that?"

"And you're my ace girl," she said. It was her dad's favourite saying.

We stood there embracing for some time, me with my ample arse squeezed into too-tight jeans (I could feel my g-string showing), and Jojo, a skeletal cartoon character.

"There's one more thing I need to ask," she said pulling away.

"Name it," I replied.

"Can you look after Widget? He can't stay at Mum's if I'm there."

"Of course," I said, deciding to finally make peace with my inner cat lady.

When we got back to the treatment room the nurse was there, disapprovingly tapping her watch. "Your afternoon meds are twenty minutes overdue." Eyeing the bulging bag of confectionary she added, "and that's not exactly packed with cancer-fighting nutrition, is it?"

"Chocolate's full of antioxidants," Jojo said, sitting down and obediently presenting her arm for the drip.

"Media hype," countered the nurse, "the sugar and fat cancel out any nutritional value."

I grabbed the bag of sweets. "Jojo would never eat this kind if rubbish. It's mine."

"I don't doubt it," said the nurse staring at my midriff and thighs. She finished hooking Jojo up to what looked like a trouser press and then bustled out of the room.

"Swap you *Heat* for Haribo," I said.

"Done," Jojo replied, launching the rolled up magazine at me. I flipped through the pages, bursting with images of actresses, singers and models and all the lurid details of their latest triumphs and scandals. And then I came to a three page spread on Dylan. I gasped.

"You okay?" asked Jojo. I held the magazine open and turned it around towards her. There was a massive photo of Dylan, looking pin-up hot, hair as thick as the thatch on a cottage. On the next page there were some photos of the toupee incident, and then a candid of Dylan with his bald patch consulting a hair transplant specialist.

"Bloody hell," she said wide-eyed. "What does it say?"

"He's going to have plugs."

Jojo looked thoughtful. "Is he leaking?"

"Hair plugs," I explained. "He's going to have a hair transplant."

"Does the donor have to be alive or dead?" she asked. "Any mention of his gorgeous assassin?"

"Let's see," I said. I read on in silence and horror. *Losing your hair is a big deal. I guess it's a bit like a woman losing her breasts.* I muttered "arse" under my breath and Jojo stopped eating her chocolate.

"What did he say?" she asked.

"That I was a no one," I said non-nonchalantly, desperately hoping she wouldn't ask me to read the article out loud. I've never been good at improv or lying.

"Arse indeed," Jojo said, looking thoroughly offended on my behalf.

"Do you mind if I take this?" I asked, already shoving the copy of *Heat* into my bag.

"Not at all," Jojo smirked. "I have a feeling I'm not going to want it back once you've confronted Dylan with it."

"You're probably right. Little shit. I better go," I said, as the nurse reappeared in the doorway.

I kissed Jojo on the cheek and she gave me a firm embrace with her tiny bird arms. "Don't be too tough on him," she said, "you know how the press like to twist things." It was a fair statement. Given what I knew about Dylan's brother the cancer comment just didn't make sense. I guessed that Kerry was behind the whole thing but still, Dylan was media savvy and I held him responsible for letting the article go to press. I scanned my phone for his number while I stomped across the hospital concourse, nearly bumping into a heavily pregnant woman. I shot through the revolving main door like an Exocet missile as I asked Siri to call Dylan, my cheeks burning with indignation.

Chapter Forty-Four

Finding Chemo

My call went straight through to Dylan's voice-mail. I was relieved; it was a chance to say my piece in full, uninterrupted. "Hiya," I said, sneeringly, "just saw your interview in *Heat*. I'm not quite sure how male pattern baldness is comparable to breast cancer but I'm sure in the context of your career it makes sense. That's what counts, after all. Sorry about pulling your wig off. In fact sorry I ever met you. Have a nice life." I hung up, shaking with anger and marched to the Tube, commuters parting like the Red Sea to give me and my rage a wide berth.

When I resurfaced at Brixton I had three voice-mail messages from Dylan. He was profusely apologetic, his voice frantic and pleading. He explained that when he told the interviewer that he was rather sensitive about being prematurely bald it was she who had made the breast cancer comparison. He tried to put her straight immediately, but she had run with her own version. Everything he said was plausible and I could see how the interview going to press in the state it did was Kerry's doing. Total cow, I thought to myself, I hope she ends up dating someone who vomits all over her Versace suit.

I texted Dylan immediately, *Sorry I flew off handle. Heat made me see red x* He got back to me two minutes later, *No problem. Drink? xx* Not wanting to lead him on I replied, *Giving booze/ dating wide berth for now. But would be great to catch up and Jojo would love to meet u xx* I walked back to my flat, calmly and slowly, hoping that dropping the "let's-just-be-friends" bomb wasn't going to backfire. I pictured Dylan with and without hair and wondered if there was any way I could fancy him. No. Handsome, funny, talented and

284

stratospherically successful as he was, I felt the same way about Dylan as I did about kombucha; I knew that it was good for me, everyone else seemed to like it, but I just couldn't do it.

As I was opening the door to my apartment there was the ping of Dylan's reply, *I'd love to. When?* It was a Monday and I knew that Dylan wouldn't have a show so I decided to strike while the reconciliation iron was hot. *Now? xx*, I chanced. He responded in under sixty seconds, *Text me the details xx* I was bursting with excitement as I did a one-hundred and eighty degree turn back to the Tube.

Fizzing with positivity I checked my dating inbox as I walked, hoping that this miraculous change of fate might have created an avalanche of suitors. My heart sank as I opened the only message, from Funny Boy; *Finally uploaded a photo. Come on Matron, give me a chance? x* When I clicked the link it took me to a photo of Kenneth Williams. I laughed. I took a deep breath. And against all common sense I typed, *Meet me by the London Eye at seven. No questions and you're paying.* I reasoned that even if he was a serial killer he was unlikely to be able to push me off the enormous Ferris wheel since the capsules on the London Eye were hermetically sealed. I logged off and decided to let Fortune take care of things.

When I got back to the hospital Jojo was napping, a smear of chocolate around her mouth that made her look six years old. "Alright funny face?" I asked as I pulled out a packet of makeup wipes from my handbag and threw them on her lap. She propped herself up on her pillows.

"What are you doing back here?" she asked yawning through a sleepy smile.

"That would be telling," I said craftily. "I've got something to show you. It'll be here any minute."

Jojo smiled, "I've got something to show you too." She pushed her iPad in front of me. In my ninety minute absence Jojo had demolished a family-sized bar of Dairy Milk, power-napped and made herself a new dating profile. I shuddered to think what she would be capable of once fully-recovered. She'd called herself "The Naked Truth" and her profile picture was a make-up free, beaming selfie. She looked incredible.

"What do you think?" she asked as she wiped her mouth.

As I read the beautifully written profile I choked back guilty tears for the less than generous version I'd once drafted for her.

"It's perfect," I said, my throat dry and my eyes wet.

"Do you think it's too soon?" she asked. "I mean, I've only just broken up with Cancer."

"Do you think it's too soon?" I said, rhetorically.

She shook her head vehemently. "No."

I passed the tablet back to her. "Well then," I replied, "fuck Cancer. He's history."

"Yeah!" she said, punching the air for effect. "Fuck Bastard Cancer. Speaking of which, what happened with Dylan?"

Just as I was about to explain that everything was fine we heard an acoustic guitar and singing outside the room. I recognised the tune, "Lola", with a new spin on the lyrics, "Jojo, J, O, J, O, Jojo. Juh–juh–juh–juh JoJo". Jojo was grinning like a maniac. There was a kicking on the door, in time to the music and when I opened it Dylan was standing there looking like a one man band, guitar on his front, backpack on his shoulders containing an enormous bunch of flowers. Jojo squealed with delight and started filming the whole thing on her phone. At the end of the song Dylan took a deep bow and his toupee flopped forwards, revealing "Hi" tattooed in marker pen across his head. Jojo and I were convulsed with laughter.

Sometimes life is like a movie. Occasionally like a horror, more often a farce, and then there are those rare, precious moments that occur once in a lifetime, when everything just falls into place. What happened next was magical. Dylan looked up, his toupee still flopping over his eyes. I grabbed the guitar from him, took the bag off of his back, and fixed his hair back into place. He stared at Jojo. She stared back. The room practically crackled with electricity and I suddenly felt like a third wheel.

The nurse came back into the room, irate at the disturbance. "What on earth is going on here? Cut flowers are NOT permitted," she said scowling at the bouquet. Then she caught sight of Dylan, did a double-take and her face softened dramatically.

"Alright my love," said Dylan, channeling the hairy-chested, tight-trousered, snake-hipped spirit of Tom Jones, circa 1977. The nurse mumbled bashfully, saying that she would fetch some beverages and asking Dylan if he could sign something for her niece (who I'm almost certain was fictional). Dylan offered to help make the tea and asked if anyone fancied a chocolate finger. Jojo and I sniggered and the nurse bumbled out of the room blushing madly, followed by Dylan with a mischievous grin on his face. He winked at Jojo on the way out, she winked back and I felt like I had interloped on something incredibly intimate.

Jojo was smiling so broadly that I thought she might swallow her own head. "This is brilliant!" she gushed. "Almost worth getting cancer for." I was rather proud of myself. What had seemed like a thoroughly crap result after the whole toupee incident had turned out very nicely indeed.

"You like him then?" I asked coyly.

She coloured a little. "He's amazing. I can't believe you don't fancy him. Are you sure there's nothing there?"

"Not even the tiniest tingle," I sighed. "I must need my head examined. Or my bits."

"I think you should give it another go," she said authoritatively.

"Nah, it would never work. Besides, I'm pretty sure he's met someone else." She looked extremely disappointed. I couldn't be sure if it was on my behalf or hers, but clearly she hadn't processed the fact that Dylan felt exactly the same way about her as she did about him.

"Jojo you loon, I'm talking about *you*," I said, laughing.

"Don't be ridiculous!" she blustered, her delight clearly out-weighing her embarrassment.

"Jojo," I said plainly, "'I'm pretty sure that Dylan just fell in lust with you, if not full-blown love. If this isn't the start of a beautiful romance then Dolly Parton's tits are real and I'll eat my own bra."

Jojo giggled and then looked worried again, "What about you?"

"That's very kind," I said graciously, "but I think a ménage à trois with my best friend and the man I've recently humiliated in the national press would be a bit weird, don't you?"

She laughed again, "I don't know if you're right, but I do like him. Are you sure you're okay with that?"

"Okay? I'm positively delighted. You have my blessing. On one condition."

She did her listening seriously face. "Name it."

"Do not make me wear a bridesmaid dress in lime, tangerine or anything else that makes me look like a boiled sweet."

"Deal," she said, her eyes welling up.

"Stop," I said, struggling to contain my own feelings. "Anyone would think that one of us had survived cancer and just fallen in love with a megastar."

I was picking up my bag to leave as Dylan and the nurse returned with a tray laden with tea and biscuits. "Not going already Kat?" Dylan asked as he handed Jojo a cup of tea. He hadn't even asked how she liked it. He didn't need to. Somehow he knew. He handed Jojo the mug and popped a chocolate finger in her mouth. She bit a piece off and then shoved the rest in his mouth. They were made for each other.

"Afraid so," I said, "I've got a date."

Dylan pretended to look offended. "You didn't waste any time."

"Who's the lucky guy?" Jojo asked.

"Kenneth Williams," I said. The nurse, who was still buzzing around the room on the pretext of tidying when clearly she was more interested in Dylan, raised her eyebrows.

"I don't mean to dampen your ardour, Kat," said Dylan dunking his biscuit in Jojo's mug, "but isn't he dead and wasn't he gay?"

"The truth is I have no idea who this man is or what he looks like," I shrugged, "But I've been talking to him for months. Let's see if love really is blind."

I said my goodbyes and left the room, sneaking a last glance at Dylan and Jojo through the Venetian blinds that lined the internal windows. Dylan sat down on the edge of the bed and said something which sent Jojo into peals of laughter, then he tenderly wiped some crumbs from her lips. They looked like they had always been together.

Chapter Forty-Five

Full Circle

By the time I got to Waterloo station I was ridiculously nervous. While I had become well accustomed to the routine of meeting complete strangers, I did at least have some idea of what they looked like – until now. I had never been on a blind date in my entire life and I doubted very much that Funny Boy would even turn up. I'd not bothered to log back into the site to see if he'd replied. I'd decided to leave the whole thing to chance and resolved that if he didn't show up I'd be my own date on The London Eye.

When I got to the Eye there were the usual crowds of tourists swarming around. A group of Japanese school girls were taking photographs, giggling excitedly and giving the peace sign, only they had their palms facing the wrong way rendering their gesture an "up yours" instead. A portly and serious line of Germans were standing by their leader who was holding up their country's flag on a stick to stop them from veering off course. I noticed an enormous bunch of flowers in the horde of people, like something from the Chelsea Flower Show. Some lucky woman's going to have a good night, I thought. I bustled past wishing my date was wearing a carnation and carrying *The Times* under his arm, so I'd know who he was. Suddenly I heard a familiar voice call my name. I looked back over my shoulder and saw Dave's face peeking through the floral jungle. I walked back towards him.

"Fancy seeing you here. Taking your nan out?" I asked, nodding at the bouquet.

"No," he said furtively. "I've got a date."

I laughed in his face. "You? Who would go on an actual date with you?" He didn't say anything, just held the flowers out to me. I stopped laughing. We stared at each other while I processed the horror about to unfold before me. *"You're* Funny Boy?" I stammered, eventually.

Dave shifted from one foot to the other nervously, resting the flowers against his shoulder like a rifle when I failed to take them. He smiled although his face had gone white. I felt the pavement swaying beneath my feet, as if everything I previously knew about the world was one enormous lie.

"Jesus fucking Christ," I said smacking my forehead so hard it smarted. "How did I not spot that?" Dave tried to grin more broadly, as if this might somehow disarm my rage. I was just getting started. "Have you got any idea how creepy that is?" Dave opened his mouth but words failed to come out. He just stood there gulping at the air like a landed fish.

"You're a fucking twat, you know that? Disappearing on Jojo was bad enough. Now this?"

"I can explain..." he began.

I cut him off immediately. "No need, Dave. Sorry, *David.* I understand perfectly well, thanks. You don't need a girlfriend, you need a psychiatrist. You've made a total fool of me. Easy though, wasn't it? I'm so thick I didn't even notice you used the same fucking name." I turned around and started walking away from him.

"Kat, *please* ... just let me explain."

He grabbed my wrist and I swung around to meet his gaze again.

"Look," he began frantically, "at first I was making a point. I wanted to prove that my version of your dating profile worked. So I set up a fake profile and messaged you."

"You were mercy messaging me in case no one else did? Because you felt sorry for me?" I was shaking with furious disbelief.

"It wasn't like that," Dave said, breathless with panic. "The more I messaged you the more I realised what a mistake I'd made."

"Oh charming. Now even Billy Liar doesn't want to date me?"

He looked like he was going to cry. "Quite the opposite. And that's the real tragedy."

"How will I be able to believe anything you say to me ever again?" I shouted, "How can we even be friends now? How much of what you told me was lies? The stuff about your mum?"

Dave turned even paler. "All true, I promise."

"And what about being a stock controller?"

"I did it as a school holiday job once."

"Bullshit, Dave!" I wanted to grab the bouquet and beat him to death with it. "You have no idea what a stock controller even is."

"Okay, white lie. But I did work in a stockroom once. Everything else is true. I swear, on my mum's life."

"Dave, she's DEAD! Or so you've said."

He was now frantically running his free hand through his hair. "I swear on her soul, Kat."

"The only soul you have any connection with has 'arse' in front of it."

I instantly regretted the words the moment they fell out of my mouth. Dave looked crestfallen. He just shrugged.

"Sorry for wasting your time, Kat. Sorry for stretching the truth. But don't ever doubt me where my mum's concerned. And while we're taking the moral high ground I wasn't overjoyed to know you've been telling all and sundry that I'm a womanising alcoholic and a failed comedian."

I laughed, a jagged, hollow sound, lacking all warmth and humour. "You must be fucking kidding me?

He dropped the flowers on the floor and started walking away. I knew I should still be angry, that my boiling rage was more than justified, because however earnest Dave was he'd still catfished me. It was weird, manipulative and just plain wrong, in fact probably illegal. But I needed to know why he'd done it. I picked up the flowers and chased after him.

"Hey, wait a minute. Dave, just stop."

He turned to me, hands sunk deep into his pockets, shoulders rounded with shame and defeat. "Look, I'm sorry if I was hurtful about your mum," I said, trying to sound as reasonable as I could under the circumstances, "But you have to admit this is all a bit odd. No wonder you didn't want to put a profile photo up." I forced an ironic smile. "You still owe me an explanation."

We sat on a bench, and I laid the flowers in between us, like a tribute to the car crash of our friendship.

"Explain it to me," I said staring straight ahead and still shaking.

Dave pulled his collar up defensively, too embarrassed to meet my inquiring stare.

"Well," he began clearing his throat, "I like you. Always have."

"I like you too," I said, sounding as if I didn't really like him much at all.

"No I mean, I *really* like you. More than like."

The unspoken hung in the air between us. I thought about that night at the club when he kissed me. I could feel my rage start to crack and thaw. Then I thought about the incident at the christening and my feelings froze over immediately.

"What about Marie Claude? Angie? All the girls you've loved before – whose names you can't even remember?" I expected Dave to dry up but this only seemed to spur him on.

"That's just it. None of them meant anything. Ever. The truth is I've fantasised about you since the moment that we met. But I thought – I still think – you're out of my league. With the online dating I was just testing the waters, so to speak."

I was finding it hard to see myself as the Little Mermaid to Dave's Captain Birdseye. Too much debris on the surface, let alone what might be lurking beneath. Then another thought occurred to me.

"Is this a joke?"

Dave stared at me blankly. "What?"

"I just remembered that you said, 'maybe we can go and see Dave perform together some time'. This is just research, isn't it, for another one of your shit stand-up routines?" My fury returned, full strength. "Not fucking funny, Dave. Sick, in fact. As usual you've taken it way too far."

Dave's mouth opened a couple of times, but yet again words failed him.

"That's what I thought," I said, standing up. "You absolute, irredeemable arsehole. I don't ever want to see you again."

My heart was thumping with the humiliation of it all as I walked away.

"Kat! Kat! *Kaaaaaaat!!!*" Dave bellowed. I could hear frantic footsteps behind me and then suddenly Dave was in front of me on his knees, holding the flowers, arms outstretched like the penitent Christ. Pedestrians parted around us, a few gathering at the edges, perhaps under the impression that we were one of the more avant-garde street theatre acts on the South Bank.

"Get up!" I hissed. "You're embarrassing yourself. You're embarrassing *me*."

"Katherine Wheeler," he said, looking me straight in the eye, his gaze penetrating deep into my soul, "I love you. There I've said it. If I never say it again, if you don't feel the same, if you never ever talk to me again at least I won't spend the rest of my life regretting not having taken the chance. I love you."

Chapter Forty-Six

Once More, With Feeling

Tomorrow is the Big Day. Again. Only this time I feel a lot more secure about it. I am, in fact, absolutely, positively one hundred percent sure that he is definitely and without a doubt The One. I have never been more certain of anything in my life.

I look at my reflection. I love my dress. Jojo chose it for me and it's simply perfect. The pale champagne-coloured, shot silk reflects the light, framing my best assets and smoothing over those that could use a more rigorous regime on the treadmill. I even like my hair, which is still in a reasonably short, sleek bob, by choice – I don't feel the need to hide anymore – and it gives the whole outfit a tasteful 1920s vibe. Jojo comes back into the bedroom with two glasses of champagne. She gasps. For a moment I think I have misjudged my appearance and I do in fact look bloody awful.

"You look stunning," she says.

"Really?" I ask, not quite sure. Jojo hands me a glass.

"Positively editorial," she affirms. "To us and our wonderful lives."

"To you, and your wonderful life," I amend.

We clink glasses and the happiness is too much. I grab my best friend and hug her, biting back joyful tears. "I love you Jojo," I blub into her shoulder and spill champagne down her back, but at least she's still in her bathrobe. She laughs as I grab a towel to dry her but she has already removed the robe. She slips into her own dress and I zip her up. She looks absolutely breathtaking.

It's a perfect late summer's afternoon. We walk from the little guest house through the quaint Welsh village until we come to the chapel. The churchyard is a riot of wild flowers and silent apart from the buzzing of bees and the faint bleating of sheep far in the distance. As we get closer to the tiny chapel all I can hear is sedate organ music. For a moment I panic that the invitations haven't been sent, or that everyone has got lost on the endless winding roads that are the only way to access this remote location. But as we push the creaking wooden doors open we see that the place is packed to its ancient rafters.

The aisle is scattered with rose petals and on the altar sits an enormous floral arrangement of two swans, their necks wound around each other inseparably. It gives me a big lump in my throat, which is silly, considering I ordered it. Admittedly it's a bit gaudy, like something from *My Big Fat Gypsy Wedding*, but I liked the sentiment: swans mate for life. Jojo and I stand in the vestibule, fussing over the veil and the train and the bouquets. When we are certain that everything is perfect we squeeze each others hands and take a deep breath, *Thelma and Louise* with a much happier ending. I nod to the white head of the organist, who appears to be almost as old as the church, and she starts playing the Wedding March with surprising attack for her years. Jojo and I begin to make our way down the aisle. I move like one of the elephants in *Fantasia* while Jojo glides with the grace of a ballet dancer. I wouldn't have it any other way.

I see Bil, Ben and the kids, sat at the very back of the church in case one of them starts crying – Ben gets very emotional at weddings. Hope sits on Ben's lap and when she sees us she says, "look Daddy, a princess and a great big fairy." There is a ripple of delighted giggling from the crowd of family and friends. Hope's baby brother Jai is wrapped up in Bil's arms, gurgling contentedly. He was named after his surrogate mother's hometown of Jaipur (thankfully he wasn't named after his birthplace, Illinois). As we pass Ben puts one hand on his décolletage as if wearing an imaginary set of pearls. "Gorgeous," he whispers, tears in his eyes. Hope mimics him to perfection but can't quite get the consonants in the right order. "Rorgus," she beams.

We move further down the aisle and I spot Wendy and Giles. Wendy is smiling warmly. A lot has changed since they had couples counselling; Wendy is the primary breadwinner and Giles works from home managing investment portfolios for a small, select client list, including Dylan strangely enough. Giles calls himself a house-husband but it's a perfunctory role, like Oxford or Cambridge awarding an honorary degree to a thick-as-two-short planks celebrity. I think the acronym SAHD somehow suits him better. Jake and Lulu have been left with the new nanny, a dead-ringer for Mrs Doubtfire, Marie-Claude having departed suddenly after Lulu's christening.

Out of the corner of my eye I see Kerry waving an A4 manilla envelope. I roll my eyes. I can't believe she's brought the renewal contract with her for the musical I've been starring in for the last year. Then smirking she holds up a piece of paper with capital letters in marker pen that trumpet, "GOTCHA!". I still don't quite trust Kerry but I like her.

As we near the altar Mum and Dad smile at me and then glance adoringly at each other. Patrick looks a little embarrassed squashed between them in the pew, but since his divorce he seems much happier and more relaxed. The ding in his nose from the accident has given his profile a handsome, Romanesque quality. He gives me the thumbs up and a big grin.

Then I see Dave. He's wearing a suit with a tie, a carnation in his buttonhole. He looks masculine and handsome. My heart skips a beat. It's still doing that after eighteen months. He turns his lovely, silly face to me and mouths, "You're next." I mime cutting my own throat, but secretly I'm delighted. My stomach somersaults making me even more aware of the tiny swelling in my belly that we haven't told a soul about yet, especially not Kerry.

As the vicar welcomes the congregation I take my seat next to Jojo's mother Francine, and my best friend takes her place next to the man she is about to marry. It seems like the most natural thing in the world and I'd put money on them spending the rest of their lives together. I look up at poor old Jesus hanging on his cross and I pray that Dylan and Jojo will grow very, very old together. With five embryos on ice they are already assured a large family.

Dylan looks up at Jojo with absolute devotion as he stands on tiptoe to lift her veil. They just look so right together. I catch my breath and wish I'd stuck a couple of Kleenex in my cleavage. Francine retrieves a pack of tissues from her handbag and passes them to me. I dab my eyes and look over my shoulder at Dave. His eyes are moist and he's making a funny little noise in his throat which makes him sound like he has a nervous tic. He coughs loudly when he realises I've caught him having a moment but then he mouths something at me. And I mouth it right back. "I love you."